Full Medical

Full Medical

Steven M. Moore

Copyright © 2006 by Steven M. Moore.

Library of Congress Control Number: 2006907445
ISBN 10: Softcover   1-4257-2677-1

ISBN 13: Softcover   978-1-4257-2677-5

All rights reserved. No part of this book may be reproduced or transmitted in any form or by any means, electronic or mechanical, including photocopying, recording, or by any information storage and retrieval system, without permission in writing from the copyright owner.

This is a work of fiction. Names, characters, places and incidents either are the product of the author's imagination or are used fictitiously, and any resemblance to any actual persons, living or dead, events, or locales is entirely coincidental.

This book was printed in the United States of America.

To order additional copies of this book, contact:
Xlibris Corporation
1-888-795-4274
www.Xlibris.com
Orders@Xlibris.com

35469

Another September is approaching...
This one is for you, Carlitos.

Acknowledgments

Thanks to my loving wife and best friend, who had the germ of the idea; to my friends at Unicorn, Pat and Chuck, for their art and conversation over the years; and to my friend Mike, the best digital graphics and cross-platform guy I have had the privilege to know.

Prelude

In the Virginia countryside, Saturday, May 2053 . . .

The escape from the Center was only a partial success. The three had been carefully planning it for a long time but bad luck happens. At least, two of them believed it was just bad luck right up to the point when they died. The third knew better; she still died.

It all began just past 3 am. The three ran quietly out from under the trees to the tall wire fence topped with barbed wire and high voltage lines. The young man known to his comrades as FS2 was familiar with high voltage. He had made a point of studying lots of things, as they all had, although he liked the technical stuff better. He knew exactly how to throw the coiled wire that he carried so that it would short out that whole section of fence, and it worked just as he had planned. Bright sparks filled the night sky, just like he predicted. The Guardians within the Center would be alerted, perhaps thinking there was an intruder from outside, though that didn't matter. They would be over the fence and speedily on their way before the Guardians either came to investigate or got the electricity in that section of the fence back on.

All three were young and athletic, so they climbed up the fence with the agility of caged monkeys. They weren't unlike those friends from the zoo either—they had felt caged for months. And threatened. At the top the young man known as HJ1 took the wire cutters out of his pocket and snipped through the barbed wire and the high voltage lines. The woman, SW1, headed down first, then FS2, and finally HJ1. At the bottom they all clasped hands.

"Have a good life," SW1 told the other two.

The two men smiled and kissed her on the cheek.

"It'll be a life on the run," said HJ1, "but I don't care. At least we're outside the Center."

The other two nodded in agreement. They all thought it was better than the alternative.

"Yeah," said FS2, "and now it's time to move out, kids."

They split up and headed off into the Virginia countryside, running at first, and then slowing down to a fast-paced walk. They had bottles of water and snacks in their backpacks, enough for a good 48 hours. However, they weren't going to get far unless they found transportation. But they knew where to find it.

The police had reports of stolen cars from three different locations that early Saturday morning. It was the plan the three escapees had all agreed upon. None of them had ever driven any kind of vehicle before. However, they knew the theory and didn't find it difficult. A few banged fenders and bumpers were irrelevant in the long run, anyway. They also all knew they would have to steal other cars as they moved away from the Center; otherwise the Guardians might find them.

FS2 headed north, keeping off the thruways with their autopilot signals. He was wiry and the shortest of the three. His unruly mop of red hair would make him stand out in a crowd but he had no money to buy hair dye. Instead, he put on an old baseball cap he found in the back seat of his stolen car. He drove methodically, concentrating on the road, learning the controls as he went along.

He was known for his bad temper, though he usually managed to keep it under control. That control came in handy as he passed through the back roads of New Jersey. The other drivers on the road seemed aggressive and dangerous to him, some waving their fists at him, others making obscene signals. He got good at doing the same back at them. It was a rush. He was free.

HJ1 headed south, into southern Maryland. He had the build of a football running back and the craggy good looks to match. Although all of them would be off the scale in any standard intelligence test, he wasn't nearly as smart as the other two. What he added to the team was patience and steely determination during their planning sessions.

His vehicle was a stolen behemoth, its past owner either having lots of money or poor environmental sensibilities. HJ1 didn't much care—he was comfortable in the car. The roads were practically deserted. He stopped once to take a pee, drink some water, and down a package of oreos. He then continued on into the Chesapeake dawn.

SW1 was the leader of the three. She was a striking beauty, even in this day and age when physical imperfections could be treated by either the geneticist's magic before birth or the surgeon's tools after. At 1.8 meters, she was a statuesque brunette with the pouting looks of a cinema sex queen. She was quicker and more creative than the others, so she got the farthest after they split up.

The car she stole was from a nearby shopping center. She had walked around the parking lot for over an hour until she saw an early morning shopper, a nurse, who looked something like her. SW1 swung the woman around just after she had placed two bags of groceries on the front seat. She decked the surprised woman with a left hook that would have made any boxer proud, leaving her victim sprawled on the pavement. She then drove sedately to Dulles Airport where she used the woman's national ID card to buy a ticket and get on a plane. No one checked to see if the fingerprint, retinal pattern, and DNA information recorded on the ID matched those of SW1, a slipup due to the early morning hour. Besides, she was leaving the US, not entering it. The airport security was focused more on detecting terrorists entering the country. Their computers simply registered that a certain woman whose profession was nursing was bound for Manila.

The three young escapees from the Center were all young, strong, and very intelligent. Their only problem was not possessing enough practical information about the everyday workings of the complicated world existing outside the Center.

No, it was not their bad luck. The men and women who had organized the Center anticipated many events and tried to assure the most favorable outcome for themselves. Their wards had been kept in the dark on purpose. They knew that any escapee would make mistakes, making him easy to find. It was only a matter of time.

Chapter One

Lexington Park, Maryland, Sunday...

Old Bob stared into the lifeless eyes of the corpse. The hour was just past 8 pm but the evening was still warm, so he wiped some of his sticky sweat off with a sleeve that was even dirtier than his brow, wondering if he were dreaming at the bottom of the bottle again. It was a late spring night in the little southern Maryland town of Lexington Park.

In the US of May, 2053, the number of homeless had reached a hundred-year high. It was partly due to a bad economy but mostly it was due to the fact that there were just not enough good jobs in the world for all the people in it. Bob Martin was just one of many who had no job, no benefits, and no home. Most of the time he preferred it that way, or just didn't care. Alcohol was his drug of choice to wipe out his ability to care about anything. But that night he couldn't remember drinking anything all day, so he cared. It made him depressed and hungry.

He had just lifted the lid to the trash bin behind Cindy's Olde Towne Family Restaurant. It was usually good for some edible scraps, especially after the dinner hour when the customers graduated to dessert, coffee, or after-dinner drinks and the dishwashers, Josh and Ray, started throwing out the garbage.

He backed away quickly from the eyes, suddenly wishing for a drink instead of food. He hadn't seen a dead man for a long time now but he knew those eyes did not belong to the living.

He had looked into his first dead eyes as he had searched a dead raghead for ID near a little town on the Iraqi-Syrian border. He would see many more as a soldier in five years of war in the Middle East, both on his side and theirs. His was the third major war there of the new millennium. The most recent one started in 2038 and his years in it had not been good for his mental health, although his physical health hadn't started deteriorating until he began to hit the bottle. Until then he was just another muscular marine who brought a fistful of medals home to a family that didn't care. *Especially Julie. Fuckin' bitch was already sleeping with Jimmy before I landed in Norfolk.*

The drinking had only started with the divorce and loss of custody of his children. Now he had no idea where Julie or the kids were, although he wished he had Julie there to ask her what to do. *The old Julie, not the slut that was screwin' around while I fought ragheads over there. The old Julie, she was the smart one.*

He found a partially filled pint bottle of cheap bourbon in one of the deep pockets of the soiled tan raincoat he always wore. A quick nip gave him courage to approach the trash bin again. He tugged at the rings in his ear and scratched his mohawk, pleased with himself. Another sip emboldened him enough so that he could lift the lid again. *The problem with this corpse is that he's naked. Big naked mother fucker. Maybe a yachtsman?*

Lexington Park had a few pleasure boats visiting from time to time although their owners usually ate in the new yacht club over on the Patuxent River. Cindy's mostly catered to the locals, fly boys from the Naval Air Station, and the less mobile vacationers, like those who rented summer cottages.

It was a nice town, away from DC and Baltimore with their teeming millions, their crime, and their cloying, swampy humidity. Here there was not much traffic, not much crime, and not many politicians and lawyers. A little more freedom, too. He hadn't renewed his national ID card in years.

There were plenty of military around, as the whole southern tip of Maryland was filled with them. The crew, for example, who flew that new fangled Navy radar plane that looked like a flying saucer copulating with an airplane. *Well, not so new anymore. But it had been pretty new when I was in the service.* There were other Navy personnel who flew the new spy plane that could spot a farmer taking a pee from 18 klicks high and sift out of the ether the lowest level spread spectrum communications signals that the new Iranian stealth fighters emitted. They were in and out all the time, testing the new planes and shaking out the old ones after maintenance. There were a lot of goings on over at Dahlgren and St. Inigoes, too, and not just Navy.

He supposed they were all good people though, in general, and for understandable reasons, he didn't want much to do with the military anymore. He supposed that somewhere, in some computer in the Pentagon, there was a database with his DNA, fingerprints and retinal pattern, taken when he entered the military, rather than be drafted. *Maybe I can apply for veterans' benefits when I'm older and see if I can get into a VA nursing home some time before I die. Then I'd probably need my national ID card from the Department of Homeland Security, my taxpayer's ID card from the IRS, and my military ID* card from the Department of Defense, so I can get my Medicare ID card from the Department of Health and Human Services.

Bob walked out through the alley, deep in thought, still trying to figure out what to do about the corpse, when he crashed into John Milton, county sheriff, who was coming out the front door of Cindy's. The sheriff was heavyset, so he didn't suffer much from the collision, although it made him angry.

"Bob, if you'd lay off that shit, you wouldn't be running into normal folk," John observed. He tried to wipe away the spot of cheap bourbon on his uniform.

"Sorry, John. How you doing? Where's Dolores?"

"At her mother's, if it's any of your business."

"Guess it isn't but you got no cause to get riled. I'm just trying to be pleasant to someone I crashed into and spilled good drink on. Just a carefree bachelor tonight, then?"

"That's the way it is. Now let me go home and nurse the heartburn produced by Cindy's Mexican meatloaf." Sheriff Milton strode off down the crumbling sidewalk.

Bob stared after him, remembered what he had just seen, and abruptly made the decision to pursue the sheriff. He usually tried to avoid the law. However, the sheriff had often been kind enough to let him sleep it off in a warm cell on cold winter nights. He felt comfortable with the man, as comfortable as he could be with anybody, he guessed.

He caught up with the sheriff as he was opening the door to his patrol car. He froze a moment at the sight of the sawed-off but then recovered his nerve.

"See here, I got a problem, John."

Sheriff John Milton was as straight-laced as they come. He still had his marine haircut, which hid the fact that his crown was starting to go bald. He was sandy-haired and blue-eyed. His family was local and a member of it had fought in every war the nation had participated in, beginning with the French and Indian wars from before the country's independence. Considering that history, it was strange that no one from his family had ever died in a war. Many had come close. He seemed to remember the story of a great-great-granduncle that had been killed during shore leave during World War II, though. Now this Milton felt the country was fighting in another war, a war involving rampant crime in the cities, from the hoodlums and gangs, and terrorist attacks everywhere, from chemical plants to shopping malls.

Milton had once been a cop in Philly. He awoke one morning in a hospital with worse wounds than he had ever received during the last Middle Eastern war, Bob's war. Three weeks later he accepted the job in St. Mary's County and moved to Lexington Park, as a temporary replacement for the sheriff who had died of a heart attack. When he won the election the following November, he made the town his permanent home.

"Bob, you've got lots of problems. Most everyone understands where they come from and leaves your sorry ass alone but, I swear, I'll haul you in for vagrancy if you push me. I'm off duty, man."

"I know, I know." He scratched his crotch and wondered casually when he had peed last. "But I don't have a cell phone. How could I inform Sam or George?"

Sam and George were the sheriff's two deputies. The three of them were usually enough to keep the peace in the small county, although some of the towns, including Lexington Park and St. Mary's City, also had a small police force.

"OK, so what's to inform, Bob? And it had better be good."

"There's a body in the trash bin."

Even though Bob had said it with a straight face, the sheriff smiled at the report.

"You don't say? You seem sober enough but I bet you're imagining things."

Bob managed, however, to convince the sheriff to take a look. He led the stocky law officer to the back of Cindy's and pointed to the bin. Milton opened the lid and looked into the dead eyes of the corpse.

"I'll be damned," said Milton. "I apologize, Bob. This is worse than one of your drunken visions."

"You see, you see? Dead and naked. Male hooker, you think?"

"More likely pimp," suggested Milton. "He's pretty fat. Or just big, anyway." He turned the body around to where he could see that the back half of the head was gone. "Explosive hollow point. Lots of firepower to waste on a pimp. I saw stuff like this in the military, Bob."

"You and me both. Maybe he's military."

"No, I know who he is. I just saw him on the newsnet. I was watching it at Cindy's. He's that Johnson bastard. No, actually, our victim here looks younger than the guy on the newsnet. He's also trimmer, if you can believe that, and has more hair. Maybe he's Johnson's younger brother. Help me get him out, Bob."

"Shouldn't we put on rubber gloves or something?"

Milton reached into his coat pocket and handed the drunk a pair of latex gloves. He put another pair on himself. They soon had the body laid out in front of the trash bin. Milton took off his gloves, took out his wallet, and handed a twenty to Bob.

"For services rendered, Bob. Go have a snort at the cost of the government. I've got to call in Claude Turner. You don't want to be here."

Claude, the county coroner, was Bob's brother-in-law. They hadn't spoken since the divorce. The drunk thanked the sheriff and hobbled off.

Claude was not very happy to be called away from his beer and TV. It was also a twenty minute drive up from St. Mary's City. When he arrived he was astounded to see the cadaver.

"Hank Johnson sure doesn't look so menacing tonight," he observed.

"If he's Hank Johnson," said Milton. "I just saw him on the newsnet, by the way. Kind of creepy, seeing him naked here now."

"Naked and dead." Claude turned the head around. "Not death from natural causes, I'd say, whoever he is. I'll need to phone Patty to bring the standard equipment. Lend me your phone."

"Yeah, just tell her to not give anything out to Bouncer, OK?" Bouncer Mann ran the local newsnet post as well as being a freelance writer for some of the major nets. Milton actually liked the kid although he thought he was way too nosy.

"He's probably screwin' that new gal of his anyway," commented Claude. "He knows there's no news on a Sunday night in Lexington Park. Or St. Mary's County for that matter."

When Patty Smith arrived, she was driving the county coroner's van. She drove right into the alley next to Cindy's and met them in the parking lot in the back where the dumpster was located. She didn't look too happy about being called out on a Sunday evening either. She was a good-looking, athletic redhead who had been a soccer star at the University of Maryland. She had gone pro but her career ended with a knee injury that left her with a permanent limp. She was excellent at the forensics stuff, though, so much so that Milton thought she was wasting her talent staying in rural Maryland.

"Hell of a way to spend Sunday evening, John," she said, climbing into the dumpster. "And this guy's nothing to look at anyway. Looks like some damn football player. All brawn and no brains."

"Especially now," said Claude. "Wouldn't want you to ogle him anyway, honey. Professional detachment and all that. Besides, he might be big time."

John caught Claude looking at Patty's thin waist and naval where a huge syntho ruby was encrusted. Patty was in good shape. He gave Claude a wink.

"I'd have to be pretty horny to get turned on by a corpse. And quit looking at me like I was the only coed at a frat party. I was vacuuming when you called and I didn't bother to change. You should be ashamed. You're both married."

"Ma cherie, c'est vrai, but we're also not dead," said Claude. "I certainly would like to watch you clean house some time."

"Fat chance. Anyway, my first guess is that this Mr. Universe was killed somewhere else and then dumped here. We may not find much, unless there's something that indicates where he was really killed."

"Well, he might have come in on one of the yachts today," suggested Claude.

"Already checked that," said Milton. "Three boats in today are all local summertime people. No big Washington honchos. No new people over on the Potomoc side either. And none of the locals are connected with the present administration."

"DC? Why DC?" asked Patty.

Milton explained the corpse's uncanny resemblance to Henry 'Hank' Johnson, Assistant Secretary of the Department of Homeland Security. Patty nodded her understanding. Johnson had been in the news a lot lately. Both he and his boss were carryovers from the previous Republican administration.

"Well, if he's any kind of Republican, he's not from around here. This town has been Democratic for as long as I can remember."

As Patty had prophesized, there was nothing on the body or in or around the trash bin that was useful. They took the body to the morgue in St. Mary's City.

Milton sat and watched as Patty helped Claude with the autopsy. Her training was in criminal forensics. Still, she had picked up a lot from Claude and didn't seem to be squeamish about the procedures. After Patty washed down the body, they started with the usual fingerprints and retina scans.

"Bullet entered the top of the head and exited his lower jaw," droned Claude for the benefit of the recorder. Later he would download the file to his computer which would use its voice recognition software to turn what he said into an official coroner's report, correcting his grammar as it did so. "Probably 38 or 45 Jersey expander. There are some titanium fragments along the path. Death was instant."

"Cause of death?" asked Milton.

"That's pretty obvious," said Claude, momentarily turning off the recorder. "You think there's something else? You stick to your business, John, and I'll do mine."

"No sense in getting hot under the collar," Patty told Claude. "John just wants you to be thorough. Shouldn't we at least do a tox workup?"

"Shit, Patty, it's Sunday evening. This case is closed, except for knowing who the guy really is. It's certainly not Hank Johnson, as much as he looks like him. Hank Johnson is a lot older. You should take the fingerprints and retina scans and work on that, John. We can get DNA later."

"Now who's butting into who's business?" asked Milton with a laugh. "I tell you what, you do the full workup. Then I'll have a better description to send out."

"All right. Given that there might be political nuances, we'll do the whole thing. Let's just get him right-side up."

"Easier said than done," said Patti, lifting a heavy arm of the corpse. "This guy's a ham."

"Wait!" said Claude, taking the arm from her. "Get me that magnifying glass."

"He's a shooter," guessed Milton.

"Maybe not a willing one," said Patty, handing Claude the magnifying glass. "Certainly looks clean to me."

"No, there's an injection track right here." There was only a slight red mark where he was pointing. "We're definitely doing the toxicology workup now."

An hour later they had the results. Milton stared at the computer screen, a little confused by all that he saw.

"What's your call, Patty?" Claude asked her.

"You haven't given me much practice with this, Claude, though I'd say you've got a man who OD'd on heroin."

"You'd be wrong. The heroin didn't kill him but it sure as hell put him under for a good while. And this isn't the poor grade you might buy ten blocks from the White House. It's rich man's stuff. No sign of the usual impurities."

"So he was out when they shot him," observed Patty. "Why not just give him more heroin? Or, on the other hand, why not just blow his head off and forget the heroin? It's high class stuff with a high class price."

"I saw stuff like this in the last war. The Ayatollah's intelligence services would interrogate prisoners using high grade heroin from Turkey or Afghanistan, and then blow their heads off and dump the bodies where the Allies could find them. Sends a message."

"Do you think this is someone sending us a message, Claude?" asked Milton, a tired frown on his face. "How do we read it?"

"No, I don't think anyone's sending a message to us, in particular. I think someone reading this report will get a message."

Just then there was a knock at the door. Milton went to the door and opened it, then backed into the exam room, hands held high. Three men and one woman followed him into the room, all with automatics covering Milton and the other two. The woman went over to the corpse and turned the head to look at the face.

"It's him," she said simply.

"Who are you?" demanded Claude.

"Since the information will do you no good, I'll tell you." She flashed a badge which only Milton had seen before when serving as a Philadelphia cop. "DHS, at your service. I'm afraid that you already know too much." She gestured to the smaller of the three men. "Kill them."

John Milton barely had time to wonder what it was that he knew when the bullets began tearing through his body.

Scherzo One

"I'm afraid your mother needs a liver transplant."

The doctor was sad for being the bearer of bad news. It was a common thing in his profession these days.

"A full liver? Part of mine won't do?"

Art Lindstrom, a portly man who looked like he might be in need of a bypass in a couple of years, was obviously also weighted down with the worries of attending to an elderly parent.

"Mr. Lindstrom, she needs a full one. Not a partial. I'll put her on the charity list."

"Charity list? My mother has medical insurance, doctor."

"She doesn't have full medical, Mr. Lindstrom."

"You mean, she worked thirty-five years as a civil servant for the government and she's only a charity case?"

"I'm afraid so. She only has what the government provides as part of her pension package. They keep lowering those benefits periodically. She doesn't even have as much coverage as a veteran. With her age, it's all on her deductible."

Mr. Lindstrom ruminated on that a bit. Then:

"So, what's the average wait on this charity list?"

"Two to three years. You would still have to come up with the difference for the operation and other care, that is, make up for the difference between what the government pays and what full medical would pay. You'd better get started now. Sell her house, maybe. Can she live with you?"

"I suppose so, I suppose so."

Lindstrom looked like a basset hound with a bad case of indigestion as he contemplated the additional stress on his marriage when he moved his mother in to live with his wife and three children in their tiny three bedroom ranch.

Chapter Two

Boston, Massachusetts, Sunday & Monday . . .

The car was bearing down on Chris Tanner through the sheets of rain. It was a new model black Toyota/Ford Daredevil, a car heavier and faster than most of the environmentally friendly cars that had been produced that year. He knew it well, since he had taken one out for a test drive only three weeks ago. He and the rest of the members of his car co-op had decided they liked it although he couldn't afford his part of the monthly payment on a cop's salary. Fortunately the co-op had decided to wait another year for their upgrade.

The headlight beams seemed to be seeking him out through the obscurity of the thunderstorm, trying to slice and dice him like some nimble cook from a Japanese steakhouse wielding his cooking knives. He dove to one side to avoid being hit. Half immersed in a rapidly growing rain puddle, he watched as the car jumped the curb and slammed into a brick wall. *At 100 klicks per hour or more, not much chance an air bag saved this guy.*

Chris ran down the street towards the car which was sparking and leaking its fuel mixture onto the ground. Vacant eyes followed him as the homeless, camped out on the street for the night, managed to show some curiosity in what was going on. Death was not unknown to them, not even violent death. Statistics showed, however, that they died mostly from lack of medical care or just plain starvation. It was not that any of them cared about the driver of the car and they had little energy to hate the cop that chased after it, yet they were still human, and human beings are curious.

Fortunately the driver's door was not jammed. He wrenched it open and pulled the man out from behind the airbag with considerable effort, thanking his luck that there were no passengers. He dragged the man a good twenty-five meters before the car blew up, sending parts of it flying into the air. The blast knocked him off his feet and a piece of aluminum-strengthened fiberglass sliced into his right thigh.

"Shit, what the hell just happened here?"

He had been walking home from a party, minding his own business, not even on duty. *Sometimes trouble just finds you, I guess.*

Still on the ground, he turned the body over. It was a young kid, maybe twenty-five, but probably less. Wiry build, a redhead. He was clearly dead. The face looked familiar although he couldn't quite place it. He found his cell phone in his raincoat pocket and speed-dialed the precinct.

"Chris Tanner, badge 13417, reporting a car accident. You there, Marcia?"

Marcia, the night dispatcher, was there. Her face came on the screen.

"Chris, my sweetness, what are you doing at a car accident? I thought you were going to Denise's birthday party."

"I was walking home from it. Polcari's is only five blocks from my apartment, you know. I'm at Marlboro and Clarendon. Get an ambulance down here, will you."

"How many accident victims, honey?"

"One dead, one wounded. I'm the wounded."

"Shit. Hold on a second." Her face disappeared from the cell phone screen. He heard her trigger another channel, making a call to the nearest black and white as well as the nearest ambulance. "This is not a homicide case, I take it," she said when her face returned to the screen.

"Doesn't look like it, unless I was the target. And I'm not dead. For a moment I thought the guy was trying to kill me but he may not have even seen me."

"Well, just keep talking to me, baby. Your cell phone will help them localize you."

"Yeah, that's great."

He looked at the growing pool of water around him and the corpse, noting the oily, black-red color of it, then realizing it was his own blood mixing in with the water from the storm. The feeble streetlights were only slightly helped by the fire in the car and the fires of the homeless trying to keep dry. He switched the cell to his left hand and felt his thigh with his right. It came back covered with blood. *I'm losing a lot. They might not get to me in time.*

He spotted a hooker peering around the corner at the scene, afraid to come near, afraid to get involved. For the homeless, nightly tenants of the street, she excited more curiosity than Chris or the burning car. She wore very tight shorts, calf-high boots, and a purse, all made out of simulated black leather. He thought at first that she wore nothing from the waist up until he noticed some matching black pasties on the nipples of her synthetically enlarged breasts. The pasties had little tassels on them that waved hypnotically in the thunderstorm's wind. Their motion matched the motion of her pony tail that sprouted from her otherwise bald head. The pony tail swayed in time with the tassels, all blowing in the strong wind coming up the cement canyons between the skyscrapers. Chris thought that she was too underdressed for Boston in May and that she might be cold because of it. He felt cold himself. *Actually, I'm really cold. The cold of Death, coming for me finally.*

Four years of service at the end of the last Middle Eastern war had given him a lot of battlefield smarts. He had been wounded once for every year of service and had survived. *This isn't any different. Just a different battlefield.* He managed to raise himself on his left knee enough to whip off his belt. It provided a crude tourniquet. In the distance he heard the sirens. The hooker heard them too, and ran away. The homeless didn't bother. They knew the authorities would ignore them, as they always did, unless there was a body to pick up. To Chris the sirens actually seemed to be getting further away, not closer. He faded into unconsciousness.

He awoke in a hospital bed, somewhat confused, memories of the war clouding his brain already fogged by the leftover anesthesia. Morning sun streamed through the window. A matronly nurse looked kindly down upon him.

"Well, Detective Tanner, feeling better?"

Chris considered the question. He wasn't a large man. At 1.7 meters, most of the other male detectives were taller. He was wiry and fast, though, often beating his sparring partners to the punch at the police gym. He enjoyed both softball and boxing, probably more the former than the latter, as there wasn't so much hurt afterwards. Now it felt like he had received heavy blows all over his body. *A full fifteen rounds of being a punching bag. Lots of hurt.*

Chris slowly remembered. The party at Polcari's Bar, the storm, the car. *Shit. I'm lucky to be alive.*

"Did they find out who the kid is?" he asked.

"What kid?" asked the nurse.

"The driver of the car. He was dead."

"Well, the coroner took him, then. We wouldn't get him here. And we'll want your bed just as soon as you can get out of here. The city makes us take you, though frankly, your cops' benefits suck."

Just then Captain Denise Rivera walked into the room. She was taller than Chris and carried herself in a regal manner. She had come up through the ranks the hard way, starting as a patrolwoman. At fifty-three, she was often called 'Old Ironsides,' like the famous old ship in Charlestown Naval Yard that hardly anyone could visit anymore because of the steep price of admission. She was a pleasant woman, though, and not above carousing a little with the troops. Most thought her quite capable and considered her a prime candidate for police commissioner when the present one retired.

"You can only visit a few minutes," warned the nurse. "He just came out of it."

"Perfect timing, then," said Denise. "You look like shit, Chris, and I know it wasn't the beer. You hardly touched the booze last night. How are you feeling?"

"Like a truck hit me," Chris admitted. "But it was only shrapnel from the fuel explosion. You ID'd the kid?"

"First things first." She held up a recorder. "I'll turn this into a prelim for you, when I get back to the precinct, just so I can get your version in quickly. Later, when the black and whites and the coroner are done, I'll want a full report, of course, combining their findings with yours. Just to keep the computer files clean, you know." She smiled and licked her lips. She usually wore no lipstick because of the habit. Some of the guys found it sexy. Chris mostly ignored it. He had his own quirks. She seemed to be studying the battery level of the recorder. Then: "You can start anytime."

Quickly and succinctly Chris told Denise the story. She only nodded a couple of times, and grimaced when he told how he had put the belt on his leg. When he finished, she turned off the recorder.

"Now, for your question. We haven't ID'd the body. The Toyota/Ford was stolen earlier yesterday, apparently from a parking lot next to the old Colonnade Hotel, another stolen car left in its place. The parking lot ID'd your driver as the thief, although we still don't know who he is. There is one thing about him that is curious, though. Marcia King picked up on it right away. She's got a good eye."

"What's that?" asked Chris.

"Your dead car thief looks very much like a very young Frank Sweeney. You know, the Secretary of Defense. He's a local boy."

Chris only nodded. Now he knew why the face had seemed familiar.

Scherzo Two

He was known as Sand Viper. His short cropped black hair was turning a little gray at the temples but he still felt strong and capable of doing Allah's work. Yet again. He never tired and would not stop until the world was rid of the infidels and the sons and daughters of Islam took their rightful place as citizens of a new Arab world empire.

The teenage boy looked admiringly into his eyes. Sand Viper saw a little of himself in this boy. The others had brought the teen to the cheap motel in the outskirts of Houston. Too bad, he thought, but the boy will be a martyr for our cause.

He handed the boy the vest of plastic explosives.

"Do not deviate from the plan. If you fail, Allah may not forgive you. You are doing his work."

"I know," said the boy. "You don't need to worry. I've got the route down pat."

Sand Viper knew that. He also knew that the others had prepared this one well. He had been approached just outside that broken down high school of his, just after some white crackers had beaten the shit out of him. He was an easy recruit—religious, proud of his family's heritage, and hating American infidels.

The boy did not fail the Sand Viper. The straight-A student drove to the mall and took the TV box out of his car trunk, as if he were returning it to the big electronic superstore there. Once inside, he ducked behind the plants in the central garden where the fountain was, took the vest out of the box, and strapped it on. Then he walked to the mall's food court, where there was not a seat to be had due to the noon-time lunch crowd, and detonated the explosives.

He died immediately. So did twenty-seven others. Over thirty more were injured, and three of those died in hospitals from their injuries. Most of the second floor food court collapsed into the first floor below. It was a big item on the local news, although it was only a small AP note in the New York Times, which long ago had become electronic: "Double-click here to see photos of the terrorist attack in Houston."

The Sand Viper moved on to another city.

Chapter Three

Washington, DC, Monday . . .

Jay Sandoval stopped jogging long enough to take the call. Always cautious, she had the video switch in the off position. The person on the other end was mixing words in Spanish and English with sobs but she still recognized the voice.

"Dolores, that you? What's up, amorcita? What happened?" She flicked on the video in order to see her friend's face. Tears were streaming down her cheeks.

"Jay, John's dead. Claude Turner and Patty Smith are also dead. I don't know what to do." The last was almost a wail. Then more sobs. Finally, her friend continued. "The place is swarming with cops, and they won't let me see John."

"Hold on." Jay suddenly felt the stitch in her side. She always got it when she cooled down too fast. She was still sweating profusely on that humid Monday morning. Her running shirt was soaked, clinging tightly to her heaving breasts. She could feel the sweat trickle down her legs into her shoes. She started walking in circles, to keep the muscles loose. "How did he die?"

"Someone shot him." More sobs. "They were down in the morgue at the coroner's office in St. Mary's City."

"They were doing an autopsy? On Sunday night?"

"I guess. But they say there's no body. So no one can figure out what they were doing there. They're all shot up."

"OK, just keep cool. Remember, when the gangs used to be out and we'd hide from them? Keep cool like that. I'll be down as quick as I can. Love ya, kid."

She pressed the END button and then speed dialed Crime Fighters, her place of work. It was 6:45 am in the nation's capital. The night desk would still be in.

"Crime Fighters E-Zine," came the voice. It was Ben Ito, technically one of her bosses, and also a good friend. Then the video signal synched up and she was looking at a man in his late thirties with dark circles under his eyes. *Being on the night desk is not easy.*

"Ben, Jay here. I've just got a tip on a good story down in St. Mary's City."

"St. Mary's City, Maryland? Are you kidding? Nothing happens in southern Maryland. Even the crabs get so bored they jump into the pot."

"Triple murder. County sheriff, coroner, and forensics specialist."

"Wow! I take back what I just said. Are you going down?"

Any hint of a good story excited Ben Ito.

"Beats wasting another day down at the precinct. Tell Olaf for me, will ya?"

"OK. I hope to be reading about it soon."

"You bet. Catch ya later."

She had nearly finished her circular path around the park, so her car was only about 200 meters away. She ran to it, thinking of Dolores all the way.

Her friend had been her constant companion as they survived together the tough LA streets of their childhood. They escaped that bad environment when they walked into the marine recruiting office together. The marines force fed them an education, molding Jay into a top recon and photo interpretation expert and Dolores into a computer and communications specialist. The first was a far more dangerous specialty than the second, being closer to the front lines, so it was ironic that Dolores came out of the war wounded, not Jay. An RPG killed her comrades in a hummer although she survived. In the hospital Dolores met John Milton. By the time he became county sheriff, she already had a flourishing software business established. Since she worked out of her home, the move from Philly to Lexington Park was easy for her, although Jay suspected that both John and Dolores sometimes missed the excitement of a big city.

Jay knew her friend would not suffer economically. But John and Dolores had been soul mates, pre-destined for each other in all karmic senses. Dolores would suffer in many other ways.

So where does the bad karma come from? Jay asked herself as she drove back to her apartment, not far from Dupont Circle. *What queer twist of fate rolled the dice so heavily against my friend? It isn't fair.*

She didn't take long in the shower. The water rationing was already in effect anyway, so she couldn't dawdle. She threw down a few ibuprofs heading out the door, still feeling the knotting in her leg muscles brought on by the abruptly shortened cooling down period from her run. She usually spent as much time doing that as in the actual run; no hot shower could be a substitute for it, even a lengthy one.

She had left the car on the street. It was one of the classic hydrogen models from the thirties. Sleek and fast, she had driven it for five years now, and loved it. It might be faster to take the maglev to Fredericksburg, although she would have to then rent a car there, so she decided on the drive. By the time she hit

Springfield and put the speeding car on the I-95 autopilot system, her legs were in complete rebellion.

But it was a beautiful spring day. The hazy sunshine and overgrown vegetation along the roadway reminded her again why she now lived on the east coast.

Yes, California was wonderful, if you could afford to play there. There are the mountains, where the snow is tucked away in the winter where it's supposed to be, not bothering commuters. There's the crashing surf and pine cliffs of Big Sur, where a blue-green roiling ocean yearns to play tag with the pale blue sky. There's always really good, authentic Mexican food hidden away in the little mom and pop restaurants around LA. Those were some of her favorite California things. But there are also the street gangs, killing the elderly for a fix and raping the defenseless for kicks. And the cops who think that every Latino girl is either a gang member or a gang member's whore. *One white nazi almost raped me in San Diego once. Come to think of it, the guy that saved me then was a marine. No wonder I like marines.* The east coast was in some ways more civilized, or, at least, uncivilized in different ways.

Fact was, the whole country was in a shambles. Led by President Fulton, it seemed unable to handle the waves of crime and terrorism, no matter how much money was thrown at these problems and others, no matter how many of the rights were trampled on.

It was all fair game for her e-zine. Crime Fighters was not the only one that reported on the crime occurring throughout the nation, although it was probably the most read on the internet. One of Jay's own stories had even been nominated for a Pulitzer, even though the video landed her cameraman in jail for six months, another victim of the guilty-until-proven-innocent policy of the DHS. *Actually, if it weren't for the Pulitzer nomination, he might still be rotting in jail.*

"Read" was perhaps being too kind—when available, streaming video illustrated the stories. Its Hundred Most Wanted was not sanctioned by the DHS but it was honest and was always up to date. With a terrorist suicide bomber blowing up a shopping mall or some other place at least once a week or so, the DHS hardly had the right to complain. Tips to Crime Fighters that were passed on to federal agents had contributed to the arrest of many perpetrators. The DHS, along with the FBI, CIA, and similar agencies therefore reluctantly acknowledged Crime Fighters' usefulness.

Jay's birth name was Jayashree Sandoval. Only half Latino, her father was Guatemalan and her mother Indian, as in Hindu, not Native American. She was height and weight challenged, her mother used to say, in order to be politically correct, yet the marines had taught Jay a lot about hand-to-hand combat that made up for her lack in size. At 1.6 meters and 50 kilos, she still toppled many bigger guys and gals down at Perry's Gym where she worked out. Some of the guys were embarrassed by that. Some of the guys resented it. And some of them asked her out. Actually, some of the gals did too, though she didn't swing that way. In their early teens, she and Dolores had tried it once, with very little success and much embarrassment.

Since the car was on autopilot, she adjusted the mirror and applied a little makeup. She never used much. Her face was flawless and her skin had a perpetual golden tan that really wasn't a tan. The raven black hair and mischievous dark brown eyes were present in both sides of her family, the high cheekbones came from her father's side, from his Native American blood. The flashing white teeth and gentle demeanor were also his. Her perseverance came from her mother, though, although her father called it stubbornness.

She left the freeway just before Fredericksburg, turning onto the old US route 301 to cross over the Potomac River into Maryland. 301 did not broadcast autopilot signals, so Jay took the wheel of the speeding vehicle. The GPS computer plotted her course into St. Mary's City via the old Maryland routes 234 and 5, which she decided were badly in need of repair. *Like a lot of infrastructure in this country. We're not much better than a lot of Third World countries now. In fact, maybe there's no Third World anymore, just the poor, the poorer, and the poorest.*

Personally, she felt she was well off compared to a lot of people. Most months she paid her rent on time. Most months she ate healthy meals about seventy per cent of the time. She also had no serious medical problems. It was just as well. Her deductible had become so high that anything serious would wipe out her savings completely and probably force her to find a cheaper place to live. She knew she lived on the edge. Most people did.

In a short time she pulled into town and headed directly for the Hamilton Building, where the Coroner's Office and other county offices were found. There were still a lot of official looking cars all over the place. She didn't see any TV vans, though. She pulled into an empty parking place. A young cop approached her.

He was good-looking, with sandy-colored hair, blue eyes, and plenty of muscles. There was a little fascist swagger to him, though not much. *He'd get rid of that in DC, but not here. Not for a while, at least.* She decided she liked him anyway.

"You got business here, ma'am?"

There was only the slight hint of a southern drawl. He sounded a lot like John Milton.

"I'm a friend of Dolores Delgado," said Jay.

"You mean the sheriff's wife?"

"Yes. Dolores Milton. Can I see her?"

The cop examined her with suspicion in his blue eyes. He pointed to a decal on her side rear window.

"That's a DC police press license. You must be some kind of reporter."

"Very observant. You'll get the Sherlock Holmes merit badge if you keep that up." She offered a slender hand. "My name's Jay Sandoval. I'm a reporter but I'm really here as Dolores' friend. We go back a long ways. I'm not here professionally."

"Too bad. We've got a triple murder." The cop shook her hand. "Name's Roger Colman."

"Well, Roger, can I see Dolores?"

"She's talking with Sam Fletcher now. Everybody's trying to figure out what happened. All I know is that we lost some mighty good people."

"No leads yet?"

"I can't speak to that. They've got me out here directing traffic."

"And you're doing just fine at that, Roger. Is Dolores inside?"

"They're in the County Clerk's office. The forensics specialists are still working down in the morgue. We've also got guys from Quantico here."

"FBI?" Roger nodded. "Well, they didn't have to come as far as I did, at least. Buy me a drink later?"

"I'd be pleased to, ma'am." He winked at her good-naturedly. "The County Clerk's office is on the first floor, last office at the end of the hall."

Jay went inside to find Dolores, more red-eyed than she had been on the cell phone, yet also more in control of herself. Sam Fletcher was sitting with her, taking some notes.

"Jay, you made it." She got up and they hugged.

"I said I would, amorcita. Aqui para consolarte."

They hugged again and then Dolores introduced her to Sam. He seemed to be nervous and defensive. She estimated that he was trying his best to run some semblance of an orderly investigation. He was overwhelmed, no doubt, starting with the realization that he was now acting sheriff, a curious version of the famous Peter principle. She didn't know who Peter was—the origins were lost in the dim past—although his principle was almost a universal law of nature.

"Perhaps I'd better leave you two and get back to my duties," he suggested.

"Not so fast," said Jay. "Did you figure out yet whether the three victims were actually doing an autopsy?"

Sam Fletcher looked at her, studied her for a moment, and then smiled. Jay decided it was a nice smile and was sorry that she been so abrupt.

"Sheriff Milton wouldn't be participating in that. He might be observing."

"I'll rephrase. Did you—"

"I know what you mean," interrupted Sam. "Just setting the record straight. In case you write about this."

"Where'd you get that idea?"

"Both John and Dolores have spoken highly of your journalistic abilities."

Jay looked at the acting sheriff, studying him for a moment, waiting for him to go on. *He's no country hick. He'll learn fast because he'll be forced to. He probably chose to be in down here in the middle of nowhere for a good reason. Running from something? A woman, maybe? Or maybe he just lives out here because he finds it peaceful. Or, should I change that to past tense?*

Jay had known Sam and George, John Milton's two deputies, for years, yet she knew them mostly secondhand from John's accounts. Sam had the most seniority, which is why he had become acting sheriff. He was a large, corpulent man that was not quite a Friar Tuck, except for the head with his bald crown and sandy brown hair, now with some streaks of gray, making the crown look like some huge ostrich egg in a nest. For that reason, he wore his hat most of the time, except when it was very windy. He generally had a good sense of humor, his blue eyes often twinkling over some private joke. But not now. His boss and best friend had just been killed. As well as two close associates. The sorrow would set in later—at the moment he was just quietly pissed. Jay could feel the pent-up anger in the man. She could hardly blame him.

"Anyway, the exam table was clean," continued Sam. "Cleaner than one might expect. The killers removed the body, if there was one, and cleaned up the table right well."

"And no one knows why they were killed?"

"I would think that's obvious. They were probably examining a body that they weren't supposed to examine. Or even see, maybe. John hadn't started a report yet, so, if there was a body, we don't know where it was found. And Claude's tape recorder is gone."

"Dios mio, no one saw them pick up a body and bring it here? This isn't a very big town."

"That's what I said," commented Dolores. "I was at Mom's, helping her hang some new curtains, so John ate at Cindy's. In Lexington Park. I suppose the investigation would start there."

"How about it, Sheriff Fletcher?" asked Jay. "Have you checked Cindy's?" She knew the restaurant and had eaten there on several occasions.

"This is a murder investigation, a triple murder, and we're checking several things at the same time. I've sent George White to talk to Cindy. One of the local cops here from St. Mary's is driving out to Claude's and Patty's places to see if there are any clues there. I've got another cop checking the phone records."

"Good. You don't need a warrant for any of that, considering that they're dead. Looks like you have all the bases covered. Dolores, come with me."

"Where are we going?"

"I need a margarita, and you could use one, too. We'll gather up Roger and go visit Cindy's."

"Who's Roger?"

"He's on duty," growled Sam Fletcher. "Besides, he's from here. I mean, St. Mary's."

"I think you can spare him. I feel a little shaky, you see. A strong, supporting male who can take good notes would be a godsend."

"John was right. You sure do have a way with words. OK, get the hell out of here. And tell Roger he's officially off duty."

"His boss is the St. Mary's City police chief, although I guess Roger would appreciate your confidence in him."

"Billy Joe Hammond is on vacation. So I'm also temporary police chief."

"No wonder you look tired. Come on, Dolores."

They left Sam Fletcher scratching his head.

Scherzo Three

The campus of MIT had changed a lot over the last fifty years. If anything, it was even more crowded, as bigger and newer buildings had been packed into that little corner of Cambridge by the Charles River. The dome, which had collapsed in the aftermath of a terrorist attack, had been replaced by a fifteen story building that could best be described as a truncated pyramid, a modern Pharaoh's tomb with its top lopped off. It had huge sections of one-way polarized glass stitched together by chrome-covered girders. It looked very impressive, especially from the Boston side of the Charles.

The view from MIT's highest buildings had always been better than Harvard's, especially at night when the Boston skyline gleamed across the Charles like a scaled-down version of the New York City skyline from the Jersey side. It was a view that many people had admired. It made offices in those buildings the subject of many turf wars between professors, graduate students, departments, and schools.

Muhammad Obaid didn't have time to admire the view from his tiny tenth story office. It was a sunny day and the Boston skyline gleamed as he was concentrating on putting the final touches on his thesis defense.

MIT had been an important participant in the non-biological sciences and engineering advances of the twentieth century, yet it made a bold leap into the new century of genetics and bioengineering with their selection of their new president in 2004. Muhammad's work was in the spirit of that now fifty-year tradition.

He was proud of his achievements, although he had little time to think about them except in the context of his preparation. In collaboration with the scientists at Brigham and Women's Hospital, Massachusetts Eye and Ear Institute, and the Harvard Medical School, he had designed a new artificial eye. It only worked, of course, if the optical nerve wasn't damaged, just the eye itself, yet there were plenty of people in those circumstances who could benefit from his work.

There were already other artificial eyes on the market. His would be better and cheaper—better because his software was better since the tiny computer chips were the more complex, partly organic ones; cheaper because those tiny new chips were made from a process inherently less expensive than those previously used. Of course, the physicians had to make the connections—he was not a surgeon. But all the engineering was his.

He already had post-doc offers from MIT, Stanford, Caltech, and several other schools. He had fifteen patents in the mill, with only three co-authored by his thesis adviser, Professor Olsen, who fully admitted that he didn't completely understand the complex signal processing algorithms that had gone into the vision software. Olsen was pushing hard to make the transfer of the new algorithms to his own specialty of robotic vision.

There was a knock on the door. Thinking it was an undergraduate looking for help, Muhammad ignored it. Normally he would generously give up some of his time to work with the younger students. That was what it was all about, after all. But his thesis defense came first today.

Suddenly there was a loud crash as the office door was forced open. He was suddenly surrounded by a SWAT team.

"Muhammad Obaid, you are under arrest for plotting terrorist attacks against the citizens of the United States," said one of the men, motioning with a sinister-looking automatic rifle.

The PhD student raised his hands, an expression of pure terror and confusion on his face.

"You must be mistaken. I was born in Chicago. I'm as American—" He was interrupted as the man clubbed him full in the face with the butt of the rifle.

"Cuff him," the DHS agent ordered.

At 4 pm when Muhammad didn't show up for the thesis defense, Professor Olsen came up from the seminar room to see what had happened. It was too late. All he found was the splintered door and a pool of blood on his student's desk, mute testimony to an unthinkable atrocity.

Five months later, after interventions from the President of MIT and the two Massachusetts senators, Muhammad was released by the Department of Homeland Security. They had made a mistake, they said, and they apologized. The brilliant student returned to Chicago to his parent's house where he still sits, staring at the walls of his room, trying not to sleep so that the nightmares of the tortures he underwent, mostly psychological, won't come back to haunt him. Needless to say, he hasn't finished his PhD. There is some consolation in the fact that twelve of his patents were approved. Some of them are making him very rich. He doesn't seem to care.

Chapter Four

Boston, Massachusetts, Monday . . .

Chris Tanner struggled up the old stairs and into the homicide detectives' area of the precinct station. Like all rookies there, he shared a desk with another detective, a fellow from the third shift.

As he entered, some of the regulars were ushering out a prisoner who was bound in handcuffs and leg-irons. One of them bumped into him accidentally, making him wince with pain. His colleague looked at him strangely and then shook his head, an expression of disbelief on his face. *Yeah, I know what you're thinking. Everyone knows I almost bought the flag and bagpipes dirge last night. You're wondering what the hell I'm doing here. Well, I can't afford to stay in a hospital, that's what.*

For years the Boston Police Department had deployed three shifts, instead of four, due to restricted budgets. The first ran from six a.m. to three p.m. The second, his shift, ran from two p.m. to eleven p.m. The third ran from ten p.m. to seven a.m. The rookies rotated shifts every month, while the veterans got their preferences, in order of seniority, along with their own desk. The system actually worked out well and there was a great deal of camaraderie among the officers, although the shifts always became much longer than the nominal duration because they never had enough time to write up their reports.

The days of having a partner were also long gone. Even with the reduction from four shifts to three, budget cuts had made it impossible to keep a double payroll. Having a partner wouldn't have worked well for Chris anyway. He was very much a loner. He was building a solid reputation with his superiors, though, as someone who got the whole job done—investigation, arrest, and conviction of perps. He had also won the respect of his peers, something not easy to do, since they were a tough bunch. He was especially admired for his ability to not get flustered in the court room. A lot of detectives got very nervous with a hostile defense lawyer coming at them. Chris had only lost his cool once; even then the judge was quick to defend him and jumped all over the defense lawyer.

"Welcome back," said Harry Carson, one of the veterans. "Quite a party you had last night. How's the leg?"

Harry was a beefy individual that always seemed to be on some kind of diet, yet he had a good heart. He was nearly bald, his black pate doing an acceptable job of reflecting some of the feeble light from the dirty fluorescent bulbs. An ugly scar started just in front of his right ear and ended at the tip of his chin, a grim reminder to all that a knife could be as deadly as a gun. The odd thing was that Harry could have had it removed via plastic surgery, since he was grand-fathered into the old medical coverage, which was more generous than the current one.

"Still bandaged, stiff, and sore. My head is spinning from the pain killers. Can you believe they gave me less than a day in the hospital?"

"The wonders of modern medicine. You're lucky you didn't need a kidney or some other critical body part. Then you'd be put on a waiting list, where you'd wait maybe a year or more, unless you died first or you could afford to buy one on the black market. Your medical benefits probably wouldn't cover the operation anyway, since you weren't on duty." That was a lot coming from Harry, who usually didn't have much to say to anyone. Chris wondered if the old guy liked him. "Yeah, lucky, lucky. By the way, Denise wants to see you."

The captain looked up as Chris knocked. She waved him in, a haggard look on her face. She often looked over-worked, and probably was, since most everyone else fell into that category.

"Come in, Chris. Ready for a case?"

"I guess. Aren't you going to ask me how I am?"

"Chris, you're here, you're not dead, so get over it. There's a shooting over at Cleveland Circle. Want it or not?"

"All right. Did the coroner find anything out about our John Doe?"

"Report's probably in your video-mail. But it can wait. I need you at Cleveland Circle."

As a consequence, Chris didn't see the coroner's report until much later. He first dictated the Cleveland Circle report into the computer, emitting the usual string of expletives as he corrected by hand the mistakes the old voice recognition software had made. In the quiet moments following that, he opened up the video-mail corresponding to his Sunday night encounter.

The first thing that caught his attention was that the driver of the car had been killed by ricin poisoning, not the crash. He had to look that up, since he was not familiar with it. He found that it was a simple organic poison obtained from the waste mash produced when castor oil is made from castor beans. As a consequence, it was cheap and plentiful, which once made it a favorite of terrorists and assassins. Nowadays synthetic poisons were generally preferred, since they were more deadly, faster acting, and harder to detect and trace than ricin. Nevertheless, the latter was deadly enough. He wondered how his John Doe had come into contact with it.

Chris also noticed that the coroner had made no attempt at matching fingerprints, retinal patterns, or DNA with the national ID database available on-line to all law enforcement agencies. *That's strange, considering the circumstances. It's something that should automatically be done.* He would have to follow up on that, since otherwise the man would remain a John Doe.

Out of curiosity, he performed a search in the same database in order to bring up anything on Frank Sweeney, the Defense Secretary. As he suspected, there wasn't much detail, as a lot of the file was off-limits to him, requiring a security password. That made sense because the man was still in public office. But the ID information was there.

Chris also saw that Frank Sweeney gave his permanent residence as Wellesley, Massachusetts, not Washington, DC. That also made sense, because these database entries for politicians and political appointees were often not changed—government agencies knew full well that in four years they might have to change them again. Nevertheless, another address in the Georgetown section of DC was given.

Another item in the file caught his attention. Sweeney had a record. Nine years ago, before he had become Defense Secretary, he had been charged with abusing his wife and she had taken out a restraining order. Apparently they had reconciled, as the Wellesley house actually belonged to his wife's family, a wealthy Bostonian one dating back to revolutionary times.

Chris frowned at that information. He didn't care much for men that beat up on women. His father had done that, and then on him if he objected. His experience in law enforcement was that the abuser never really reformed, although anger management courses and other counseling sometimes helped them control their anger. His own father had learned to leave the house and take a walk around the block until he cooled off, not a mean feat when it was a negative fifteen degrees centigrade outside.

Now, where was Frank Sweeney last night? And did he know he had a look-alike?

Scherzo Four

President Fulton usually enjoyed himself at these special events. The long-winded political speeches were always hard to take, especially as he got older, though part of the POTUS obligation was to sometimes assume the ceremonial role still handled by monarchs in certain European countries, notably England. He shared those ceremonial duties with Stephanie Williams, his VP, and tried to be fair about it. She was going to run in the next primaries and could use the media exposure. She was also a lot more photogenic than he was.

Nonetheless, he took his fair share of those duties because it got him out of an office that he was growing to hate after eight years. His hair had gone from coal black to silver gray during his two terms. He had never wanted the job. Others had pressured him into it, telling him the country needed his guidance in these troubled times. *Needed, yes, but did anyone really listen? I didn't want the job then and I don't want the job now. Now people are just too damn adverse to compromise and consensus. Everyone has a personal agenda.*

Congressman Pratt from Louisiana had already spoken and Congressman Sanchez from Texas was finishing up. *Almost time to cut the ribbon.* He looked out across the water, up and down the shoreline and out to sea. Windmills. Thousands of them. One of his successes. It made him smile.

He had started on day one of his first term laying out his aggressive energy policy. Some of his predecessors had done good work there, work he could build on. But he had accomplished a lot himself in eight years.

The windmill farms were only part of the plan, of course. Cheap solar energy, aided by semi-organic photovoltaics, was also helping to produce more and more electricity independently of coal and oil. This was a good thing, considering that both would soon go the way of the dinosaurs.

Harnessing the wind had been around for centuries, of course, and modern engineering had made the windmill farms one of the wonders of the modern world. The windmills could be out in deep water because they floated; they didn't have to be anchored because they were stabilized by gyroscopes. A combination of wave action and rotational motion of those gyroscopes actually generated even more electricity, a trick patented by a young high school student at the turn of the century. That same trick kept buoy lights permanently on and allowed carpets of wave-gyroscopes to generate electricity where the larger windmill structures were not practical.

The semi-organic photovoltaics, however, were cutting edge technology, a synergistic product using diverse technologies from material science, electrical engineering and biogenetics. Contrary to what many futurists had believed at the turn of the century, the 21st century was not the century of biology and genetics. Instead, it was the century where old technologies were greatly improved by combining them with new life tailor-made for a specific function.

Initially, the rabid environmentalists, who wanted to keep the environment absolutely pristine, and a good number of the rich and wealthy, including senators and congressmen, who didn't want these solutions to the energy problem in their backyards, fought these alternative technologies. As oil reached the three hundred dollar per barrel plateau and the only coal left was not suitable for power generation, the world first thought of turning once again to nuclear power. But the problem of radioactive waste had never been solved. So governments finally began in earnest to pump funds into the development of alternative sources of energy. Now extensive solar energy regions in the desert and many wind farms off shore were providing a clean, environmentally safe way to generate power. Of course, his predecessors had to get past the oil companies, too, who still wanted to sell oil, even and especially at exorbitant prices. A lot of that work had been done for him, yet he would go down in history as the president who had put it all together. By the time his second term was up, the US would be largely independent of foreign oil.

President Fulton smiled as he stepped up to the microphone. *Yes, some days were all right. Now, if this sun weren't so bright, I could maybe get rid of this headache caused by a mostly sleepless night on Air Force One.*

Chapter Five

Paris, Monday . . .

Vladimir Kalinin could swear fluently in ten languages. His choice of language often seemed to be random, which puzzled him, since he prided himself on his orderly mind. He hadn't become successful by being unfocused. Thus the stream of German expletives coming out of his mouth, his reaction to the call he had just received, surprised him, since he was in Paris.

He snapped shut the cell phone and stared down at the Rue de Rivoli, the main thoroughfare that ran alongside the Champs d'Elysees. At this time of the year most of the would-be summer tourists from the US were only beginning to anticipate their adventures into the renowned and revered French culture, yet the tour buses were still snarling the traffic. His nose wrinkled at the thought of the uneducated swarms that would be coming to this beautiful city. His opinion was that most didn't deserve to be close to all this wonderful culture. *Of course, the French people, especially the Parisians, don't deserve it either. During the Roman Empire, Paris was not much more than a dunghill. And Napoleon was just a fat little fascist with a little man's inferiority complex! Put him beside DeGaulle and you have Laurel and Hardy, a comic fascist duo. What a farce!*

He smiled, humored by the fact that he was thinking badly of the French, in German. It took a little of his anger about the call away. He shook his head, clearing out the German, and started to think in English. Although it wasn't his native language, it was more practical than any other for clear business-oriented thinking. Life was all about business and English was its language, no matter what the French or the Germans said.

For him, business was a general term, a religion almost, a guide to efficiently living your life. In his Living the Good Life 101 course, "Have good business savvy" would be bullet number one on his first presentation chart. The first sub-bullet would be "Know your competitors' weaknesses; exploit your own people's competence." *Of course, a good business manager knows he cannot do everything, so he must delegate. And that's where the shit hits the fan. If the people I delegate to are incompetent, then all my planning is for nothing.*

Some close associates called him Volodya, although there weren't many that could claim to have that familiarity. Lethal accidents had befallen some who had thought they possessed it. Even the prostitutes he used to satisfy his enormous sexual appetite called him Mr. Kalinin, or the formal equivalent in the language of their country.

He not only looked down at the street but also at his partial reflection in the window. He had a Charles Bronson visage tempered by a Kirk Douglas chin and Sean Connery eyes (they were three old 20th century actors that he truly admired). His curly black hair now had the touch of gray around the ears common to many men his age.

He had to admit that at fifty-four he was slowing down. In a given night he would still take on two or three of Paris' finest "demoiselles de la nuit," although now he would often just do one and make the other two do each other, something that amused him to no end. It was all in the name of stress relief.

His was a stressful life. As CEO of the biggest drug company in the world, he was constantly traveling. He had even been into space, checking up on microgravity experiments financed by his company. That hectic business life produced some of his stress, though only a small portion.

The real stress came from his special "business projects," the ones very few people knew about. Most of them were run by people who only knew him as a disembodied, electronically distorted voice that gave orders over the phone. They were the aces he was holding, his real purpose in life.

He decided to go out for a walk. He went back to the bedroom where three naked women were sleeping. One stirred uneasily and then looked at him with wine-blurred eyes. He tossed a good number of euros onto the bed.

"You can use the shower if you want," he said in French. It was gutter French. In addition to his ten languages, he knew many of their dialects, using the dialect appropriate to the person being spoken to. He considered it a sign of good breeding to speak his guests' language. Even if they were whores. "Just be gone by the time I get back."

The woman who was awake nodded and picked up the money. She was smart enough to spread the bills out on the sheet and count them. Apparently satisfied, she put them on one of the nightstands, smiled and called him a bastard, then rolled over to go back to sleep.

Vladimir left the room and took the elevator down to the street level. He walked out of the hotel and turned up the Rue de Rivoli. Crossing the Seine via the Pont Neuf, he was soon in the Latin Quarter. All the while he was walking, he was thinking about the call, though he stopped to have a café au lait in a sidewalk café on St. Germain. By then he was perspiring since the early spring day was warm and humid.

Vladimir Kalinin had grown up in a Leningrad slum with another name, a name that mattered little neither then nor now since he didn't know who his father was, other than through that name. His mother, a prostitute, died from TB at twenty-seven. The young boy of ten became a ward of the state, an orphan in a country in chaos.

The fall of the Soviet empire had left his native country in a shambles. The ethnic strife throughout the old empire, unleashed after years of harsh control by the Kremlin, could not be controlled by an underpaid and overworked police force. This chaos was a breeding ground for corruption and crime. The smart young man had known how to take advantage of it.

He had taken the name Vladimir Kalinin when he saw it on a grave in the suburbs of Moscow. The original Vladimir had been born in the same year as he was. With the inefficiencies of the Russian bureaucracy, there was little chance that anyone would ever find out that he was not the authentic one. He adopted the same tactic in a number of countries. Thus it came to pass that Interpol had several files on him, not knowing they all corresponded to one and the same person.

The file on Vladimir Kalinin was clean, though, and as CEO of a huge company he was considered a VIP by most governments, a fact that made his work all the more easy as he moved around the world attending to his legal business empire as well as the illegal one. He donated large sums to all three US political parties and was not unknown in the halls of power in Washington DC, as well as many other capitals. He had a chalet in Switzerland, a villa in Italy, and a large estate in Connecticut, yet he rarely visited any of them, living mostly in expensive hotels where service was first class and the people were discreet about his own goings and comings as well as those of his guests.

He sipped at his café au lait and pondered what he should do about the telephone call. The idiots had slipped up. He didn't like incompetence. Various plans of action started forming in his head. He smiled. *Oh, I'm good. That's why I survive in this dog-eat-dog world.*

Chapter Six

In the Virginia countryside, Monday . . .

RP1 sat on the little bench in the garden and waited. The high fence around the garden was nearly as tall as the two young trees and certainly taller than the bushes. It was white and sterile, as was the main laboratory building. He didn't know it was a laboratory, of course. He just knew it as home. It was the only home he had known for twenty-one years. Everyone called it the Center.

The garden, while small, had lots of plants and flowers. He found it peaceful. It was a good place to wait, even though it was well past midnight and all the lights were off. He looked up and saw a patch of open sky. Some stars were peeking out around the clouds now as if to announce that the day's thunderstorms were over.

RP1 knew that out there people were beginning to explore the solar system. More close to home, a new section was being added to the International Space Station, or so he had heard. *Someday I'll be out there.*

It was a relaxing moment away from his training. The Center was part of a special NASA program, so there were classes and training sessions every day, including all sorts of physical exercise and endurance tests. Under the watchful eyes of their tutors, they all prepared for one of mankind's greatest adventures, a trip to the nearest star system. To avoid distractions from the outside world, the Center was patrolled by a well trained security force. The future astronauts and the other Center personnel—doctors, nurses, scientists, and engineers—called them the Guardians.

Their only contact with the outside world was via the newsnets. They could watch them all they wanted, although it was all pre-recorded. Most of RP1's colleagues thought the outside world was in pretty bad shape and were glad that they were shielded from it. It allowed them to concentrate on the business at hand, namely learning all the things that would be necessary for first the long journey, then the future colony. Some courses were required for all, others were required for some that had certain skills, and still others were elective. There was a lot of camaraderie among them, though they couldn't fraternize much, since their classes were often small and only limited team projects were allowed.

Some of them complemented their classes by teaching themselves other things, using e-books and e-journals from the library. Overall, they were generally much more educated than the average US citizen. For example, their knowledge of anatomy, basic bodily functions, genetics, diseases, and so forth was at least equivalent to that of a second year medical student. In particular, RP1 knew all about the differences between males and females. He was sure his feelings for SW2 were much more than simple sexual attraction, though. *Where is she?*

As if on cue, she stepped into the garden. He stood and she slipped into his waiting arms. Her warm body made him feel electric. Her full lips brushed against his.

"I've missed you," she whispered. "They did more tests on me today. Will they take something from me like GW1? Or am I going to die like FT2?"

Some months ago GW1 had been taken somewhere else in the complex, a place where they were not allowed to go. When she came back five days later, she announced rather sadly that she had been operated on to remove a diseased kidney. A month after that, they said that FT2 had died of a heart attack. SW1, FS2, and HJ1, the rebels in their small group, had thought that odd and snuck into a place where they shouldn't be. The three of them claimed that they had seen FT2 with his chest laid open. By his side, packed in ice, was his heart. It looked fine.

That began a lot of ugly talk among the group, some believing the three rebels, others thinking they were stupid or making up stories to get attention. Both RP1 and SW2 were in the latter group but SW2 was a little scared about all the talk.

Then the rebels simply disappeared. The rumor was that their colleagues had jumped the fence, escaping into the mysterious world beyond the Center. RP1 couldn't believe they had been killed like FT2, if FT2 was indeed killed, although he also didn't think it was that easy to jump the fence. *And why would anyone want to? They were being prepared for the longest and most wonderful journey ever undertaken by human beings.*

Just about every day they were told they were genetically perfect representatives of the human race. They would be sent out on the first expedition to go outside the solar system, bound for the Alpha Centauri system. They would not see the end of the journey, although their great grand-children would.

Since they had been told that all their lives, RP1 had usually not questioned it, thinking it was just an established fact, like "you must brush your teeth." But lately he had started to question things, especially since FT2 was allegedly killed and the three others left.

It also made a difference that he was now in love. Or, at least he thought it was love. He had no one to tell him whether it was the real thing or not. He wasn't about to ask the Guardians, or the other personnel, for fear they would stop him from seeing SW2. He wasn't about to ask any of his colleagues either because he didn't want them to laugh at him.

"I don't think you have anything to worry about. They need us for the mission."

"But that scares me, too. What happens if there are ugly alien monsters out there?"

"You watch too many science fiction movies," said RP1. "If there are alien people out there, they'd probably be just as scared of us as we are of them."

"Yes, but there could still be monsters. I mean, think of the T-Rex in that old movie we saw just last week."

"That was an old classic. I think we're seeing the second in the series tomorrow night. Remember, dinosaurs existed millions of years ago. And cloning them is really impossible."

"I just mean, well, if aliens had come to Earth millions of years ago, wouldn't they call T-Rex an alien monster?"

"Come on, let's sit on the bench. Why worry about aliens? Only our great grand children have to worry about alien creatures anyway. Not us."

She kissed him on the cheek and tussled his hair. He liked her to do that. He took her hands in his and stared in her eyes. She blinked nervously and licked her lips.

"That sounds like a romantic suggestion," she said.

He took her in his arms.

"It's more than a suggestion."

Scherzo Five

Christy Vargas strode to the podium. She had given many speeches in her political career but she was always nervous. This hot summer evening in Miami was no exception, even though she was dressed in her trademark short skirt and half blouse that showed her well tanned midriff. Her black hair waved defiantly in the stiff sea breeze.

"Ladies and gentlemen, I am here today to start a movement." She waited for the Miami crowd to settle down. "As Congresswoman for this district, I'm very much aware of the general sentiment here that Washington is neglecting Floridians, and, in particular, the citizens of this great city. Our adults are burdened with taxes and the costs of medical coverage. Our children have to study in schools that are run down and outdated, using twentieth century textbooks in many cases. Our workers, those who have jobs, see their standards of living diminishing day by day as the middle class slowly disappears." Cheers interrupted her. She held up her hands to quiet the crowd. "Washington is too far away to care about us, my friends." She was ready for the trump card. "Today, I am resigning from the US Congress to head up a new movement, a movement inspired by the great patriots who founded this country. As those patriots struck a blow for freedom against a tyrannical overseas power, I will dedicate myself to strike a blow for freedom against the tyranny of Washington DC. Our movement will promote the secession of Florida from the United States of America. Our goal is a free Florida by making it a new nation, a nation where all Floridians may enjoy the fruits of their labors and live together in peace and harmony without the tyranny of the federal government."

The cheers were raucous now. The crowd was ready to be whipped into a frenzy.

We'll make the riots and protests in California, Michigan, and Texas look like child's play. A new social revolution is spreading throughout the country, and I'm going to ride it as far as I can.

Off to one side of the crowd, a man in a light tropical suit frowned. He was a DHS agent. They were just keeping tabs on Christy Vargas, who had become something of a firebrand as she refused to play along with the status quo. She was another germ in a disease that was spreading like wildfire across the country, attacking its very nervous system. But her actions by themselves were not what bothered the DHS. Free speech, up to a certain point, still prevented them from doing much beyond giving her warnings about crowd control and not promoting violence, yet the agent knew that such movements were also fertile grounds for terrorist recruiting.

Christy Vargas certainly had no desire to provide recruits for terrorist cells; her own father had been killed in an attack on a financial building in downtown Miami. In other words, she meant well, however crazy seceding from the union might seem to a lot of people. Nevertheless, the agent would infiltrate her movement and try to pick off the terrorist leeches when they came to look for their new recruits.

Chapter Seven

Lexington Park, Maryland, Monday . . .

   Cindy's Old Towne Family Restaurant was a refurbished church. Cindy, now white-haired and portly, was only five when her grandfather purchased it many years ago. The archdiocese shut it down and used its sale to help pay for the lawsuits it had lost in the pedophilia scandals at the turn of the century. In that way the Church of St. Francis became very much a secular institution, though the secular Cindy was influenced by her St. Francis as if she were a modern St. Anthony, tending to her flock with the good humor and good counsel characteristic of the best of priests. What her food lacked in flavor and presentation was compensated by her walk-throughs where she talked to the regulars and welcomed the newcomers, although over the years there were more of the former and fewer of the latter as the demographics of Lexington Park waxed and waned, but mostly waned.
   Lots of hanging drapes and old quilts on the walls deadened the sound of the dining customers, their chatter and laughter muted to a contented murmur punctuated by the soft percussion of clanging pots and pans. The little naves where the saints used to be made nice private dining spots. The altar where the priest used to say mass, calling for the Lord's light to shine down upon his charges, had become a performance stage, although it was usually dark. On some Friday or Saturday nights there would be a volunteer that would strum a guitar and sing a few songs on that stage, especially if Cindy prodded the amateur crooner with a few beers from the well-stocked bar at the front of the church where they used to keep the proceeds from the collection. These weekend events were random but enjoyable ones that made the white noise hum of the local dining crowd increase in intensity, the noise often interrupted with hoorahs or cat calls, depending on the skill of the entertainer. In addition, on Thursdays there was always karaoke, except on Thanksgiving, of course,

when Cindy's was host to the many people around—widows, widowers, and other lonely people—Cindy's friends who didn't have a family holiday dinner to go to. Occasionally the restaurant would even be hired out for a wedding—not a church wedding, of course—yet it made it very convenient to have the wedding and the reception in the same place.

As she crawled into a booth on the main floor across from Dolores, Jay studied her friend. Roger, the cop, had unfortunately been called to get a cat out of a tree, so he had been left behind in St. Mary's. Jay had mixed emotions about not having him with her. *Good looking guy, though this is probably not the time to flirt with the gendarmes anyway.*

Dolores had been putting on a little weight. Hippiness was in her family, so she was fighting against genetics. The flat-chested teenager with the devilish glint in her eye had given way to a serious, mature woman who was sure of her place in the world and the goals in her life. At least, she had been, until her husband's murder.

She and John Milton never had children, although Jay knew they had tried. Neither had wanted to go the route of fertility pills or artificial insemination, even though both were commonplace for couples who wanted a baby. They also had avoided the bureaucratic nightmare of adoption, having neither the time nor the money to hire an adoption lawyer. Their baby had turned out to be Henry, a large golden retriever, who happily slobbered around the big, rambling house the couple owned.

"Are you calmer now, amorcita?"

The question seemed to break the dam to a flood of tears. Jay was surprised that her friend still had some left. On the other hand, for a woman that had just lost her soul mate, Dolores was holding up well.

When there were no more tears and a few nose blows indicated a readiness to talk, it was Dolores' turn to quiz Jay. She had noticed that Jay's hand shook when she picked up the margarita. Jay had also downed a good third of it on the first sip.

"You're not so strong yourself, hermanita," Dolores said. "This affects you a lot too, doesn't it?"

"Of course. I've reported on a lot of crime scenes, though never one involving my best friend's husband. But it's just a case of nerves mostly. One's own mortality, and all that."

"You were always the philosophical one."

"That's probably why you got a man and I didn't. You know how—" Jay stopped in mid-sentence as a shadow fell across their table. She looked up at a hulk of a man—nearly two meters and 150 kilos, she guessed. He had a black beard that covered his chest but he was completely bald. "Blackbeard the Pirate?" she asked.

The giant chuckled and offered a meaty hand.

"No eye patch, ma'am. That's the give-away. My name's Gunther Mann, though my friends call me Bouncer."

"Are we friends?" asked Jay, looking at Dolores, fearing the answer, whether it be yes or no.

"Bouncer is a freelance reporter," explained Dolores. "He does a lot of his work on the internet with his computer up in a cavernous loft he calls his apartment. We have a lively e-mail and video-mail correspondence, mostly about new software and new computer gizmos. Bouncer, this is my friend, Jay Sandoval."

Jay looked with curiosity at the wires plugged into sockets implanted behind Bouncer's ear. They ran down his massive neck and disappeared into the shirt collar. Obviously he was connected to the internet all the time and controlled his computer with one of the new devices just out that used modern speech processing algorithms and special sensors to detect subvocalized commands. They were very expensive and the software was not even fully tested. She wondered if Bouncer was a beta-tester for the equipment. A lot of hackers got fancy stuff that way and it all represented a good investment for the company making the devices, since the beta-testers usually worked for free.

"I've heard of you," he said. "Mostly John reminding me that I'm scum and my work sucks and I should be a good reporter like you, work for a decent e-zine, hold down a steady job, and all that." Dolores scowled at him. "Sorry 'bout that, Dolores. I didn't mean to insult his memory. He was a good man. I feel your loss."

"So?" asked Jay, waiting for one of them to continue.

The giant squeezed in beside her. Jay decided he couldn't fit in beside Dolores, so it was the only practical choice. But she was immediately aware of his body odor and wished that his choice had been to go away.

"First, I'd like to offer condolences to Dolores. Second, I want to make you an offer, Jay."

"I'm not that kind of woman," she said with a pleasant smile. Again the giant chuckled.

"Acerbic banter is just my cup of tea. Actually, now that you got me thinking of beverages, I believe I'll have one of those that you guys are drinking. Waiter!"

By then Jay had decided that Bouncer Mann was just plain annoying. The reporter or hacker or whatever he was had the manners of a barnyard swine and the bacon to match. He certainly wouldn't be doing any ads for a physical fitness club, that was for sure.

He finally got settled and comfortable with his margarita, and raised it in a toast.

"To John Milton, a noble man, friend to most, yet feared by the bad guys."

"Don't make light of his death," hissed Dolores.

"Sorry, that wasn't the intention. You shouldn't take it that way. John was one of the few friends I had in Lexington Park. Or anywhere else, for that matter. Present company excepted. Now, Jay, back to my offer. I'd like to go 50-50 with you on your story."

"What story?"

"The story you're going to write about this case. That's what really brings you down here, right?"

"Wrong. I came down to give some comfort to Dolores. The story was the excuse I gave my night editor for coming down. Lots of stories don't pan out. He won't hold this one against me. I don't plan on writing it."

"It may pan out whether you want it to or not," he whispered while looking around the restaurant as if to see if anyone was listening. "I've got a lead."

"What?" asked Dolores. "Why didn't you tell the authorities?"

"They're too slow. Besides, then it wouldn't be a story."

"On the contrary," said Jay, "finding John's killers would be quite a story, whether the police did it or not. And whether I write about it or not. That should be our goal, monstro mio."

"Well, it's not much of a lead. So, anyway, are we 50-50?"

"Since you ignored what I just said, sure, you can have half credit for anything I write about this case," agreed Jay.

The giant's face exploded into a toothy smile.

"Oh, I get it. You're not writing anything, so 50 per cent of nothin' is nothin', correct?"

"You learn fast, big man."

"Oh, this one is a bruja," Bouncer told Dolores, "and she has me under her spell."

"Callate, amigo, and give with the lead. I've had a long day."

"It's Bob Martin." The giant looked smug.

"You're kidding. Bob can't see anything beyond his next bottle of booze."

Bouncer turned and leaned towards Jay, and winked at her.

"You see, I've got sources. Shirley, the busty redhead over there, told me that she saw him run into John, literally run into him, as John was leaving here. They exchanged words and went off somewhere together."

"Off somewhere?" asked Dolores. "What does that mean? In a car?"

"No, they were walking. Shirley was on a break, so she didn't see when they came back, though on her next break, the sheriff's patrol car was gone. That's the lead."

"They walked . . . ." Jay was staring into the foggy lime green transparency of her margarita. "This Bob, where does he live?"

"Mostly where he can find a place to lie down and sleep it off. Right now, with these warm nights, he's probably hanging out under the old railroad trestle, if he's not out looking for a handout. Want me to drive you there?"

"No, I first want to take a walk. Bouncer, why don't you take Dolores home?"

"You'll come stay with me tonight, right?" her friend asked.

"Sure. But I want you to go home and just take it easy. And Bouncer, meet me at the A&W stand in about a half hour. I saw it on the way in."

"But that's too far. The trestle's real close, just over on Summer Street."

"I have my reasons."

She watched Dolores and Bouncer leave, then put down two twenties and left herself. Bouncer hadn't paid for his drink, of course.

She walked around the block containing the restaurant but didn't see anything of interest. A couple of teens whistled at her from a passing car, showing Monday afternoons in Lexington Park were clearly slow. She then walked into the alley bordering Cindy's. It opened up into a small parking lot with a dumpster at one end. It was probably part of the old parish parking lot, although some of Lexington Park's expansion had probably eaten up a good chunk of it. Again, nothing much to see.

She looked up at the church. The afternoon sun lit up the ornate stained glass window that was over the altar, momentarily hiding the cobwebs and dirt of neglect. She could barely make out the scene since she saw it in reverse view. Even though the colors were dull, she could determine that it was St. Francis surrounded by his usual entourage of animals. It brought back memories of her childhood.

There was no bell in the church tower, although there was a place for it. She could imagine how it would toll a century ago, calling the faithful to mass. In her own childhood she had been innocently devout. Her experiences with the rough street gangs had killed her innocence and the suffering and dying she saw as a teen were only intensified by her present occupation as a mature woman. *And now John Milton. How can that be part of God's plan?*

The cooking smells of the restaurant, dominated by garlic and onions, caused her nose to twitch in distaste, again bringing back memories of the sleazy eating spots of her childhood. *Or is it the smell of the restaurant garbage in the dumpster?*

She went over to the dumpster and walked around it. She was tall enough to raise the lid but not tall enough to peer inside. Right then she wasn't about to climb in. Then she noticed that there were marks on the ground around the dumpster suggesting something or someone had been dragged. *Is the dumpster the source of the body?* She took out a tiny digital camera from her purse and snapped a few pictures. Then she returned to the street in front of Cindy's, got into her car, and headed for the A&W stand.

Scherzo Six

"I don't understand your point, Mr. Adams. Why would this bill hurt your company?" The senator glared across his polished oak desk at the lobbyist. He had always disliked the unctuous little bastard, yet his company was a big campaign contributor and provided many jobs in his state.

The Senate office building had been refurbished in 2019. It was showing its age again. Fortunately, there were still only one hundred senators, yet over the years staffs had grown. Office space was at a premium. The senator's office was spartan for that very reason. His desk, while elegant, was small. Some members of his staff were actually housed in his home state because of the lack of room in DC, a perfectly workable solution to a vexing problem most of the time, thanks to modern communications. Staff meetings were routinely run through videoconferencing, for example. There was also the added benefit that the staff in the home state could directly sample the voters' opinions, face to face.

Paying for all that staff was not an easy matter. His state provided some funds, of course, yet he needed other sources. There were usually leftover campaign donations as each senator became more and more entrenched, making the would-be challenger's job more and more difficult. Those leftovers, sometimes via legally questionable routes, made their way into the general coffers and paid for that staff. Since it was all to the benefit of the home state, the senator usually didn't think about it too much. It was the way the game was played.

But Mr. Adams, being the little rat that he was, reminded the senator about how questionable some of these practices were, even though they had well over a century of history.

The lobbyist didn't wilt under the senator's glare, though he did look nervous. He fidgeted in his seat. The senator's office was nicely air-conditioned, yet he thought it was stuffy. *Or do I just hate my job?*

"You understand, senator, that there is a waiting list for transplants. All kinds. We are in the business of saving lives. If this law goes on the books, we can be prosecuted for buying organs of dubious origin, even if we are the innocent victims of some black marketer. And the people these organs could save would suffer, perhaps die."

"Yes, but if we don't make it a federal crime, won't it encourage the black market in organs?"

"Oh, I don't know about that. Highly debatable, I think."

"And all those people you save, aren't they the filthy rich ones with full medical? Your company doesn't pay for any transplants in their lower tier medical plans."

"I'm not sure I approve of the adjective 'filthy' being used in conjunction with our most esteemed clients. They have to be financially well off to afford our full coverage, it's true, but we're still saving their lives, important lives, the best of our country's best." He leaned forward slightly. "You're one of our clients, if I remember correctly."

"Yes, so what? My whole family has full medical with you. So do most senators."

"I see, the whole family." Mr. Adams shuffled through some papers. "Your daughter, Sally, now she really shouldn't be covered by us anymore, should she? She's over twenty-five on one hand, which we could overlook if she were a student still, though both you and I know she'll quit graduate school for a semester so she can accompany you on the campaign trail."

"You bastard! Get out of here."

Mr. Adams paused at the door.

"Do I have your vote, senator?"

The senator nodded, feeling numb.

Chapter Eight

Boston, Massachusetts, Monday . . .

Chris Tanner looked up as a visitor, blocking the overhead light, cast a shadow over his desk. He iconized the file on Frank Sweeney, not knowing who the person was.

"Detective Tanner?" The voice was a woman's but it was hard to see her features against the harsh glare of the light.

"I'm about to go off duty," he replied.

"Mary Beth Grogan, DHS." A badge was offered. He could see her picture on the badge better than he could see her face. Unlike a lot of pictures on badges, hers was not a bad picture. "I'd like a word with you." Chris waved to his guest chair. He thought the chair had been purposely designed to keep interviews short, yet it was the best he had. "In private."

"How about an interrogation room?"

"That's fine. Lead the way."

He did so.

They sat down face-to-face at the old, scarred wood table, which dated from the previous century. The precinct was that old. Initials and other graffiti had been etched into the table's surface, not by prisoners, but by generations of cops who also used the interrogation room as a conference room when working up a case.

The walls of the room had places where the paint had been knocked off, exposing plasterboard underneath. The old fluorescent fixtures cast a harsh light and the air was heavy with the moldy odors of an old building. In the old days an interrogation would get so heated that a prisoner would vomit or lose bladder control, especially if he was stoned or drunk, thus adding just the right police station finish to the spectrum of odors. At one end of the room, above the old steam radiators that were no longer functioning, there was a one-way mirror. Behind it observers could watch the interrogation without being seen.

Chris studied his visitor more carefully. She was not a knock-out beauty yet she was pert and pretty. She was prettier than her badge picture too, thus re-establishing the norm. She was dressed in an expensive business attire which was carefully chosen to accentuate her best features. With short, blond hair—probably natural, he guessed—unblemished complexion, and piercing blue eyes, she would turn heads. Boston, New York, Philadelphia. Almost anywhere except out west or Florida where the smart business suit would have to give way to much skimpier and simpler clothing, thus reducing the synergism between wardrobe and wearer.

"How can I help you, Agent Grogan? What brings you up from DC? I know it's a short hop by shuttle, yet it must be important to make you come in person instead of sending someone from the local office."

"It's important enough for me to come up, yes. I work directly for Hank Johnson, the Assistant Secretary. I fly all over the country, sort of an agent at large, and also representing him sometimes. He's a busy man."

"Yeah, I've seen how busy he's been, in the news." Everyone knew that Hank Johnson had just recently been involved in a sex scandal, an embarrassment to the Fulton administration. "Are you representing him now? Or is this part of your agent-at-large identity?"

She smiled. It was a nice smile, although the eyes became cold and distant. He knew those eyes. He had seen them many times, belonging to several different varieties of sociopaths. They made quite a contrast with the pert little face. He was beginning to get an uneasy feeling.

He had a thing about eyes, always had. One could learn a lot about a person by looking him straight in the eyes. He remembered the eyes of his father when he grabbed Chris by the shirt, drawing him close, ready to punch him out with a fist already covered with his mother's blood. He remembered the Iranian soldier's eyes, filled with hatred, as Chris blocked the knife thrust, plunging his own knife into the man's chest. These were the eyes of violence.

There were strange eyes, too. He remembered the imploring eyes of the sexual predator, standing over the little girl's mutilated body, eyes that asked Chris to kill him, eyes expressing the searing mental anguish as he realized what he had done. Or the vacant eyes of the man sitting on the steps of a building, a gun barrel in his mouth, while inside some of his victims still writhed in agony as they bled out.

Yes, eyes told him a lot. Sometimes he would wake up at night in a cold sweat, seeing those eyes. The police psychologist said it was part of who he was—battered youth, ex-soldier, now a cop. *She said I have to learn to live* with it. *Not much help there. She wasn't paid enough to be any good. And my medical plan won't cover the cost of an outside shrink.*

"Let's just say we are interested in one of your cases, and leave it at that."

"You're here about the ricin poisoning victim?" he asked, already knowing the answer.

"We're not just interested in the fact that he's a victim of an accidental poisoning. We're also concerned about his features. The report from this office was that your John Doe has an uncanny resemblance to the Secretary of Defense, Frank Sweeney."

"A very young Frank Sweeney, I'd say. A lot of people have look-alikes, Agent Grogan. Las Vegas is still full of Elvis look-alikes, even after all these years. Why does a look-alike interest the DHS high command?"

"The ricin and the resemblance to Frank Sweeney combine to send up a red flag. We're always on the outlook for terrorists and any new tricks they might come up with. We have such an open society that it's very easy for them to infiltrate and set up their cells."

"The society is a lot less open now than it was fifty years ago but I get your point. So, you want to hear my story first hand?"

"I would appreciate that." She took out a tiny recorder. "Do you mind?"

"I'll keep what I say strictly professional, then. I'm not going to have my conjectures thrown back at me."

"Oh, I would never do that." She smiled a disarming smile. It was still a nice smile, although now there was something a little twisted about it, in addition to the cold eyes. His cop's sixth sense, cued by the eyes, was going into overdrive. A healthy paranoia, Denise often called it. He had come to trust it. "You can begin."

He gave it to her straight, including the conversation with Denise in the hospital room.

"Well, that's quite a story," she said when he finished. "You did a lot of quick thinking for someone who was off duty."

"What do you mean by that?" he asked defensively.

"I understand that you had a few beers under your belt." When he started to object, she raised a hand. "Off duty, I said. Nothing wrong with that. We all need to unwind at times. We have stressful jobs." She consulted some notes she had been making. "You have no clue as to who this John Doe might be, then?"

"None of the standard ID checks are in the coroner's report, something I'm going to call him on. I just haven't got around to it yet. There's nothing on the body or in the car that gave an ID either. Except for that, we've pretty well shut the book on the case, I guess, except for my checking with the coroner and writing up my final. Our John Doe was a car thief, by the way. That part is solved. I guess it will remain an unsolved homicide, though. We get a lot of those. The crime statistics aren't good."

"Yes, I know, especially with terrorism. DC, Philly, Boston, Chicago, LA—and not just the big cities. A minor league baseball game in a small town in Alabama was hit last Friday. We seem to be getting further and further behind. After three wars with the Arabs, you'd think they'd have learned their lesson." She cleared her throat. "No need to tell you about that, I guess."

"How so?"

"A four medal man from the last one. Quite a record."

Chris felt uncomfortable. Was she trying to get on his good side?

"I guess it prepared me for the war on our streets. Like last night."

"About that. We'll take over from here. Just in case. I have some forensic agents picking up the body now."

"I think you're wasting your time."

"You said no conjectures," she observed with another smile, pointing to the recorder, which was still running. She turned it off. "In spite of some bad press, we do know our job and we try to be thorough. Like I said, it's the ricin and the possible Sweeney connection. These guys are capable of anything."

Her statement was so matter-of-fact that he could almost believe her. She seemed to be studying him for a moment. Chris wondered whether she was sizing him up professionally as a cop or whether he turned her on a little. Some women liked him immediately while others, especially the ones he seemed to be interested in, often ignored him. He knew he had some rough edges, yet he also knew that there were a lot of guys out there with less class. Normally he would ignore it when a woman gave him the once over, knowing that lasting relationships rarely came from love at first sight. But Mary Beth Grogan's study of him somehow had a deeper meaning.

"I suppose they are," he said. "That's why they're terrorists."

"Correct. Good day, detective. You've been most co-operative."

Chris watched her go. His sixth sense was still telling him something was amiss.

How did she know the ricin poisoning was accidental? No one had concluded that. Or did she think the Frank Sweeney look-alike was a terrorist who had been planning on using ricin in some future attack? Quite a stretch, when there are so many other better poisons available.

Scherzo Seven

Helen Rialto looked out over the Sunday morning crowd. The church was two-thirds full, not bad for a hot, almost summery day. It took some dedication to come and sit on the old, hard pews in the faulty air-conditioning. The church was starting to show its age, yet the congregation was steadfast. And they weren't just old-timers either. There were young faces in the crowd, looking at her with expectation as they waited for her to begin the sermon.

She launched into the parable of the prodigal son, bringing it into the present context, relating it to their everyday lives. She was good at it. It was what she had studied and trained for; it was what she had wanted to do since she was a teenager.

Many people depended on her, using her as support in their times of crisis. The old and the young, they came to her. In these poor neighborhoods, she often served as marriage counselor, youth guidance counselor, even psychiatrist, because the people she served couldn't afford anything else and wouldn't be comfortable going anywhere else.

As Helen talked, she noticed one young man sitting alone in a pew, a third of the way back from the front. She noticed him because he was sweating. Dark sweat stains were visible in the collar and the sleeves of the light brown, short-sleeve dress shirt that he wore. His forehead had beads of sweat that glistened in the heavy, stale air. Helen knew the air conditioning was bad, though not that bad. The man also fidgeted, like he had a bad case of hemorrhoids. However, the pews were old-fashioned and hard, so she soon forgot about him and his discomfort as she got more into the sermon.

She never wrote her sermons. She just jotted down general ideas on a 3 by 5 and then let inspiration take over. When she found a good place to end, to sum up the lessons learned for today's congregation, she brought it to a close.

This Sunday was like every other, for the last eleven years. She finished but as she told the congregation to bow their heads and pray, the fidgety young man stood up, and the church exploded.

Helen survived, in a way. She was blinded and crippled. Many of her congregation did not. The terrorist group Bravo Islam claimed responsibility. Helen found a hard time finding forgiveness in her heart for them—not so much on her account, but for her congregation. In addition to the lives lost, they had lost their church, and, with it, their safe harbor in time of need.

Chapter Nine

Lexington Park, Maryland, Monday . . .

"We're being followed."

Bouncer almost bit his lip upon hearing that observation. Jay reached over the steering wheel and wiped some whip cream off his moustache. It was the remnants of the two root beer floats he had put down, while she had struggled with one. *Oh, but it had been so good!*

"Followed? In Lexington Park? Who'd follow me?"

"Who'd brutally murder the sheriff, the coroner, and the forensics expert? Pull in here!"

It was a little neighborhood shopping mall with a drugstore, a pizza shop, and a few other stores. Jay got out and strode purposely towards the entrance to the drugstore, her digital camera in the palm of her hand. As she entered the store the angle was just right to get a picture of the front of the car that had been following them as it swung into a parking place. She bought a diet Coke for appearances, which she couldn't really drink after the root beer float, and left the store.

"What was that all about?" asked Bouncer.

"I've got his portrait, monstro mio. I have a friend in DC who can trace any license plate. I'll call tonight."

"Actually, I could transfer it right now. I've got a direct link to my computers." He pointed to the wires coming out of the side of his head. "New technology. It senses subvocalized commands. It's still pretty experimental but a pal up at Carnegie-Mellon set me up with it."

"Yeah, I wondered about that. If it's so experimental, isn't it risky to have it plugged into your head?"

"Well, it's not attached to my brain, you know. It picks up the subvocalized commands and I can hear things back from the computer. Someday they'll have video too. They got the bandwidth limitation licked a long time ago, though the optical nerve connection is tricky. Those with the new artificial eyes would have no problem. They're working on that up at MIT and other places. Real soon now for real eyes, I bet."

"Enjoy your toys. As for GeeBee, I think I'd better send the request. He might get spooked if he receives a request from a stranger, even if it's in my name. He knows I move in unsavory company sometimes."

"I'm not unsavory, am I?"

"Uncouth and unsavory. But stow it. We need to talk to Bob. Is there anyplace nearby to where he hangs out that could be taken for our destination?"

"There's a Good Nites Motel just a hundred yards beyond the trestle. We could be going for a romantic afternoon."

Jay laughed. It didn't seem to hurt his feelings. She then decided to play it straight.

"Can we walk back to the trestle without being seen from there?"

"There's a big stand of trees between the trestle and the motel. It should be possible. You really think we're in danger?"

"Maybe. Maybe not. Someone was following us, that's for sure. So I don't want to put Bob in any danger either. OK, romeo, onward to the Good Nites Motel."

"Amorcita mia, your wish is my command. I promise to be gentle."

She studied him for a moment.

"Excuse me, but I think that must be impossible. You're twice my size. You'd squash me, you know." The off-color banter with Bouncer was improving her mood, which had been at its very lowest point when she had sent Dolores home with him.

"You could sit on my lap," suggested the giant with a wink.

She didn't know what to respond to that, so she resumed looking behind for the car that had been following them.

They actually checked into a room to maintain their cover story. The motel, like many in the area, always had a few visitors of the type they were pretending to be. It was built like a U, the open part facing the street. There were three two-story buildings, two forming the sides of the U and a third the base at the back of the complex. At each end of the back building there were two corridors, one with coke machines and ice, and the other with various toiletries, including condoms, even the fancy kind with erection enhancing drugs included. One normally could use either side to get to an alley in the back of the motel, although a tall latticed fence with a locked gate held them back. Jay picked the lock of one of the gates. They crossed the alley and were immediately into the woods.

"Where'd you learn to do that?"

"Not much to it with locks that old. Nineties vintage, I'd say. You'd be surprised at some of the tricks I know."

"Nein, fraulein, I don't think I would."

Bouncer led the way. His size made him move with care through the foliage and over the intertwined roots. Jay almost skipped along in his wake. They were soon underneath the trestle.

Bob Martin was standing and watching them, scratching his mohawk and full of curiosity.

"You sure make one hell of a racket," he observed.

"I can't help it. I'm a little too big to be a boy scout." Bouncer shook Bob's hand. "Bob, this is Jay Sandoval. She's a friend of Dolores Milton. She wants to know if you know what happened to John."

"The sheriff?" asked Bob, studying Jay from top to bottom, nodding his approval. "What about the sheriff?"

"He's dead, Bob," said Jay. "And Claude and Patty, too."

Bob looked suddenly sad.

"No shit, how did that happen?"

Jay and Bouncer explained the scene at the coroner's.

"So, do you know anything about a body?"

"Sure thing. I found it."

"In the dumpster behind Cindy's?" asked Jay.

"Now, how'd you know that?"

"A guess. It looked like a body had been dragged there. Was there anything unusual about the body? Enough so that someone would want it back?"

"Only that the sheriff was struck by how much the stiff looked like Hank Johnson."

"Hank Johnson? Who's he?" asked Bouncer.

"Henry W. 'Hank' Johnson, Assistant Secretary for Homeland Security. You know, that bloated sack that's been in the news."

Indeed he did. Hank Johnson presently was considered to be a political liability for President Fulton due to Johnson's escapades with a nineteen year-old Georgetown coed.

"That can't be. I caught the eye-opener newsnet this morning. Hank Johnson was fishing with President Fulton on a lake in Minnesota. He certainly didn't look dead."

"I saw that same news down at the appliance store this morning." Bob bobbed his head in agreement. "I stood and watched that a bit. The guy with the President looked a lot older than the stiff. I only said the corpse looked like Hank Johnson."

"What did John do?" asked Jay.

"He was going to call Claude. That's when I lit out, see, 'cause Claude and I don't get along well. Guess that won't be a problem now. I'll actually miss them all, even Claude. John and Claude were good men, and that Patty Smith, she was one hell of a soccer player. Good looking woman, too, like you, Jay. You got good taste, Bouncer, but what about Sandra?"

"So they were going to do an autopsy?" asked Bouncer, ignoring the man's question.

"I guess so, since he called Claude. 'Course that doesn't mean necessarily that Claude would do it, especially on a Sunday night. He doesn't have to do one if the cause of death is obvious, I suppose. And it was. Half the back of the guy's head was blown away. I figure the corpse was at least a half day old. He probably was put in the dumpster late Saturday night or early Sunday morning. Otherwise Josh or Ray woulda seen'm."

"Josh? Ray?" asked Jay.

"Joshua Corning and Raymond Burton. They're Cindy's dishwashers. A little addled at times, but nice guys." Bob looked straight at Bouncer, daring the younger man to contradict him.

"Both are a little slow," explained Bouncer. "I doubt that they would have noticed anything anyway."

"Oh, don't underrate those two country boys," said Bob. "And they don't drink like I do. I betcha they'd noticed that fat slob in their trash bin. That's why I'm giving you the timeline like that. There's no garbage pickup on Sundays either."

"I guess that's about it," said Jay. "So much for your lead, Bouncer."

"At least we know there really was a body and it looked like Hank Johnson," countered Bouncer.

They thanked old Bob and returned to the motel the same way they had come. Once inside their room, Jay peeled off her shirt.

"Hey, we don't have to make it look that good," said Bouncer. "Unless you're throwing yourself at me for my irresistible good looks."

"Don't kid yourself, Don Juan. Since we have this room, I'm taking a shower before I go out to see Dolores. You can take a nap on the bed for a while."

"What for?"

"We do have to wait a while in order to convince whoever was following us that you're getting laid in here. If we leave too soon, he'll think that you suffer from pre-mature ejaculation."

"Heaven forbid. I wouldn't want Sandra to think that. We've only had a few dates and things are starting to heat up."

"So who is this Sandra? Do you mean you have a girl friend? I'm proud of you, Bouncer. Worried for her, though. Is she a geek like you?"

"Sandra Chapman is a pharmacist. But I wouldn't call her a geek if I were you. At least, not to her face."

"I'd love to meet the competition."

"Like I said, we're just getting started, and she's the jealous type. You look pretty good in just a bra, you know."

"I know. And that's the best look you're getting, so Sandra's safe. I'm heading for the shower. Actually, while I'm in there, give a call to Sam Fletcher and see if he has any more information. Also, call that cop from St. Mary's City, Roger Colman. I think he has the hots for me, so he might give up info the acting sheriff doesn't want me to know."

"All right. You take all the fun out of reporting."

"Who said it was fun? It's just a job. But I do want to find John Milton's killer. That's a personal thing."

Scherzo Eight

In the years following September 11, 2001, an important discussion began in the US. Often posed as an argument between conservatives and liberals, the discussion really centered around the delicate balance between citizens' rights, on the one hand, and the need for public security, on the other. It was a discussion that had been postponed after the Bill of Rights, those first few amendments to the US constitution, was ratified. It was only continued every so often in times of national crisis. The Civil War was one such time. 9/11 was another.

The issues were often confusing. For example, while it was desirable to maintain a citizen's privacy, how much was the government allowed to know about him or her for national security purposes? With the advent of modern computers, that question became all the more important since it was easy to collect and maintain an enormous amount of information about each individual. Linked to this discussion, was the call from time to time to create a national ID card, a card that would legitimize a person's stay in the country, a card that would carry information that could be cross-checked in one of the government's databases. More than a passport, driver's license, or a Social Security card, such a card promised enormous advantages for preventing terrorism and other criminal acts. The demands for such a card were spurred on by the fact that over time it was found that real terrorists trickling over the borders from Canada and Mexico generally found it easy to get all the documentation they needed, either through completely legal means, or by using the many illegal services available to illegal immigrants. It only took money and a few connections.

The discussion seemed to end with the creation of the national ID card in 2019. With it every citizen and permanent resident over the age of six was required to have their fingerprints, retinal pattern, and DNA characteristics on file in Washington, DC, together with basic personal information like current address, place of work, etc. This database was accessible to most government agencies. In particular, federal and local law enforcement groups used it extensively. Contrary to the fears of many, it did not become a Pandora's box that let out a fascist society. For the common man, it simply replaced a number of other cards that were his or her responsibility to possess. Since it was virtually impossible to forge, people grew accustomed to using it and trusted it.

The ACLU, however, had always argued that a national ID card was unconstitutional, just as they argued that many forms of wiretapping were, even though most of the public thought these were also necessary practices to guarantee some level of public safety. Besides, the card seemed to be a moot point when there was so much information available about each and every person already. However, the ACLU, and rightly so, was more concerned over controlling potential abuses. The simplest way to do that would have been to not have the card, which did not seem to be a practical position to most. But people listened because the ACLU often made some good arguments. One that resonated with many was when they argued that the DNA information could be used by medical insurance companies to deny coverage to people with genetic risk factors, something the public was more worried about.

Although the ACLU took the government to court several times, the card was never declared unconstitutional. The ACLU did win one concession, a big one, however: medical coverage could not be denied to people on the basis of genetic risk factors alone.

The consequences of that Supreme Court decision for family budgets were immediate as the law of unintended consequences took effect. Medical insurance premiums skyrocketed as the insurance companies tried to provide themselves a cushion to the fact that more and more genetic risk factors were being discovered with the data from the Human Genome Project. Shortly after that, the multi-tier insurance plans were offered, from full medical to no medical, leading to inadequate health care for most of the world's population, in spite of astounding advances in medicine, some of them generated by the same Human Genome Project.

The criminal underworld, not to be outdone by the insurance companies, created the black market in body parts. It was a brave new world but not the one imagined by Huxley.

Chapter Ten

Lexington Park, Maryland, Monday . . .

Jay had been to John and Dolores' house several times before yet had actually socialized more with them when they came up to DC, which was not infrequent, as both her friends liked theater and classical music. The Kennedy Center was not exactly Lincoln Center, although it had some very good performances. Jay would often meet them for dinner either before or after, yet she rarely went to concerts with them—her musical tastes leaned more towards Latin American folk music, especially the kind with heavy Native American influences, like the music of Bolivia, Paraguay, northern Argentina, Peru, and Ecuador, along with that from her father's native land.

She sadly walked up the four steps to the front porch and rang the bell. It was a wide porch with several comfortable wicker chairs, ideal for sipping cool drinks in the summer and just chatting. She could imagine her friends doing just that, John with his lazy drawl, not quite Southern, but certainly not Northern either, and Dolores spicing up her conversation with the Spanish obscenities and expressions that amused John.

"Come on in, Jay," Dolores greeted.

Jay gave her a hug and went inside with her.

The living room reflected Dolores' taste for simple comfort but John had also given it character with his comfortable reading chair and wall of books. He had built the bookcase that lined the entire wall, giving it the little personal touches, like cubby holes for computer magazines and special slots for their old CD collection. The floor was hardwood that John had redone only two years ago; scatter rugs marked off the conversation area from the bar and the bookcase. A long sofa and a few more straight-backed chairs invited one to sit down and talk or just listen to a classic performance of some musical piece.

Dolores started up the music system with a recording of Rodrigo's Arenjuez Concerto and then went to the bar.

"I'm just going to get some spring water. Want something, Jay?"

"I'd like something really strong, though I'd better keep the synapses clean. Just give me what you're having."

Dolores went into automatic with the ice and spring water, watching Jay all the time with her large, expressive eyes. Finally she spoke.

"You know, I already miss him. He's not gone twenty-four hours and I miss him. It's like losing my leg all over again."

"Come again?"

"I mean, it's like I've lost a part of me. Actually, something more than a leg. We were so close, Jay. And we'd come through so much. It really hurts, way down deep inside."

"I know, amorcita, but you have to focus. You have to go on."

"No!" Her face turned ugly as it contorted into an angry mask. A glass went flying towards the wall, its death throes leaving dripping spring water sliding down the old wood to spread out among the shards on the floor. "No es justo! All my life I wanted what we had. I wanted it so bad. And then mi Dios gave it to me. So why does He take it away now?"

"You're not being punished for anything, Dolores," Jay quietly told her. "You know I don't believe in that crap that God works in mysterious ways. This is not God's work. It's not even the Devil's. It's the work of some human scum. He, she or they took out a good man in his prime. They'll pay."

"You promise?"

"I promise."

"I'll clean up the mess."

"Let me help you."

Then Jay listened to Dolores. In the living room. In the kitchen. While she laid out some of her extra pajamas for Jay in her office. While Jay brushed her teeth. Her friend rambled. The intense pain of losing her leg. How hard the PT had been as she got used to the computerized prosthetic. John's compassion. The hell of Damascus. The hordes of crazy Shiites in Teheran. It all came pouring out, a lifetime of emotion and pain. The one good thing in her life being John Milton.

Somewhere along the way they had grilled cheese sandwiches and hot cups of chocolate. It was 10:30 before Jay could put her to bed.

She was as nearly exhausted as her friend, yet she still had some things to do. Her promise to Dolores was all that kept her going.

Dolores' office, a drafty loft above the garage reachable from a stairway out of the laundry room in the back of the house, was full of the latest computer equipment, but Jay only used some of the really standard stuff, not daring to touch a lot of it. She hooked up her camera to Dolores' desktop, one of the old 128-bit two CPU models, and downloaded the photo of the car that had been following Bouncer and her that afternoon. Using one of the standard programs, she cropped the image, blowing up the license plate to fill the image. The numbers were clear although a little fuzzy—both the camera and the computer had plenty of pixels. It was a DC plate, though not official. That didn't mean anything, of course, since plenty of official cars had ordinary plates these days.

She downloaded the picture to GeeBee, her contact at the DC DMV. George Bernard Jones, otherwise known as GeeBee, wouldn't see it until the morning, yet that was good enough. She also sent him a video-mail explaining some of the things that were happening, thinking that otherwise he might ignore the request.

It was 11:15 before she crawled into bed. Dolores' sofa bed was a relic from her single days and filled one corner of her office. The mattress was hard and thin, making one very aware of some of the springs underneath, but Jay fell asleep immediately.

Scherzo Nine

Annie Petersen checked the water level again and then jotted the datum down in her notebook.

Another two centimeters over last year. Where's it going to stop?

Fifty years ago scientists had begun to notice the increase in sea level and the minute changes in sea salinity and temperature due to the melting polar caps and glaciers. A combination of global warming, controllable by man, and natural climate change, which wasn't controllable, had left many cities fighting the good fight of Venice in Italy. Venice itself was now protected by a seawall, not unlike the seawalls in Holland. The East River, where Annie had just taken her measurement, was a good two feet above the roadway passing in front of the UN headquarters, on the average, so the roadway now was also protected by a seawall, as the East River's level increased and decreased with the Atlantic tide.

The planet was beginning to lash back at its profligate sons. Fishing grounds, once providing for millions of mouths, had disappeared, the fish either killed off by the lowered salinity or increased temperature, or moving on to different areas in the world's oceans. The worst consequence was famine, although there were also simpler health consequences, like those from the change in people's diets. Somewhere between were the numerous small wars and local skirmishes fought over fishing rights.

There were many consequences for the world's weather patterns as well since the whole evaporation cycle that turned sea water into much needed rain was perturbed.

Annie knew all this. She was studying it all at NYU. Like many others, she was highly motivated and hoped to do something about it. She didn't yet know quite what specifically, so she just took the data for her professor. In time she would find a definite proposal to make, and hopefully a thesis would come out of it.

She shook her head sadly. *Another two centimeters.*

Chapter Eleven

New York City, Tuesday . . .

Vladimir left the board room tired. In spite of the fact that he had helped finance the campaigns of the current American President, that fool Fulton had now become a thorn in his side. He had said as much at the meeting. *Now I even have to watch my back on my legitimate capitalist endeavors.* He knew he could work within the parameters proposed by the Fulton administration, although he didn't want to have to do it for long. The word was now out to his legal department and his lobbyists: Go after them.

He was still suffering from jet lag. He knew it. There was only one way to relieve the stress. He called and made the arrangements. Two out-of-work Broadway actresses would show up at his hotel at 9 pm to put him to bed.

His first priority over, he made two more calls. The first was to a general in the Pentagon. Naturally, there was a blank image on the video. *Ah, national security, isn't it wonderful!*

"Buenas tardes, mi general. Soy Ramirez." The general only knew him by that name. He spoke quickly using a Caribbean dialect. A Spanish speaker like the general might guess Dominican, Cuban, or maybe Atlantic Coast Colombian. In Madrid he could speak Castilian or any of the other dialects from the Spanish provinces. He had a good ear for the nuances of language and loved fooling people with his ability.

"I can't play golf tomorrow," said the general in English, after hearing the usual banalities of polite phone conversation in his native language. It was a simple signal that he had someone with him or the line was not secure. Of course, secure for Vladimir and the general meant that some NSA spook could still be listening in as part of his job.

"All right. I just need to know what your handicap is today."

"I'll have to figure it out and tell you. Some of us played last week. I'll get back to you."

Vladimir knew it was a risky code, since most dedicated golfers knew their handicaps without any hesitation. But he liked to live dangerously. It amused him that he could have a conversation with someone in the Pentagon, giving them information and getting information back, just using ordinary language. He had just asked the general for an update on one of his pet projects and had been told it would be forthcoming. The general would call him at his hotel that night.

The second call was to a woman, one that he admired greatly, even though she had never succumbed to his charm. Her voice was strong and authoritative.

"Be quick," she said in German. "I'm very busy."

"As you should be with the important position you have."

"If you're calling about Fulton's latest moves, you're wasting your time. I think he's right on this one."

"From the perspective of getting votes, perhaps. From my perspective, it will mean money lost. That should be important to you. Anyway, I'm not calling about that, liebchen. What are you doing about the new fugue I heard the other night? It was quite a Wagnerian blast, I thought."

"Your fugue is being revised and edited as we speak. It will be taken care of. Anything else?"

"When will you allow me to take you to dinner, meine frohliche frau?"

"These days I am too busy to be happy. I'll call you. We still have to be careful."

"I'm only a campaign supporter, you know."

"Yeah, and I'm Davy Crockett. Good day, Volodya."

Vladimir looked doubtful, although he smiled at her use of the familiar version of his name. The woman was hard to read. Most times he could tell whether someone was competent or not just by looking them in the eyes, face to face. The skill had served him well over the years. But she was different.

He got up and walked over to his bar. He tossed down a straight shot of his best vodka, and then made a more socially acceptable vodka and tonic. He sipped it at the window, overlooking Fifth Avenue. He was counting on a lot of people. *Perhaps too many?*

Chapter Twelve

In the Virginia countryside, Tuesday . . .

"What's bothering you, son?"

RP1 jerked to attention.

"What do you mean, Dr. Tyler?"

"You seem very distracted today, RP1? This class is voluntary, you know. It's not required. If you don't want to pay attention, you shouldn't take up the time of the others. But I'm really teaching something useful here, and all knowledge you receive from us will make you better prepared for your long trip."

RP1 looked at the others in the class, then back at Dr. Tyler. He really admired the man. In some sense, he was the father of them all, at least spiritually. He had made them, the perfect humans who would go to the stars. But he was also afraid of Dr. Tyler, afraid that he would discover what he and SW2 were doing.

The class was studying the Human Genome Project. It was generally an interesting subject, since, in some way, they were learning about themselves, how they were bioengineered to be free from genetic diseases and programmed to be as long-lived as possible. In that way not that many generations would pass during their long trip through interstellar space.

"Dr. Tyler, where did SW1, FS2, and HJ1 go?"

"We're still looking for them, son. Perhaps they'll come back. You know it's a dangerous world out there, however, so they might not come back."

"You mean the crime and the terrorists?" asked PW2.

"There's that. There's also disease. They aren't protected from viruses and bacteria out there. Malaria, polio—you know all about them. You're not protected because we're trying to insure that you don't take any of that out to the stars. Just the pure human stock, boys and girls, just the pure stuff."

It was a favorite theme of his. RP1 thought Dr. Tyler even looked fatherly as he smiled first at RP1 and then the rest. He was a big Santa Claus of a man, with a bulbous nose with veins standing out on it, and large black bushy eyebrows flecked with white. His hair was graying around the ears, too. He had a big Santa Claus belly which also shook when he laughed, which was often. He just didn't have a beard.

RP1 knew better than to believe in Santa Claus. He read the e-zines and watched the newsnets channels, even though they were pre-recorded and censored for them (the Center staff called it 'editing'). The world was indeed a mixed-up place. That's why he was sometimes scared of Dr. Tyler. RP1 knew Santa Claus really didn't exist.

"So why did they leave?" asked RP1.

"I don't know. Maybe some of you know more than me. I'd like to think that they just wanted to get out and explore."

"Maybe they thought we're in a prison," observed SW2. "People try to escape from prisons."

"Well, it's not really a prison," said Dr. Tyler with a frown. "We keep a tight security here so that you won't be exposed to the germs and viruses from the outside. And also, so others won't get in here, of course. The Guardians are here to protect you."

RP1 looked at SW2, and she smiled back at him. He wasn't really thinking of her, though. Instead, he was thinking about the Guardians.

Mostly, they were quiet, scary individuals. Big, strong men who silently patrolled the grounds of the Center dressed in long gray coats and black boots. RP1 knew there were guns under those coats. They all wore little black berets and looked similar—their steel gray blue eyes moved continuously, surveying all. They all had that special little implant behind the left ear that allowed them to communicate with the Center's security office and among themselves. He had watched them do it, their throats barely moving as they gave the subvocal commands to their com links and networked videocams, which were everywhere throughout the Center, even in the bathrooms.

No, I think the Guardians are here to keep us here and to keep others away from here. They were very upset when SW1, FS2, and HJ1 escaped. And that's the word I would use. Escaped.

RP1 turned his attention back to what Dr. Tyler was saying. He had returned to the Human Genome Project and what it signified. RP1 couldn't focus too well. His mind began to wander again, until Dr. Tyler's cell phone rang.

"Andrew Tyler here," he said, answering it, after apologizing to the class. "Yes, yes, OK. I'll ring you back from my office." He looked at the class. "I'm really sorry. I have to make an important call. That's all for today. Tomorrow we'll take up where we left off."

Tyler quickly walked down the corridor, turned left, and took the elevator down to the laboratory level, which was off limits to all his charges. Adjacent to his lab, he had a small office. He quickly dialed a phone number from memory.

"I hope you're on a secure line," Tyler said to the man who appeared on the screen.

"And hello to you, too, Andy." There was irony in the voice, yet there was no smile. "You always lacked the social graces when you were my graduate student. Considering the salary you now make in your new babysitting job, I would think you would be more civil to your mentor, the person who made it all possible."

"Cut the crap. You said something about needing money. Why come to me?"

"Let's say I've become accustomed to a certain lifestyle and inflation is high this year. My consulting fees have to increase correspondingly."

"Fucking lot of consulting you do. And why are your money worries my problem? Take it up with the committee."

"Your precious committee meets at their own convenience, not mine. I prefer not to wait. You have more direct connections with some of the members than I do. It's a paltry increase in my demands, at any rate." He named a figure. Tyler didn't look pleased. "You think it's exorbitant?"

Tyler's immediate scowl turned to a worried frown. His mentor was asking for a lot, considering he did so little for the committee now.

"I think you're full of shit. That's a lot of money for anyone, even the US government."

"Oh, I'm in complete agreement. But the cost of living here on the West Coast is not going down, Andy. I really do have needs."

"Yeah, I know about those needs. You should have been a priest."

"Don't be nasty. It's all consensual. Anyway, this conversation is already boring me. Pass my request on to your contacts. I think the usual method of payment will work just fine." His face faded from the screen.

So much for civility. The bastard's got some nerve.

Tyler reached and dialed another number, cursing silently to himself.

Scherzo Ten

Humberto Prieto looked at his nephew, astonishment on his face.
"You joined a militia?"
"Estoy harto con este gobierno, tio," said Jose.
The old man slapped him.
"Your father didn't send you to UCLA to learn Spanish, idiot. Speak to me in English. That's the language of international business and commerce."
Jose spit on the concrete floor of his uncle's office. High above the factory floor, the office window looked out over the workers toiling below, making the robotic arms that were shipped all over the world to handle all sorts of things that were too dangerous for human beings to handle. Huge, specialized ones were being used at that moment to make additions to the International Space Station.
"That's what I think of your international business and commerce, tio. All those people down there are exploited by you and by the government."
"Where do you get that caca?" asked Humberto. "Those people down there all have full medical. I've seen to it that they're well taken care of. They're very specialized workers, all of them with smarts and skill sets you don't have."
"Maybe so. I'm just a chemical engineer. But there's no work for me."
"That's because the processes you learned were superceded by better ones. Go back to school. In one or two quarters at UCLA, you will have marketable skills again. I'll pay for it."
"I'm tired of studying. You shouldn't have to study all the time. I want an easy job, like yours, where I can get rich."
"If you only knew. My job isn't so easy, chico loco! I burn the midnight oil many nights keeping up with the micro-circuit technology, the new CPUs, the mechanical engineering, and the new software. I have ten full time engineers continuously working on projects, developing new or improved ideas. Life's a bitch sometimes, though it can be fun. There's adventure in creating new things, seeing them take off in the market."
"OK, so your job isn't easy. Anyway, I don't want to work that hard."

77

"And what's this militia going to do?"

"We're going to protect ordinary citizens from the Zionists who are trying to control the world."

"By Zionists, do you mean the Israelis? Their economy isn't exactly healthy now, by any means. The whole Middle East has run-away inflation."

"I mean the Jews, tio. All over the world they're trying to control everything."

"I repeat, where do you get that shit? Your father must be turning over in his grave."

"My father was a victim. I don't intend to be."

"Where is this militia located?"

"They have a camp in the foothills above Fresno. They'll take care of me."

"How? Where do they get their money?"

"Several businessmen and politicians support us. They're all patriots."

"They're stupid fools!"

"Say what you want to, old man. You won't change my mind."

"So why did you come here today?"

"Just to say good-by. You did a lot for me after my father died. As much as I hate who you are and what you represent, I'll give you that."

"Que generoso," mumbled Humberto. He stuck out a hand. "Bien, buena suerte. I certainly can't stop you. I only hope you come to your senses."

Jose looked at his uncle's hand for a moment, shrugged, turned and walked out, without ever shaking it. Humberto looked after him, sadness on his face.

Chapter Thirteen

Paterson, New Jersey, Tuesday & Wednesday . . .

Dr. Kalidas Metropolis looked at her afternoon's work on the computer screen and was satisfied. To a casual observer it might be just another journal article, yet to her it was a labor of love and a personal triumph. It represented five years of hard work, mostly done late nights and weekends in the lab or at home. It would be her crowning achievement as a scientist. *Hey, Jose, I'm still pretty good at 67, no matter what they say upstairs. I make them rich, yet no one will remember what I did for the company. But now I can retire with the personal satisfaction that I actually did something worthwhile for the human race.*

She told the computer to submit the preprint. It was 7:49 pm and time to go home. Tomorrow it would be on the journal's preprint board and she would see the reaction of her scientific colleagues to her work.

She had always been fascinated with the body's genetic evolution and the interplay of random mutations and inherited genetic change. In high school she had won a science fair and a full scholarship with her first project on the theme. Fifty years and two doctorates later, she believed she was close to a universal solution to the transplant rejection problem. In twenty years the business of finding matches for liver transplants and so forth would be over if she was correct. *Jose will be happy. She hadn't had any matches and had died.*

It was in high school that some people began to call her Kali. Especially one girl. Josefina Botero took her to both the junior and senior prom. Kalidas didn't particularly like the shortened form of her name, and generally found Jose's constant use of it annoying. After high school they didn't see much of each other until Kalidas entered grad school and Jose's father passed away. A long courtship during which Jose became a pediatrician and Kalidas became a well known research scientist ended with a marriage that lasted until Jose died of liver cancer at fifty-eight. Kalidas threw herself more into her work after that.

Kalidas knew that she was privileged. Her parents had been immigrants, so while they had to struggle to make ends meet while tolerating the bigotry and prejudice of polite American society, she was second generation. She had reaped the benefits of their endeavors, from upbringing to education. The first had instilled in her the work ethic of her parents. The second had given her the tools to hone and develop the ideas of a free mind to the point where she was tops in her field, although, more importantly, making significant contributions to the human race's knowledge base. She knew that her children would not have had her work ethic. She also knew that they would have been children spoiled by the fruits of her success.

Most likely, anyway. Like most third generation children. But now I'll never know.

She had debated sending off the preprint for two days. It certainly wouldn't buy her any kudos from the upstairs crowd in the company. The manager and marketing types at Dalton Biomedicine Inc were looking for more immediately marketable items. But that wasn't the reason for the hesitation. It was more fundamental.

Did she want to be remembered as the scientist who made human cloning easy? It was only a corollary of her work, a mere byproduct, still she had seen it immediately. *Of course, I didn't spell it out specifically. Maybe others won't see it.*

She knew she was kidding herself. Like most scientists at the cutting edge of their specialty, she moved in a small circle of individuals, people she saw at conferences and congresses year after year. Research was so specialized now that it was hard to even get graduate students to come to work with you. Many of them thought they were more employable as generalists. The truth of the matter was that Dalton didn't really need her either. In 2053 she was a vanishing breed, someone who's scientific curiosity gave more weight to the why and the how, rather than to the "is it marketable."

During the maglev ride and the car ride home that followed, she thought mostly of Jose. A sweet woman, Jose had loved children. She was always a gentle person with everyone, though, not just kids, rarely using a four-letter word, in contrast to Kalidas, who often used a much more colorful vocabulary to express herself. Jose often called Kalidas her beautiful Greek goddess with the foul mouth. *It would have been fun to have grown old with her.*

Kalidas' townhouse in Upper Montclair was small, yet comfortable. Except for the stairs up from the garage, it was all one level. It had two bedrooms, one serving as her study. She hadn't spent much time there lately. A cot at the lab was often her bed.

She put a frozen dinner into the micro and made herself a vodka and tonic. It went down in three gulps as she sat down at her home workstation and sorted through her e-mail and video-mail. There was a little spam that had passed through either the text or video filters. She told the filters to watch out for those, easily picking off the tell-tale words and offensive pictures. There were always new ones. Still, the filters were getting pretty good. Another program searched the internet for things of interest to her but she decided to wait on its latest report. She went to her bedroom and stretched out on the bed. *Just a few minutes until the micro is done.* It was her last thought before she fell asleep.

She awoke the next morning before the alarm clock. Instead, the annoying sound of the micro's periodic warning buzzer had interrupted her slumber. *Guess I needed the sleep.*

It didn't take her long to gulp down some cereal, shower, and dress. Although in public she was rather shy about it, she had an excellent contralto voice and had once sung the part of Carmen many years ago in college. Jose had enjoyed singing with her, often accompanying her on the piano and joining in with her unsteady soprano, though more often she had just listened to her with a happy smile on her face as Kalidas mangled the French and Italian or the Spanish of Jose's beloved zarzuelas. Now Kalidas just sang in the shower, to an audience of one, herself.

As she was drying off, the mirror told her what she already knew from many similar mornings: she was getting old, although she had escaped her mother's fate. Where her mother had been gray and bulgy, her hair was still black and she was not overweight. *Oh, girl, you've got some sags here and there, but you could still attract attention if you wanted to.* She had experimented a little with that a few times, beginning four years after Jose passed away; still she couldn't get beyond the loss of her one true love. *Yeah, the sex was great but the love wasn't there. At least not like with Jose. Nice women, all of them, but they weren't Jose.*

She was in a good mood in spite of the thoughts about Jose, the traffic to the maglev station, and the crowded maglev, at least until she got to her office. Brian Wilson was waiting for her, sitting comfortably in the chair behind her desk as if he owned it.

"Kalidas, we've got a problem."

He put his hands together and touched his fingers to his little goatee as if he were praying. She looked at the slick hair, eye shadow, and ring through the left eyebrow and wondered how his wife could put up with the prick. He was her immediate manager and, generally speaking, they didn't have a bad relationship. But there was always the little irritation, like from a skin rash, that this man hadn't done any real science in his entire life, probably didn't even deserve the doctorate he had, and yet was her boss.

"Spit it out. Whatever it is."

He handed her an envelope and she opened it. A quick glance told her what the papers were.

"You're firing me?"

"You're retiring, Kalidas. You deserve it."

"I didn't ask to retire."

"It's better than the alternative."

"I'll take you to court for age discrimination, you know."

"No, you'll sign the papers, including the release from all future lawsuits."

"Why would I do that? Do you think I'm stupid?"

Brian squirmed uncomfortably in the chair. Kalidas noticed he was nervous and sweaty.

"No, you're too smart for your own good. You see, Dalton had a visit from the DHS this morning. Because of your connections with the terrorist group Greek Liberty, your clearance has been revoked. And you must have a DHS clearance to work here, among others."

Kalidas was dumbfounded.

"I've never heard of such a terrorist group," she said. "And, even if exists, I'm certainly not a member. I've been in the US since I was eight. I became a citizen with my parents. What the hell is going on, Brian?"

"I don't know. Don't kill the messenger. This comes down from on high."

"I bet. And that's where I'm going. I'm going to raise hell all the way to the top until I find out what the fuck is going on here."

"No, you won't. The security guard is waiting outside to escort you out of the building and off the grounds. Your personal effects will be FedEx'd to you in a few days." Brian stood up. "I'm sorry, Kalidas. I wish I knew more about what was going on. But I don't. Good luck."

As he strode out of the room, the security guard came in.

"Bum deal, Doctor Metropolis. But I got to do what I got to do."

"Do you have any idea what's going on?"

"Are you kidding? I just started working here a month ago. Fat chance I'd know something. So far it's been a good job, though now, seeing what happened to a VIP like you, I'm not so sure."

Kalidas shook here head in disbelief and then realized she had been standing for the whole interchange. Suddenly her legs felt very rubbery. *Hold yourself together. Maybe it is time to retire. You were thinking about it just last night. You can't work forever.*

But she was kidding herself. She wouldn't rest easy until she found out what was going on. *First, why the trumped up terrorist charge? Second, why did Dalton put any credence to it?*

No, she wasn't going to retire. She would be working harder than ever.

Scherzo Eleven

President Fulton looked up as his Chief of Staff entered the office.

"Bad news, sir," said the woman.

"Don't sugar coat it, Hilde. I can take it straight."

"Your bill was defeated in the Senate. By one vote."

"Why would they do that? This was a no-brainer. Everyone knows the damn insurance companies are buying body parts on the black market for their full medical customers. If we can't prosecute them, what can we do?"

"I guess we'll just have to keep attacking the problem at its roots, sir," Hilde said.

"Yeah, we know how effective that's been," growled Fulton.

He turned to the news report describing Christy Vargas' threat to resign from Congress. She belonged to his party. *I admire her for her independent thinking but what the hell does she think she's doing?*

Chapter Fourteen

Boston, Massachusetts, Tuesday . . .

The next morning, before his shift began, Chris went to visit the coroner. Ka Wah Fong was a wiry old Chinese gentleman with white hair and a raspy voice. He had worked closely with Chris on quite a few cases and the detective had always been impressed with the doctor's competence and ability to explain complicated concepts.

"Doc, any stuff about our John Doe that didn't get into your official report?"

Ka Wah was looking tired that morning. He was getting a little old for the job's long hours but never complained.

"Could be, could be," Ka Wah said with a wink. "Off the record?"

"Off the record," Chris agreed. "Just curiosity."

"Yes, yes, but I believe it's more than curiosity. I heard about your DHS visitor. May they all rot in hell."

"How so?"

"They deported my cousin's daughter a year ago. They accused her of working with the Indonesian Muslims."

"Didn't your cousin try to stop it?"

Ka Wah threw up his hands, a gesture of helplessness.

"What can you do? You're guilty until proven innocent. And we had no proof they were lying. She isn't even Muslim. Anyway, she got an internship back in China. In Beijing. They know the value of doctors trained in America. She'll do fine. Maybe it's all for the best. She found a husband, too. From Shanghai."

"Good for her. So, give already. What's the scoop on our John Doe?"

Ka Wah spread his hands as if preparing papers on a university lectern.

"Well, first of all, your visitor's friends confiscated all the DNA evidence, did you know that?"

"No, I didn't. Why would they do that? Just because he looked a little like a young Frank Sweeney?"

"Ah, you will understand better when I tell you the off-the-record story. Do you know anything about telomeres, Chris?"

"Telo-whats?"

"Telomeres. They're at the end of DNA strands. A DNA molecule of a typical chromosome contains a linear array of genes, encoding proteins and RNA, interspersed with much noncoding DNA. Included in the noncoding DNA are long stretches that make up the centromere and long stretches at the end, the telomeres. These are crucial to the life of the cell since they keep the ends of the various chromosomes in the cell from accidentally becoming attached to each other."

"OK, I think I understand that. But what's it got to do with our John Doe."

"Patience, young friend. The first clone was a sheep named Dolly. Analysis of telomere length in Dolly's cells revealed that they were only eighty per cent as long as those of a normal one-year-old sheep. Shortly after making Dolly it was discovered that this need not always be true. On the contrary, it was found that clones could have even longer DNA tips, or telomeres, than the original cells, and also show other signs of youthfulness." Ka Wah cleared his throat and smiled at Chris. "However, we now know that what often happens in the cloning process, although it's unpredictable, is that sometimes there is telomeric cleavage, i.e. the tips are broken off, if you will. It is also sometimes seen with transplant patients and leads to transplant rejection."

"I'm glazing over here, doc. Help me out."

"Well, they couldn't take all the DNA evidence, you see." Ka Wah tapped his forehead and smiled again. "What's up here belongs to me. Anyway, your young John Doe had telomeres as short as an eighty-year-old. Since he didn't look to be eighty, I would suspect that he's one big transplant rejection—in other words, a clone."

"How could that be? That's illegal."

Ka Wah shrugged and straightened his white hair nervously.

"I'm just offering my opinion. Illegal or not, I think he was a clone. And since he looks like Secretary Sweeney, I'd say he was a clone of Sweeney, though I'm not going to put that in any report. In fact, this is just between you and me."

"Why? It sounds too important to leave out. And can you prove it?"

"To answer your first question, it's because I value my job. I'm sure that I wouldn't have it if this leaked out. Your visitor from the Department of Homeland Security, remember? I'm just going to ignore it all and hope it goes away."

"You can't do that."

"Oh, but I can. And you should do the same. It wouldn't help your career either, Chris. Believe me. Forget about it."

"And if I can't? How do I follow up on this? It's a homicide, after all, isn't it?"

"Not clear. The ricin definitely did our Frank Sweeney clone in. Whether someone gave it to him, making it a homicide, or whether he accidentally picked it up, toss a coin, if you will." Chris thought of Mary Beth Grogan's matter-of-fact statement, probably unintentional, that it was an accident. "As for following up on the case, what can you do? How do you ID a clone?"

"That's what I don't understand. And it comes back to my first question. Aren't clones like identical twins?"

"Hmm. Yes, but the cells may be differentiated differently. Especially if someone bioengineered the final product. There's a technique called blastocyst reprogramming. It has promise for producing new organs. I could get a clone of you, for example, and grab it before the nuclear genes take over its development, which in humans is at the 4-cell stage. Then I could turn that into a new heart for you and avoid most problems with transplant rejection."

"Doesn't that require an egg?"

"That's the unsolved problem. Where do you get all the eggs? Actually, you really shouldn't need them. You're you. In some sense you just have to take one of your differentiated cells and run them backwards until you get an undifferentiated cell, then let it run forwards to get the differentiated stuff you want. You shouldn't need the egg if all you want to do is make Chris stuff."

"Can that be done?"

"No. Like I said, an unsolved problem. It was once thought that stem cells were the answer but only very simple specialized cells can be programmed that way. A few very specialized researchers are still working on this. The best known scientist in that area is a Dr. Metropolis. I believe her first name is Kalidas."

Chris took out a PDA and input the name.

"But did you check John Doe's DNA against Frank Sweeney's or not?" he asked.

"Not enough time." He tapped his head again. "There's not enough room in here to store a full DNA workup. From what I remember about the partial results, there were definite similarities, still they weren't conclusive as yet. And now we'll never know. So right now your best bet is Dr. Metropolis. Perhaps you should give her a call. Off the record recommendation, of course." He gave a final wink. "And if you really want to pursue the case, which I advise against."

Chris smiled and nodded.

Scherzo Twelve

Little Karen Simpson looked up at her father expectantly.
"I want the double decker."
Harold Simpson was actually enjoying the time with his daughter. His wife had taken off for the mall. It was raining, a perfect day for it. Unfortunately for Harold, that left him as the babysitter. Although he'd much rather be at home watching baseball, Karen had become fidgety, so he promised to take her for ice cream.

The economic problems plaguing the country were not new yet Harold and his family had been untouched by them. He had worked in his father's accounting firm and took it over when the old man retired. He was well off, enough so that he could afford full medical for his whole family. It was somewhat illogical, therefore, that he was attracted to the newsnet reports on Christy Vargas. He knew there were things wrong with the economy, even though he was relatively insulated against them.

As he helped his daughter climb onto the stool at the ice cream counter, he extrapolated on what he knew and on what Christy Vargas had said in various speeches. *The globalization of our economies has increased on a par with the increase of ethnic strife as the Third World groups become stronger economically. We are not immune to this. The destruction of the middle class began with that president at the turn of the century—I can't quite remember his name—and was caused by the globalization of the American economy—outsourcing and all that. That destruction proceeded in spite of the fractionalization of the US into powerful interest groups. At first it was just East Coast and West Coast factions united against the Middle and South. Today it's worse but it was that president that started it all back then. What a legacy. It's a wonder we have a country left!*

He and his daughter were actually at another mall, across town from where his wife was. She liked the department stores better in the one she had gone to although it was farther away from their house. The ice cream was more urgent.

87

"You want sprinkles on it?"

"Whipped cream, sprinkles, and a cherry."

"You heard the woman," Harold told the robot waiter. Just in case, he said it all again in very clear language, and then he swiped his debit card. Some of the many arms of the ice cream counter, that is, the robot, began to move faster than the eye could follow. Soon another arm was offering the delicious concoction.

They decided to go to a table to sit down and eat the dessert together. They each had a spoon. By splitting the ice cream with Karen, Harold could honestly say to his wife that he had only bought ice cream for Karen, not for himself. He was getting a little belly on him. His wife was always trying to make him watch his calories but he was a stress eater. *And what is more stressful than taking care of an energetic and demanding little girl while thinking of the world's problems?*

"Daddy, isn't that man going to be hot, putting on that vest?"

Harold looked where she was pointing.

"Oh, shit," he cried out. He managed to cover her before the blast hit.

A half hour later as the EMTs and forensics experts went through the rubble, they were amazed to see a little girl walking towards them. There was spattered blood all over her and she had been crying.

"I need you to help me find my daddy," she wailed.

They never did.

Chapter Fifteen

Lexington Park, Maryland, Tuesday . . .

On Tuesday morning, the computer woke Jay. She had finally fallen asleep on Dolores' sofa bed.

She had been dreaming about her life in the marines. It hadn't been a bed of roses, yet it had been exciting. She missed her comrades. Especially the ones that were gone. *Too many lives. Three too many wars. Four, if you counted the Gulf War of last century. Would it have been different if we had just let the whole Middle East settle their own differences? Maybe so. But in other places that had led to ethnic cleansing. The Kurds were still besieged by everyone around them. And the UN seemed helpless most of the time. Look at Sri Lanka, Southeast Asia, and Ireland. What a world!*

The computer was simply announcing a fax coming through. Almost immediately, the phone rang. She picked it up and started to look at the fax. The voice on the other end was GeeBee's. The fax was a DMV registration record.

"As you see, I got your registration info. Please note who the owner of your car is." Jay read it and smiled. "It looks like you're playing games with the feds, Jay. I could really get in trouble for this, you know."

Jay knew that GeeBee was somewhat paranoid. Living in Washington, one would normally think that he would believe it was the politicos that were out to get him. Instead, he believed it was the bureaucracy, especially in DC. *I guess being part of it makes him like that.*

"You've retrieved info for me before. No one will be the wiser."

"Yeah, but the data has been on crime suspects and terrorists. I can't recall getting involved with the feds before."

"Just cool it. And by all means, don't talk about it. By the way, if your life was in danger, and you had some special information, where might you put it?"

"What they usually do in the mystery novels is put it in a safe deposit box and send a letter to their lawyer with the code and power-of-attorney to open it in case you're found dead. Unfortunately, after Goldman versus US, the feds don't have to respect attorney-client privilege after you're dead, so they can raid the box themselves. If they don't beat the attorney to the box, Popov versus US allows the feds to subpoena it from the attorney—all the originals and copies. I would take another tact."

Jay was getting tired of the legal mumbo-jumbo. GeeBee was also an amateur lawyer and well read on the latest Supreme Court decisions, though he wasn't helping much, not this early in the morning.

"I'll invent something. Thanks for the info."

"Is your life in danger? Quit while you're ahead, senorita."

"I'm not sure. It could be nothing, yet something smells fishy down here and it isn't last week's leftover crabs."

"Well, if you ever need a place to hide, remember where we all went that Fourth of July. Take care."

She turned to see Dolores standing in the door with two coffee cups. Her friend looked worried.

"Is your life in danger, Jay?"

"Oh, that's just GeeBee. He gets excited. Is one of those for me?"

Dolores looked pretty in her silk pajamas and fluffy bathrobe, her dark, long hair draping over one shoulder. The legs of the pajama pants were long, yet she didn't have slippers on, so the prosthetic was completely visible, a mute and terrible reminder authenticating service to her country. The dark circles under her eyes showed that she had spent the night crying, at least when she was awake. Jay could not really find the words to comfort her. *I'm so bad at this. I almost get a Pulitzer but I can't find the right words now.*

"It's the full octane. I thought you'd need it. I know I do." Dolores sat down on the couch. "So, are you going to tell me what's going on."

Jay quickly brought her up to date.

"I'm thinking that John's killers were not from around here. They're probably back in DC. Or elsewhere."

"Do you think the feds have something to do with all this?"

"I'd rather think they're just snooping around trying to find out who did it, thinking maybe there might be a terrorist connection. I'm not much into conspiracy theories. They're the material of pulp fiction, not real life. You know, a shopping mall in Silver Spring was hit on Saturday by a suicide bomber. Maybe they think there's a connection."

"But what about this Hank Johnson look-alike? If his demise started the whole thing, shouldn't we start with him?"

"You mean, the real guy? Actually, that's a good point, though 'we' is one too many people. I will talk to him. But you stay put and just try to get a grip on things. You've had a rough time. Get a margarita when you need it. Call Bouncer for conversation. Whatever you need to get through this."

"You're going back to DC?"

"Actually, I'm going to Quantico. I know one of those forensic guys. Sam Fletcher's given me squat. And Bouncer hasn't got anything either. But first I need some ham and eggs. Got those, amorcita?"

Dolores laughed. She was always amazed by her friend's appetite. In spite of her size, Jay could pack the food away.

"Hermanita linda, I'll whip you up my LA special."

"Don't tell me you have some real chilis?"

"Es verdad. Mamacita got them from one of our cousins in New York City. FedEx'd them down to her on the shuttle."

It was not a breakfast to begin a long drive, in spite of the strong java. Fortunately Quantico was just across the Potomac River into Virginia.

Scherzo Thirteen

Claire walked through the metal detector yet again. She had been doing it for over twenty years. She knew it was to protect her as much as the kids, yet the junior high teacher hated the whole idea of it.

She had no office, even though she was science department head. She shared the teacher's prep room along with all the other teachers. Only the principal had a small office, although even that had peeling paint and plaster hanging from the ceiling.

Only the poor sent their children to public schools anymore. The problem, at least in DC, was that every year there were more and more poor. And every child that left the system using a voucher, which paid only a small fraction of their private school's tuition, made the public school poorer, as that portion destined to materials and infrastructure was lost.

"Hey, girl, you look gloomy today," said Felipe Garcia, one of the biology teachers, when she entered the prep room. "Today's your big day. Cheer up."

"Oh, yeah, my big day. A visit from the superintendent. He's going to tell us to do more with less. Rah, rah, rah. Wave the flag, 'cause we're the bastions of democracy. Rah, rah, rah."

"Get rid of the attitude before he comes," said Jonas Smith, a math teacher, "or we'll all pay the price. My god, he could cut the budget even more."

"Or increase the size of the classes," said Claire.

He did both.

That night Claire went home with a handful of personnel files. She had to decide who to lay off.

Chapter Sixteen

Upper Montclair, New Jersey, Wednesday . . .

Kalidas burst through her front door, fuming. She was so angry, she forgot to close the door. She went immediately to her study and sat down at the computer.

"Compose mail," she said simply.

The e-mail window came on the screen, the 'To:' flashing impatiently.

"Phillip White." The computer searched her address book and came up with the correct address. "Message: You will recall that we met last March at your wife's birthday party. You said if I ever needed a good lawyer to let you know. I must confess that I usually stay away from lawyers nearly as much as I avoid doctors, although now I do need a lawyer."

It took her only a few minutes to dictate the e-mail to Phillip White, a lawyer who had gained some media fame for winning big pension and age discrimination cases. Just sending it calmed her down enough to realize that it was probably a waste of time.

So she checked her journal submission. The note the editors had electronically attached to the preprint file left her dumbfounded. They had rejected the submission by order from the DHS. *Holy shit, what's going on? Are the fucking feds next going to strip me of my citizenship and send me back to Athens?*

Then came the surprise return e-mail from Phillip.

"My dear Kalidas, I'm so sorry, but the Department of Homeland Security has contacted me. I've been threatened with the loss of my federal license to practice law if I take your case. My only suggestion is to contact your senator or representative. Regards, Phillip."

She stared at the screen. She had just sent the e-mail. The feds must be intercepting it. She reached for her cell phone and then decided against it. If they were intercepting encrypted e-mail, they certainly would not have any problem with a cell phone call. He might not answer the phone anyway, and leaving a video-mail message was just as bad as e-mail—worse, actually. She could always deny she sent the e-mail but the video-mail message would have her voice and image.

She felt she really needed advice, though, and Phillip was the best one to give it to her. The little clock at the bottom of the computer screen said 11:32. Phillip would be at his office. That was no problem. He lived in Montvale and worked in Upper Saddle River. It was a quick ride up the old parkway. She would grab lunch on the way.

White was not particularly happy to see her.

"I really can't help you, Kalidas," he said, as his secretary showed her into the plush office that made either of hers, work or home, look like a slum. He always called her by her full name. Most people did. Jose had been the one exception to that rule. "They were quite insistent."

"I know. It'll be off the record. No one can overhear us here, can they?"

He smiled. It was a fatherly smile. White was a big black man that carried his age well. Only the short-cropped hair hinted at his seventy-seven years. He was vigorous and strong. He had a deep baritone voice that added to his fatherly image and probably gave his clients a great deal of confidence in him.

"I suppose you're right about that. I don't think they've had time to bug my office. No reason for it, until you came along."

"I'm not a member of Greek Liberty. I don't think there's any such organization."

"I know that, dear woman. Someone is pulling a fast one. Nevertheless, my hands are tied."

"Can you at least say who that someone is?"

White looked a little uncomfortable. His bushy white eyebrows danced a little, and then he smiled and shrugged.

"They probably wouldn't want me to, so I will. It was the personal aid to Hank Johnson."

"That guy that's been in the news?"

"That's the one. At least he authorized it. The aid's name is Mary Beth Grogan. In other circumstances, she might be a pleasant person, still I found her rather annoying. She also packs a gun."

"OK. That's the DHS angle. They won't let you play with me. How about some unofficial advice? What about the age discrimination?"

"Did you sign the papers?"

"No. Of course not."

"Then Dalton fired you. That normally would make it easier."

"And why not now?"

"Because you're a suspected terrorist. Hale and Rivera versus the US, 2019. 'The court concludes that any suspected terrorist, citizen or not, has no recourse to civil suits in the US or its territories until said suspicion of terrorist activities is proven to be unfounded.' In other words, you're guilty until proven innocent. They reversed a decision from 2004, mostly bowing to public outrage caused by some big terrorist attack. There's been so many, it's all a blur to me now. Anyway, I'm afraid the court system has become more of a pawn to the Justice Department and public opinion and less of an independent check and balance on executive and legislative abuses of citizens' rights. And everything is hidden under a cloak of secrecy, arguing national defense interests."

"You're kidding me. And just how am I going to prove the suspicion is unfounded? The feds could keep me in limbo for years."

White shrugged again and looked sadly at her.

"It's unfortunate, still that's the way things are in the land of the free in 2053. You really only have two options. The first, the normal and most often used recourse and the least likely to succeed is to contact your senator or representative. The second, which is only slightly more likely to succeed, is to go to the media."

"The media? How can they help?"

"Sometimes the only thing that stops these people is the glare of negative publicity. Freedom of the press doesn't mean what it meant one hundred years ago, thanks to Supreme Court decisions along the lines I quoted, but it's the best thing around. Find yourself a good reporter. It works for me."

"What do you mean?"

"I would have less success than a black man at a Ku Klux Klan meeting if I didn't work the press. The corporations feel the pain of negative publicity somewhat, and the more they think people are going to boycott them, the more they feel it. Do you know a good reporter?"

"Holy shit, of course not. Why would I?"

Phillip White smiled his fatherly smile again.

"Indeed. Why would you? You live in another world, Kalidas. Do you ever read e-zines?"

"Sometimes my personal search engine brings back e-zine articles. I don't make a habit of reading many of them. They don't seem to contain any facts."

"You should. They can be entertaining. And they do have facts in them, even statistics, though maybe not the kind you like. I got addicted to them as a young lawyer and have been entertained by them ever since. And they serve another purpose. You know, old-fashioned papers and magazines, some of which are still subscribed to by the filthy rich, have an exorbitant tax on them for a reason."

"And what's that?"

"We discovered years ago that the negative environmental impacts of getting a newspaper dropped on your doorstep or a magazine delivered to your mailbox vastly outweigh those of receiving the same information through a computer or a handheld electronic device like a cell phone or personal digital assistant. Pulp paper is a very resource-intensive product, hence the government tax. You can still use it if you want to, although you pay the price. I, personally, prefer a paperless office, as much as possible. And e-zines are so much more fun. They're generally a combination of the old-style newspaper, weekly news magazine, and in-depth bi-monthly. Most are interactive and also have lots of visual aids to boot."

"Phillip, you've convinced me. First, I should read e-zines. Second, I'm terribly old-fashioned. How do I contact one of these e-zines?"

"Don't look for extra special attention, except on the message boards. But there are alternatives. Here's the name of an e-zine reporter. Use it wisely."

He handed her a slip of paper. It read simply: Jayashree Sandoval, Crime Fighters.

"How do you know this person?"

"Jay served under a friend of mine in the marines. I was a marine too, before I became a lawyer. She's quite a little dynamo. I've met her on a couple of occasions, at parties at my friend's house. She's quite interesting, and very intelligent. She almost won a Pulitzer. You'll like her. I e-mail or video-mail her occasionally. She's very busy but I'll bet she'll listen to you and at least connect you up with the right reporter to help you."

"And what about my journal submission?"

"File it away for now. When and if things are squared away, maybe you can re-submit. Your first steps are to do what I suggested. Unfortunately, I know neither of our senators nor your representative personally. I don't even know my own representative. They're all a rather useless bunch anyway. You're on your own there. As for Jay, give her my regards. That should be enough."

"This is all so crazy," Kalidas said, as he led her to the door. "Everything's happening so fast."

White opened the door, and then surprised her by giving her a peck on the cheek.

"When this is all over, my wife and I will have you over for dinner and we'll laugh about this."

"I hope you're right," were her parting words.

Scherzo Fourteen

Stanley Morgan had five best-sellers to his credit, plus two other novels, and three collections of short stories. He considered his newest novel to be his best so far. It was ready for publication but his publisher was still waiting for the DHS approval. A mere technicality, said the publisher.

Stanley couldn't wait to see how reviewers received his new book. He was therefore crestfallen when he received the following letter:

Dear Stanley,

I regret to inform you that the DHS license was denied. One of your characters, Paul Lecompte, bears too much resemblance to the present Secretary of Defense, Frank Sweeney. This character is treated as something of a buffoon. The DHS perceives that, given the war between the terrorists and the US, it is not appropriate that one of the US leaders involved in that struggle be publicly ridiculed in an e-book that would have a large circulation throughout the world.

Perhaps we can do some creative editing and re-submit.

Sincerely,
Bob Reese

Stanley dropped the paper to the floor, his mouth agape at the absurdity of it all. His novel, The Quest for the Shield, was set in a fantasy kingdom where Paul Lecompte was indeed the Defense Minister. It belonged to the standard fantasy genre that had existed for over one hundred years.

He found his cell phone and dialed his lawyer's number.

Chapter Seventeen

Washington, DC, Wednesday . . .

The Lear jet touched down at Reagan National Airport and Vladimir watched with amusement as one of the VPs from his drug company ran out onto the windy tarmac. He hadn't been to the Washington office for a while, so the fellow was probably trying to maximize his ass-kissing time.

It was a short ride to his hotel in one of the company's executive limos. After thanking the driver and going through some banalities with the VP, Vladimir was alone. He needed to continue his work on countering the administration's moves against the drug industry.

The US government periodically tried to control the international drug companies. Through their numerous lobbyists and campaign donations the companies usually managed to get their way. Money was always the clincher. Those with the money, bought power, and therefore ruled as de facto masters of the world. It just depended on the whims of the market place who had the money at any given time.

Capitalism is wonderful. Uncontrolled capitalism is better. Without controls, we can stomp all over the middle class, getting them to pay dearly for products that they don't even need half the time. And their taxes even pay for most of the research program in my drug company via NIH grants.

He chuckled and served himself a vodka on the rocks from the minibar. Then he sat down at the luxurious desk of the hotel suite to open up his laptop. After it booted he connected to one of his own personal servers in Switzerland. The computer software automatically set up the coding. His computer people had guaranteed that not even the NSA could break through the code, though there was also added security in the fact that his signal bounced through several satellites and other earthly connections from India to Iceland. It would take the best hackers in the world to even determine the source of the log-on to the server.

Vladimir typed in a name in the search box and looked at the file that spread out on his computer screen. It was something he did every now and then, since a personnel file often gave him a clue to an exploitable weakness. He had once bribed a Boston city council member with two tickets to the BSO, a miniscule bribe for a very important vote. In spite of home theatre music systems and quality telecasts around the world, some people still preferred live music. Despite their exorbitant price, the BSO's tickets were always sold out in advance before the beginning of the season. The councilman had made an off-hand remark to that effect in a local interview which Vladimir had seen.

The file he was looking at was more complex, though, because the man was more complex. Pierce Hamilton, Fulton's National Security Advisor, seemed to have no weaknesses to exploit.

The man was the most powerful person in Fulton's administration, excepting the President and Vice-President, of course. Hamilton was an ex-priest but he had never gone high in the Church hierarchy. True to his parish priest roots, he was concerned about the plight of the common man, a concern anyone that was a bishop or higher church prelate often lacked, even if they hypocritically pretended otherwise. As a result, Pierce Hamilton was a progressive liberal that worked well with John Fulton. He was a no-nonsense Massachusetts liberal and proud of it, once saying in an interview that if it weren't for Massachusetts liberals Americans would still be singing "God save the King."

There is nothing in the man's record that I can use. No obvious weakness, except the obvious political one that all the Jesus-freaks in the southern Bible belt probably hate his guts, being both a liberal and a Catholic. That's why Fulton's from mid-America. No one has been elected president from either coast since George Prescott Bush and he had pretended to be Texan.

Yes, Pierce, you are so dull it's frightening. What planet did you come from?

Then a glimmer of an idea struck Vladimir. He smiled.

If there's nothing in the man's record, I'll put something there.

Chapter Eighteen

In the Virginia countryside, Wednesday . . .

Wednesday evening RP1 and SW2 snuck into Dr. Tyler's office. It was GW3 who had figured out how to trick the videocams using an alternate feed from a memory stick that played the same video scene over and over again. He was able to do it all via computer.

GW3 was probably the most intelligent one in their whole group. He wasn't much interested in the Center's classes—they were too slow for him. He would spend hours on end in the library, though, absorbing ideas, mostly technical ones, from the computerized system that had most of human knowledge stored in its terabytes of memory. That same system was supposed to go with them to the stars, receiving periodic updates from Earth via transmitters already positioned in space.

GW3 wasn't really a rebel, either. He just liked an intellectual challenge, so fooling the Guardians was more of a game for him, rather than anything serious.

For RP1 and SW2 it was serious, though. GW3 had taught them both how to break into Dr. Tyler's computer.

RP1 had become obsessed with two questions. What happened to SW1, FS2, and HJ1? And why were most of them twins, or even triplets and quadruplets? The first question was related to his suspicion that the Center's official story was, at the best, misleading, in spite of learning about nuclear ramjets and astral navigation. As for the second, neither he nor SW2 could think of any particular reason why having a duplicate would be advantageous on a voyage to the stars.

Dr. Tyler's answer to the second question had been as equally puzzling as his answer to the first. He had said that they didn't want to lose any of their gene pool, that it was limited to begin with. They had been carefully chosen to have the maximum diversity in a small number of individuals so they couldn't afford to lose any of that diversity.

RP1 thought that answer strange. He had never been attracted to SW1, even though she looked just like SW2. *How could I ever have children with either SW3 or SW4 if I ever lost SW2? It just doesn't make sense.*

It took them several nights of prying through Dr. Tyler's files before they had answers to those questions. Along the way, they learned a lot more about the Center. In particular, they learned that it really wasn't part of NASA. The doubts kept growing.

Not very far away that first night and at the same late hour, the head of the DHS financial section made two computer transfers. One was into an account on the west coast that had been used before on numerous occasions. The sum was large, yet not as large as the one that he transferred to a numbered account in a Zurich bank. He had no idea what either of the transfers was for; he just did his job, taking orders from on high. He had a wife and three kids. The oldest kid was a senior in high school, hoping to get into a college the family could actually afford, considering that his wife had health problems. He couldn't afford to lose his government job, even if it didn't provide full medical. So he didn't question his orders. He never did.

Wheels were set in motion by the Zurich transfer. A manila envelope with an address, phone number, and photo, together with a huge amount of cash and a first-class ticket to San Francisco, were put inside a carry-on bag and placed in a baggage locker at the Zurich airport. A day later a tall, thin blond woman wearing an expensive business suit and leather boots, opened the locker and removed the bag. She was caught on the airport security videocam, yet there was no videocam in the women's rest room when the tall, thin blond became a tall, thin man with short cut brown hair.

He looked at the ticket and smiled. The flight was in five hours. He would have time to check into the airport hotel and sleep at least two. The rest of his sleep would be on the plane, although he didn't need much.

Scherzo Fifteen

"Senator Pollard, you got up in the Senate today and made a threat that your state will secede from the union if some tax relief is not forthcoming. Can you comment on that?"

Rick Pollard, senior senator from Wyoming, looked at the CNN reporter with astonishment.

"Comment? What do you want me to comment on? We're having our life blood sucked out of us by the federal government. Our taxes are going to pay for all these wars, and we don't get anything back. What little trickles back to the people goes to social programs in the big cities of the east and west coast. What comment can I make? These are facts. The federal government is not doing its job. And it's not only Wyoming that's suffering. Utah, New Mexico, North and South Dakota, Idaho—we've got taxation without representation."

"But Wyoming has two senators just like every other state."

"Sure, and two representatives, also. That makes four of us in DC. How many does California have?"

"But the senator from California had similar angry words on the Senate floor just last month. Is there any connection?"

"California has a different problem. There the north is out of step with the south, and the Big Valley is pissed at everybody else. We actually have quite a bit in common with the San Joaquin Valley people. Just look at the riots in Modesto last week. People are getting tired of paying, paying, paying. They have high taxes and they can't afford medical coverage anymore, not without high deductibles, anyway. Everyone is living on the edge. The Californians think, why do we have to pay for a wheat subsidy in Wyoming? And my people think, why do we have to pay for a social program in an LA slum?"

"But haven't you put your finger on the problem, Senator?"

"How's that?"

"People have lost compassion for other people."

"Oh, I think in good times, it's easy to be compassionate. But we're in bad times now. People turn inward and look out for themselves."

"So, do you think this is wrong, then?"

"What I think matters little. I represent my voting public. If I don't, I'll get voted out of office as quick as you'd get bucked off a wild horse. I haven't got solutions for these people, not within the context of the status quo, anyway. That's my comment."

"Thank you, Senator."

Chapter Nineteen

Paterson, New Jersey, Wednesday & Thursday . . .

Representative Eddy Lemoine offered his hand as he stood to welcome her. "Dr. Kalidas Metropolis, it is a pleasure to meet you. Please, let's sit."

Kalidas sat down in a tall leather wing chair obviously designed to keep a visitor uncomfortable so that his stay would be short. Lemoine sat down at his desk which had very little on it, probably so the visitor could see his reflection in the highly polished wood. What items were there—a small onyx pencil and pen holder, an engraved paper weight with no papers under it, and a picture of a woman—were arranged in impeccable order.

The important man himself was handsomely dressed in the latest business fashion. Immaculate fingernails and white hair that had been to the beauty salon more recently than hers bore witness to the fact that here was a true man of the people.

"Are you affiliated with one of our local community hospitals?" he asked. "I have co-authored several bills to give them more funding, you know."

"Wrong type of doctor. I do research. Bioengineering. I just got fired at Dalton Biomedicine."

"Oh my. How can I help?"

"The excuse they gave was that I am a member of Greek Liberty and therefore a suspected terrorist." She plopped down her resume on top of the beautiful desk, adding some chaos to the order there, and rather enjoying it. "There's no such organization as Greek Liberty, in Greece, or elsewhere. As my resume shows, I have been far too busy trying to solve the transplant rejection problem to bother with such nonsense." Lemoine picked up the resume and began to study it. "In any case, the DHS canceled my clearance, which I need to continue working at Dalton."

"You could file an age discrimination suit," suggested Lemoine.

"Not with a terrorist accusation hanging over my head. Hale and Rivera vs. US, 2017."

Lemoine looked impressed.

"I'll assume you're right about that. I wasn't much good as a practicing attorney, so I went into politics." He paused a moment, knowing from her frown that she didn't find that amusing. "Anyway, I really don't see how I can help you. I can't buck that Department. Our local police would never get another dime from them."

"Why do they need the Department's money?"

"Because, whether they pay for it or not, we have to provide police presence when they declare a terrorist alert. Or when there's a motorcade. Or whatever. I'd rather have their money than take it from our local coffers which are always stretched to the limit."

"Whatever happened to personal freedom and innocent-until-proven-guilty?"

"We have lost a lot of that since 9/11, haven't we? The war on terrorism is very real."

"Yes, I've seen a lot of it during my life. Still, all of our attention to it and all our trampling on individual liberties doesn't seem to do any good, does it? The terrorists still strike, almost with impunity. And we've fought three wars in the Middle East this century without gaining much ground there, either."

Lemoine drummed on the top of his desk, clearly uncomfortable with her words.

"What do you want me to do?"

"I'm not asking you to buck the DHS. I just need something to work with here. A clarification. Where did they get the idea that I'm a member of Greek Liberty? What are the details of the accusation?"

"Even that may be taken rather negatively by them," said Lemoine. "There are rumors, you know."

"What rumors?"

"That Pat Gramza ran such a successful campaign against Helen Shizuru down in Elizabeth because he had secret financial backing from the DHS."

"Do you have proof of that?"

"Of course not. But one hears things. I can't risk it. This district needs my seniority in Congress. It's my obligation to the people."

"You have an obligation to me. I voted for you in the last election."

The tapping at the desk began again.

"Tell you what I'll do. I will write an inquiry and send you a copy. I can't do any more than that, though."

She was not happy with his decision, although she decided that something was better than nothing. She left him her e-mail address and cell phone number.

When she returned home, her front door was open. She walked in. A stocky, short, balding man was writing a note.

"Ah, Dr. Metropolis, I presume." He held out a badge. "Curt Forrester, Department of Homeland Security."

"What the fuck are you doing here? How did you get in?"

"Your landlord let us in, of course."

"Us?"

"My team. I was just leaving you a note. We confiscated your computers, backup data cubes, and a few other things. Sorry. It's part of an ongoing investigation. You have a good day now."

He started to walk out the door. She moved in front of him and grabbed his arm.

"Just a fucking minute! You can't steal my computers. They're my property."

Forrester looked at her hand on his arm with obvious disapproval.

"Hmm, I can see another charge of obstruction of justice coming your way."

She let go of his arm and moved aside.

"You fucking bastard. May you rot in pig shit. Oh, I forgot, that's what spawned you, so you'd be right at home. Get the fuck out of my house. And if I ever see you again, I'll cut your balls off. If you have any, that is."

He only smiled at her and took out a pair of handcuffs. She fought him but he was strong. Minutes later, after a cell phone call, a sleek black limo pulled up in front of Kalidas' townhouse. Two agents hopped out and escorted her to it, handcuffed, and swearing like a sailor.

The trip into Newark was fast and uneventful. By the time they took her into the New Jersey DHS HQ, she had lost all sensation in her hands from the tight handcuffs. From an underground parking lot, they went directly to an elevator, which rose rapidly to the 11th floor of the building. They got out into a dimly lit corridor. She could see it was lined with cells. Most of them were full.

"What is this place?" she demanded.

"Your new home," said Curt Forrester with a smile.

They stopped in front of one of the empty cells. He waved an electronic key and the door slid open. A hand belonging to one of the agents accompanying Forrester gave her a push in the small of the back. She went flying into the cell, stumbled, and fell to the floor.

"Have a nice life," said Forrester. All three left. She went to the small cot to sit down. Then she cried.

A half hour passed, then Kalidas saw and heard the cell door open. A burly woman stepped inside and waved an electronic card, shutting the door behind her.

"Who the hell are you?" demanded Kalidas.

"Be nice, or I'll have to slap you around. I'm here to give you these." She handed Kalidas an orange prison uniform. "Take off your clothes."

"I will not!"

"Honey, you'll take them off one way or the other." The woman waved a night stick suggestively. "I can do it either way. Unless you want to be strip-searched by Forrester or one of his cronies."

"You've got no right to do that."

"Don't go all liberal on me, honey. I've got all the rights and you ain't got none. You lost them by becoming a terrorist."

"I'm not a terrorist!"

"That's what they all say. Now, what's it going to be? I have fun either way. You see, I don't like your kind at all."

"You don't know shit about what's going on, do you?"

"You're here, that's all I need to know. Now, I've got a job to do. Get naked, honey."

The strip search was thorough and maddeningly invasive of her privacy. The prison uniform actually felt good when she put it on afterwards.

The rest of the day and night seemed like an eternity. She didn't sleep much, pacing most of the time. Early on she discovered the surveillance camera high up in one corner of the cell and would make an obscene gesture directly at it when her pacing brought her close. She realized it saw everything in the cell. She wouldn't even be able to go to the bathroom without them seeing her. Or hearing her. *Bastards. What have I done to bring down their wrath upon me?*

She had heard of such travesties. She figured that there had been many over the last fifty years as the war on terrorism droned on and on, yet the media no longer gave them much attention. If they did report on them, it would always be accompanied with a statement about how some civil liberties had to be given up in order to make the general population safe. Sometimes an outraged congressman would make angry statements to the press but such abuses were being tolerated more and more.

Even for me, it was an abstract, intellectual thing, until I became the victim. Now it's an outright abuse of power.

She wondered if she had a right to a lawyer. Probably not. There were plenty of court decisions favoring the DHS on prisoners' rights. There were stories of people being locked away for up to five years, without trial and without a lawyer. The practice had started back at the turn of the century and had become more prevalent over time.

She spent the worst night of her life in that cell. She had been given a miserable dinner the night before and an even more miserable breakfast. Surprisingly the coffee was good, although she had to drink it black.

Some time after breakfast, the cell door opened again. It was the burly woman guard that had strip-searched her.

"Looks like you got lucky, honey," she said, tossing Kalidas her clothes. "The big shots told me to tell you that this should be a warning. About what I don't know."

"And what if I sue the government over this outrageous treatment?" asked Kalidas.

The guard laughed. It was a deep, contralto chuckle that made Kalidas shiver.

"Let me just offer you a piece of advice. Go home. Forget about this. Get on with your life. And, like I said, count yourself lucky. Most people that come here end up in Alaska. We've got a nice place up there for terrorists."

The guard accompanied her down to the same garage where Kalidas and her captors had entered. The guard walked her up the ramp into the busy, grungy daylight of a Newark city street.

"How am I going to get home? They took my money and all my personal belongings."

"Imagine that," said the guard. Then she looked at Kalidas, who seemed about to cry, with a little more compassion. She took a twenty out and handed it to her. "You can catch a bus a couple of blocks down that will take you to Montclair center. Have a nice day."

Scherzo Sixteen

Tulinagwe was proud of his new country. Formed from parts of the old Kenya, Uganda, Rwanda, Burundi, and Tanzania, it was a multiethnic nation that circled Lake Victoria. The AIDS epidemic had decimated its population in the first decades of the twenty-first century but people learned to leave the old ways behind. Unfortunately, it was still a poor country.

Tulinagwe had never seen a doctor in the flesh before, so he was more fearful of the old black man in the white coat than his daughter was.

"Tulinagwe, you have a brave little girl," the doctor said in his perfect Oxford English. "But she is very sick. She needs an operation on a heart valve to repair a birth defect."

"So? Operate on her, then," said Tulinagwe.

"It's not so simple. I will gladly donate my time—I have an opening in my calendar in three months—but everything else is beyond my control. Even to transport her to the capital will be costly, as she may not survive the long bus ride."

"What can I do?" asked Tulinagwe. He felt helpless.

"Perhaps you can take up a collection in your village."

Unfortunately, although he was poor, the rest of the people in Tulinagwe's village were poorer. He could only collect 213 US dollars altogether. When he told this to the doctor over the one cell phone that the village had, the doctor said he was only about 23, 800 US dollars short. Tulinagwe handed the cell phone back to the chief of police with tears streaming down his cheeks.

Two weeks later a strange man showed up in the village, looking for Tulinagwe. He found the young farmer laboring in his field.

"Tulinagwe, we must talk."

They sat down in the shade of a tree that had bark that was all shiny from where the oxen rubbed against it.

"You are from the city," Tulinagwe observed.

"Yes, and I heard of your problem. I would like to make you a proposal."

And that was how Tulinagwe went to the capital with his daughter. They both had operations on the same day. The father gave up one eye, one kidney, and part of his liver so that the daughter could have her heart valve fixed. He considered that it was well worth it.

Chapter Twenty

Quantico, Virginia, Wednesday . . .

Asako O'Brien had a Japanese mother and an Irish father and was born in Johannesburg, South Africa. Such were the ways of the modern world.

She was only slightly taller than Jay, yet looked more delicate. Her black hair was usually cut shorter than normal. She dressed simply but always looked regal all the same.

Jay often thought of Puccini when she was with her, which was absurd. First of all, neither of them really liked opera much. Also, Puccini wrote other operas besides Madame Butterfly. Jay even liked La Boheme a little but her favorite opera, if any could be called a favorite, was Carmen. Too bad it was in French instead of Spanish. *What was Bizet thinking, writing an opera in French about bullfighting? Of course, Hemingway had written a novel in English about bullfighting. Now why didn't the Spanish, or even the Portuguese, write a novel about bullfighting? Instead, the most famous Spanish novel was about that nut who went tilting after windmills. That should have taken place in Holland. This world has always been strange.*

"I shouldn't even be talking to you," Asako told Jay. She sipped her tea between mouthfuls of a hearty ham sandwich.

"You can't have a social life?"

"I'm an FBI agent. Even worse, I'm a forensics expert. We have no life, social or otherwise." She took a bite of her dill and made a face at its tartness.

"But you knew Patty Smith better than you know me, right?"

"So what? I don't need a grudge to do a good job."

"I know that. But wouldn't you like to get her killers?"

Asako lifted the top off the second half of the sandwich and slathered more hot mustard on it. When it was uniformly thick, she seemed satisfied, and pointed the knife at Jay, as the latter stole a few chips.

"I don't deny it. But I didn't ask for the case. My superiors knew that Patty and I were friends. They still gave me the case. And they haven't said anything. What do you want me to do, go off the case?"

"You're going down a road that I had no intention of going down. I just think that knowing Patty so well would motivate you to give me any information you have so I can help out on the case. I made a promise to Dolores."

"That's not an easy promise to keep. This is not an easy case. We have nothing, absolutely nothing, except three shot-up corpses. No motive. No suspects. No reason for their deaths. My bosses are ready to close the books on this one."

"From the FBI's perspective?"

"Yeah, who else?"

Jay told her about the car registered to the DHS. "Are they in on this?" she asked.

Asako considered her answer for a moment, and then shrugged.

"Over the last fifty years, the DHS has developed its own bureaucracy. Its head is a cabinet secretary, after all, on par with the National Intelligence Director. The FBI and the CIA are often marginalized from the inner workings of the DHS bureaucracy, even though the FBI and CIA directors nominally report to the National Intelligence Director. The DHS has closer ties with the NSA and the DEA and, in fact, receives information from them often before we do. When they started mucking around with the intelligence services at the turn of the century, they created one god-awful mess. Over the years that hasn't been helped by the fact that when we have a strong National Security Advisor, like, for example, Pierce Hamilton, the National Intelligence Director becomes little more than his errand boy, even though it has now become a cabinet position. The left hand many times still doesn't know what the right hand is doing until we start tripping over the bureaucracy's big feet. So, to answer your question bluntly, I don't know. We were called in to help by the acting sheriff, since they lost their sheriff, coroner, and criminal forensics expert in one fell swoop. I think Sheriff Fletcher would have told us if they had also called in the DHS. So my guess is that DHS is acting alone, not in cooperation with the sheriff."

Jay nodded. Most of what she heard she already knew, and the last confirmed her suspicions.

"How hard is it to clean up after a body has been placed on an exam table?"

"Not hard. You're supposing they were there to do an autopsy?"

"I know they were doing an autopsy." She explained about the body that Bob Martin had found.

"My lord, you do pick up information, don't you? A Hank Johnson look-alike, huh? Now there's a real prick, if there ever was one."

"Have you had dealings with Mr. Johnson?"

"Not personally, but he's no friend of the Bureau. He's quick to point fingers, especially when he's covering his own ass. Ben Knowland, his boss, is a much more square dealer. By the way, I'll have to pass on this information, though your name won't be mentioned. I protect my informants."

"Works for me, too, so give. What do you know about Hank Johnson that might influence this case?"

"Nothing, absolutely nothing. His problems with that Georgetown coed stirred up a media frenzy for awhile, as you know, but I don't know if he's ever been in Lexington Park. He's originally from Minnesota, I think."

"St. Paul. I think it's time to learn more about him, maybe to pay him a visit."

"You're not just going to go up to him and directly ask him why he had a dead double in Lexington Park?" Asako raised an elegant right eyebrow in a quizzical expression.

"Maybe. How long does it take FBI info to get over to the DHS?"

"Longer than we like to admit. It depends on the urgency. We do a triage but anything that goes over has to pass a minimum threshold of urgency. Sometimes we accumulate info on a person for years before any direct action is taken, and, even then, the FBI may go it alone, especially if it's more oriented towards traditional crime, not terrorism. The CIA works similarly with info gleaned overseas by its operatives. The dotted line to the DHS is really a dotted line. In fact, they probably have closer connections to the military, and, like I said, to the NSA and the DEA, the latter because so much terrorism is financed by drugs."

"So this info I gave you might never make it over there?"

"I didn't say that. It will probably be classified 'Very Urgent' and be passed over immediately, all because of the Hank Johnson connection."

"Will he see it?"

"Almost certainly—again, because it's related to him." Asako licked some mustard off one of her long, delicate fingers. "You're thinking you might as well go ahead and ask him, then?"

"Just to see his reaction."

At that moment, Jay's cell phone rang. The face of a pretty black woman came on line.

"Jay, this is Sandra, Bouncer's friend. He asked me to call. Bob Martin is dead."

"Where? How?"

"They found him under that trestle where he hangs out in the summer. I guess they don't know if it was death by natural causes or not. Sam Fletcher is really pissed at Bouncer for not telling him what Bob had seen. He's got Bouncer locked up for obstructing justice. And I'm sure he would like to lock you up too. He's going to get some expert from the FBI to come over and tell him if Bob's was a natural death."

"That would probably be me," said Asako.

"Want to ride with me?" asked Jay.

"Only if you're coming back this way. The Bureau frowns on unnecessary car rentals these days, since we have a nice fleet of our own."

"All right, let's go."

Scherzo Seventeen

Oliver Whitney felt comfortable inside the air-conditioned van, even though it was nearly 40 degrees centigrade outside. He sat next to Cathy Jones, his nose twitching a little from the scent of her perfume. There was no getting away from it. He wasn't exactly allergic to it, although he was definitely uncomfortable. Besides, she was one good looking woman, a single mother, and generally very pleasant.

At the moment, she was swearing as they listened to a conversation between two terrorists. They called them X and Y, and the DHS had been tailing them for three months. In their present conversation they were finalizing plans to blow up one of the largest hotels in Las Vegas. The city had long been the target of extremist Muslim groups, since they felt it represented the decadence of America. Three years ago they had managed to blow up part of the largest casinos in Monte Carlo, yet so far the DHS had managed to foil every plot against Las Vegas since the original one in 2014 that had ripped apart the Egyptian.

"I think we have enough to move in on them," suggested Oliver. He started to get up so that he could swing around to the other side and call for a SWAT team.

"Wait," said Cathy, grabbing his arm and holding him down. He was surprised at her strength. "Listen."

They both listened as X told Y that Allah would be smiling down at them since two other comrades were simultaneously planning to hit Hoover Dam. The venerable old dam had also been a target for nearly fifty years, although the terrorists had never gotten close.

Oliver began cursing to himself. Now he swung around and opened up a channel to the local DHS office. They would need two SWAT teams.

Neither one of them participated in the following action, as they were com specialists, illegally listening in on conversations, tapping into computer networks, and so forth. Normally, anything they recorded would never stand up in court. Once Oliver had listened in on the planning of a bank robbery yet the bank robbers got off because they were Americans. But spying on non-US citizens had been declared legal by the Supreme Court over twenty-five years ago. Most terrorists were not US citizens. Most terrorists, in fact, entered the country illegally.

Both SWAT teams encountered heavy resistance. They had their orders on what to do in that situation. Three terrorists were soon in a Las Vegas morgue. The fourth, wounded but not critically so, was in heavy security as DHS agents grilled him, trying to obtain information about how he entered the country, if there were any other plans in the making, and their groups' methods in general. He would never be released. When the DHS agents were done with him, he would be flown to a high security prison near Juno, Alaska. In most respects, he would no longer be among the living either.

Chapter Twenty-One

In the Virginia countryside, Wednesday . . .

The sleek limo pulled up behind the other parked in the semi-circular drive of a mansion in the Virginia suburbs. A woman got out, went to the front door, and rang the doorbell.

Hank Johnson, the owner of the house, opened the door.

"Good to see you again, Stephanie. Always a pleasure. Senator Preston is already here. Come on in."

The woman nodded curtly and entered the house. "Roger is never late when his ass is on the line," commented the Vice President. "Have someone get me a gin and tonic. It's damn hot, you know."

She knew her way and walked imperiously towards the living room. Hank Johnson followed her meekly.

Roger Preston stood when she came into the living room. She frowned. She hated the man, although he had his uses. He was dressed in tennis clothes, obviously coming from the club. *Of course. Why would he be doing the job the people of Indiana actually wanted him to do, expected him to do, elected him to do?*

She sat down facing Hank and the Senator. She was still a striking woman. She was not in as good a shape as she had been as an actress, which had been years ago. Still, she knew she was still photogenic and people all over the country immediately recognized her. She was also fairly healthy, which was important, since there would be challengers in the primaries. When Fulton stepped down, she would have the advantage over all contenders, though she needed to be in peak physical condition to endure the lengthy campaign. Especially with those assholes the other parties were going to throw at her.

She looked at both men, who were both obviously waiting for her to say something first, not wanting to risk starting their meeting off on the wrong footing. *But I don't have time to be amused by their temerity. I tolerate them only because they both have their uses.*

"We have a problem. I want it solved. Sweeney's off at NATO HQ, and anyway I don't want to call a general meeting. You should be able to handle it, Hank."

Johnson looked uncomfortable. He had been low in the ranks at the DHS when Stephanie Williams was Secretary. He knew she was a lot smarter than he was. *I've been kissing her ass for a long time.*

Johnson's athletic build from college had given way to some serious middle-age spread. He still considered himself to be a lady's man. The affair with the coed had only become a debacle because he was caught at it, caught in a photo taken by some paparazzi who sold it to the Washington Sentinel, an e-zine with the goal of embarrassing as many political fat cats as it could, in either party. Hank still thought they made a handsome couple. The coed was now going out with the quarterback of the University of Maryland football team after dumping him because of the negative publicity.

Johnson would always believe that women were attracted to big, strong men who moved in the circles of power. Except Stephanie. She could leave any male feeling like he had just been castrated. He had seen it happen many times in their overlapping careers. She was also not seduced by strong men. Even as an actress, she had been a loner, eschewing the traditional husband-swapping of Hollywood. Some thought she was lesbian. Johnson knew better. She had enjoyed numerous lovers during her long life; she just didn't keep any of them around long.

"Yeah, well, this whole fiasco isn't my fault," said Johnson. "That was a major cluster fuck at the Center."

"And Richter?"

"He was asking for more money."

"Greed is such a basic human emotion," she observed. "Well, like I said, I want our problem solved. Controlled. Whatever."

"The Richter problem will be solved," said Hank, watching Preston squirm uncomfortably. "And I'm pressuring Andy to kick some ass. What about the others?" Preston squirmed some more.

"Roger, you're playing with the big boys now," said Stephanie, frowning at him. "It won't help things if you pee your pants."

"Don't be uncouth, Stephanie," Preston said.

"I'm just a realist. Most of us have been in this a long time. We're very certain about where we're going with this and how important it is for our country. You're the new kid on the block. As much as I was against it, you were brought into this."

"And I love you, too," muttered Preston.

The Vice President ignored him and returned her attention to Hank Johnson.

"I'm leaving it in your hands. Do what you think is necessary. Just don't get me into an embarrassing situation. And for god sakes, keep your pecker in your pants. You and it have had too much press lately."

"So why am I here?" asked Preston.

"It's only a slightly related issue. I need some action in a committee you're on. We need some new legislation proposed. It's time to earn your pay."

"He hasn't worked a full day for a long time," commented Hank.

"It's the connections," said Preston with a smile. "I'm valuable for my connections. I've been a senator for a long time."

"Precisely my point," said Hank.

"All right, cut the crap," interrupted Stephanie. "Let's see how good those connections are. If you can get this legislation onto the floor, I'll drum up enough votes to get it passed. My immediate problem, however, is how to get it out of your committee."

She began a lengthy explanation of what she wanted. It didn't interest Hank much, so he soon became bored. But he couldn't leave the room. The VP hadn't dismissed him yet. Forty minutes later, she ended the meeting. She left as imperiously as she had come.

Scherzo Eighteen

General Ahmed Ayoubi was a great admirer of American military discipline. That didn't mean he liked the country necessarily, just that their military discipline was a thing to be admired. Especially the marines. And special forces.

He had been fighting Americans one way or another for a long time. He had killed his first American in Sadr City, the Shiite section of Baghdad, when he was twelve, almost fifty years ago. He had moved from country to country, one step ahead of the infidel invasion. The guerrilla had kept on fighting even when the creation of the new Palestinian state had generated an uneasy peace between Israel and the rest of the Arab world. The only thing he knew how to do was fight.

The Arab world actually had mixed emotions about the peace their leaders had brokered with the Israelis. Many of the followers of Mohammed professed a tolerance for other world religions, knowing full well that the modern world was a place where the profit and loss ledgers of the huge international corporations held more practical importance compared to reading materials from the Koran, the Bible, or any other religious texts. There were still those of the old school who were quite successful in obtaining new recruits for their cause, though, making them believe that Islam was the only true religion, that the world-wide corporations were the work of Satan, and that those who didn't believe that deserved as ignoble a death as possible. Whether the old school actually believed that or not was irrelevant. They, and their recruits, were unified in their desire for payback, a desire to slap down all those deemed responsible for their lackluster, poverty stricken lives—they were not about to lead quiet lives of desperation, but to strike out, destructively and lethally. For them it was the eternal, endless war that a certain American president had started at the turn of the century. It would not end until the last infidel was dead or they were all dead.

Yes, the only thing Ayoubi knew how to do was to fight. But he was tired. He studied the CIA agent sitting across from him.

"You are taking a big risk in coming here." His English was heavily accented, although he knew it was good enough. He had learned it listening to CNN. His French was better. He often made trips to Paris to buy arms on the black market.

"Obviously you're interested in my deal. Otherwise, I'd be dead now. I realize that. So let's get to it. We'll provide you with ten million dollars in weapons if you do this little chore for us."

"But I have no quarrel with the Sultan. I may not like the fat life he leads but I have other priorities. Still, I will do what you say if you tell me why you're interested in deposing him. And why you don't do it yourself."

"For your first concern, it looks more legitimate if it's just a power struggle between you folks. For your second, I have secret knowledge that the Sultan is going to sign an exclusive oil export agreement with the Chinese. We can't allow the Chinese to get their hands on more cheap oil. We're in a full blown economic war with them, and have been for most of the last fifty years. You know that. It wouldn't be to your benefit for them to get more cheap oil either, because that would probably mean more arms deals with the Arab governments that are friendly to the US, the ones you're fighting. It's a strange world we live in, General."

"Indeed it is. Just a little business deal, right?" said the General. He handed a tea to the CIA agent. "I guess it makes sense to me."

Three months later the Sultan's motorcade was attacked by guerrilla forces. The Sultan died of his wounds three days later. The contract with the Chinese was never signed.

The CIA agent met once more with the General on the outskirts of Baghdad. He congratulated the General on a job well done.

"I guess you won't need to be going to Paris this year," the agent told the terrorist.

"Oh, I'll still go. Your weapons help, but I will need more. And we have very wealthy backers."

"Well, bon voyage, then," said the agent.

Chapter Twenty-Two

St. Mary's City, Maryland, Wednesday . . .

Bouncer wasn't actually locked in a cell. He and Sandra were having coffee with Sam Fletcher.

"Ah, the other perp from the let's-keep-the-sheriff-in-the-dark gang. Nice to see you again, Jay. And Agent O'Brien. So nice to see you again, too."

"Sam, I think your irony is lost on Jay," observed Bouncer.

"Since she's a big city crime e-zine reporter? Have you solved the mystery yet, Jay?"

"Hey, we were going to tell you," objected Jay. "You haven't been exactly forthcoming either. Colman shut up tighter than a clam."

"Well, why do I get the idea that you two are working on a conspiracy theory or something? If so, forget it. This is St. Mary's County. There are no conspiracies here, and no secrets either, beyond the usual classified government stuff at the Air Station, St. Inigoes, and so forth." Sam jerked a thumb at Asako. "Let's go take a look at old Bob. I believe he died of heart failure, though I could be wrong. There's not a mark on him, so he probably brought it on with the juice. Can you do autopsies, Agent O'Brien?"

"I just watch them. I have no medical training per se. Did you want an autopsy?"

"Only if I can't pin the cause of death down satisfactorily."

"Well, a start would be an exterior examination of the corpse and a tox workup. I can certainly do that. Otherwise, I would need some help."

"I suspect that will be enough, which is why I just called you. It would probably be hard to get an autopsy done on short notice anyway. I didn't know you were consorting with the enemy, of course." The sheriff looked from one woman to the other. "I don't believe in coincidences, you know."

"Let's get started," suggested Jay, trying to change the subject.

"Oh, it will be just Agent O'Brien and me. I may tell you what we find later." He gave her a wink. "Or maybe not." He guided Asako by the arm towards the stairwell that led down to the coroner's office and morgue.

"So what did you learn from Asako?" Bouncer asked her after the sheriff and the FBI agent had left.

Jay flopped down in a chair. She smiled at Sandra Chapman. The black woman was pretty, although she had a few extra pounds. She was nearly as tall as Bouncer. She dressed much better than Bouncer, though, and had a degree of sophistication that he would never have. Nevertheless, they seemed well matched, for two giants, anyway.

"Asako knows very little. She didn't know about the Hank Johnson connection. We had just decided that my next course of action should be to approach him when Sandra called. Did you tell the sheriff about the car?"

"I didn't want him to shit another brick. By the way, did you mention Bob Martin to GeeBee?"

"Yes, I guess I did. You don't think—"

"Yes, I think they eliminated him. They're cleaning up. We may be next."

"Absurd. You're not really a conspiracy theorist, are you?"

"Not in the way most people think. But stuff is going on here that I don't like. I've lost four of my friends. In a very short time." He took Sandra's hand. "And I would like to keep the count limited to that. You included, by the way."

"Well, thank you. I suggest we wait to see what Asako turns up."

They didn't like the answer when they heard it. The sheriff had been right. Bob died of heart failure, though it was not brought on by alcohol. His alcohol level was actually low enough to even drive a car. Instead, the tox report showed a high level of heroin in his blood stream; he had died of an overdose. In another homeless person, this might not have seemed unusual. However, it was well known that Bob's older sister had died of a drug overdose when he was a boy, so he had never used any drugs his entire life. Even the booze was a recent thing since he returned from the war.

"You think someone wanted to murder him and make it look like it was his own doing?" asked Jay.

"Looks that way," said Sam Fletcher. "Anything you people want to tell me about this?"

Jay looked at Bouncer, and he nodded. Apparently he trusted Sam enough and wanted his help, considering the news they had just received. So she told him about the car that had followed them and her later determination that it belonged to the DHS. Asako chirped in that she knew of no involvement by the feds, other than the FBI, at Sam's request.

"I'll have to make some discreet inquiries," said Sam. "Something strange is going on, and I'm not liking any of it."

"Do you mind if I approach Hank Johnson?" Jay asked.

"That's not exactly discreet. And why do you think he'd tell you anything? To him you're just a nosy reporter."

"I don't think it can hurt," said Bouncer. "And it might save our skins if he knew a lot more people besides old Bob know the corpse that was found in the bin looked like him."

"Oh, please," said Asako. "You are into conspiracies."

"That's my Bouncer," said Sandra. "I take it that he's free to go now?"

"If it weren't for the paper work, I'd book both you and Jay for obstructing justice," Sam said. "But ok, get the hell out of here. Watch your back, though."

"Sounds like you believe in a conspiracy," observed Jay, with a wink and a smile.

"Not at all. This sounds more like a murderer trying to cover his tracks. It's probably not even related to the Hank Johnson look-alike. I expect there might be a Philly connection. John made a lot of enemies when he was a cop up there. One of them almost killed him."

"Yeah, Sam, so why did they take the body of the Hank Johnson look-alike?" asked Sandra.

The sheriff frowned.

"I don't know. Be careful. All of you."

Scherzo Nineteen

Imre Horvath knew he had little time. He made a hand sign to Nao Takahashi. The other Interpol agent nodded slightly and counted to five as Imre moved around to the back door. Then Nao broke down the front with one expertly placed kick.

"Interpol! Hands in the air."

He actually said it in French. They had come to the dirty Parisian slum, filled with foreigners, mostly from the Middle East, on a tip from the American CIA. It was reported that General Ahmed Ayoubi, one of the most feared terrorists in the Middle East, was hiding out there. The tip said he had come to Paris to buy weapons on the black market.

There were three men and a woman in the dingy five room house. None of them felt like putting their hands in the air. They all went for their guns. Nao hit the ground, firing his automatic weapon with deadly accuracy. At the same time, Imre broke down the back door and began firing.

Only the woman survived. She was bleeding from several wounds, though. Nao looked down on her in pity, watching her as Imre checked the three bodies. Then Imre came over and knelt down beside the woman.

"Mademoiselle, vous etes blessee. Je peux demander un medecin."

She spit in his face.

"Hungarian pig, go fuck yourself," she said in English.

"Ah, well, have it your own way." He grabbed her by her hair. "Irish bitch, you've been running with a rough crowd. How long have you been with General Ayoubi?"

"Who's General Ayoubi?"

"Your boyfriend over there, your boss, who knows what he was to you," said Nao. "And how did you know my friend here is Hungarian?"

"I know his face. We know a lot of your faces."

"Shit," said Imre.

"That way we can kill you if we see you. Interpol, CIA, DHS, MI6—they're all our enemies. But we know your faces best."

"You still didn't answer my question," said Imre, jerking her hair again. "Let's rephrase it, since I may have been impolite." He tightened his grip a little more and she winced. He also bent her arm back, exacerbating one of her wounds. "Is that General Ayoubi?"

"Yes," she hissed.

Imre let her go and stood up. Nao kept the gun on her, knowing she could still kill them in a moment, wounds or no wounds.

"We'd better get her a doctor," Nao suggested.

"Yeah, fix her up good, so she can spend the rest of her life rotting in jail. I just don't get it. Good looking bitch, and she throws her whole life away for that bastard."

"Fanaticism is not logical," said the stoic Nao.

It took some time but the news of General Ayoubi's death at the hands of the Interpol eventually reached a certain CIA agent in Baghdad. That night he permitted himself a small celebration, eating a nice meal at a very good restaurant. He even snuck a small flask of grappa in and put it in his coffee when no one was looking.

He only felt a small twang of remorse that Becky O'Neil, whom he had seduced to get information, would spend the rest of her life in jail. They were in a war.

Chapter Twenty-Three

Washington, DC, Wednesday . . .

Daniela Romano looked around the Georgetown townhouse with a smile. "This is a lot better than the apartment I shared in New York," she observed.

"Don't get used to it," said Vladimir Kalinin "but enjoy it while you're here. Remember, though, from now on you don't know me. This is the most important acting job you've ever had."

"I'll do it so well you'll even start believing it."

Her laugh is soft and tinkling, like a wind chime. And she's smart. Too bad she's had such bad luck as an actor. Broadway is not known for its fairness.

Daniela was a pleasant woman who had recently been effective in relieving his stress in New York City. Vladimir liked that she took pride in her appearance. Even now, in blue jeans, she still had her hair done up nicely and wore light makeup. Her loose, soft green sweater, barely hinting at her magnificent breasts, almost matched the color of her eyes, which he guessed was produced by contacts. Her only jewelry was a pair of small and tasteful earrings.

She didn't look like a kept woman. Which is exactly how Pierce Hamilton's mistress should look.

They had agreed on that. After studying the National Security Advisor's history, they had decided that Daniela should be the quiet and charming but sexy type, someone Hamilton could discreetly have an affair with.

Vladimir found Daniela's personality an intriguing one. He had always been interested in actors. He admired a lot of the old ones and knew quite a few of the current ones. He also knew that they were at their best when they got so immersed in their role that they became the person they were playing. He was fairly confident that Daniela could have been one of the good ones. Fickle fortune had not favored her, though. The roles were hard to come by. Rather than wait on tables or serve drinks at a bar, she had augmented her earnings by attending to the needs of rich men who could pay big money for her body.

They continued to walk through the townhouse. She looked happy, even coquettish.

"Vladimir, is this the way all you rich people live? It's weird to see so much luxury that's tangible, not just something on an entertainment center's holo-screen. You know what I mean?"

"This is nothing. The rich spend their money wisely sometimes, foolishly others. The truly rich don't care that much about money. But Hamilton is not rich. He's just comfortable. He could afford this if he wanted it, and he would want it for a mistress like you."

"I wonder if I'll like him."

"You'll probably never meet him. It might be better that you don't."

"Because he could fuck me better than you?"

He smiled. She had the audacity to tease him. He liked that.

"I wouldn't think so. But he might stir up your Catholic guilt."

"Ah, yes, the ex-priest. I have a brother that is a priest. He thinks I'm a starving actor."

"You are a starving actor."

"Not now. This is a well paying gig, when it's all said and done." She stopped at the entrance to the master bedroom. It contained a huge king size bed with the usual furniture. However, one whole end was tiled. The master bedroom and the master bath were one. "Not much privacy here when someone is doing poopers."

"The combined bath and bedroom goes in and out of style. I suppose this would be considered retro and it is practical if you're mostly living alone." He didn't want to bore her with encyclopedic details, yet he couldn't resist elaborating a little. "This townhouse dates back to the Georgetown gentrification of the last century. At that time it was thought to be a fine example of well bred hedonism. Everything you need in one room in order to take care of all bodily functions."

"Well, that's absurd, because you don't have the kitchen. Eating is an important bodily function to me. Especially when I'm getting a lot of exercise." She nodded towards the bed and winked. "How about a freebie? I'm in the mood. This place turns me on."

Vladimir looked at his watch. He went to a small bar and poured pale ales for the two of them. He offered her the glass.

"I guess I wouldn't be much of a gentleman if I killed that mood."

The wind chimes tinkled again, liltingly, drawing him closer to her. She hadn't seen what he had poured into the ale. It was a tasteless, white powder. Her preparation would begin. It would be enjoyable for her, probably more than for him. He was working now, a willing tool in his own plan.

Chapter Twenty-Four

In the Virginia countryside, Wednesday . . .

Gossip about what RP1 and SW2 had found out in Tyler's office spread like wildfire through the Center. Not all their colleagues believed that they were being lied to, not on something as important as going to the stars. The disbelievers promised to keep quiet, though, since no one liked the Guardians. It was left to RP1 and SW2 to plan their next move.

"I'm at a loss," said SW2. "We know that we're being lied to, that we're some kind of bioengineering project. The whole Center is dedicated to keeping us here under the watchful eyes of Dr. Tyler and the Guardians."

"Maybe we can only find out the truth by escaping," said RP1.

"But what if Tyler isn't lying about what would happen to us out there? Maybe that was what happened to FS2, HJ1 and SW1."

"Their files didn't even mention their escape. The last entries in them were weeks before they left the Center. Maybe they're still alive. But they're not our problem. Don't you want to know why we're here?"

"That one file, that report, talked about us like we're lab rats. I don't like being a lab rat."

RP1 considered that a moment, and smiled.

"With white fur you'd be nice to snuggle up to," he said.

"Get serious."

"Well, I'm at a loss, too. I sort of like it here, though now I'm scared."

"Me too. So we're going to have to escape. But first we can dig deeper. We just got into Tyler's desktop. Maybe there's a server somewhere with a lot more files. Maybe in Tyler's lab."

"And what about the other labs? We don't even know what goes on there."

"Maybe GW3 can help us get in there, too. He's always up for a challenge."

They went to find GW3.

At that moment in Menlo Park it was just past 7 pm. A small townhouse belonging to Professor Wolfgang Richter was filled with the strains of one of Mozart's four horn concerti. A few other single senior Stanford professors lived in the complex, yet most could not afford to live in such expensive housing, even with the subsidy that the university provided. Over the music Peter Kendall heard the professor's doorbell.

"Can you see who that is?" the professor called to him from the kitchen.

Peter was the professor's current favorite. As a second-year law student, the good food, wine, and money the professor threw at him wasn't even necessary, as his family was one of the richest in San Mateo County. He actually liked the professor, although he knew that eventually the older man's attention would turn elsewhere. Wolfgang had quite a reputation in the gay community as a person not overly keen on long-term relationships. In particular, he tended to go after the young undergraduates, so Peter considered himself lucky.

Peter was dressed in the plush bathrobe the professor had loaned him. He thought it was a little too warm even though the professor had the air conditioning in the townhouse on high. *That's not unusual, considering it could be another wild night. How dare someone interrupt our evening.*

Peter was slighter of build than the professor. His blond hair and blue eyes qualified him as a poster boy for the Nazi youth corps. His well muscled body offered visual evidence of many workouts at the gym and laps around the pool. As an undergraduate he had been on the swim team. *The other members of that team probably would have shit a brick if they had known I was gay. Not even Dad and Mom know. Maybe it's time to come out. Let everyone know who I really am.*

Peter went to the door. A tall, thin man was about to push the doorbell again.

"Can I help you?" Peter asked.

"I'm looking for the professor," the thin man said. "I'm from the DHS. His sister's quite ill."

"Oh, I'm sorry to hear that. Come on in. The professor is in the kitchen."

"Thank you. I really hate to interrupt his plans for the evening with bad news."

"I'm sure he would want to hear about his sister, even if it's bad. I'm surprised that they just didn't call."

"No family in the east, I dare say. I'm from the San Francisco office. I'm sure the news will just kill him." As Peter turned towards the kitchen, a strong arm reached around him. The visitor's knife hand made a quick, expert pass at Peter's throat. "Just as it did you."

Peter gave a gurgle and slumped to the floor as the visitor let him fall. The visitor then moved towards the kitchen.

"Who is it, Peter? We really don't need interruptions tonight."

The visitor stepped into the doorway. The knife had disappeared. In his hand was a modern pistol with a long silencer. He shot the professor between the eyes, smiling at the man's astonishment.

"I really must apologize for ruining your evening," he said, putting the gun back in the holster under his armpit. "But I have a bit of jet lag, you see." He turned an opened bottle of wine around so he could see the label. "Californian. I happen to like your local Zinfandel. So I'll just have a glass." He poured himself a small serving and took a few sips. "Not half bad. But I really prefer French wine. Once they finally learned how to play the marketing game, they've been giving your local stuff a run for the money. I do believe competition has been good for you both." He picked up a piece of the expensive dill Havarti, enjoying the burst of flavor that seemed to favorably chase after the wine taste. "I do give you credit for having good taste, Professor. Maybe that makes up for your overbearing greed. A good night to you, sir."

The thin man bowed to the professor's corpse and then made his way out of the townhouse. As he passed Peter's corpse, he noted the foul smell of feces and urine. *The Greek god Apollo has become despoiled.* The thin man shook his head, lamenting the loss of innocent life. *It makes my chosen profession so hard sometimes.*

Scherzo Twenty

Jackson Pfeiffer floated lazily in the zero gravity environment of the space station and watched Julie Dembner expertly work on her experiments.

"It's all a waste, you know."

"What do you mean? My work here?"

"Yeah. I've thought about it a lot. You're doing these micro-g experiments for a drug company conglomerate. Suppose you're successful. How many people will it benefit?"

"You mean, how many people will be able to afford the drugs, I suppose. I've thought about that, too."

"So what's your conclusion?"

"I think it's not my problem. If they didn't finance the research, the discoveries couldn't be made. It's like playing the lottery."

"Yeah, only in this case, if you win, the drug company gets rich. It's happened before. Many times."

"Yeah, I know. Maybe the problem is in the patent system. Or there should be more government controls so that the companies can't get too greedy. Like I said, not my problem."

"Maybe you'll think differently when you're elderly and know you're dying because a drug that could save you is too expensive."

"My, you're the cheery one today. Don't you have something better to do than needle me?"

"Yes, but it's not as much fun."

Chapter Twenty-Five

Washington, DC, Wednesday . . .

Pierce Hamilton, National Security Advisor to President John Fulton, sat across from the President's desk in the oval office. While Fulton shuffled through the papers—when would the old man use classified e-mail and video-mail like everyone else?—Hamilton looked around the office.

The White House was showing its age. It had gone through various repairs and upgrades on both the inside and outside, the last major one two years before Fulton took office. But a lot of the furnishings could only be classified as very old and worn antiques. That didn't seem to bother Fulton. He was something of an antique himself.

President Fulton had won the election his first term with a populist and antiwar platform. In the primaries, his only strong contender had been Stephanie Williams, who was known for her tough anti-crime positions and America-first ideas. She had become his VP on the ticket and they had won in a landslide. The other principal party's candidate, associated with the war and foreign policy failures of the previous administration, didn't stand a chance. The third party was almost a no-show.

Pierce Hamilton was a small, wiry and bookish individual who had become associated with John Fulton when the man was governor of Missouri. His unruly mop of rust-colored hair, blue eyes, sunken cheeks, and Pinocchio nose often caused people to underestimate him. In his everyday life and in his role as National Security Advisor, he had the kind of analytic mind that often allowed him to leap beyond the ordinary solutions achieved by small, conservative, strictly logical steps to really novel solutions derived from bold intuitions. He needed every bit of his mental capacity in order to manage the vast intelligence network which would degenerate into chaotic and often competitive bureaucracies without his guidance. He needed that network to be working well, as it provided him with the data that allowed him to counsel the President with what he hoped was the right solution for a given situation. Some of those in that network often feared or despised him, although, in spite of the power he wielded, he was a firm believer in justice and fair play, so most respected him. Many called him the President's conscience.

John Fulton needed no conscience, however. He had grown up in poverty in a black St. Louis slum, starting out his political life as a sixteen-year-old volunteer in a heavily contested presidential campaign. His conscience was honed by his parish priest, a staunch fighter for the common good, who often was at odds with his bishop. When Fulton's father died at the age of twelve, the parish priest became the father figure.

A stint in the US Army had taught Fulton that war usually doesn't solve the real problems, even though there often was no choice but to fight. He wasn't a believer in turning the other cheek, yet he was a believer in talking through problems if at all possible.

He was also a believer that US foreign policy had been wrong for a long time. Too often Washington had paid homage to the adage that the enemy of my enemy is my friend, causing the US to get into bed with some rather unsavory bedfellows over its short history. The whole Middle East problem of the last hundred years or more could be attributed to fallout from that failed policy, in Fulton's opinion, beginning with support for the creation of the Israeli state and the Shah of Iran. While America couldn't be held responsible for the Crusades, they hadn't been very successful in bringing stability to the region. The support of Al Qaeda when they were fighting the Russians in Afghanistan and the support of Saddam Hussein when he was fighting Iran were two more examples, the last made even more ironic because of the fiasco with the Shah.

Yet Fulton had always been a pragmatist. He knew the motivation behind most Middle Eastern policy was oil, now more than ever, as the world's oil supplies dried up. He had made a campaign pledge to promote alternate sources of energy. He wasn't sure they would win the race to become independent of foreign oil before their economic competitors did but he was doing the best he could. However, the stress of this and other aspects of this job were taking its toll.

Still he was in excellent health and worked out three times a week. He was tall and muscular, making quite a contrast with Pierce. Since the two were often seen together, more than one political cartoon had picked up on their differences in physique.

"I guess the first order of business is this mistress thing," Fulton began. Pierce looked uncomfortable. "I know you've denied it to the press. I want you to deny it to me."

"You know me better than that, John. When and if I want to play the field, I will do it as much out in the open as the next guy. But no, I don't know this woman, and I've certainly never had relations with her."

"Just checking," said Fulton with a smile. "You know I've encouraged you to find someone. Otherwise, you're going to die a lonely man."

"If the right someone comes along, I'll know it. Most people die lonely anyway, John. You don't see many old couples going out together. I had an uncle who was a widower for thirty years."

"Well, he should have remarried," countered Fulton. "Now, about this report."

He thumbed through it, glancing at Pierce, then returning to read and examine the photos.

"Is Knowland privy to this information?" Fulton finally asked.

"I sent it as a 'FOR YOUR EYES ONLY' just ten minutes ago."

"So what are Senator Preston, Hank Johnson, and my VP up to, do you think?"

"I asked Knowland if he knew," said Hamilton. "He hasn't responded. Since she is your VP, and has clearly displayed publicly her dislike for Preston, it seems unusual. By the way, this came via the FBI quite by accident. They had two men on a stakeout. The house across from Johnson's is owned by one of our local mob members."

"Serendipity. It will get them every time. Tell Jake to give those agents a pat on the back. They were alert and thinking outside the box."

"Actually, I think they were just trying to get photos of Johnson's next girl friend. They didn't know it was going to be Stephanie."

"I doubt that. She's too old for Johnson and once was his boss. He likes young coeds who are dazzled by his power. That also counts Stephanie out, since she's contemptuous of anyone's power, including mine at times. Now, Stephanie and Preston, there's an interesting pair."

The conversation lagged. Seeing that Fulton was anxious to get on to other business, Pierce took his leave. He was also wondering about Stephanie and Preston. *Now that was a match made in hell.* His mind wandered as he sat at his computer. Then he thought of his mystery woman. *Maybe it would be nice to have a mystery woman.* He had lied to Fulton a little there. He valued his privacy too much to have a public relationship with someone. Actually, he would value her privacy even more. He would probably have to quit.

He had worked for about a half hour when his phone rang.

"Mr. Hamilton, I have a call from Peter Barkley," said his secretary. "Do you want to take it?"

Pierce smiled. Peter had been the wild one in high school, always playing pranks on fellow students and teachers. He was also very intelligent and had become a NASA engineer.

"Well, a voice from my past," said Pierce, looking at his friend's bearded face. The beard had been grown when Peter was a teaching assistant in grad school. He had not wanted to look younger than his students.

"Yeah, hey, I send you video-mail occasionally. If you look at them. 'Course, I'm not as important as the National Security Advisor. You rarely respond."

"I plead guilty. My life is not my own, it seems. I'm a workaholic."

"Yeah, I was almost happy for you when I saw you and your supposed Georgetown bimbo in the newsnets, but then I knew it couldn't be true. You just couldn't have any fun even though you gave up the collar. You're just married to your work. Not even time for a mistress. Take my advice: getting naked with a woman does wonders for stress relief."

"Crass as always. I'd have to be rather desperate to take your advice on women. How many divorces is it now?"

"Still just the three. I learned my lesson. I fool around a little still, although I'm even getting too old for that." He frowned. "To not waste your time on pleasantries, I've got an intellectual itch that needs scratching, and I think you can do the scratching."

"How so?"

"Internal bureaucratic contradictions have been my nemesis before, yet now I've really got a whopper. I have heard a rumor that NASA has a starship project."

"Well, that's news to me. You'd think that would be on the newsnets."

"Precisely. We're on the same wavelength. I've checked around. NASA doesn't have a starship project."

"Ah, the contradiction."

"Yes, but investigating the rumor further, it seems that I just assumed it was NASA. The real rumor is that the government has a starship project and it's top secret special access only. Now, who do you think I know who could set me right on this rumor?"

Pierce laughed. The same old Peter. Always looking to know something no one else knew.

"Well, you've got me. I don't know about any such project."

"'Course, if you did, you couldn't talk about it on an unsecured line. Should I call you back on a secure one? I've got a clearance, you know."

"Not high enough to talk to me about black programs. Anyway, Peter, your rumor is wrong, as many rumors are. The Pentagon has its own space activities, of course, many of which NASA is involved in. But there is no starship project. Nil, nix, nein, nyet."

"OK. Though next time I'm in DC, I'm looking you up, and I'll see if you stick to your story. Over a nice Rioja at that Spanish restaurant you like, OK?"

"Sounds good to me."

Peter signed off, leaving Pierce wondering about his friend's rumor. Peter was not one to swallow tall tales. He obviously put some credence to the rumor or he wouldn't have called Pierce to satisfy his curiosity. *I'll have to keep my eyes and ears open. The rumor has piqued my curiosity too. More so than the scandal with my supposed mistress.*

Scherzo Twenty-One

UN Secretary General Ricardo Gomez looked at the report on his computer screen. It was a good piece of news in a rather bad news day. The cholera epidemic in Indonesia was winding down. *It all started with that damn earthquake. Of course, the contractors can't build anything reliable, can they? Anything to cut expenses. Live on the edge until the edge whacks you in the balls.*

He had rushed WHO doctors to the scene as soon as he could, and Doctors Without Borders and the Red Crescent had arrived soon after. Still, they couldn't rebuild sewer systems and aqueducts. With all the dead around, it was no wonder they had a cholera outbreak.

Polio. Cholera. Malaria. Sleeping sickness. Yellow fever. Smallpox. These and more were diseases where a cure was available. *Add that to AIDS and TB, and you'd have to say the world is pretty well screwed.*

Part of the problem was getting the medicine to the people. Being a doctor who had grown up in the Amazons of Peru, Ricardo could well understand the difficulty of attending to people in remote regions of the world. Still, most of the problems actually stemmed from the fact that the medicines cost so much. But he could do something about that too.

He picked up the phone and dialed a number he had long ago memorized. "President Fulton?"

"This is his Chief of Staff, Dr. Gomez. What can I do for you?"

"Not in today, I take it?"

"No. He's in New York City. A fundraiser."

"Well, speaking of funds, I was at a state dinner a month ago in the White House and we talked. Could you remind him of that promise to push another UN payment through that Congress of yours? It could really help some people, you know."

"I'll remind him tomorrow, sir, when he returns. And how are the wife and children?"

"Fine, fine. Yours?" The answer was affirmative. "Well, don't forget to remind him. 'Ta luego."

"Ciao, Dr. Gomez."

Chapter Twenty-Six

Boston, Massachusetts, Thursday . . .

Chris was still in his apartment Thursday morning, working at his computer in an attempt to implement Ka Wah Fong's suggestion. Some preliminary internet searches had led him to the Society of Molecular Medicine. In its member database he found two persons named Kalidas Metropolis. One was a graduate student at UCSF. He eliminated her as not having had the time to make a name for herself. Besides, the time zone difference made it impossible to call her anyway. The other was at Dalton Biomedicine Inc in Paterson, New Jersey. He called the company.

"I'm afraid Dr. Metropolis is no longer with us," said the switchboard operator at the company. "She just retired."

Chris looked at his PDA for the date. It was not the first or last of the month. A strange day to retire.

"Do you have a cell phone number for her?"

"I'm sorry. We can't give out that information."

So Chris called the precinct. Harry Carson found the number he needed using the police tie-in to one of the law enforcement databases.

"Dr. Metropolis?" he asked when she answered. "You don't know me. My name is Chris Tanner. I'm a Boston police detective and your name came up in a discussion about a homicide I'm working on."

"Oh great," said Kalidas. The video was slightly distorted but Chris liked the woman immediately. Her voice had a tired and edgy quality to it. "I've just been fired from my job, spent a night in a DHS prison, and now you connect me to a homicide."

"I'm not connecting you to a homicide. Just consulting with you. I apologize for calling you at home. I called your former place of work and they said that you retired."

"That's the official spiel. I never signed their damn papers. The DHS has accused me of being a Greek terrorist, so I lost my clearance. No clearance, no work, at least in my discipline. Of course, they then had to show who's in charge by making me stay overnight in one of their fucking prisons."

The mention of the DHS caused Chris to stir uneasily in his chair. His cop's sixth sense was working overtime again.

"Any chance that an agent named Mary Beth Grogan was involved?" he asked just for shits and giggles. He was surprised at the answer.

"I don't know about Dalton Biomedicine but she was the one who warned a lawyer friend not to take my case. Threatened to disbar him. She's Hank Johnson's personal aid. And I had a visit from another bunch of agents who confiscated my computers and some other things, and, when I objected, they made me spend the night in jail." There was suddenly silence as the woman in the tiny screen of the cell phone pursed her lips and glared out at him. "Hey, Detective Tanner, I'm giving out a lot of information here. I don't know you are who you say you are. Why don't you show me your badge? And what's your consulting question?"

He held his badge up to the videocam and then told her everything about the case, including the theory that the John Doe was a clone of the Secretary of Defense, without mentioning Ka Wah's name.

"I thought you might give me an indication of whether that was possible or not."

"Sure, it's possible. Not very likely, though, with present techniques. Right now you need an egg to make a clone. However, I just sent off a preprint about transplant rejection. An easy extension of the technique I've discovered would make clone production easy. You wouldn't need eggs. I've only done it with pigs, of course, since I can't and won't experiment with humans."

"Is it possible that someone has already applied this to humans?"

"Not likely. I would think quite a few years would be needed to perfect my technique. However, while unlikely, your clone may have actually come from an egg. If it's a clone, that is. Given the common connection with the feds, I'd say there's too much of a coincidence here. Something's rotten in Denmark and it isn't Hamlet's farts." Chris laughed. He felt that this lady was already a friend. He needed one right now, as he was beginning to feel that he was bucking a huge and dangerous bureaucracy. "By the way, my lawyer friend gave me the name of a reporter to contact. I think this might turn into a story she can't resist. Do you want to contact her too?"

"How about a conference call?" he asked.

"Yeah, I can set that up. Give me your number. I'm beginning to feel better already."

Scherzo Twenty-Two

President Fulton called UN Secretary Gomez rather reluctantly.

"I guess you heard the bad news, Ricardo?"

The full size image of the Secretary's face on the com link screen was not a happy one.

"What's the matter with those people, John?" he asked.

"Too many drug company lobbyists, I guess. Some of these companies make more money than the GNP of a lot of your Third World countries. You know that."

"Well, what happened to the famous compassion of the Americans?"

"Oh, you'd probably not have much of a problem convincing a large percentage of the American public, Ricardo. If I could put it to a vote, I'd probably win. I just can't budge our senators and representatives. At least, not enough to get a majority. You know I busted my ass on this one."

"Si, senor Presidente, I saw their lame excuses on CNN. Everything from the bloated and inefficient UN bureaucracy—which you know damn well is not bloated and inefficient anymore with all the budget cuts—to our national problems come first—as if the world's problems, especially the economic ones which disease and pestilence can generate, don't affect your country too. Senator Preston even had the audacity to suggest that there are just too many people in the world and we can't take care of all of them, a nice little twist on an old argument."

"What argument is that?"

"I believe it was conjured up by Malthus centuries ago, namely, the way to control population growth is with war and pestilence."

Fulton frowned at that. Senator Preston wasn't one of his favorite people.

"The Senator is out of touch with reality," observed the President. "He's also pretty provincial. He's never left his native Indiana except to go to Washington. His policy has always been 'first me, then my state, then America, and fuck the rest of the world.' Though they keep re-electing him, even with his limited number of upper brain functions. Thirty years in the Senate now, and counting."

"John, I know you think your system is pretty good but it sure can be one hell of a cluster fuck sometimes."

"Tell me about it. All these protests and demonstrations against the federal government. Politicians from different regions of the country pitted against each other. People from Texas hating people from New York. It goes on and on. There was a poll taken just last week where sixty-eight percent of Americans feel their regional interests are not sufficiently represented and that they think their region would be better off as a separate country. Just between you and me, many in that sixty-eight percent are not able to even locate their state on a US map. And California basically thinks it's three regions already—the Bay area, the LA area, and the Big Valley. Of course, California has always been crazy. Five Hollywood stars as governor and still counting."

"Well, you might have another one as President, too."

"Actually, most of the time I think Stephanie Williams would make a good President. She's tough and smart. Still, I sometimes find her scary." Fulton coughed slightly, thinking he might have said too much, even though the com link was secure. "Anyway, that's not one of your problems, Ricardo. At least it's not one you can do a lot about. What's your plan now?"

"What I've always done in the past. Media blitz and a motion for censure against the US for not paying its bills."

"That will really get them riled," said the President. "Go for it. I can certainly add to the media blitz. I'll call in my press secretary right now. I never have babied Congress, not even in my first term. Of course, now I've got nothing to lose, so it's even more fun."

The Secretary laughed.

"That's why I enjoy working with you, John. We have similar world views."

Chapter Twenty-Seven

Falls Church, Virginia, Thursday . . .

The sleek black limo pulled into the heavily guarded back entrance of the new Sheila Remington building in Falls Church, Virginia. Renamed after President Remington, who had died in the terrorist attack in 2037 that had led to the last Middle East war, it was a twenty story black obelisk, built after the second war as the new HQ of the Department of Homeland Security. Its roof was full of antennas of every shape imaginable, except for the area set aside for the helipad. The building also went a full seven levels below the surface, three of which were dedicated to a parking garage. While the FBI and CIA still struggled with their antiquated facilities, the DHS bureaucracy enjoyed much more modern comforts and conveniences.

The limo speeded by the four saluting marines at the entrance to the parking garage and went down into the first level, stopping by the underground entrance to the building where elevators would take its occupants up into the office levels above or the lab levels below. Hank Johnson, the Assistant Secretary, got out, followed by his two bodyguards and Mary Beth Grogan, his personal aid and also an armed agent herself. As the group moved towards the entrance to the elevators, Jay Sandoval stepped out of the shadows. The bodyguards immediately jumped in front of Johnson and Grogan, drawing their pistols.

"Easy boys," said Jay, flashing her press badge. "At the street entrance they said I could wait for Mr. Johnson down here. I'm doing a story. We help you. You help us."

One of the bodyguards took her badge and examined it.

"It's OK," he growled. "She's got all the right stamps and stuff. She's from that e-zine, Crime Fighters."

"I know her," said Mary Beth, a thin smile on her lips. "How are you, Jay?"

"A little busy. I've got a deadline to meet. I just wanted to give Mr. Johnson a chance to comment on the story."

"What story?" asked Johnson, speaking for the first time.

"Is it true that your agents discovered a terrorist who was your double and eliminated him? Together with the county sheriff, coroner, and forensics expert? I'm speaking about the Lexington Park case, of course."

Mary Beth exchanged looks with Johnson. In the dim light of the garage Jay had a hard time reading their expressions, or even if they had any reaction to her story.

"I don't know what you're talking about," said Johnson. "I don't know where Lexington Park is. Isn't that right outside Boston?"

"No, that's Lexington," Jay said. "Lexington Park is in Maryland."

"Well, anyway, if that's your story, it will be censored immediately. I can't have false stories about terrorists circulating around. You know better than that."

"To my knowledge, terrorism is still a crime. That's what I write about. Is it possible that your agents acted without your knowledge?"

"Of course," said Johnson. "But highly unlikely. Why would they do such a thing? I'm sure you've got your facts mixed up. Who gave you that information?"

"I was down there. I talked to the homeless man who discovered the body. Old Bob Martin said Sheriff Milton thought the man in the dumpster was a younger version of you, Mr. Johnson. I checked. You have no siblings and no close living relatives other than your elderly parents."

"Good for you," said Johnson. "So you concluded that the man in the dumpster must be a terrorist who looks like me. My god, you people really have active imaginations, don't you?"

"The body existed. No one imagined that. And then it disappeared. Three people were killed. No, four, counting old Bob. I'm looking for a DHS involvement because a friend and I were followed by a car registered to your Department."

"Perhaps they were on another case and you just thought they were following you," suggested Mary Beth.

"I don't think so. Still, you're right. There is another similar case in Boston. I've been in contact with a detective named Chris Tanner. Seems he was almost killed by a Secretary Sweeney look-alike. You're personally involved in that one, Mary Beth. You picked up the body." She got a response on that one, as Mary Beth scowled at her. It was time for the *coup de grace*. "I think both these John Does are clones."

"Why would you think that?" asked Mary Beth.

"Because the DHS got Dr. Kalidas Metropolis fired from Dalton Biomedicine. She works in the area of genetic engineering. She submitted a preprint describing a new technique to prevent transplant rejection. A corollary to her work is the potential for making clones without an egg. You confiscated her computers and other notes. Curt, I believe you were the culprit in that case."

"Even if I understood it, I don't have time for this," said Johnson. He reached for the entrance door to the elevators. "Bring her badge, Curt."

"You can't do that!" Jay protested.

"Oh, I can. We issued it."

As Johnson and the two bodyguards entered, Mary Beth took her by the arm and led her away.

"I'll try to get him to send it over to your office. Just go. Forget this ever happened. And your story."

Jay heard the unctuous and false sympathy in that mousy voice. She shook off Mary Beth's arm, thinking about whether she should deck her then and there. She had never liked the woman. It would be sweet to spin her head over heels into a concrete wall. But that might not accomplish anything, except get her thrown into a DHS cell. Unlike Kalidas, they might not let her loose.

"I'll consider what you said," Jay said. Mary Beth turned to walk back down towards the elevators. "Do you want me to send the registration information on the car? What did you learn about Tanner's John Doe? And why is Kalidas being persecuted?"

"About the car, do what you want. I won't answer any other questions. And don't write that story."

"Is that a threat, Mary Beth?"

"No, it's a friendly warning. For your career. See you around, Jay."

Grogan entered the bowels of the building, following the path of her boss.

Jay walked up the short ramp to the public lot where her car was parked. One of the four marines on guard at the garage's entrance winked at her as she came into the sunlight. She winked back. As she headed for her car, she dialed the day desk. Olaf Johansen answered, his face contorted in anger. The editor of Crime Fighters did not seem happy to see her.

"Where the hell have you been, Jay? Ben said you were working on a triple murder."

"Actually, five now." She explained quickly what she knew. The irascible editor calmed down a little. "So, it's shaping up to be a good story, but right now, we can't publish. They'll censor it. Though we can go with the story that they took a reporter's badge away. They can't censor that, and it will stir up some interest."

"Actually, they can," said Olaf. "But I'll try it. We'll get the e-mail synopsis out on it right away before they can even act on it. We've got congressmen and a whole lot of other powerful folk that subscribe to that, a lot of them just itching to get the goods on these feds. Johnson won't be able to close us down before a lot of these people read it." Another phone rang, Olaf took it, and asked the person to hold. Then: "So, how are you going to follow up with this?"

"I'm not. I want a month's leave of absence. I made a promise to Dolores."

"It'll be a leave without pay, then."

"Olaf, I get paid on commission."

"So? There's the usual precinct stuff you cover. Who's going to do that for me? The public needs its usual diet of murders and muggings. Not to mention a terrorist or two. We're shorthanded as it is."

"Please, Olaf. Dolores is my best friend. John was a great guy."

"So, are you going to play detective and whistle blower at the same time? You got your funeral expenses covered, honey?"

"Olaf, are you telling me to be careful? There is a soft spot in you somewhere, I guess."

"From past experience, I know it wouldn't do any good to tell you to be careful. Nevertheless, live long enough to get the story. When you do, I want it, leave, or no leave. Then I'll go to your funeral."

"Entendido. Ciao, amigo."

On a hunch, Jay turned and started back down the entrance ramp to the parking garage. The winking marine stopped her.

"I can't let you back down there, ma'am. Your permission's been cancelled. I just got the word. Sorry."

"Soldier, how long have you been a marine?"

"Two years, ma'am."

"Well, I was one for six. Cut me some slack. I dropped some notes back there in the garage. My editor just chewed me out for it. You saw me on the phone." She put a pouting expression on her face. "I could get fired."

"Sorry, ma'am. Can't do it."

"Soldier, are you acquainted with Crime Fighters?"

A broad smile appeared on the marine's face. It was clear that he had just recognized her.

"You're that Jay Sandoval?"

"Yes, I am. So let me go down and pick up my notes. No one will be the wiser."

The marine gave a thumbs up sign to the other three, and nodded to Jay.

"OK. But be quick about it."

Jay hurried down the ramp. Johnson's limo had parked at one end in a specially designated place, although she wasn't particularly interested in it. She went up and down the other official cars, all alike, checking plates. She soon found the one she wanted. It had been washed recently. On a chance, Jay tried the driver's door. It was unlocked. *Of course. The driver would feel safe leaving the car unlocked while parked in one of the most secure parking garages in America.*

She slid in and went through the glove compartment quickly. An old laundry bill gave her the name of the car's driver—Mary Beth Grogan. She smiled. *So Johnson's personal aid is up to her perky little tits in this shit pile, even if Johnson isn't.*

As she walked past the marine again, she patted her bag and mouthed a silent thanks. He nodded and smiled.

Scherzo Twenty-Three

Marcus Brown tried his best to comfort his wife. He looked at the doctor helplessly.

"I heard you right, didn't I? Even though there is a standard procedure that will save her father, you can't perform the operation because we can't afford it?"

Dr. Pierre Jolicoeur looked uncomfortable. This was happening way too often.

"I didn't exactly say that. I said that unless you can pay the minimum that we would get from any standard medical plan, the hospital has to refuse treatment."

"Well, how much is that? Maybe I can scrape it up—sell the house, or something."

"Your wife's father can't wait that long, I'm afraid. The aneurism will blow at any moment."

"But we can't cover the cost, then. How can I save him?"

"Unless Mr. Allan has full medical, there isn't much we can do. In this type of situation, I often donate my services, but that is only a small part of the cost in this case. We've already run up a bill of more than eighteen thousand dollars. The hospital could take me to court even for that."

"They can take you to court?"

"Of course. I ordered the workups on your father-in-law, knowing that he didn't have full medical. I hoped it would be something simple. It's not. I can do the surgery if you can find the money, Mr. Brown, though it'd better be quick. Mr. Allan is not likely to live out the week."

He didn't.

Chapter Twenty-Eight

Washington, DC, Thursday & Friday, three weeks later . . .

During the next three weeks Jay made little progress in obtaining more information about either the Lexington Park murders or the Boston case. Kalidas educated both Chris and Jay about how difficult it is to make human clones because the differentiation of the blastocyst already begins at the four-cell level. It would be a major feat for even the best-equipped genetics lab, so it was hard to imagine terrorists achieving it. The plans for their attacks were usually low budget ones designed to create the most panic in the population affected. It was not clear what they would gain from having young versions of Johnson or Sweeney around. They couldn't be used to get close to any of their older look-alikes. On the other hand, even though both John Does had been much younger than their older twins, they were still in their twenties. How cloning technology twenty years ago could have been as advanced as today's was beyond Kalidas' comprehension.

The three of them began to have doubts, wondering if they were seeing conspiracies where there were none. No one involved with the case was threatened or harmed. Jay received her press badge back from the DHS. Things seemed boringly normal.

Yet Jay plodded on and encouraged her new friends to do the same. Clones or no clones, she wanted John Milton's killers. She called Bouncer and heard that Sam Fletcher had filed the cases away as five unsolved murder cases, one John Doe and four Lexington Park townspeople. Denise Rivera also suggested to Chris that he put the Boston murder in the database of cold cases. Kalidas bought a new laptop and attempted to reconstruct her preprint, hoping to make more progress along those lines, although she also began asking around in her small community of scientists about any secret government research.

Jay was still on leave and very frustrated when Asako dropped by her apartment. Jay was shabbily dressed in blue jeans and a checkered blouse. There were paint smudges on both, since that very day, while she thought about the case, she had decided to finish a painting she had started some months ago. Asako, in contrast, was dressed in a smart business suit.

"Amiga mia, how are you? Come on in."

"I'll just be a minute, Jay. I was downtown and I'm on my way back to Quantico, so I can't stay long. Still, I thought you might be interested in this." She handed a few papers to Jay. "Got a coke?" The DC summertime heat and humidity were turned on high.

"In the fridge. Help yourself." Jay sat down to read.

It was a report from the CIA about a terrorist interrogation gone bad in the Philippines. The Filipino army had captured a suspected terrorist in an apartment in Manila. The woman had allegedly been planning an assassination attempt on President Fulton on his visit to Manila next month for the Pacific Rim Economic Summit. Asako had underlined one portion which read: "The terrorist bears an uncanny resemblance to Stephanie Williams, Vice President of the United States, when the Vice President was a movie star twenty years ago."

"How does the CIA analyst know this suspected terrorist looks like a young Stephanie Williams?" asked Jay. "And where did you get this?"

"The analyst is Simon Multani, who works at Langley. Coincidentally, he happens to be a fan of the young Stephanie Williams."

"Let me guess, when she went topless, like in 'Shakedown in Rio.'"

"Especially that one, but also other films she made, before she turned to politics. Simon's really a nice guy, though, not a pig. We've dated a couple of times. The last time maybe I talked a little too much about your case. He knew I was coming in today and met me for lunch on M Street in Georgetown. We both like a Middle Eastern restaurant there. It's become expensive over the last few years so I pay part of it with my travel stipend and he picks up the rest. He had these papers for me."

"Don't worry. I'll forgive you for blabbing about my business if it helps me find John Milton's murderers."

"So, do you think this Philippine case is connected?" asked Asako.

"Apparently you do. You're not going to get yourself or your friend in trouble for this, are you?"

"No, I don't think so, and I think you should really talk to Simon. He may have more information that's not in the report. You saw the addendum?"

Jay turned to the second page. It read: "Addendum: the terrorist was an apparent suicide this morning." Simon's name, the time of day, and a date corresponding to three days ago, followed.

"I'm really getting confused here," Jay said. "We have a bunch of possible clones, or at least young look-alikes, corresponding to three key members in the Fulton administration. Maybe Bouncer is right. Maybe there really is a conspiracy."

"But what would be the purpose?" asked Asako. "Especially in this case. Stephanie Williams is at least fifteen kilos heavier now than when she was a movie star. You'd have a hard time making the connection unless you were an old movie fan like Simon."

"With a CIA analyst's experience in seeing connections," added Jay. "Maybe that's the point. Our John Doe in Lexington Park was heavy set, like Hank Johnson, yet maybe it was more muscle than fat on that John Doe. Didn't Hank Johnson play football?"

"Hank Johnson was an All-American fullback at Stanford," informed Asako. "Hugo Martinez, Hugh Murphy, and Hamilton Kiefer were the rest of the backfield, all good, two of them also All-American, with Kiefer, the quarterback, even nominated for the Heisman. It was a dream backfield, often called the 4-H Club, and the line was great, too, with Sandy Brown at left tackle, also All-American. They won three national championships in a row."

"Dios mio, I didn't know you were such a football fan."

"Oh, I don't really know much about the game. Remember, I was born in South Africa. Soccer's really my sport. I was a fan of Patty Smith's even before I knew her. I just like to look at football players." Asako smiled. "They generally have pretty good bods, don't you think?"

"Hey, I'm way too small to have one of those behemoths on top of me. Some of them make Bouncer look like a midget."

"Oh, I don't know, Bouncer's a big boy. Anyway, who says you have to be on the bottom?" Asako licked her lips suggestively.

"I thought you didn't have time for such things," said Jay. "You always complain you have no social life."

"I don't have much of one. Still, when I play, I play hard."

"So, is Simon going to be a playmate?"

"I don't know. He's kind of bookish."

"Cielos, Asako, you're kind of bookish yourself. You've always got your nose in some journal."

"That's work related. I think Simon might be bookish all the time. But he's the only fresh meat in the supermarket right now, if you know what I mean." She winked.

"Yeah. I know what you mean. My playtime has also reached a new low right now." Jay gave a shrug, implying that that was a sore topic for discussion. "Anyway, I think we're on to something. Let's suppose, as a working hypothesis, that all the John Does, including this new terrorist, were young and healthy copies of the real old-timers. That's got to mean something. Any ideas?" Asako thought a moment and then shook her head. "Well, keep thinking about it. I need all the help I can get. Anyway, I agree that I need to talk with Simon. Can you give me his number?"

Asako pointed at the pile of cheap cell phones on Jay's kitchen counter.

"You'd be hard put to give him yours. What gives with all the phones?"

"Kalidas, Chris, and I decided we should communicate with each other using a bunch of different throw-away cell phones. We each have twenty. When I want to call Chris, for example, I pick one of my phones at random and dial one of his numbers at random."

"Kind of hard to carry all those, isn't it?"

"Well, we only randomize the calls when we're at home. We also only talk to each other about the case when we're at home."

"Wow! That sounds all cloak and dagger. Like those spy movies. Maybe you should go to Hollywood and be in one."

"Yeah, like 'Shakedown in Rio'? I don't have the tits. Nor the height, for that matter. Hollywood only likes leading women that look like someone from some male hedonist's wet dream." Asako laughed at that and nodded her agreement. She too was petite, although taller than Jay. "So what's Simon's number? I'm just going to set up a meeting. No long conversations about any of this. And you should be careful, too."

Simon Multani met Jay the next evening after work, Friday, in a small bar in Alexandria that they both knew. It had a bartender who minded his own business and six TVs, all on different cable channels, that combined to make a close approximation to a white noise background. Jay got there first and five minutes later Simon slid into the booth across from her.

"Wow, my prospects are looking up. First I meet Asako, then you. Hell, the number of good-looking, unattached women in my life has taken an upswing."

"Don't get any ideas. I'm not interested in any ménage-a-trois relationships. If you're dating Asako, you're not dating me."

"Now that's real funny. Asako and I aren't actually dating steady. Or, if we are, it's a surprise to me. Not for lack of interest on my part, by the way. But I count myself lucky that a woman even talks to me." He pulled his goatee and smiled. It was a nice smile. "I'm sort of the male wallflower type, you know."

"Now there's an odd word," observed Jay, "and I'm not even sure what it means, although it sounds as negative as it does ancient. Anyway, maybe you need to let women see your inner being."

"Yeah, 'cause the outer is kind of dumpy. Anyway, you didn't come here to be my spiritual adviser, I take it, or to analyze my erudite vocabulary."

"That's right. I guess Asako blurted out a little more of the story than I would have liked. Still, no harm's done. I saw your report. Is there anything else that you might think of that is significant and didn't get into it?"

"Just my suspicions," said Simon. They had to wait as the bartender brought them two beers. He downed half of his immediately. "This damn town is just too hot in the summer. And everybody has to wear these damn dark, formal business suits. We should dress like in the Bermudas. White shirt and tie are OK, but Bermuda shorts. That would make more sense in this swamp." He took his coat off and loosened his tie.

"You were saying? Your suspicions?"

"Oh, yeah. I found the coroner's report on the suicide rather incomplete. And the whole terrorist plot just didn't seem to hang together. I can't put my finger on anything in particular, just a *je ne sais quoi* feeling I have that maybe the story was invented."

"Can you elaborate? Are you familiar with the Filipino terrorist movement?"

"You bet I am. That part of the world is my specialty. I speak both Spanish and Filipino. I have a knack for languages. I thought about being a UN interpreter once, but that requires listening in one language and speaking in another. That gives me a headache. Then I thought about the NSA, because they monitor a lot of stuff in different languages. The CIA made me a better job offer."

"Still, why the government? You could have gone to work for business and made a lot more money."

"Yeah, I know. But—and this will sound crazy—I really want to do something for my country. These fucking terrorists drive me nuts. We've become like Israel, except we get them from all over now. Not just Arabs anymore, but Chechnyans because we're friends with the Russians, Colombians because we're helping the fight against terrorism down there, Filipinos because we're helping the Filipino government, Serbs because we're helping the Bosnians, Irish Catholics because we support the peace accord in Northern Ireland—everyone that has a grievance with the US now becomes a terrorist, it seems. I want to do my small part to put a stop to it."

"Me too, but I already fought a war. I want to find a good man, get married, have a couple of kids, and try to live a peaceful life."

"Well, just don't let your kids go to a shopping mall or an amusement park. They might get blown up."

Jay nodded. "OK, that was therapeutic, but let's stop baring our souls for the moment." She raised her beer mug in a salute. "I respect your choices. Now, about your suspicions?"

"Well, like I was saying, I know the Filipino situation well. I get fed prescreened stuff from the NSA, regional stuff they consider of possible importance. Although they use sophisticated computer programs that evolved from the internet search engines at the turn of the century, it's still too coarse a cut on the data. So I then sift through what remains and try to pick out the really important stuff, making the connections computers still have a hard time with. It's generally boring work mostly. This case interested me because of the terrorist's resemblance to Stephanie Williams, though Asako probably told you about that."

"Yeah, 'Shakedown in Rio.' She told me."

"Hey, she was a good actor, too. I look beyond the tits. Like you say, to the inner being."

"Don't get all defensive with me. Is it possible, Simon, that these people are not terrorists?"

"I don't know about your John Does, but I'd say there's definitely the chance with mine. You see, to be in the Filipino movement, you must be Filipino. They're complete xenophobes. I've never come across a foreign mercenary in the Filipino movement. And Stephanie Williams is definitely not Filipino."

Jay lost herself in thought a moment, looking into the amber glow of her imported beer. *If not terrorists, who were these people?*

They talked a little more, and then Jay left the bar first. Then it was Simon's turn to leave. As he was walking towards his car, he noticed a balding, dumpy-looking man across the street, leaning against the characteristic Alexandrian brick wall of a building housing a drugstore. He was talking on a cell phone. Simon wouldn't have given it much thought if it hadn't been for the conversation with Jay. It was still quite warm yet the man had his suit coat on, not draped over an arm as most did after hours. Although DC was known for its punishing dress code, Simon felt something was amiss.

The man looked up and smiled at him. Simon decided he was being foolish, and went on to his car. As he bent slightly to put the key in the car door, there was a pfft! and the window shattered. He had received some training at Langley about what to do in case of a terrorist attack, so he dropped flat on the ground and looked back down the street. His nerves caused him to sweat even more. He felt an overwhelming desire to pee. And to run. He now understood what the psychologists were talking about when they described the fight-or-flight syndrome in human beings. And he had no desire to fight.

He slowly got to his knees and looked around. There was no one. He stood, crouched as low as possible, and reached for the door handle. Another pfft! was heard and a large hole appeared just above the handle and below the window—rather, where the window had been. Rapidly he jumped into the car. He was trembling and perspiring so much that he dropped the keys twice. He finally got them into the ignition. The motor caught on the first turn and he was off, gunning the engine and leaving tread marks on the hot asphalt, running for his life.

Scherzo Twenty-Four

"The reason we are all here," said Bertrand Hammer, "is to see if we can stop this Fulton juggernaut." He looked around the board room. It was a hot day in London and some of the weirdos were bathing in the fountains in the parks below. Hammer didn't particularly like London, but he was CEO of the biggest oil conglomerate in the world, so it was as good as place as any to have a meeting.

"Stephanie Williams is not exactly John Fulton," observed Ken Wong, in from Saudi Arabia. The Saudi royal family still managed to hang on to power, largely through the open direct support of Europe and the US, and the hidden, covert support of the oil companies. "Maybe she can be bought."

"I'd prefer to throw my lot in with her opponent," said Kay Houston, in from Venezuela. She was dressed in a low-cut dress that Bertrand would normally find distracting, although at present he was too damn annoyed to think about her predominant physical assets. "He's got a good track record of helping business fight off all these environmental activists and social welfare nuts. He also knows how to go after laws that might be detrimental to our interests. He's tied up a lot of them in lawsuits. I hate to say it but sometimes you need a good lawyer."

That brought chuckles to the executives seated around the table.

"I'm thinking along those lines myself," acknowledged Bertrand, "but I think we should hedge our bets. My suggestion is that publicly we pump equal amounts into both campaigns and meet with both candidates to try to come to an understanding. I'll repeat, that's publicly. Privately, I'm going to make funds available to each of you so you can personally donate heavily to Stephanie's opponent, since I agree that he's my favorite among the two horses. Are we agreed?"

Everyone around the table nodded.

"OK, that agenda item is done." Bertrand checked off the first item on a short list. "Now, I want to go to the second item. We need to pump some money into the insurgents in western Colombia. The oil fields there won't ever be developed if we can't get rid of that damn government down there. Kay, I would like you to come up with a detailed plan on how to do that. Let's have dinner tomorrow night to discuss it."

Everyone there knew what that meant. Still, Kay didn't even blush.

The meeting dragged on for another two hours.

Chapter Twenty-Nine

Washington, DC, Saturday . . .

Pierce put down the phone, trying to control his anger. He counted to ten slowly, breathing deeply, all the time staring at the woman on the computer screen. Although he was a firm believer in a free press, tabloid reporters could be very obnoxious.

The woman is devilishly pretty. At least the public will think I have good taste.

The scandal had taken on a life of its own. Headlines were now everywhere on the internet. "National Security Advisor Hamilton Is Only Human" was one of the better ones. "Hamilton Humps Hussy" was one of the worst. Photos of Pierce entering the Georgetown bungalow of Daniela Romano, photos of him with her at Starbucks and Peets, at the Georgetown Mall, at the Air and Space Museum, and so forth, were all over the news.

He had already offered his resignation to Fulton. The President had simply told him to not wimp out, to fight it.

"Pierce, you're effectively in charge of every intelligence organization in this country. Surely you can find out who this woman really is and prove these stories false. I'll give you a week. I don't want to hear anymore about it now. I've got a speech to work on."

Pierce thought about that statement for a moment. He had known Fulton for too many years. The man now fully believed the stories were false and really wanted him to get beyond this. Still, Pierce was somewhat saddened by the fact that Fulton didn't think he was capable of having a relationship. There were stories in the tabloids that Pierce was gay, that he had done choir boys as a priest, that he had caused Fulton's divorce years ago, and on and on. Pierce chuckled. Yes, maybe Fulton thought Pierce was still abiding by his priestly oath of celibacy, even though the Vatican had changed the policy on married priests over ten years ago. Pierce thought that that was the best thing that had ever happened to increase applications to the seminaries.

Yet he couldn't really fault Fulton for thinking him incapable of maintaining a relationship, with a woman or otherwise. He never had time for intimate relationships, not even with the President's family and friends. He worked between ten and sixteen hours every day, seven days a week. That was why the whole scandal was absurd.

Pierce decided his initial feelings were correct. He had left the Oval Office feeling buoyed by the President's confidence in him on one hand, yet scared on the other hand by what an effective slander job the woman was mounting. It was a big waste of his time and he didn't have a lot extra to waste. Moreover, he didn't understand it, and when he didn't understand something, he got annoyed.

With a brain fart born out of desperation, he had considered holding a press conference in order to tell everyone that none of what was appearing in the media was true and, even if it was, he had a right to his private life. Cold logic won the day, however. There was time later to go before the media wolves, when he was better prepared. He needed to know the facts first.

In fact, as Fulton had suggested, with the people under his command, it didn't take long to cobble enough facts together to shoot holes in the woman's story. Apparently he had never been at the places in the photographs at the time the media said he was. As near as the FBI could tell, all the pictures were expertly doctored, using techniques as good as any of the high-tech special graphics labs out in Hollywood, techniques that could even take a still shot of a man and make him walk or run. They usually required a model, a wire figure, or even some other person doing the action, an e-frame to hang the pixels on. So it was probable that some other man had been there with Ms. Romano and Pierce's image had been substituted for his. The FBI's take on it was that someone was trying to discredit the conscience of the Fulton administration and, in the process, attack Fulton.

By Saturday evening, Jake Hanlon and his FBI agents had passed the details of their findings to the White House Press Secretary. He would take it from there, and Fulton would consider the problem solved. For him and most people, the scandal would become now a non-issue, although doubts about Pierce Hamilton would continue in some minds, especially those who were Fulton's political enemies.

Pierce kept the FBI on a short leash, though. He wanted to know who had set this up. *Who would play this dirty?*

Not knowing the answer, he decided he needed the afternoon off. He called to see if he could still play golf with some friends who had invited him three days ago. He figured the exercise would relieve the stress, even though it too would take up valuable time of which he had so little.

Chapter Thirty

In the Virginia countryside, Saturday . . .

Even in the dim red light, RP1, SW2 and GW3 could see that the lab was stuffed with modern equipment. They walked quietly between the work tables, only partially understanding what they saw there.

The computers were even strange. There were several new workstations, together with their huge screens, voice interfaces and data keypads, computers that made GW3's eyes shine in anticipation. He sat down at one and started to play.

"Are you sure you should touch those?" asked RP1.

"Give it a rest," said GW3. "You may not know what the fuck you're doing, but I do. This is the latest stuff. For me, it's better than sex." He glanced at SW2's cleavage. "Although I'm pretty good at that too."

"In your wildest dreams," she said.

RP1 and SW2 continued to walk around the lab, not worried about the videocams, since GW3 had figured out how to fool them again. They could be there for three hours, the time when the videocams would stop repeating the movie strip GW3 had fed them and return to their normal surveillance.

There were several high-priced optical microscopes and one of the more expensive electron microscopes scattered around and between the work tables, together with specimen slides, both used and sterile. Also available were two gas chromatography machines, a mass spectrometer, several scale/beam balances, hydrometers, and laser spectrographs. There were several cell culture hoods and high-speed centrifuges plus three new DNA analysis machines that were networked with the workstations. On one side of the lab there were shiny stainless steel cryogenic tanks and blood diagnostic machines.

RP1 and SW2 recognized most of these instruments from courses they had taken, though they were so shiny and new that the two of them knew they were state of the art and certainly not cheap. Some very expensive research was going on here in their Center. The idea made RP1 frown. *Was it about them? Where were the researchers?*

"I think they come in from outside, every day, through there," whispered SW2, as if to answer his thoughts. She pointed down a corridor. There were two turnstiles, two metal stalls, and two devices for checking fingerprints and performing retinal scans, just like she'd seen in pictures of security stations at airports. A sign above the door on the other side of the turnstiles said "To Parking Garage." Just before the turnstiles was another sign that said "Have your ID ready. All personal belongings are subject to inspection." Yet another sign in the corridor had a caricature of Uncle Sam pointing a gnarled finger at the sign reader; the sign said "National security begins with you. Did you close your safe today?"

"What are they talking about safes for?" asked RP1.

GW3, who was still intent on breaking into the workstation, pointed across the room. Several upright Mosler safes, filing cabinets with formidable electronic locks, lined the wall. Such safes were not used for paper anymore; instead, they were used to house removable hard disks from the computers, including their backups. Most government offices were now paperless. Some workers still printed out hard copies for meetings and the like where computers were not available but these would be shredded at the end of the day. It was all the more reason for good computer security.

"We're some kind of top secret government experiment, I bet," he whispered to them.

"Oh, come on," said SW2. "We know what all the secret is supposed to be about. They didn't want anyone to know they made us especially to send to the stars."

"We know that's crap," said GW3. "After what you found in Tyler's office, only some dumb ass could believe that. It's just some cover story, just in case some nosy reporter gets wind of this project. What we do know is that it has nothing to do with NASA on the one hand, and on the other somebody is running a state-of-the-art genetics lab here. Also, we geniuses, we're probably its most important product. For what reasons I don't know. This is all too hush-hush." He paused for a moment, as if for dramatic effect. GW3 liked to be the center of attention. "I've got it! Maybe we're some kind of special biological weapon. I bet that's it! I bet this is a DoD facility. It's a fucking bioweapons lab. We know the terrorists have them. I bet our government does too."

GW3 liked cursing. He thought it was smart. SW2 looked at him with a frown.

"So, Mr. Smarty, what kind of weapon are we?"

"If I can get into this computer, I might find out. Though maybe the answer's in those safes."

"In which case we'll never find out," said RP1. He walked over to the first safe and spun the dial on the top drawer. He stopped beside another door. "I wonder where this leads?"

GW3 jumped up and came over beside RP1. He took a small tool from his pocket that looked something like a metal toothpick. He stuck it in the keyhole and moved the tool around a little.

"It's probably just a janitor's closet or something. Otherwise they'd have a combo lock on it." He kept twisting and turning the tool until there was an audible click. "Old technology. They're pretty confident that whoever comes down here is already cleared into this facility." He swung the door open. "Suivez-moi, mes amis. Bienvenus chez le Marquis de Sade."

He turned on the light and immediately dropped his little tool and flashlight, regretting his prophetic words. It was not a janitor's closet. Instead it was a large storeroom with a seven meter high ceiling, the floor area as large as half a football field. It was filled with several rows of tanks that were a little bigger than a good-sized man. Each tank was hooked up to an elaborate snake's nest of coiled wires and tubes and had a square meter window on one side.

RP1 went to one of the tanks and looked in, then drew back, his face filled with horror.

"What is it?" asked SW2, taking a look herself. Through the window she saw a little twelve or thirteen year-old girl, apparently asleep. But the girl's long hair floated in the liquid she was immersed in. Her fingernails and toenails were at least seven centimeters long. What had shocked RP1 and even more SW2 was that the girl looked just like SW2 had looked when she was that age.

"Shit," said GW3, as he went from tank to tank. "We're all here. And more. What the fuck is going on? They're not training any of these kids. They're unconscious."

RP1 ran his flashlight over a plaque above one of the windows.

"Brainless homonoid, SW-type, Jan. 17, 2040," he read. "What does that mean?"

"It means that we were the first but that they've perfected the technique," said GW3.

"And what does that mean?" asked SW2.

"They made us for something, the devil knows what, and then found out that they really didn't need the final product to have a brain. Brainless homonoid means they don't have a brain, amigos mios."

"You mean, they're just growing there?" asked RP1.

"That's what it looks like."

SW2 shivered. "That means they probably don't need us, because we do have brains."

"Unless they have to wait until these reach maturity," observed RP1. "Let's do a census. How many here are mature copies of us?"

They began running up and down the rows. The oldest swimmers in the tank were the age of the SW copy. All the rest were younger. Some could still be classified as embryos.

"Looks like we're safe for a few more years," said GW3 breathlessly with a smile. "How about that?"

"How about getting out of here?" said RP1. "This information is dynamite. We have to tell the others."

"A sage observation," said GW3. They left the storage room and closed the door behind them. GW3 locked it in much the same way he had opened it.

"I wonder what this is?" asked RP1, pointing to something beside the door. "There's a small keypad, though on top it looks like something else goes inside it." He stuck his finger in the hole.

GW3 looked where RP1 was sticking his finger.

"You dumb fuck, it's a security checkpoint."

"Do you think the Guardians check periodically down here as well?" asked SW2, fear showing in her eyes. She had never liked the Guardians and often had nightmares about them.

At that moment, they heard the elevator motor start. They had sent the elevator back up to the first level. Did the Guardians have any way to tell that it had come down to the third?

"Damn, he's coming here," said RP1.

GW3 ran to the workstation and shut it down while RP1 and SW2 tried several doors, looking for somewhere to hide. SW2 found one, an unlocked storage room that was much smaller than the vast warehouse they had been in. It was filled with boxes of supplies. They managed to all fit in, GW3 enjoying the close proximity to SW2 way too much in RP1's opinion.

They watched as the Guardian swung a flashlight around the lab, and then walked over to the security checkpoint. It was just a routine security pass but SW2 still squeezed RP1's hand until she drew blood with her nails. The Guardian left.

The three decided to call it an evening.

The next morning another Guardian was about to enjoy his donut and coffee. He was fast forwarding the lab's night time videocam readout. It was just another boring part of his boring job until the donut stopped halfway to his mouth as he noticed the time stamp that the computer automatically put on the image just before it was recorded onto the hard disk. He backed up the video file and then moved it forward, normal speed. The night time Guardian was supposed to hit the lab security checkpoint during a fifteen minute window but the computer didn't show the usual image of his colleague.

"Bring up the checkpoint file," the Guardian told the computer. That file was an independent one that registered the exact time his colleague put his key in the security checkpoint. It was within the fifteen minute window.

The Guardian forgot all about his coffee and donut as he picked up the phone. Something was not right. *Thank the Lord it didn't happen on my watch.*

Scherzo Twenty-Five

"Why so glum today, partner?"

Tex turned away from the computer screen. He had been watching and listening to his video-mail, beamed to Mars from Earth every day on a tight spread spectrum signal. It was easier to do video-mail than to suffer the time delay in a direct link, not to mention negotiating the different time zones on Earth.

This time, however, he wished he could just pick up a cell phone and call his wife. Maybe he would, delay or no delay.

Dr. Chandrakanta Gupta, known to her comrades at the Mars colony as Chandy, was technically Dr. Clayton Pratt's boss. But Chandy and Tex were old friends, and Chandy knew Tex' family well.

"She and the kids will be here in a few years," she said, trying to help his mood.

"Maybe not," said Tex. He turned the monitor so she could see it.

The video-mail from the young geologist's wife was shocking. In it Tex' wife told the story of how the Pratt family home and other assets had been seized to pay for Mrs. Pratt's complicated brain surgery. A tumor had been discovered some time ago but had only been declared malignant that very day. The prognosis was good and their insurance, together with their assets and savings, would cover the costs of the surgery. However, Mrs. Pratt, a double PhD in astrophysics and chemistry, was declared a health risk and was scratched from the list of passengers that were going on the next flight to Mars. She had decided to keep the children with her.

Tex waited for his friend and boss to get the gist of it.

"Well, maybe you ought to go home," suggested Chandy after a moment's reflection.

"That means five years instead of two and a half," objected Tex.

"I know, Tex, I'm sorry," was all Chandy could say.

Chapter Thirty-One

Boston, Massachusetts, Saturday . . .

Denise Rivera looked over the lip of her coffee mug to see Chris Tanner standing at the doorway to her office. She frowned. Chris decided he liked her smile better.

"I thought you had the day off?"

"I do, but I came in to make a request." He toyed with a PDA, nervously tossing it up and down in his right hand. He had always used one, finding the standard memory in the police-issued cell phones inadequate for both his work and private life.

"Denied. Since you're here, I have a case for you."

"How'd you know what I was going to ask?" It was his turn to frown.

"You're here on Saturday, on your day off, so you're going to either ask for time off or ask for a raise. Considering that even you aren't so stupid to ask for a raise outside of the union, I concluded that it's extra time off. Have you been talking with Ka Wah Fong again?"

"How'd you know that?"

This time his captain smiled.

"Ka Wah tried his conspiracy theory out on me first, you know. I told him he was full of shit. And so are you, if you believe it."

"Well, he's not. And I'm not. I believe it. I think you should hear what I have to say."

Chris filled her in about what he had learned in conversations with Jay and Kalidas. The story seemed to change Denise's opinion about the case. But she was still doubtful.

"So you think these three Fulton administration look-alikes are clones? Come on, Chris. Next you'll be telling me you still believe in Santa Claus."

"You'll admit there are a lot of unusual and coincidental circumstances here. It sets off all my detective's warning alarms. I'm on to something here, Denise. Don't deny it."

"Yes, you might be. But I don't think we should tangle with the DHS. I'll take their money but they're harder to live with than the FBI."

"We've got an unsolved murder case," Chris reminded her.

"Yes, we do, but I shelved it. And just what do you propose to do?"

"Go down and help Jay and Kalidas solve this case."

"Not on my time. But I'll meet you half way. Frank Sweeney's got a mansion in Wellesley. See if you can talk to some of his staff to see if any of them can remember anything strange on the night of your attack by the Sweeney look-alike."

"It wasn't an attack. He was already dead."

"And you almost were, so it might as well have been an attack."

"All right, I'll do it, as a first step."

"We'll talk about the next steps after you finish the first one. Now get over to MGH. They've got a gunshot victim who is just coming out of surgery. Her husband was also shot, though he's dead. I want his killer."

"What about my day off?"

"I told you, you just forfeited it by coming in."

It didn't take Chris long to interview the gunshot victim. She hadn't even seen the carjacker. Chris received a call from Marcia King saying some black and whites had just apprehended him after he ran a red light on Congress Street in the couple's car. He had entered 93 going the wrong way, causing five minor accidents. He was flying high on cocaine.

Chris told the woman.

"How is it that such animals are allowed to roam the streets?" she asked, tears rolling down her cheeks.

"Drugs can do bad things to people," was all he could say. She thanked him and dozed off again. He shook his head sadly as he left the room. Her question had been a valid one. The carjacker had a long history of violence in support of his habit. He also had two previous jail terms. This time he would get life without parole. Another person had self-destructed because of drugs. He didn't know what to do about it. Some blamed all the crime on people getting desperate—with their financial circumstances, their marriage, or their addictions. While he thought that that was true in some cases, Chris knew from experience that desperation played second fiddle to pure meanness. *Staying on the high moral ground is more and more difficult with the quagmires that modern life generates around us.*

He headed for Wellesley. As Chris drove out of Boston towards the suburbs, his thoughts turned to history. In particular, he was thinking about how little use he had for it and how much people in the area were into it.

The weekend aficionados who pick up their toy muskets and practice the re-enactment of the famous battles of independence. The fathers driving their families to the history tours of Walden Pond and the North Bridge. The children's school tours on their visit to Orchard House. People focus on the past because they're dissatisfied with the present and afraid of the future.

All wastes of time as far as he was concerned. He was more practical. If he ever had a wife and children, his outings would be to natural places, away from the city, yes, but focused on the wonders of life on this small planet, enraptured with our evolutionary history, not the history of some popular myths.

Speaking of nature, take Thoreau. Now there was a nut. Almost everyone considered him to be the father of conservation, a transcendentalist in love with nature. Forget the fact that he almost starved his family one winter. Forget the fact that he almost burned down Walden Woods. And forget the fact that his writings contain some of the most misguided and syrupy words ever written in a misguided Puritan culture touting itself as liberal. He was an icon. And that was all that mattered. The historians declared him to be an icon, so he was. Caveat emptor.

After an hour's drive through horrible traffic where he was thankful for the autopilot signals on the Mass Pike, he turned off and entered the town of Wellesley. He couldn't help but admire the stately homes with their manicured lawns and glorious old trees. Yet the general decay of the American infrastructure could be seen even here as well as in the city. *This once posh suburb of Boston is showing the wear and tear of time, yet it would still be impossible for me to live here. Not many places I can live with just a cop's salary.*

The Sweeney mansion was tucked in behind the college. He got a little lost but the GPS in his car saved the day. He felt a little uncomfortable leaving his ten-year-old car in the circular drive in front of the main entrance. It badly needed a wash and wax. *Maybe I should go park around back so the neighbors won't talk?*

The knock on the door was answered by an old woman, a little bent and crippled, yet still elegantly attired. She said her name was Mrs. Hutchins. She looked at the offered badge.

"I would like to talk to all of Mr. Sweeney's staff in regards to a homicide case I'm working on."

"You should have made an appointment," the woman scolded.

"I thought Captain Rivera did so, ma'am. She suggested this trip."

"Ah, Captain Rivera." The woman smiled. "That would make sense. I'll see who's around to talk to you. Please come in and have a seat in the living room, detective."

Chris waited patiently some ten minutes before the old woman returned, followed by seven others. Three were clearly groundskeepers. They stood, apparently fearing that they would soil the elegant furniture. The other four were chambermaids. One looked very much like Denise Rivera. Mrs. Hutchins introduced them all, finally coming to the Denise look-alike. *Another clone,* thought Chris.

"And this is Patricia Rivera. She is your captain's sister."

"She never told me she had a sister."

"I'm Denise's youngest sister," said Patricia, with a smile. "We have four others, detective."

"Well, I guess there is a lot that I don't know about Denise. Did you suggest to her that I should come talk to all of you?"

"Well, not you in particular. We do have some information that might bear on your case, though."

"In good time," interrupted Mrs. Hutchins. "And let me set one thing straight, detective. We are not Mr. Sweeney's staff. We are Mrs. Sweeney's staff. She runs this house. It has been in her family for a long time."

"But she's usually not here, right?"

"She is usually in Washington at her husband's side," said Mrs. Hutchins. There was an unspoken implication that Mrs. Hutchins considered that nothing more than Mrs. Sweeney's social obligation.

Chris explained some of the circumstances of the case and the fact that he had nearly been killed by an already dead Frank Sweeney look-alike.

"Was either Mr. Sweeney or Mrs. Sweeney here that night?" he finished.

"They both were here," said Mrs. Hutchins. "They had dinner guests. Judge Parkhurst and his wife and daughter were over. The daughter is an assistant professor at Wellesley College. The Parkhursts are old friends of Mrs. Sweeney's family."

"And were Mr. and Mrs. Sweeney here all night with them?"

"No, Mr. Sweeney left suddenly," said Patricia. "He received a call which he took in the study." She pointed down the hall. "Jack?"

One of the gardeners, a burly fellow, nodded.

"Yeah, I was in the shed back of the house working on one of the lawnmowers, trying to get it fixed for the next day. Because of all this rain, the grass was growing a lot, and Monday was going to be sunny, so I didn't want to miss it. Anyway, Franky—"

"Mr. Sweeney," corrected Mrs. Hutchins.

"I call the bastard Franky. He ain't no Mister, the way he treats his Missus sometimes. If I ever treated my woman like that, she'd crown me with a frying pan."

"Jack gets a little carried away," explained Mrs. Hutchins, obviously annoyed with the gardener for airing dirty linen.

But Chris already had surmised that all was not well in the Sweeney household.

"Please, go on, Jack."

"Like I said, Franky comes busting out of the study like his rear end was on fire and hops into that fast car of his. He tore out of here leaving gravel spraying all over my lawn. I had to pick it all out before I mowed the next day."

"Does anyone know who he received the call from?"

"I can only say it was from Washington," said Patricia.

"And how do you know that?" Chris asked.

"He was using the red phone. He calls it his hot line. He only receives government calls on that. And to use it he has to punch in a special code."

So Secretary Sweeney had gotten a call on a secure line and raced off in the middle of a rain storm.

"What time was this?"

The time was just before Chris had almost been run down by the dead Sweeney look-alike.

After thanking Mrs. Sweeney's staff, he called Denise and was about to tell her what he had learned when she cut him short.

"Make your report to me, here, in the station, in person, Chris. It will wait until you get here."

On the way back to Boston, Chris didn't notice the car that was tailing him.

That evening Mr. and Mrs. Sweeney came home. The woman had obviously been crying in the car, yet prim and proper Mrs. Hutchins didn't say anything. Mr. Sweeney went straight to the bar and fixed himself a drink and then sat down on the sofa. He spotted Chris' card.

"Mrs. Hutchins, was this cop here today?"

"Yes, sir," said Mrs. Hutchins. "He asked the staff some questions about a murder."

"What murder? In Boston? It says he's a Boston police detective."

"He works for Denise Rivera, Patricia's sister."

"Did Patricia open her big mouth about something she shouldn't have? You people are supposed to be discreet. I should fire you all."

"You can't do that, Franky," said Mrs. Sweeney, getting some of her courage back. "These people work for me."

"I'll have them declared a national security risk, then they can work in Leavenworth. How 'bout that?"

"May I go now?" asked Mrs. Hutchins.

"Sure. Get the hell out of here. I have ways to find out what the detective wanted without talking to you or any of the other servants. None of you have any brains anyway."

"Franky, please, you're in a bad mood." Mrs. Sweeney sounded tired.

"Yeah," he said. He stood up as Mrs. Hutchins left the room. "I'm real tired. Tired of you, bitch." He slapped her across the face. "Don't ever contradict me in front of the help again."

His wife started crying again.

"I won't, Franky," she said.

Scherzo Twenty-Six

Bruce Phillips grunted and heaved. The shotput sailed out over the field.
"Not bad, son," said Coach Bob Smith.
The Arkansas sun bore down on the two unmercifully. Yet most of the track team was out practicing. None were as famous as Bruce, two-time All-American in the decathlon. His muscles ached from the workout he had given them. The jacuzzi would feel good.
"So, today's the big day, huh?" asked Coach Bob.
"Yeah, I'll here from the Committee tonight. Everybody says I'm a shoo-in, but I'm still worried. They could select Randall in place of me. He's been really good the last three months."
"I wouldn't worry. Even if Henry gets the first spot, you should get the second. You beat Randall in LA last winter."
Bruce balanced another shot in his big hand and looked across the field at some runners. That was the hardest for him. His running game was the weakest, including the hurdles. But he had beat Randall in the 100 and hurdles, much to his surprise, and Randall's.
He worked out for another two hours, did the jacuzzi, showered, and slowly made it back to the athlete's dorm. He got the call at 8:05. He was not going.
His first reaction was to throw his engineering thermodynamics book at the wall so hard that it split, its pages fluttering all around the room. Then he called Coach Bob.
"I know, son. I heard. I don't understand it. Let me do some checking."
The next afternoon Coach Bob approached him as he was warming up for discus throwing.
"You're not going to like this but I found out what happened."
"So, give," said Bruce. "Where did I screw up?"
"You didn't screw up, son. I didn't believe it when I heard it."
"Heard what?"
"Randall goes to IU, right?"

"Yeah, the Hoosiers. It's got a good, solid sports tradition. But they don't have anyone on the Olympic Committee to pull strings, if that's what you mean."

"No, but Randall's aunt has donated heavily to Roger Preston's senatorial campaigns over many years."

"A senator has that kind of power?" asked Bruce incredulously.

"Roger Preston does."

Chapter Thirty-Two

Washington, DC, Sunday . . .

Roger Preston didn't like Washington much. In summer it was swampy; in the winter it was icy. His Hoosier state was much better. Born in Terre Haute, he hadn't left it until he won his first bid for Congress. Being a senator required even more time away from his beloved state.

He knew the Northeastern liberals often called Middle America the flyover zone, referring to the planes that crisscrossed the country back and forth, flying over the Midwestern states for the most part. There was a lot of truth to it, of course, but the phrase ignored a very important fact: Presidential elections were often won in Middle America. The urban sprawl around Chicago had made both Illinois and Indiana important states to be reckoned with. Preston had often leveraged that to his benefit.

He sipped his iced tea by his pool and wondered if tomorrow he should go into his office. As one of the senior members of the Senate, he had a nice one, but he knew work was waiting for him there. Yes, maybe tomorrow he'd make at least an appearance. Right now he would just lie here and try to think of ways to solve more pressing problems.

He really didn't trust the others. Maybe they were capable but they had made mistakes. Too many mistakes could spell disaster.

His wife waved to him from the diving board. He estimated that the board was smarter than she was but she was good to look at, and that's what counted. At thirty-three, she had a perfect body and was not letting herself go, either. Not like the two before. They had cost him, in both alimony and votes, but a senator had connections that led to lucrative business deals. He could afford the alimony and the votes were still enough to keep him in office.

Gina was topless, as usual. She knifed into the water from a perfect back flip. *Wow, that's something. I wish I had the guts to do that.*

He really didn't like the water and had never learned to swim. His stint in the Navy was a joke, since he had spent it behind a desk in San Diego. Still, he didn't have to like water to admire a topless Gina. She was spectacular. Dumb, but spectacular.

His admiration for his wife was interrupted by the arrival of Frank Sweeney.

"Playing hooky again, Senator?" the Secretary of Defense asked.

"It's Sunday, Frank. The Lord's Day. We're all supposed to rest."

"Yeah, and you're sure doing the Lord's work getting a hard on while watching your wife's tits fly through the air."

Preston frowned. The Defense Secretary could be uncouth at times. He chose to ignore it for now.

"What brings you here, Frank?"

"I was in Boston yesterday. I think this detective, this Chris Tanner, is nosing around too much."

"I thought Mary Beth had that under control. She picked up the body, right?"

"Yeah, she did, but Tanner almost got killed, so maybe he's got a grudge. I would. But I really came to ask you a question."

"My god, you couldn't call me?"

"You don't have a secure line. I don't want any of the others to hear the question. And, if you repeat it to anyone, I'll kill you. So there."

"What's the question?" Preston's smile was one of egotistical self-confidence. He wasn't particularly afraid of Sweeney. He considered him a stupid hothead. A technological Neanderthal. "It must be very important for you to threaten to kill me."

"You and Stephanie aren't exactly bed mates yet, so I thought you might have an independent take on things." Sweeney hitched up his slacks nervously. Preston could see him admiring Gina from the corner of his eye. "A lot of us, including you, bought into this later than Hank and her. Do you think they're losing control?"

"Suppose that I did, what would you do? Or have me do?"

"I'd be doing the doing. I've got some wet teams no one knows about, Roger. They're experienced overseas. Real professionals. Taking out those assholes would be a piece of cake for them."

"And the Center?"

"The kids there would be casualties of war. Too bad."

"Well, I understand your concern. I'd wait a while, though. As much as I dislike Stephanie, she's tough and resourceful. She's also coldly calculating. She's not likely to lose her temper, unlike some people I know."

"Oh, please. Spare me the anger management lesson. I've got to where I am by being quick and decisive. With the new scramjets we can strike anywhere in the world with only a couple hours delay. I have to be quick on my toes to do my job. You people on the hill fuck around for months before you can decide where to take a pee."

"You wanted my opinion. You have it. What are you going to do?"

"I'll take your advice. I'll wait. But I'm getting antsy. Stephanie's capable, but Hank's pretty slow sometimes. I don't want him to drag us all down. The fiasco at the Center showed me that he hadn't thought through the security issues enough."

"Yes, that was particularly unfortunate." He caught Sweeney stealing another glance at his wife. "Not enough action at home, Frank?"

"Oh, my wife's a pretty good fuck but she's a simpering idiot. Too much inbreeding in that rich family of hers, I'd say. How 'bout a drink? We'll watch the tits together."

Scherzo Twenty-Seven

Sean O'Reilly tossed his knife lazily.

"Benny, do you know how they catch a lot of knife murderers?" he asked his colleague.

"Nope, how do they?"

Benny Jackson was on guard duty with Sean. They were dressed in thermal suits. Even with the protection of the guard hut, they would die from exposure without the suits. They were lightweight, new models, the technology borrowed from spacesuits. It made guard duty on the Aleutian island bearable.

Not far away were the huge phased-array radars that continuously scanned to the west, ready to detect, track, and identify any ICBM launched from Asia. Or so the manufacturer claimed. Conceived over fifty years ago, the radars and the interceptors that were tied into them were now largely just another example of corporate welfare the DoD didn't want to spend but the Congress kept making them do it. Together with the troops, it was another drain on the American taxpayer, a dinosaur that in its youth possibly provided some protection from an isolated attack of a few missiles (fortunately, it was never tested in real battle), although in its old age it was ready for mothballs.

Sean and Benny didn't care about that. They mostly cared about keeping warm.

"It's easy," said Sean, looking at the knife. "This is a military knife. It's got a protector on it. If I knife someone with it and I hit bone, my hand won't slide onto the blade. The average person, when they knife someone, they use a kitchen knife or a steak knife, or one of those Swiss jobs, and there's no protector. They cut themselves, so the blood gets on the person they killed. Since everyone has to have their DNA, fingerprints, and retinal patterns registered to get an ID card, they've got you."

"What do the fingerprints and retinal patterns have to do with it?"

"Nothin', stupid. They just need the DNA. I'm just saying they get that when you do the ID card."

"And if you don't hit bone?"

"I guess you got me there. I bet you hit bone a lot, though. We've got a lot of bones. Thousands."

"Yeah, and all mine are cold. Think of something warm to talk about."

"Yeah, like being stationed in the Philippines? My brother's over there."

"Good enough. It's gotta be warmer than here."

"You'd better believe it. It's a fucking swamp. And they got skeeters and leeches. He hates the place."

"You should trade places with him."

"Nah, I already got a leech. You."

Benny gave Sean the finger and they both smiled.

Chapter Thirty-Three

Upper Montclair, New Jersey, Monday . . .

With the strains of Mahler's Ruckert-Lieder filling her townhouse study and her second glass of French burgundy, Kalidas Metropolis should have been able to vanquish some of her anxieties. Instead, her paranoia and puzzlement were increasing. She had just made a call to Italy. She hung up the phone, dumbfounded. *No one is talking to me.* Every scientist in her close circle of fellow researchers was shunning her. The last one she talked to, Antonio Magliozzi in Rome, looked like he was scared of his shadow. *Hey, girl, your deodorant can't matter over that many miles!*

The lines of the last lieder seemed to mock her. "I am out of touch with this world where I have spent so much of my time . . . ."

It seemed that no one wanted to talk about human cloning anymore. True, the United Nations, along with more than seventy other nations, had outlawed it, though researchers still discussed it. *Someone has put a tight cap on that discussion, at least among scientists who have a right to more than a layman's opinion about it.*

She tried one more call. It was three hours earlier in Palo Alto but Professor Wolfgang Richter's department secretary answered the phone.

Kalidas explained who she was. The secretary remembered her from her trip out to Stanford University seven years ago. Wolfgang Richter had been a pompous ass, harassing her all the time during her presentation. But she knew for a fact that he was smart and had lots of DoD contracts.

"Is Professor Richter there? I need to ask him an important question."

The secretary looked uncomfortable. Kalidas at first thought it was only the good secretary protecting her boss. Yet when she spoke, the answer shocked her.

175

"Professor Richter was killed by thieves that broke into his house. Didn't you see it in the e-zines?"

No, she hadn't seen it. She didn't read e-zines. Maybe she should start. It was the second time that had come back to bite her.

"I'm so sorry. How did it happen?"

"I'm really afraid to talk. It was so violent." The secretary was clearly in distress. "From what the police said, the professor was shot and a young student's throat was slit."

"Holy shit!" exclaimed Kalidas. "Have they caught the thieves? What did they steal?"

"As far as I know, the police have no clues. It seems they took several valuable coin collections the professor had. He was quite the collector, you know."

"Well, that should be easy to trace. Maybe they will catch them soon. My condolences."

"Thank you. Can I be of any further help?"

"If it's not too much trouble, yes." She thought about how to phrase the question, given the circumstances, but then decided to just go boldly forward, ignoring the secretary's sensibilities. "Do you happen to know if any of his projects had to do with cloning?"

"I only know about the unclassified ones, Dr. Metropolis. All of those dealt with cloning."

"Do you know who were the sponsors of the classified ones?"

"I'm not sure I should give that information out."

"Well, I'm doing a survey of who funds research in our field for one of the journals. I suppose I could go to the finance department. They have to divulge the information, you know. Not the research topic nor even the titles of the projects, which might also be classified, but they have to give the names of the sponsors and the dollar amounts. That was the result of a big lawsuit back in 2047, I believe." It was all a lie. There was indeed such a lawsuit but the decision rendered was exactly the opposite: the corporation suing the University of Chicago for unfair competition was denied access to the sponsors' names by the Federal Court of Appeals. Kalidas hoped that the secretary was not acquainted with the intricate details of that case.

"Well, I suppose I may as well tell you then, though the exact dollar amounts you'll still have to get from the finance department. I don't have those."

"All right, that'll do for now. I don't think I need the exact dollar amounts anyway."

"Well, then, Professor Richter worked with both the Department of Defense and the Department of Homeland Security."

"Did he have a long standing relationship with DHS?"

"I knew him for eleven years. He had several projects with them every year."

"Thank you for your help."

Kalidas hung up, deep in thought. *So Wolfgang Richter was working—rather, had been working—with both the DoD and the DHS. Sweeney and Johnson? Am I grasping at straws here? Are we believing too much in conspiracies, or was Richter killed before he talked about his research? Was he doing research for them as far back as twenty to twenty-five years ago?*

She considered how to go about answering that last question. Many classified projects start as unclassified ones. It was only when the government realized that a project was so new or so innovative that it was necessary to hide it from enemy eyes that it became compartamentalized into a black program. It took an expert to trace a thread of research in the open literature to where it disappeared under the cloak of secrecy. But she was an expert.

She went to work, tenaciously burrowing into the old references, helped by the fact that just about everything since 1990 was somewhere stashed electronically in some computer database—even preprints. As much as she hated computers, she knew how to use them. It took a little over five hours but the literature search paid off. There was a clear line of two years' research starting twenty-five years ago that, if continued in the open literature, would have led to results similar to the ones in her recent preprint, and beyond. Yet, suddenly, twenty-three years ago, that line of research disappeared from the open literature. There were no subsequent disclaimers for errors and no retractions during the following years. Richter took up completely new topics for his unclassified research. It wasn't concrete evidence, yet she could only conclude that the original line of research had become classified. *No wonder they confiscated my stuff. But why is the work classified? Wouldn't it have benefited a lot of people?*

Her detective work also explained why she had probably duplicated Richter's results. She had been working in an entirely different area ten years ago, being led to her recent research from the concern with making transplants safe. She had only back checked the previous five years of research. Richter's line of work had gone undercover eight years before that.

That realization didn't improve her spirits any. It was uncomfortable knowing that the work reported on in her preprint was probably re-inventing the wheel. Richter had most likely done it earlier. Much earlier.

With each paper she ever submitted she questioned the originality of her ideas. She never wanted to be criticized for stealing someone else's intellectual property. Her papers were riddled with references that read "private communication" as she gave someone their due credit for a remark made in a hallway conversation at a conference or an idea suggested in an e-mail or video-mail. She was known for being a zealot about academic honesty. She was therefore troubled. *Did I steal ideas from Richter?*

She thought long and hard about the last years of her research and decided she hadn't stolen anything from the pompous ass. She knew it was easy to make mistakes there. Watson and Crick drew on the work of Rosalind Franklin when they described the double-helix structure of DNA, for example. Kalidas had often wondered if they had downplayed her role. Disputes like that were hard to resolve, especially after the particulars were dead.

She decided that it didn't matter anyway, since her most recent result had not been officially published. *The question really is, did Richter's work become classified because he was cloning humans? If so, why? We suspect that the John Does are clones. Why do they want them?* She might have found the how behind the conspiracy, if there was one, but not the why.

Farther down the eastern seaboard, Simon Multani pulled into Asako O'Brien's apartment complex, somewhat ashamed and embarrassed. Here he was running to a woman so she could protect him. Actually not her, since he knew Asako was not trained in dealing with violence. She only handled the aftermath. Still, maybe her FBI friends would help.

He had driven around all weekend, sleeping two nights in the car in two different rest stops. Rather, trying to sleep. Paranoia oozed from every pore. He was a rumpled mess but Asako didn't seem to mind when she heard the story.

"Nice little slug," she said, after studying the car and pulling the bullet out from some padding on the door on the passenger's side. She held it up to the fading sunlight between latex-gloved fingers. "Without a microscope, it's hard to say, but from your description, the gun had a silencer. I might be able to confirm that. I don't expect I'll find the barrel striations registered in my database." She gave Simon a squeeze on the shoulder, trying to cheer him up. He was sweating profusely in the early summer heat. "It's probably a warning. If they wanted you dead, you'd be dead."

"Thanks for the comforting words," said Simon. "Now, other than I drive a junky old car, what could they be warning me about?"

"They probably want you to stop talking to Jay. Who else sees your reports, Simon?"

"They're just passed up the chain of command."

"Do they ever go to the DHS?"

"Of course. But someone higher than me decides on that. It's probably the same at your place."

"Yeah. Well, I'd say you're probably safe for now. Stay here tonight, and tomorrow go back to DC. Act like nothing happened. I'll let Jay know."

"Thanks, but maybe I should just drive back. I don't sleep well on a couch."

"Simon, who said anything about sleeping on a couch?"

Scherzo Twenty-Eight

Ben Hartnell leisurely swung along using the hand rings until he got to the galley.

"I didn't call any meeting, guys," he said as he entered.

"Surprise!" yelled the rest of the crew.

Ben looked astonished. Then he remembered.

"Hey, my birthday's not 'til tomorrow."

"Well, which day it is depends on where you are on Earth," explained Patty Clark. "We just jumped Zulu time a bit to the next day. That way most people are awake."

"How long have you been planning this?" Ben asked them.

"Oh, 'bout five hours," said Lindsay Thornton. "Craig was asking everyone how old they thought you were, so we made bets. When we looked it up, we saw that your birthday is tomorrow, or rather, today."

"So you know I'm old enough to want to forget about it," said Ben.

"That's why there's no number on the cake," explained Patty with a smile. "But get with the program, Ben. How often is it that we can eat cake?"

"Not very often," admitted Ben.

As captain of the Anthelion, all of these people were under his command, yet he felt they were all his friends. He didn't begrudge them their small pleasures. Patty Clark was his second in command but she was also an astrophysicist. Lindsay Thornton was a navigation and computer expert, while Craig Fox was an astrophysicist and com expert. Many of the others had multiple skill sets. He himself was an MD, mechanical engineer, and linguist, although he didn't expect the last discipline to have any application where they were going.

The Anthelion was headed out from Mars towards Jupiter. An expedition due to last many years, the small group of twenty-three specialists remained in contact with Earth via a big dish antenna that sat on the Anthelion's hull.

In many ways, the ship looked like a floating junk yard. It had been constructed in Mars orbit and would never land on a planet, atmosphere or no atmosphere. It was more a floating laboratory, although far away from the habitation areas there was an engine spewing out enough stuff that would make it a bright star to their Martian comrades below for many months to come.

After they each had a sliver of cake—it was only pound cake—and the rest of the slices were set aside for those either sleeping or still on duty, Craig broke out the rum and coke. It was becoming a rather nice party until Yolanda Gomez broke in. She handed Patty a note. Patty turned white and hastily left.

After the party, Ben passed by Patty's quarters, not much more than a closet, yet it did have a fairly comfortable bunk and fold-down desk. Her head was on the desk and she was crying.

"I guess something's happened," said Ben. "Do you want a shoulder to cry on? Or maybe just tell me what's going on?"

Patty looked at him.

"It was a message from my mother. My father's gone. Passed away."

"I knew that he was sick. How'd it happen?"

"A stupid, really stupid, freaky accident. He fell in the bathroom and bumped his head on the toilet. He started to have a really bad headache, so my mother wanted him to have an MRI. They're so good now, they can really let you know what's going on with the soft tissue. Anyway, his HMO denied it. They gave him medicine for a migraine."

"It obviously wasn't a migraine," said Ben. "What was it?"

"Well, like a lot of migraine medicines, it dilated the artery which loosened the clot. It got stuck in a more vital place. It was like an aneurism blowing. The MRI would have shown that, Ben."

"I'm sorry," Ben said, feeling helpless. He knew Patty and her father had been close. He had met both their parents before the crew left for Mars. "I'm canceling your shift. Yolanda can cover for you."

"No, don't do that. The work will take my mind off this."

Chapter Thirty-Four

Falls Church, Virginia, Tuesday . . .

"I'm not sure you understand the gravity of the situation," said Mary Beth Grogan. "These people are tenacious. This Metropolis woman feels she's been wronged. The detective has quite a rep for sniffing out people responsible for crimes. And the reporter is dedicated to bringing her friend's husband's killer to justice. She was seen talking to that CIA analyst, the one who did the report on the Philippine terrorist. Curt gave him a little warning, though I don't think that's enough. They're all intelligent and persistent. We should eliminate them all."

"There's been enough killing," insisted Hank Johnson. He looked out his office window. It was a million-dollar view. Soon he would have a better one when he took over from Ben Knowland. "We just have to last through the election."

"Well, I disagree, Hank. This kettle of fish may boil over before the election. And if the press ever gets wind of it, it could mean losing the election, too. Our whole agenda would come crashing down around us. Think about it."

"I will. The committee meets next Thursday night. I'm sure we'll hear many suggestions about the possible actions we could take. You may get your wish. Both Vladimir and Stephanie are not known to flinch at applying a little old-fashioned 'terminate with extreme prejudice.'"

"That's not my wish. My wish is that these people would just get bored and go away. I warned that reporter."

At that moment, a message flashed onto his computer screen. It had a three-line cover:

Top Secret / Blue Hammer
Handle via Special Access Channels Only
For Your Eyes Only

He typed in his user name and password and looked into the retina scanner. All three were needed to open the document and turn the scrambled text inside to English. An angry expression washed over his face.

"The detective was out at Sweeney's house. And that Metropolis woman called Stanford to inquire about Richter."

"So, what could they find? Nothing. Mrs. Sweeney's staff doesn't know anything. And we cleaned up the Stanford connection."

"I'm always worried about loose ends. I worked for Stephanie, remember. Perhaps you're right. The safest thing is to get rid of these people. I'll propose it next Thursday. There's too much at stake."

The report Hank Johnson had just read also appeared on a computer in a Pentagon office. Frank Sweeney stopped his analysis of a package of presentation slides on a new weapons system long enough to read it. He smiled as he did so, because no one knew about his hack into the DHS network. It only depended on the classified intranet link between the Pentagon, NSA and the DHS. The techie that had set it up for him had died overseas—he had seen to that.

After finishing the reading of the report, he didn't return immediately to the new weapons system. Instead, he debated the pros and the cons that went into what would be a tough decision. At some future moment he might have to cut his losses by eliminating everyone and everything having to do with the Center. Stephanie's idea had been a good one twenty odd years ago, yet he wasn't going to hang for her.

He picked up the STU phone and made a call to San Diego. It wouldn't hurt to have things ready, just in case. It would take some planning. *If the shit hits the fan, they will only need a coded message from me to begin the cleanup.*

Elsewhere in the Pentagon, General Roberto Vargas, head of the Joint Chiefs, entertained Pierce Hamilton, National Security Advisor. It wasn't often that Fulton's conscience visited the Pentagon. He preferred to work by secure phones, secure intranet, or VTC. Since the meetings he attended with the Pentagon's top brass often involved VIPs spread out all over the country, that was not unusual. It was well known that Hamilton, as an ex-priest, wasn't particularly comfortable around the military culture, although he was a believer in a strong national defense. Roberto disliked the man for the first part and other, less logical reasons, yet he considered Pierce to be quite capable at his job. Although there was a National Intelligence Director, Pierce was the de facto leader of all the intelligence services, including the military's, in the Fulton administration. But he also knew how to delegate, and let the military do pretty much what they always had done in that area.

"This is an unexpected pleasure," said the general.

"Come now, Roberto, I know you don't like me, and you're not on my Christmas card list either. However, I respect your abilities and hopefully you respect mine." He folded his hands into a steeple and placed them under his chin as if he were about to lead them in prayer. It only served to accent his most prominent feature, his nose. "Now that those pleasantries are all over with, I have a question for you."

The general frowned. The man could be blunt sometimes. He wondered if that was why he had left the priesthood. He must have been terrible at hearing confessions.

"I'm ready and willing, if I can answer it."

Pierce picked up a paperweight on the general's desk. It was a model of the Apollo spacecraft. He tossed it in the air once, surprised at its weight.

"I want to know if you have a special access program going on that uses a NASA starship project as a cover story."

"That sounds like sci-fi to me. Area 51 and all that? Have you been watching too many conspiracy movies?"

"I don't do many movies, modern or old, although I would probably prefer the old, since many modern ones are just sanctioned pornography, S and M, and the like, with computer generated background. No, it's an honest question. I have an old friend at NASA who brought this up. I checked around with my other NASA contacts, and they know nothing about it. My guess is that it is a cover story."

"If it is, you may not have a need-to-know."

"Are you kidding?" asked Pierce. "I'm the National Security Advisor. If I say I have a need-to-know, I do."

"Point well taken. Let me rephrase that. Why do you want to know?"

"Because I'm curious about why the Pentagon would invent such a far-fetched cover story. You're very good at inventing much more believable ones. Like you said, this sounds too sci-fi."

Roberto squeezed one of those little rubber stress relaxers with a big, hairy hand. This one was a rubber doll, dressed in traditional Arab garb. Although lighthearted, it represented the focus of the Pentagon for the last fifty years. It brought back memories of the three siblings he had lost in the Middle East. He was the only son left for his parents. A tragedy for the Vargas family, a closely knit family with many cousins, uncles and aunts. Yet both his father and mother believed their children had died for a good cause.

He knew better. He was more practical, knowing full well that it was all about oil. It had been the same story for the last fifty years, although tensions were now even higher. As the liberals had warned all along, oil was becoming a more scarce commodity. The price per barrel had gone over $430 year 2000 dollars, so it was now really deserving of the name black gold. That price made alternate forms of energy all the more attractive, yet they could never replace the products obtained from petroleum. The world's economy was sitting on the edge of disaster.

He always felt frustrated that the toughest problems didn't seem to attract the smartest people. Alternate forms of energy were certainly one such problem. Terrorism was another. Unfortunately the two were related and equally confounding. He also believed that the Fulton administration didn't have any of the hard answers.

General Roberto Vargas had a reputation of being a tough but fair commander. He had grown up in Miami, survived a childhood in the slums, and ended up fifth in his class at West Point. Rumor was that he had hated the place, though the rumor was unfounded. His happiest years were those spent studying there. He had met the love of his life there, but Carl Holmes had died in the Middle East along with many others. Now he had a trophy wife and three kids and no one knew that he was a closet gay. It was also at West Point where he learned that some problems just don't seem to have solutions, like gays in the military. They were allowed now but you didn't reach the top echelons very often being gay.

"You could have just called me for that one, Pierce."

"I wanted to see your expression close up, not over a videocom system. You obviously don't know anything about it either."

"Maybe I'm just a good poker player."

Pierce smiled. He could end up liking the man. Pierce had heard that he was a model husband and father. That was important to the ex-priest. Families were the foundation of any civilized society, he believed.

"Maybe we should try that some time. I was pretty good at keeping a straight face with all kinds of outlandish confessions."

The general chuckled. Yeah, he knew how some of those confessions were in Little Havana. He picked up a phone.

"Lt. Franklin, could you check on something for me?" He outlined for his aide the information he would need to answer Pierce's question. He turned to Pierce. "She's good. It will take her ten minutes max. You're right, I don't know about such a program, and you've piqued my curiosity."

The aide came in after a short delay slightly longer than seven minutes. Lt. Franklin was a pert brunette about Pierce's height who made the dress military uniform look sexy. She also had a husky, sexy voice, one that could lend itself to late night porn calls. Pierce smiled at her and she smiled back. *It's good to not be a priest anymore. I can allow myself to have carnal desire.* But memories of the Daniela Romano scandal then made him frown, and they were not made more pleasant by Franklin's sly wink. Roberto watched the play of emotions across his face, trying to read them for his own benefit.

"There is no such program, General Vargas. Not in the Pentagon. It could be in one of the agencies, like NSA, CIA, FBI, DEA, or DHS."

"Do they have special access programs?" asked Roberto, surprised.

"Of course they do," said Pierce. "But neither of you have need-to-know." He winked at Roberto. "I'll call you soon to invite you to a poker game."

After bidding farewell by getting his hand almost crushed in the general's handshake, Pierce was walking in the hall outside the general's office, slowly, deep in thought. *Yes, all those agencies have at one time or another had special access programs. But this one is so buried that not even I can find about it. Now, where does that leave me? Is Peter Barkley smoking pot again?*

Scherzo Twenty-Nine

The ambulance pulled up to the emergency entrance of the hospital. The EMTs hurriedly lowered the gurney and ran it into the emergency ward.

"Elderly patient in coronary distress," one of them announced.

The doctor on call, an intern, quickly strode over to examine the patient. It was an elderly Jewish gentleman, clearly in pain, gripping his chest with both hands.

"His name is Solomon Weiss. One of his neighbors heard him crying out for help. He apparently lives alone."

The doctor bent over him, applying a stethoscope.

"Nurse, get the EKG machine. Now tell me, Mr. Weiss, exactly where is the pain?"

"In my chest, stupid," the man spit out. "No pills. I ran out of pills."

"What pills, Mr. Weiss?"

"My blood pressure medicine. I couldn't pay for the prescription this month. I had to eat. My medical plan, they don't pay."

"Why not?"

"The drug I need is not on their list. But my doctor prescribed it. I don't know why they don't pay."

"Who's your insurance company, Mr. Weiss?"

He told him.

"Well, that explains it. You don't have full medical."

"Of course I don't. Who can afford it?"

That was the last thing Mr. Weiss said.

"Fifth one this month," muttered the doctor.

"Poor bastard," said one of the EMTs.

"Yeah, well, we don't have full medical either," said the other. "Is that going to happen to us?"

The doctor looked at them both and shrugged. God, he hated this job.

Chapter Thirty-Five

Miami, Florida, Wednesday . . .

"I told you that I don't like to lose money."
Stephanie Williams tipped up her sunglasses and looked Vladimir Kalinin straight in the eye.
"You're a fool sometimes, do you know that? If you discredit John Fulton and his policies, you'll have an adverse effect on my electability."
"Maybe I could work better with one of your opponents." He looked across the pool to a striking brunette that reminded him of Daniela. He would have to see her again sometime. *It would be like starting fresh again with her, since she no longer remembers who I am.* "You have always misunderstood me, I think. I really want it all."
"No, you misunderstand me. I can bury you, Vladimir. I know about all your little pet projects, your crooked deals. I have enough evidence on you to get you the death penalty in thirty-one states. Don't fuck with me, you bastard. You'll lose."
"I'd much rather fuck you, though I'd probably wear you out, old woman." He waved expansively at the Miami skyline, ignoring her frown. "Your priorities are all wrong. You, and hundreds of politicians like you, think it's all about power. It's not about that at all. It's not about money either. You have no idea what really motivates me."
"So why the emphasis on power and money? Why don't you go to Tibet and become a Buddhist monk?"
"Well, first of all, all religions are bunk. Oh, yeah, some people get buoyed up by their beliefs in some intelligent super being. Or Nirvana. Or whatever. The problem with all religions is that they try to create a morality in human beings that just isn't there. We're just sophisticated social apes, looking out for number one. There is no morality beyond the simple realization that what is,

is. Certainly no afterlife, no reincarnation. That's what I'm really interested in. I want immortality. I like my life." He pointed a finger between his eyes. "I've come to terms with this person in here. I know his needs."

"You're scary."

"So are you. Considering the circumstances, I'd say we both want the same thing. Years ago you may have been in every garage in America as a pin-up, Stephanie, but you've got a brain. Just think about it and you'll know I'm right."

"Well, I still think you're a fool. Setting up this scandal will cost you plenty when the FBI finds out that you were the mastermind behind it."

"On the contrary, it gives me good reason to kill myself."

"What? Are you crazy?"

"Like a fox. You see, it's time for Vladimir Kalinin to die. I'm tired of him anyway. A little plastic surgery and spare body parts when I need them will allow me to become my own successor in all my enterprises. Yes, very soon Vladimir Kalinin will be no more."

"That's absurd. I don't know what you gain by that."

"You're just miffed because you didn't think of it. You'll have to remain Stephanie Williams if you become president. You also run the risk of burning yourself out in the job. The fact that you're a bitch doesn't mean the job won't be stressful. It's going to put a lot of strain on that old body of yours. Look at Fulton. He's aged tremendously over the eight years he's been in office. It comes with the job."

"Perhaps you aren't a fool. I had no idea that was what you were planning. Why tell me?"

"Because we work so well together." He took her hand. "No, it's really because I need somebody who will admire the genius of the idea. Someone who wouldn't dare say anything about it to anyone else."

Stephanie looked down at the hand holding hers. It was a long time since she had felt desire. Interest in the male body, yes, but desire for the person beyond the hair and muscles and genitalia had been mostly gone from her life. Thus, with some amusement, she realized that she was mildly interested in Vladimir, the person.

In many ways they were alike. Cunning, ruthless, and sure of themselves. She had made him a member of her secret committee for the Center and then watched him become her equal, steering the research along lines that would be considered unethical, to say the least, but producing a more desirable product. Andrew Tyler had played a key role in that endeavor, taking everything further than Wolfgang Richter had ever imagined.

"You're right about my ability to keep a secret but wrong about being able to tire me out."

"Ah, a challenge. I'm willing to let you try to prove me wrong."

Stephanie gestured back towards the house.

"I need to slip into something comfortable. And maybe have a vodka and tonic. It could be a long night."

"We will see, we will see."

Chapter Thirty-Six

In the Virginia countryside, Wednesday . . .

Andrew Tyler's hand was shaking as he closed the suitcase.

The last few weeks had not been good for him. First, there had been the escape. He actually smiled to think about how FS2, HJ1, and SW1 had outsmarted them all. Especially SW1. Tyler had known she was trouble from the age of two. *Ah, the terrible twos.*

Then, one of the Guardians had reported that at least one of his children that knew a lot about computers had deftly spliced in an image file to a videocam surveillance record. Since the videocam watched over one of the main labs, Tyler concluded that at least one of his children had been in that lab. He was sure he, she, or they hadn't found anything, yet it was troublesome to him because it meant that they were questioning. It wasn't just the three rebel children, who were now dead.

He called them his children and had genuine affection for them. He had been the primary one responsible for bringing them into the world. Sure, it was Wolfgang's theories and vision at the beginning, but it had been Andrew's hard work. He knew their terrible purpose. He rationalized it away in the same way that people rationalized away buying live Christmas trees: the trees are bred to be cut down. *Or, more like minks that are bred to make fur coats. Have I become such a beast that I have no conscience? I didn't even get rich off the project. Not like Wolfgang, anyway.*

Andrew thought about the other news he had received over the last few weeks, the news about Wolfgang's murder. He had a pounding headache now. Wolfgang had died terribly, violently. Andrew turned a little green as his imagination began to get the best of him.

He shrugged and picked up the suitcase. Dulles was only a few miles away. His ticket to Asuncion was already in his new name. A lot of money had been spent on getting that new name. He was almost certain that the DHS had no idea about what he was planning. They thought he was dedicated to his work. Especially the new line, the line the Committee was really focused on, the line that was his alone, not Richter's.

And he had been dedicated. *But the guilt kept growing as the kids grew up. God help them.* He knew it was only a matter of time before the Committee would decide the brainless homonoids were mature enough that they could get rid of his children. He didn't want to be around when that happened.

Not far away, in the J. Edgar Hoover building, Jake Hanlon listened to Asako and Simon's story with full attention. Both of their files were on his desk. He had studied them before they came in. They had the reputation of being competent people. Still, he found their story farfetched.

Jake had survived the bureaucratic wars of three previous administrations. They had left scars, so consequently he was uneasy with most Washington politicos. The FBI was such an easy target for Presidents, senators, and congressmen that were quick to put the blame on the agency for almost anything. Jake admitted within the walls of his DC office building that there were times when the FBI deserved the blame. Agents were human beings, caught up in the bureaucratic power struggle just like other government bureaucrats, so they could make mistakes when cold logic on a case was taken over by someone's agenda. He believed that his agency now had the mechanisms in place that kept that to a minimum, in spite of the politics that flowed down from the National Intelligence Director.

That post, nominally head of all intelligence services since the time when the second George Bush was President, had suffered ups and downs in the last fifty years, depending on how strong the National Security Advisor was. Pierce Hamilton, hated by some, loved by many, was definitely one that didn't give up power easily. He allowed the director control of the budget, since Pierce hated to get down into the weeds of financially managing fifteen different agencies. But Pierce also made his priorities clear, and neither Jake Hanlon, Ben Knowland, the DHS chief, Simon Multani's boss, nor anyone else cared to go up against him.

Jake always thought it was strange that an ex-priest like Pierce could wield the big stick so well. He admired the little runt in an abstract way. He also counted himself lucky that he had never crossed swords with him. He had almost felt sorry for him during the Daniela Romano scandal.

Jake was also Catholic by birth but not by practice. At the ripe age of thirteen he had suffered an epiphany when he concluded that God was, at best, too busy with the big picture to worry about whether any particular maggot on one particular planet circling a rather nondescript G-type star attended mass or not. With that he was bucking a long family tradition. *Grandpa Hanlon was a devout Catholic. He prayed every night for God to punish George Bush for his stupidity. Grandma Hanlon, on the other hand, believed that he should be canonized, even if he wasn't Catholic.* The fact that neither happened contributed a lot to Jake's epiphany.

"I'm having a little trouble with this story," Jake told Asako and Simon, "because I don't see a reason for these look-alikes. They're all too young to be enemy substitutes for the corresponding people in the Fulton administration. What's the agenda here, my friends? There's got to be one for this to make sense."

"I wish I knew, sir. My friends are working on it, so I'd like to request that you keep all this confidential."

"Don't worry about that," he said with a smile. "Until you give me something more to go on, I'm not talking to anyone about it. I'm not Fox Mulder, you know."

"Fox Mulder?" asked Simon.

"Sorry, that dates me. I used to watch old TV reruns when I was a kid. Some are quite good."

"I'm into old movies myself," said Simon. "But you already know that."

"Yes, I do. All right, you two. All I can say is, stay out of trouble. Someone did take a couple of shots at you, Simon, that we know. I'm not sure the FBI was the right place for you to come, but you're here. As for Asako, I take care of my agents, field agents or otherwise. You both do good work. Keep on doing it. But be careful."

Asako nodded and thanked the director. She hadn't expected too much out of the interview. It was Simon who had insisted on it. The director was right. They needed more proof. They needed to know what the agenda was.

Asako had parked her car in the parking garage. As they left, neither Simon nor she noticed as a black car started following them. This one had diplomatic plates. There were many like it around DC. The driver of this one, though, happened to be Curt Forrester. It was actually easy for him to tail them. Back in Alexandria, Curt had placed a GPS locator in the rear tire well. Not only could he follow their car, he could watch it on video, as a satellite high above, owned by the DHS, optically tracked the moving vehicle.

All the time Curt was wondering what the FBI gal and CIA pal had talked to Jake Hanlon about. *Shit, I'll be glad when Stephanie becomes President and we get rid of bastards like Ben Knowland and Jake Hanlon. They just get in the way of making any real progress.*

Ben Knowland, the Secretary of Homeland Security, was, in fact, the last one on Pierce Hamilton's list, as he made the rounds checking out Peter Barkley's story. He didn't fully understand why he was being so tenacious about it. He was playing a hunch, and like a lot of people in his business, or similar ones, it was good to play a hunch for a while, as they often represented some subconscious problem solving process that defied formal logic, the uncanny ability of the neural network in a man's brain to come up with ideas and solutions from very sparse data sets. He was doing no more than what a good homicide cop might do. He was, in a sense, the top cop of the country.

Unfortunately Ben Knowland knew nothing about a special access program using a NASA starship as a cover story. He promised to check into it.

Scherzo Thirty

The troops fanned out into the poor neighborhood, warily looking for hostiles.

"Get ready to call the air cover," Lt. Yuri Gorbov told his com man. Lt. Gorbov had been born in Moscow. The Russian had a good reputation for knowing how to fight in urban warfare. Still, the streets of Rawalpindi were just as new to him as the rest of his UN comrades.

"We shouldn't need it, sir," said Pvt. Mark Bellamy, US Army signal corps expert. "Things look quiet."

"That's because they want to take us off guard," said Yuri. "You must learn to have eyes in the back of your head. You see, there."

A shadowy form dashed along the side of a house several hundreds of meters down the street and blended in with the nocturnal shadows again.

"Constantine, take your men and move them to—" he looked at Mark's computer. He read out the longitude and latitude. "Be prepared for hostiles. Colm, take yours to the square. Your group and mine will move towards Constantine." Yuri looked at his men. "Let's move out. Weapons ready."

They moved silently on, their black smeared faces and camouflage uniforms making them appear like ghosts in the twilight.

Constantine's group was fired upon first. The battle did not last long, as the Pakistani insurgents were not well equipped. Nevertheless, seven UN peacekeepers died and four more were wounded. Forty-seven insurgents died. The insurgent survivors took their wounded with them, so the count of wounded insurgents was unknown.

Yuri clasped Mark's hand as the medics carried him to the Red Crescent truck that would take him to the field hospital twenty miles away.

"You'll be fine, Private," said Yuri.

"Yeah, I guess I'll be on the lines again soon. Take care, Lt."

"You, too."

He watched silently as the truck doors closed.

"Bet right now he's wondering why the hell we do this," said Colm, one of the Irish soldiers. He had been watching the interchange between his commander and the signal specialist.

"Probably. Why do you do it, Colm?"

"It's what I do. It's just a job."

"Yeah, and Mark knows that so well that he may not even think about it anymore." Yuri punched Colm good-heartedly on the shoulder. "I wonder if they have any vodka in this shit hole."

Chapter Thirty-Seven

Lexington Park, Maryland, Wednesday . . .

Pages and pages of information were flying across the screen as Bouncer directed the computer with skill. In addition to his usual wires, he also wore a headset, the earphones catching bits and pieces of audio output that had no corresponding video. His subvocal instructions expertly directed the search for data, unheard by Jay. Finally he turned to her.

"I've got nothing connecting Williams, Sweeney, and Johnson to Richter. Kalidas is right—Richter was heavily involved in the cloning business, although everything recent must be classified. I'm not quite good enough to hack into government systems. Besides, they're all on their own intranets—no connection to the outside world."

"Not even a partial connection? Johnson and Richter, for example?"

"Nope. There is one thing, though. Kalidas' old company and Richter were connected."

"Dalton Biomedicine? How so?"

"I don't exactly know what he did for them. He was a consultant." He flashed several pages of text on the screen. "There's a steady payout to him over a period of fifteen years."

"What are the dates?"

"From about sixteen years ago to the present, that is, three weeks ago. Just a minute." Bouncer made a quick calculation. "It's a considerable sum. On a year by year basis, I'd bet it was a lot more than he made as a professor at Stanford, and he probably was not making peanuts there, since he was a full professor."

Jay thought a moment.

"The money goes out from Dalton to Richter. Does the money originate in Dalton? Or does it come from another source?"

"There's no way I can get that info. You're thinking someone was using Dalton just to hide the money transfer? Like a terrorist organization?"

"Or something. Let me call Kalidas."

She took out her list of random numbers. Calling from Dolores' house would not make it as secure on one end but at least she was halfway protected.

Kalidas picked up immediately. Jay passed on what they discovered.

"Tell Bouncer he's a doll," said Kalidas. "I know someone in finance at Dalton. They may be able to find out if someone was passing money through the company to Richter. Give me a few minutes."

It took half an hour. When she rang back, Kalidas' expression was clearly one of excitement.

"US Treasury Department checks, and I don't think they were tax refunds," she said. "The government was using Dalton to pass money directly to Richter, over and beyond what he was getting from his scientific funding. Now, why do you suppose they were doing that?"

"Because he was working on something he shouldn't work on?" suggested Bouncer.

"Or possibly he was blackmailing some government agency as a price for keeping quiet?" suggested Jay.

"Well, I think they were cloning human beings," said Kalidas. "I still don't understand why. And I don't understand why the DHS is persecuting me. I'll have to admit that my research was at least twenty years behind Richter's. That doesn't make me feel good, though that's the way it is. I came in the back door, so to speak, by attacking the transplant rejection problem."

Jay looked at Bouncer, her expression slowly growing to a smile.

"That's a new route to check," she said. "Hang up, Kalidas. I'll get back to you when I have something concrete. It might take a while."

"Don't keep me waiting."

"What's going on?" asked Bouncer. At that moment, Dolores appeared in the doorway.

"Any luck?" she asked.

"I think your friend just had an epiphany," said Bouncer. "Come on, Jay. Give."

"Just humor me for a moment. I want you to hack into hospital records. Can you determine the surgical histories of Williams, Johnson, and Sweeney?"

"That's not an easy task," said Bouncer. "Medical records are all in electronic databases now, although they're pretty secure, for privacy reasons. You usually need some kind of e-certificate or something at least. Even if I can do it, it will take me a while."

"Let me help," said Dolores. "What's the time frame?"

"Digamos, mijita, the last twenty years."

"Before we do all this work, why don't you tell us your idea first, so we can tell you if you're crazy or not?" said Bouncer.

"Loca como una zorra," said Dolores, with a wink at Jay. "But I agree. What's in that crazy head of yours?" She put her legs up on an empty chair. The prosthetic got heavy at times. "It might help us look, too." She scratched Henry, her golden retriever, behind an ear. His tail struck up a drumbeat on the hardwood floor.

"Okay, but now that I'm going to tell you, I have second thoughts. It sounds stupid."

"Go ahead," said Bouncer. "We're among friends."

"Well, here it is: Suppose the clones just represent replacement parts?"

"You mean, like for transplants?" asked Dolores.

"Si, senora. Transplant rejection would be minimized if the donor is your genetically identical twin."

"Kalidas' solution to the transplant problem wasn't that," said Bouncer.

"Kalidas' solution to the transplant problem could lead the way to human cloning without an egg. She recognized that. Richter probably went there directly, without realizing he also had a solution for the transplant problem. It works both ways. Yet he didn't need a solution because he already had one, namely the one I just conjectured."

"It's possible," mused Bouncer.

"I'm not sure I follow you," said Dolores. "Are we to look for transplant surgeries performed on Williams, Johnson, and Sweeney then?"

"I doubt they will be that obvious. Look for stays in government hospitals for studies, etc. These people would want to keep the details from the press."

It took them three days. When they finished, they tried to call Kalidas and Chris to discuss the conjecture and the evidence. It was damning, at least in Jay and Bouncer's opinion. Dolores was still not convinced.

Neither of their friends from up north was available, though, and Jay didn't want to leave a message.

So they went over the evidence again. Williams had been in Bethesda three times for over a week for different studies that were performed on her. Sweeney had been in Walter Reed twice. And Johnson had been under study in Johns Hopkins, the study made under the supervision of a Bethesda doctor. These were in the open press. The medical records were something else, although the very first day Bouncer was able to break into Johnson's Bethesda doctor's private practice records and determine that just before the Johns Hopkins "study" Johnson had been diagnosed with acute cirrhosis of the liver. The Walter Reed computers were secure but the NIH computers were defeated. All three of Williams' stays were for DVTs, commonly a blood clot in the leg. No one thought it was very likely that she had had three DVTs.

Nevertheless, Jay's idea was only a conjecture, the hypothesis of a secret government project for a privileged few.

"If it's true," said Dolores, "who are they? Who's involved in this? I want to know. They're all directly or indirectly responsible for killing my husband."

Further north, from his Virginia office in the Sheila Remington Building, Ben Knowland picked up the secure phone and dialed Pierce Hamilton. He waited until the digital encoding settled down and Pierce's face stabilized on the screen.

"Pierce, I think we have a problem."

Scherzo Thirty-One

Brenda Santorino turned the page in her law text and read some more.

"Given that the plaintiff signed of his own free will the contract with his health maintenance organization and as such is subject to the conditions listed therein, this Court finds that the lawsuit against the health maintenance organization is frivolous and should be thrown out. Even though the medical treatment was prescribed by the plaintiff's physician, the health maintenance organization's policy did not cover that treatment, as it was not a full medical policy."

Hmm, thought Brenda. *The plaintiff didn't have to worry about the adverse finding. He was already dead.*

Chapter Thirty-Eight

Boston, Massachusetts, Friday . . .

Denise Rivera looked around the office that Friday afternoon.
"Where's Chris?" she asked Harry Carson.
"I haven't seen him, Captain. He's usually early."
Denise thought a moment. She had given Chris the OK to keep the John Doe case on the back burner, primarily on her sister's urging. Frank Sweeney was clearly an SOB who treated his wife horribly, yet Denise couldn't imagine him doing anything crooked. However, sister Patricia knew the guy well, so that was that. It also kept Chris happy and motivated enough to do his other work. *Let's face it. This job is usually pretty boring.*

She returned to her office. On a whim, she dialed Chris' home phone. *If you're sleeping off a binge, I'll be very upset.*

The phone rang and rang. *Funny, no video-mail. Either he's sleeping and won't answer, or he left without turning on the video-mail feature.* She hung up and dialed Marcia King.

"Marcia, dispatch a black and white to Chris' apartment. Something a little strange is going on."

A half hour later the black and white reported back. The patrolman was clearly agitated.

"Denise, something's really wrong here. It looks like the whole side of the apartment facing the stairs was used for target practice. The door's busted open, like with a ram."

"Any sign of Tanner?"

"Tanner isn't here but there's a fair amount of blood on the floor. The back window is wide open and the fire escape is down. Maybe he got out that way. What's going on? This looks like a mob or gang hit."

"Maybe that's what they want us to think," said Denise.

"Excuse me?"

"Just stay there. I'll send forensics over. Have them do a full workup and especially check to see if the blood is Tanner's. I'm also sending some backup, just in case anyone comes back looking for him."

At that moment Chris Tanner was crossing over the Tappan Zee Bridge from New York into New Jersey. He had been very glad to see the old bridge come into view around the bend of 287. Unfortunately he had to switch on the autopilot, as it was required going across the bridge. The system was used here more to keep cars in the same lane going over the bridge. The car communicated with small transmit/receive modules buried into the bridge's surface. It was a little like threading a needle at high speed as the car sped over the bridge at 100 kilometers per hour. Thus the autopilot was only on for a very short period of time. He hoped the NSA wouldn't pick him up that quickly.

For the second time that month he had a tourniquet around his leg. He loosened and tightened it periodically as he drove. He knew he was in danger of losing the leg if he didn't get some medical attention soon.

Normally it was a three hour drive from Boston to upstate New Jersey but he didn't know what else to do. After the attack, he had fled Boston. He was sure that his attackers were somehow associated with the Sweeney look-alike case, yet maybe he was just paranoid. Like a lot of cops, he had many enemies. Right now he felt he needed help from a person that had been very understanding so far.

Unfortunately Kalidas was not at home. He sat down on the steps to her townhouse in Upper Montclair to think. Ten minutes later he was still sitting there when she showed up.

"Chris, what the hell are you doing here?" Then she saw the blood stain on his pants just above the right knee and the belt tightened around his leg above it. "My god, have you been shot?"

"'Fraid so. With all the bullets flying, it's amazing only one hit me. Aren't you going to ask me in?"

"More than that. Go right to the kitchen and lie down on the table. I'm going to operate."

"You're not a surgeon," he objected. "I thought you might know one."

"I'm a medical doctor as well as a PhD. My medical training was years ago, so I'm a little rusty but I'll remember enough to patch you up. Unless the bullet's still in there."

"It's not. Went straight through. You sure you can do this?"

"Shit, I have to. You of all people should know that every gun shot wound treated by a regular doctor has to be reported. If it's the feds, they'd know within minutes where you are and come pick you up. By the way, you didn't use your car's autopilot feature on the way down, did you?"

"Only on the bridge. It's required, you know. I turned it off on the Jersey side."

"It's not Jersey for a while, you dumb shit. But good man. Let's hope they can't trace you crossing the bridge, then. Let's get cracking. I have to fix you up, and then we're moving out of here fast."

Kalidas did quite an acceptable job suturing the wound with dental floss and a large needle she had for darning. She first gave Chris a good slug of whiskey and then had him bite down on a wet dish towel. She liberally doused the wound with whiskey as she sewed him up.

"Just like the old westerns, huh?" he asked. "I'll smell like a drunk."

"Well, if a cop stops us, we're probably goners anyway, and not just for DWI. Except in your own precinct, they probably have every cop in the Northeast on the lookout for you and your car. Which is why we're taking mine. Let's go."

"Can I put my pants back on?"

"Well, they're pretty shot, if you'll pardon the pun. Wait a minute." She dashed off down the hall, leaving him sitting on the kitchen table. In a moment she was back, tossing him some unisex jeans that she had hoped to get back into someday. "Might be a little big around the waist and too long in the legs but use your belt and roll up the cuffs. They were once just right for me."

"Thank the Lord they have the zipper in the front."

"Yeah, just don't get you-know-what caught in it. I'm not that good of a surgeon and some people think I hate men."

Chris was about to ask what the hell she meant by that but she was already busy throwing food supplies and water bottles into a knapsack. He quickly put on the pants and then they were out the door.

Five minutes after they left a black sedan screamed to a stop in front of Kalidas' townhouse. Kalidas and Chris were already on their way south to find Jay Sandoval.

Scherzo Thirty-Two

Yassouf lowered the rifle. His target had been a small girl. He shook his head, thanking Allah that he had not pulled the trigger.

"What are you doing here?" he asked her. She was silhouetted in the doorway of the hovel. She obviously had been watching him as he rummaged, looking for food, guns, or ammo.

"I live here. What's your name? Why are you here?"

"My name is Yassouf. I'm a member of the Liberation Forces."

"You are the ones who killed my two brothers, father and mother, and aunt and uncle. Why did you kill them?"

"Well, it wasn't me. I just have this rifle, and right now it's out of ammo. I don't suppose you have any here."

"No, not even food."

"Where can I find ammo?"

"Maybe in the police station. If you haven't blown it up."

"Not even old bread here? I'm very hungry."

"So am I. If I had anything here, I would have eaten it. You've taken almost all the food here in the village."

"Again, it wasn't me."

"But you're one of them. And you're here. I could blame the Americans but you people did it. It could just as well be them, of course. You people are always fighting and ordinary people are caught in the middle."

"You're a smart little girl. How old are you?"

"Nine, but it's none of your business."

Just then Yassouf heard the high-pitched whine of the UN fighter coming in for a strafing run.

"Get out of the doorway!" he yelled.

It was too late. The rapid fire of the fighter ripped through the walls and the little girl. Yassouf, further inside, ended up with only a few scratches from flying glass. He went to her and held her hand as she died.

"Will I be in paradise?" she asked.

"I don't know. Still, it will be a better place than here, I'm sure."

When she was gone, he picked her up and put her on the single small bed in the one-room hovel. He closed her eyes, turned, and walked out into the moonlight, tears streaming down his cheeks. He was only fifteen but he had seen a lot of death already. He wondered when his time would come.

Chapter Thirty-Nine

Lexington Park, Maryland, Friday & Saturday . . .

Jay, Dolores, Bouncer, and Sandra were sitting on Dolores' front porch when Sheriff Sam Fletcher drove up. He gestured for Jay to come to his car. She leaned in the open window and he pointed to the onboard computer screen.

"Oh, Dios mio!" she exclaimed. It was a DHS APB on Chris Tanner and Kalidas Metropolis: Wanted for Terrorist Acts. "You don't believe that, do you?" The others crowded around the car.

"I don't know what to believe. I do have a suggestion, though, as a friend, not as the sheriff. I would find a nice hideout somewhere for awhile. Until this boils over. Now, let me roll the window back up. I'm losing my air-conditioning." He took off.

"What are we going to do?" asked Dolores. She looked pale. Bouncer and Sandra both shook their heads incredulously.

"Well, I've got to try and contact Asako, for one thing. Maybe she can help us at the FBI."

"Excuse me," said Sandra, "but aren't they part of the problem?" She had gripped Bouncer's arm so tight that Jay could see red blotches starting to appear, though the gentle giant seemed not to notice it.

"Well, we don't know that. And Asako certainly isn't. My other suggestion is that we each take hard copies of the stuff we found and split up. Go to a hideout like Sam said, but let's not say where, so they can't get it out of us. Bouncer, you go with Sandra, and Dolores and I will split up. That makes it three-way."

"What about Chris and Kalidas?" asked Bouncer. "How can we help them?" He had never met the detective or the scientist, yet they seemed like good people. As much as he talked about conspiracy theories, this seemed unreal to him.

"Well, they'll just have to fend for themselves for now. They don't have this evidence anyway. I never was able to contact them."

"It's not much evidence," observed Sandra, looking doubtful. "It's basically circumstantial, a good working hypothesis for now. I'm not sure I should risk my job for it."

"Come on, Sandra," said Bouncer. "You see what's happening to Chris and Kalidas. Not to mention four deaths here—no five, if you count our John Doe. I'd like to be able to grow old with you, baby."

"Is that a proposal?" Sandra asked, suddenly cheering up a little, but tightening her grip on his arm even more.

"Take it as an installment on a more formal one, if we get through this, that is."

"When, not if," said Dolores. "I'm going to see John's killers brought to justice. And you're all going to help me."

They were all in agreement on that. They went inside and made the hard copies. Then they left the house, going in three different directions.

Jay's route took her north, up old 235, then 24, then 2, closing in on Annapolis. Part of 2 was autopilot equipped but she wasn't on that stretch long, so she didn't even turn it on. Before she hit Londontown, she turned off the thruway onto a dusty old country lane that had seen better years.

GeeBee's family's country house, as he called it, was really run down. They had partied there one Fourth of July, and she definitely remembered how to find it. It belonged to GeeBee and his sister now, and she lived in Wisconsin. The garage was unattached and filled with cobwebs but she hid her car there anyway, cursing the spiders. In the tool shed in the back of the garage there was a loose board on the floor which hid the house key.

The house is filthy. But I have plenty of time. Might as well practice my nesting skills.

After many hours of hard labor, Jay managed to get part of the house in order. She felt she could now use the bathroom without worrying about disease. There had actually been clean sheets to put on the bed, although they were stale smelling and the colors faded. The kitchen was clean enough to eat in if she had any food. Dolores' early dinner had been substantial but she needed some items for tomorrow.

She remembered a convenience store she had passed on the way to the house. Since she didn't want to chance having her car spotted, she walked. It was pleasant, since the day had started to cool down. The forest alongside the dusty road was alive with the sounds of twilight. Several times she heard a rustle in the bushes as some creature spotted her and left the scene, rather than face the planet's most fearsome predator. She was only slightly perspiring as she entered the convenience store.

"A nice night for a walk," said the old geezer at the counter. He watched her with lusty eyes as she moved quickly through the aisles, filling up a cart with what she thought would make up two bags of groceries. As she bent to pick up a can of chili, she saw the old man out of the corner of her eye admiring her butt.

"You're a little old for undressing women with your eyes," she said with a wink as she put her goods on the counter.

"An old fart can still dream," said the old geezer. "Not too many good-looking women go through here, you know." He rang up the purchases. "That'll be $47.83, miss."

She rummaged in her purse, looking for cash, but found she didn't have enough. She gave him her bank card. He swiped it, and handed it back.

"I think you must be one of GeeBee's friends," said the old man.

"Why would you say that?"

"'Cause all the others living up the lane there are older than me. GeeBee comes through here every so often, usually with a different girl each time. You should stay away from him. I think he's only into one night stands."

"Well, that gives your eyes some variety. Anyway, I'm just using his house. It's a quiet place to write. I'm just a friend, you know."

"That's what a lot of them say. Wish I had those kinds of friends. Take care, and say hi to GeeBee."

She left with a smile. *So GeeBee is a Don Juan.*

By the time she got back, it was late. The walk had been tiring on the way back, carrying the two bags of groceries. Bugs were swarming all around now in the heat of the summer night. She was rather amused as a dragonfly droned along with her for awhile, keeping pace during the walk. It was so well built that she didn't notice it was mechanical and that its eyes were camera lenses, technology that was forty years old already, financed originally by DARPA and used extensively by the DHS in its fight against terrorism.

When she got back to GeeBee's, she stashed the groceries away. She stripped, washed out her underwear and tee shirt, and then took a quick shower. Finally she crawled into bed and was soon asleep, oblivious to the stale odor of the sheets.

The dragonfly still circled around the house.

The next morning the Marines arrived.

Scherzo Thirty-Three

The riots in Detroit that summer were the worst in the city's history. Street battles between secessionists and the National Guard were frequent and violent. Anarchists moved in from the Canadian side and militia moved down from the Upper Peninsula. For many days it was not clear who was fighting whom.

Things were just beginning to calm down when similar riots broke out in Miami. There the heat and humidity made tempers shorter and the fires burn brighter.

A new dimension to the riots was soon added. Bonfires were being created using national ID cards and medical insurance cards as fuel. The firemen, attending to many other fires, did not bother to put those out. Some even added their cards to the fire.

The news was beamed around the world. Many people just nodded sagely upon seeing it, since similar riots had already occurred in other countries. There was world unrest, and it finally had spread to the US.

A tired President Fulton appeared on the newsnets, pleading for calm.

"My fellow Americans, this is not the time to fight among ourselves. We must preserve our nation. We cannot allow the disease of regional and ethnic hatreds and breakdown in civil discourse that has spread across our planet to become endemic in our own beautiful country. To prevent precisely this and to ensure public safety, I have established martial law in both Detroit and Miami and both these cities now have a 10 pm curfew. Please, those who are rioting in the streets of these cities, return to your homes. Maintain calm. And keep your sons and daughters at home too. Order must be restored. Order will be restored."

The National Guard was deployed in Detroit for seven months and in Miami for five. They were the longest periods of martial law in the nation's history. More were to follow.

Chapter Forty

Washington, DC, Friday & Saturday . . .

"She's not here."
Chris looked at Kalidas through the fog of the pain.
"We've got the right address?"
"Of course. The landlady says she went to Lexington Park. I think I heard Dolores in the background when I talked to her a few days ago."
"Yeah, you said something on the ride down that she was working on a theory. Did she tell you the theory?"
"She seemed to react strangely when I said that I came in through the back door to Wolfgang Richter's research."
"And what did you mean by that? Or did you already say?"
"You're badly in need of rest, Chris. Yeah, shit, I did say. I told her I had been working on transplant rejection."
"I don't know why that would cause a reaction."
"Damned if I know either. Unless . . . ." She seemed lost in thought.
Chris' new friend at times seemed to live on another planet. He supposed all scientists were like that. Even old Ka Wah Fong, more of a practical type than a research type, often seemed to have his head in the clouds.
Chris' was starting to feel an emotional bond to Kalidas, though. In spite of cultural differences, she reminded him in many ways of his mother, a gentle, caring woman who had been trapped in a bad marriage. On the other hand, he could well imagine her thirty years ago as a stunning beauty, someone that turned quite a few eyes in the hallowed halls of science. *Too bad I didn't know her then.*
"Come on, give," he finally said. "What are you thinking? I'm just a stupid cop. You're not going to suggest that they're using the clones to harvest transplants for the people cloned, are you?"

210

She smiled and gave him a peck on the cheek.

"There, you're not such a dumb cop. That's exactly what I was thinking. I know it sounds paranoid and melodramatic but your wounded leg says we have a right to be paranoid. Come to think of it, it's only paranoia if it's not true." He managed a smile at that, so she knew that he was not completely out of it. "Since I came in from the back door, so to speak, I considered the cloning a corollary to the solution of the transplant rejection problem. Wolfgang wouldn't think that way at all. He would consider cloning itself to be the solution to the transplant rejection problem."

"That's far out," mumbled Chris.

"Oh, I know that he had his head far enough up his ass that he wouldn't see my solution at all. In that sense, I was lightyears ahead of him. He didn't try to find a better solution."

"You really buy into this theory, then?" The cop looked doubtful but the throbbing in his leg was demanding some sort of explanation. He didn't believe in random violence, at least not when the whole front of his apartment was sprayed with bullets. It was time to develop some theories.

"To buy or not to buy is not the question. I'm pretty sure it's what Jay came up with too. She's a wily one."

"But if it's true, there is a conspiracy. It's not just our paranoia. Many people may be involved."

"Many powerful people, and we know that among them are Frank Sweeney, Hank Johnson, and Stephanie Williams." She saw Chris nodding off. "Come on, lover boy, we're going to find a place to stay. We can look for Jay and the others tomorrow." She got into her car. "Actually, come to think of it, maybe it's better that we're split up."

"How's that?"

"Go to sleep. I'll find us a place."

They found a Comfort Inn in Vienna that was mostly a place where truck drivers stopped. Without reservations, it was not easy to find lodging in the DC area.

As a precaution, Kalidas surreptitiously removed the license plates and parked the car several spaces down from the entrance to their room. She used no flashlight in the dimly lit parking lot, gouging her fingers several times with the screwdriver. It didn't matter—the satellite image coming into the DHS was still clear.

"How did you explain this to the check-in clerk?" Chris asked when she got back inside.

"I just said that I hoped the young gentleman with me was worth the money."

He laughed. In spite of the seriousness of their situation, this woman could make a joke.

"Well, I don't have any energy, but I'm all yours."

"Just lie down on the bed. I'll get your shoes and pants off."

He was already half asleep when he heard her get into the shower. The room was hot in spite of the old air conditioning. Apparently the management knew this and provided a whisperfan that helped some. He was so tired he didn't care about the heat. He realized just before he passed out that he didn't really know if Kalidas had been kidding or not.

The next thing he knew light was streaming through the window. Kalidas sat down on the edge of the bed, offering coffee, donuts, and muffins.

"It will have to do for now. I don't think we should stay in one place too long. How's the leg?"

"Much better. I'll never play softball again, but I wasn't much good at it anyway. My boxing probably won't suffer much. I never did have fancy footwork."

"Well, as long as you can still make love to me, I'll be—" She stopped in mid-sentence as he put a finger to his lips. "What is it?" she whispered.

"Someone's trying the door. Get into the bathroom."

Chris took out his gun and stepped into the far corner of the room, to the left of the door, as Kalidas moved silently into the bathroom. Then all hell broke loose as the door and the entire wall was hammered by high power rounds. *Déjà vu. Just like in Boston. At least they're consistent.*

Then there came another salvo and he was hit. *Somewhere in the chest. This is it, Detective Tanner. Old tomcat, your nine lives are up.* He blacked out with the pain, crumpling to the floor.

Chris slowly regained consciousness enough to hear Kalidas' voice.

"You can't get away with this," she said. "We've talked to too many people."

Mary Beth Grogan, the DHS agent, waved the automatic menacingly. She was apparently alone.

"None of you could leave well enough alone. You had to keep picking, picking at the scab, until the blood started to flow again. I had it all cleaned up but then all of you started to meddle."

"Because you made mistakes. Why did you leave the clone's body in that Lexington Park trash bin? Why did you kill that one in Boston with ricin? You could have made them both disappear. And why go to all the trouble of preparing a fake interrogation report for the Philippine clone?"

"To answer your first question, we had some cleanup to do first. The trash bin was a temporary storage place. Who would know that Bob Martin would be there looking for a meal? As to the second clone, he was exposed to ricin in his escape from the Center. Neither he nor we knew it until after your dead friend over there nearly got killed by the clone. Finally, the clone in the Philippines was caught by the Filipino army and turned over to the CIA. If we had caught her first, there would have been no problem."

"From your answers, it looks like you had a clone breakout. From where? You call it the Center? Is it at the DHS in Falls Church? How many more are there?"

"I don't have to answer any of that. If you're so smart, tell me, what do you think we're using the clones for?"

"Well, right now, I'm certain that it's not a terrorism plot to replace or kill some of our leaders. Given the ages of the clones, they're probably not useful as doubles for them anyway. My guess is that they're walking factories of body parts destined to replace the aging ones in those leaders."

"You're good, Kalidas." Mary Beth lowered the gun ever so slightly. She was clearly impressed. "Come to work for us."

"I'd rather die first."

"I can arrange that." The gun came up again.

Kalidas stood straight. *I think I still have some good years left but would I want to live them with these people in power in this country? Jose, we'll soon be together. I hope it's better where you are.* Tears swelled in her eyes as she thought of her dead lover. *At least she didn't die violently.*

Mary Beth had been so concentrated on the discussion with Kalidas that she didn't see Chris come to his knees, pick up the whisperfan, and hurl it at her. It hit her just as she fired, making the shot go wild. Kalidas lunged at her and they wrestled for the gun. The agent was much more agile and stronger but Kalidas was heavier. There was a muffled 'pfft' as the gun went off again.

Kalidas watched as first surprise, then pain, came into Mary Beth's eyes. Then she was dead. Stunned, Kalidas noted, with the medical detachment of a coroner, that the shot had entered the right side of her jaw and come out the top left side of her head.

After helping her up, Chris touched Kalidas gently on the shoulder.

"Are you all right?"

Kalidas looked at him, sudden raw emotion ripping away the medical detachment, bringing tears to her eyes. She threw her arms around him and sobbed.

"This is horrible! I never killed anyone before."

"You didn't kill her, Kalidas. She killed herself. She pulled the trigger. Now, you've got to do me a favor."

"What's that?" She let her arms fall and backed away, seeing the pain in his face.

"Get me to a real doctor. I think this one's beyond your skills."

Scherzo Thirty-Four

Dr. Barbara Summers smiled at her patient.

"I'll take care of you until Dr. Kleinert takes over, Sonya. I just won't deliver your baby."

"What happens if you lose the case?"

"I try not to think about that. I guess I'll quit medicine."

"I just don't see how an HMO can sue a doctor. It seems absurd. You work for them in some sense, don't you?"

"That's the problem. I went to that poor woman's home and delivered her baby. Even though I didn't charge, I'm the HMO employee, so I was giving away services that they could rightfully consider should profit them. It's sort of like an employee in a computer firm signing away his rights to any software developed while working there, even though he develops the software outside of work. At least, the court is likely to see it that way."

"Is this ever going to stop?"

"I don't know. But you'll like Dr. Kleinert, Sonya. Don't worry."

Chapter Forty-One

Washington, DC, Saturday . . .

Jake Hanlon tossed some hardcopy onto Pierce Hamilton's desk.
"This is our final on the Daniela Romano scandal. For your eyes only. I don't think you want this in the press. They already had enough to get them off your back. This is just FYI."
"How is she?"
Hanlon studied the man before him for a moment. *Just like an ex-priest. More worried about saving the criminal's soul than protecting his own well-being. It's still a knee-jerk reaction with you, Pierce, even though you're mostly one hell of a politician.* The FBI director had known this man for years and still found him to be a mystery, perhaps because his own faith had disappeared so many years ago.
"She's still denying it was a setup. We even gave her a lie detector test. I don't know how it was done, but she actually believes she was your mistress. We really have nothing to charge her with."
"Is she a nut case?"
"I don't think so. Somehow she got programmed. It's been done before. And the Russians were the best at it."
"What's that mean?"
Jake gestured to the file. "It's all in there. At some of the places shown in the press photos, eyewitnesses identified the man that was with the Romano woman, the one who served as the hanger frame for adding your digitized image. His name is Vladimir Kalinin."
"I've heard of him. He's the CEO of one of the major drug companies. He's an international VIP. Even contributed to Fulton's campaign. You're saying that he set this up? What's the motivation?"

"Our people have concluded it was his way of going after the President. I hope that doesn't mess with your ego but that's the way we see it. A lot of Kalinin's enterprises stand to lose money because of John Fulton's policies."

"The whole thing sounds illegal."

"It is, at least in this country. We have a warrant out for his arrest, to Interpol."

"Because he's out of the country?"

"Correct. He was last seen in Italy. His yacht pulled into Brindisi yesterday."

"Well, let me know when you find him. I would like to interview him personally."

"Off the record, of course."

"Off the record."

Pierce watched Jake Hanlon leave. He had had problems with the FBI director before, yet, in general, considered him competent and accessible. That was more than he could say for a lot of Fulton's cabinet. The traditional presidential method of rewarding long-time political supporters positions in the cabinet was not unknown to Pierce's boss. It would have been political suicide to not dole out the pieces of the pie. Usually it worked fairly well, although even Fulton had long-time political supporters who were incompetent hacks. It didn't make the President's job any easier.

That evening, at home, Pierce received a call from Jake Hanlon. As the face of the FBI director swam onto the screen, Pierce noticed how tired he looked. *These jobs are killers. Especially if you're motivated and dedicated.*

"We found Kalinin," said Jake. "He's dead. He had a villa inland from Brindisi. There was a fire. There was enough DNA in the body to identify him, and there was a suicide note. He felt remorse for having slandered your reputation."

"Am I the only one that suspects something fishy here?" wondered Pierce.

Jake smiled, the tiredness showing through the smile.

"I'm with you there. It doesn't fit his profile."

"You have a profile on him?"

"DHS isn't the only one that profiles. We invented it, you know."

"But he had no criminal record."

"Doesn't matter. He's a VIP. We've got a lot of profiles on people who are squeaky clean on the surface. The National Clandestine Service only organizes information that the intelligence services feed it; there's still a lot of duplication. You know that. Anyway, Mr. Kalinin has been under suspicion for many years. Interpol and a lot of other agencies around the world suspect him for a number of shady deals and outright crimes. Now it's a moot point."

"If it isn't suicide, I want to know who killed him. It could be important."

"Maybe not for national security. I'm guessing it's some competitor or something. I don't particularly care if low-lifes around the world bump each other off. That just makes my job easier."

"Still, I would like to know. Keep some of your guys working on it. Don't close the case just yet."

"Will do. Sorry to interrupt your evening."

"Not at all. And thanks." Jake Hanlon's visage faded from the screen.

Pierce Hamilton rubbed his long nose and tried to think clearly. First, there had been the call from Ben Knowland about some Center that maybe, or maybe not, was under DHS control, something possibly related to Pierce's NASA enquiry. Now, Jake Hanlon had just told him about a complicated plot to embarrass him, and, as a consequence, President Fulton. For once, the man who thought he was so much in control of everything was finding it to be otherwise. *What is this Center? And was Kalinin's plan really an attack on Fulton?* There certainly wasn't enough information to go to his boss, and nothing that required Fulton's decision. Or his. His only conclusion was that he needed more facts.

Chapter Forty-Two

In the Virginia countryside, Saturday . . .

The Guardians were agitated. It took some time for RP1, SW2 and the rest to find out why. It was BH3 who overheard a conversation in the hall that gave them the lead. They soon confirmed it from other overheard conversations and another GW3 break-in to the Center's security intranet.

At the very least, Dr. Tyler was missing. At the very worst, Dr. Tyler had fled. Or escaped, was RP1's suggestion. He had come up with the idea that maybe Dr. Tyler was also kept in the Center against his will.

Those who had originally not believed that FS2, HJ1 and SW1 had escaped nor that the whole starship thing was just a lie were now coming around to thinking along the same lines as RP1 and SW2.

"What are we going to do?" asked SW3. Although she looked just like SW2, she was rather shy and somewhat stupid, at least for practical things. She was actually a brilliant physicist, though none of her work would ever see the light of day. "Are they going to kill us?"

"Now there's a thought to make you shit your pants," said GW3. "They'll grind us into hamburger and give us to the bears at the zoo." When he saw SW3's shocked look, GW3 patted her on the hand. "Don't worry. It's painless. If you think enough of your starship, it won't fucking hurt at all."

"Stop it," said SW2. "It doesn't make sense to generate hysteria. We need a plan."

"Hysteria is a good, solid emotion," observed BH3, who happened to like SW3. "She's pretty when she's hysterical."

"All the SW's are pretty," said RP1. "Give it a rest. SW2 is right. We need a plan. GW3, how many Guardians are there at any one time?"

"There are always six," replied GW3. "And they have eight hour shifts. What are you thinking?"

"You're thinking we can take them, right?" said BH3, smacking his right fist into his left palm.

"They're armed," observed SW2.

"That's where it will get sticky. There are enough of us to overpower them, I think, but with the guns, we've got a problem."

"Fish nets," said GW3.

"What do you mean?" asked BH3.

"I saw it on the Discovery channel. They use fish nets to catch fish. If we drop a net over a Guardian, he can't get to his gun. Especially if the net's sticky."

"A sticky net? Where do we get that?" asked SW2.

He told them.

It took them the rest of the day to make the nets. They used twine and string from the arts and crafts class and various jams and jellies from the kitchen. Six brooms and twenty-four wire hangers made frames over which the gooey nets were draped.

That night they went into action, two hours after the shift changed. All six guards were neutralized without a hitch, although one managed to get off a badly aimed shot. Dr. Tyler's children were in control of the Center. They only had one problem left to solve: Should they leave or should they stay?

It was easy for GW3 to shut down everything and open the gates, so they had a choice. He also convinced them that if they were going to escape, they had no time to lose, because the Guardians probably reported every so often to somewhere outside of the Center.

"That does it for me," said RP1. "Team up however you want and let's disperse. Some of us will surely escape."

"And the rest?" asked SW3.

"At best, they'll bring you back here. At the worst—" He hesitated. "At the worst, you're dead. At least you'll die free."

"I don't want to die," wailed SW3.

"Then stay here," said BH3. "I'm going. Who's coming?"

It turned out that no one wanted to be left behind.

It was another swampy summer night in the Virginia countryside as they dispersed by twos and threes to all the points of the compass.

Two hours later the Guardians and their helicopters had recaptured most of them. They were helped by men dressed in dark suits who drove black cars with regular DC plates. RP1 and SW2 knew that because they were forced to ride in one. They overheard one of the men say that they should have killed them all long ago.

But no one was killed and the search continued for the remainder.

Scherzo Thirty-Five

He was called Brother Frank. New to the monastery, he shared a characteristic with the other monks. They were all young and very fit.

Brother Frank and the rest were all ex-special forces, that is, their recruits were ex-Navy Seals, ex-Marines, or ex-SWAT team members. Their little monastery close to Salt Lake City was really a clandestine operation run by the DHS, a black program funded by a secret account in a Swiss bank. Its mission was to take out terrorists that threatened the US.

Brother Frank had known violence his whole life. The first money he ever made was in bare knuckle fighting in the back streets and back alleys of the Bronx. He was only fourteen then. When he was seventeen the love of his life was killed by getting caught in the middle of a battle between two gangs. Single handedly, and without anyone knowing, he found out who the shooters were on both sides and eliminated them, one by one, making it look like more gang killings.

He always hated school and joined the Army as soon as he legally could, even though he lied about his age and used a fake national ID card. The Army found about it, but by the time they did, he was of age, so it didn't make much sense to get on his case. They put him into special forces where his special brand of violence served God and country.

He lasted for seven years until they officially discovered he was a sociopath. They hushed up his massacre of all the people in a small village in Iran, gave him a general discharge, and bid him farewell. Two months later the DHS approached him.

He lived to perform mayhem. He knew he was in the right place.

Brother Frank's first DHS mission was in Indonesia. It was also his last. The terrorist got him first.

Chapter Forty-Three

Savannah, Georgia, Saturday . . .

Bouncer and Sandra drove all night to the outskirts of Savannah where Sandra's parents had a vacation home their family also used when her father had business trips from Atlanta. They put their car in the garage, away from prying eyes, and entered the house from the garage door which led into the kitchen.

Bouncer went around the house, studying its floor plan and checking its security, especially the front door, making sure it was solidly latched. As he turned away from it, a floor board creaked loudly.

"The house is a little run down," Sandra apologized. "Daddy's meant to fix that board for a long time now. You have to get at it through the false ceiling and insulation in the basement, so it's not easy. There's other things, like dripping faucets and the like."

"It's plenty good enough for me," observed Bouncer. "We can't expect it to be a fort. Actually, it's a good, solid southern house. Why didn't you tell me you were rich?"

"I'm not. My parents are. You should see our house in Atlanta."

"Hopefully I will. For now, this will do just fine."

"We'll get by, I guess. Do we just wait?"

"That's a good question. Better still, how will we know when it's safe to stop hiding?" Bouncer jabbed a finger skyward. "These guys may have every government satellite available looking for us. Speaking of which, I need to get wired up. Got a hub?"

"Always on," said Sandra. She took him to her father's den where the house hub was located. It had the old-fashioned fiber optics connections plus the now more standard capability of receiving high bandwidth RF spread spectrum signals from any close-by portable computer, although neither was state-of-the-art. She watched as he took cables out of his pockets and plugged them into the unit. Then she stopped him when he was about to plug the other ends into the sockets implanted behind his ear. "On second thought, don't. Maybe they can trace you. I'm unplugging the hub too."

"I think that's a little extreme. How are they going to trace me?"

"Don't you access your computer at home remotely with that system?" He nodded. "So just suppose that they now control your computer, or are listening in somehow."

Bouncer looked at her, and then smiled. "Good girl. For a pharmacist, you're computer savvy. But can't I just use one of your computers here, and just stick to your hub?"

"I guess you could do that, but do you need to? I'd prefer to exercise caution."

"So what are we going to do? I'm at a loss without a computer."

"How about a nice dinner and some R & R afterwards?" She winked at him.

"Somehow I don't think you mean R & R. Mentally, I'm willing, but my body's kind of tired, babe."

"We'll take a little nap after dinner. That will perk you up." She went to the freezer. "Mom's got some nice T-bones in here. I'd bet there's a good cabernet or merlot in the wine cellar."

Bouncer was admiring her buns as she stretched to check out the contents of the freezer. Her stretch pants were lime green and her half blouse that left her midriff bare was white, both colors cool and refreshing and contrasting nicely with her ebony skin.

"You have a wine cellar here?"

"Daddy calls it that. None of us are wine experts. It's just a rack in the cellar filled with wine bottles. Nothing fancy, but he probably has a decent selection. My family's large, and many are quirky about what they drink. I have a cousin who only drinks pinot grigio, for example, and a brother who only drinks shiraz."

"Any wine's fancy for me. That's why I only do glasses when we go out."

"And here I thought you were saving yourself for me. With these T-bones, you'll need more than a glass, though. Like I said, a nice bottle of cabernet, or merlot, or even red zinfandel. Anything red. Hey, there are frozen vegetables here too, so we'll pretend to be healthy. No salad fixings, though, and I'm hesitant about going out for some. The less we're outside, the better."

"Agreed. How long can we last here before we need to shop?"

Sandra went across the kitchen to the cupboards and started opening them.

"Lots of canned goods, chili and stuff like that. There's pancake mix and plenty of coffee. I'd say we could last a good week or more, even considering your appetite."

"Hey, you've got a pretty good one yourself." He showed her the manila envelope. "Where can I hide this?"

"Good question. Daddy's got a safe here, although I don't know the combination."

Bouncer spotted some plastic freezer bags in the cupboard. He took one out, put the envelope inside, and then sealed the bag.

"It's now waterproof. Where's the toilet?"

"Yeah, that will work," said Sandra with a smile. "Might be the first place someone looks, though."

"Yeah, it's obvious, so just maybe they won't look there." He put his arm around her waist. "Now, about those steaks."

As Bouncer and Sandra began to prepare their meal, Curt Forrester took a bite out of his hamburger and turned on his laptop. As Bouncer had feared, several satellites, one by one, had been tracking them shortly after they had entered Virginia, cued by a quick cell phone call Sandra had made to her pharmacy. Even though he had not connected remotely to his home computer, it didn't matter. Curt knew where they were. He pulled out of the highway rest stop and headed south.

Sometimes he actually enjoyed his job, although most of the time he just didn't care. It was just a job.

He had always lived a violent life. Starting in the Philly slums, he graduated to the Marines, where he was washed out when he killed a prisoner in Teheran with his bare hands. The CIA then became interested in him for wet work, although they threw him out after he raped and killed a Pakistani minister's daughter. The DHS picked him up after that. He found a niche in taking out terrorist cells in the US, achieving a good reputation in one of the black ops units. After Hank Johnson picked him to be his bodyguard, he did a lot less wet work, so much so that he thought that he might be getting soft.

Recent events associated with the escape at the Center, however, had changed all that. Even though he was still Hank's bodyguard, the wet work was taking up more and more of his time. He was trusted. He was efficient.

He closed the laptop and tossed the hamburger in the little garbage can he kept in the DHS car assigned to him. He would get a good dinner when this assignment was over. He deserved it.

Scherzo Thirty-Six

When the ACLU sued the government over the national ID card and won the concession that a bad genetic history could not be used to deny medical benefits, it was the straw that broke the camel's back. Health premiums skyrocketed as a consequence although even at the turn of the century health plans were already too costly for many people. They were also too costly for many employers who saw many years of double digit percentage increases in their medical benefits costs.

A more grim statistic had already reared its ugly head. The number of premature deaths in the age bracket of 50 to 65 attributable to lack of health insurance kept increasing year after year. By the time the US and the rest of the world went to the multi-tier system, things were already beyond the critical point.

It is hard to blame either the ACLU or the Supreme Court for something that was already out of control.

The multi-tier system was a bad fix to a bad problem. Not unlike cable coverage for their digital televisions, the insured were subjected to a system that ran from full medical, only affordable to the rich (also available from some private doctors' organizations for a hefty yearly fee), to basic coverage with a huge deductible (prescription plans not included). Of course, even the basic coverage was no longer affordable to many.

Unfortunately, the phenomenon was not confined to the US. Most of the industrialized world, from England to Singapore, was forced to change to similar systems as the costs of the vast plans of socialized medical coverage became more and more of a tax burden. Sweden, long the shining example of government-sponsored benefits programs for its citizens, was actually the first to change its medical system in 2017, with Canada following the next year. Norway, once the envy of Europe because it was saving billions from its oil revenue for the future, was now drawing down heavily on those savings and had only managed to postpone using them all up by slashing services in ways paralleling both Sweden and Canada.

It seemed that the whole concept of medical insurance no longer functioned, even with tort reform, lower physicians' fees, and streamlined efficiencies in the world's hospitals. The only real result of the first was that more people died from medical errors that went basically unpunished. The second produced droves of physicians leaving the field and unfilled spaces in the medical schools. The third usually meant that corners were cut in giving care to patients as well as increases in operating room infections, errors, and premature releases of patients.

During this time, a black market for body parts began to operate worldwide, rivaling the illegal drug trade. From 2040 to 2050 reported crimes in this area showed a steady increase in their percentage of the total crimes reported.

Chapter Forty-Four

Baltimore, Maryland, Saturday . . .

By the time one of the marines took Jay's hood off, she already knew she was somewhere on the docks in Baltimore. There was the smell of diesel, decay, and salt air. *Apparently an abandoned warehouse. In this economy, there are so many of them. I bet I know who owns it.*

"Sit," said the marine sergeant, as another offered a chair.

"Always the gentlemen," said Jay. "Tell me, who are you working for?"

"They're just marines, Jay. Obeying orders."

Stephanie Williams entered the dark room that had probably been the foreman's office in times gone by. Jay looked from the marines to the Vice President.

"I figured this went as high as you, Stephanie, because of the clone in the Philippines, your look-alike. Does it also involve President Fulton?"

The woman smiled at Jay. An enigmatic, Mona Lisa smile. She was still a beautiful woman. *Helped along by new body parts, or just a skillful plastic surgeon?* Jay couldn't tell from the ex-actor's expression what was going on in her mind. If she was uncomfortable with Jay and her friends' discovery of her plan, she didn't show it. She made a gesture and one of the marines brought her another chair. She sat down, still smiling.

"Do you know what it takes for a woman to get ahead in politics in this country?" she asked.

"Enlighten me," replied Jay with a scowl.

"Actually, not just in politics. We are not that far above the baboons and other great apes, you know. Striving to be the alpha male is part of our evolutionary curse. A successful man is often called strong, masculine, industrious—a whole host of positive sounding adjectives. John Fulton is a successful man. A successful woman is often called ballsy, bitchy, overbearing—a lot of negative adjectives. I'm a successful woman, so I get a lot of those adjectives thrown my way. It's the way the world is, I guess."

"I've had some of those adjectives applied to me sometimes, though I haven't committed murder. So what's your point?"

"Yes, you're a ballsy bitch. I actually admire you, because you too have succeeded, at least up to now, in a professional world dominated by strong, masculine, and industrious men." She coughed a little. *Maybe she needs a new transplant?* "John Fulton is successful but he's also stupid. No, he has nothing to do with this project. Do you know I was once an intern working with then Senator Sheila Remington?"

"Actually, I do," responded Jay. "I'm not sure you learned a lot from your internship."

Stephanie Williams ignored the barb, or pretended to.

"You think I'm a B-movie actor that became a political hack, I suppose. However, that internship, done just before I ran for congress, started me out on my career. Sheila did me an immense favor. She took me aside once and told me that I was destined for great things. I served my dues as representative in the House; I served a stretch as Secretary of DHS; then as junior Senator. But just when I was ready to move in on the big one, John Fulton came along with his progressive 'Take Back the Heartland' movement and derailed my run for the Presidency. I think I put up a good fight, good enough that he had no choice but to take me on as his running mate. After two Fulton administrations, I'm ready again."

"You won't get the chance," warned Jay. "This scandal will bury you politically."

"What scandal? You say too many people know. I don't think so. My agents are on their way right now to clean up the whole mess."

"What do you mean, clean up?"

"Why, you, this Boston police detective, Chris Tanner, and that meddlesome scientist, Kalidas Metropolis, will soon all be history. Plus a few others that have been a nuisance, like that sentimental Dolores Milton and that giant friend of yours, Gunther Mann."

"Did you learn those tactics in your stretch at the DHS?"

"I honed them to perfection there, my dear. They have served me well."

"When did you hatch your cloning plan?"

"Over twenty years ago, of course. I had access to the best scientists the world could offer. Wolfgang was a sweetie pie, too. All I had to do was keep him supplied with young men and plenty of money. Until he got greedy." She smiled unctuously—her best baby-kissing politico smile. "And we didn't have to waste our time experimenting on animals. There were plenty of young girls in the Third World that donated their eggs to the cause."

"What happened to them?"

"I suppose that most of them were left barren. It was a small price to pay. While they were with us they weren't getting raped and slaughtered or maimed by some female circumcision procedure. In the process we also contributed to population control."

"Stephanie, have you always been a fascist?"

The VP looked at her and frowned.

"As a journalist, you should know that's an odd, old and misused word. In particular, it doesn't have much meaning when we are constantly fighting against terrorism. I know the enemy. My father died in the World Trade Center on September 11, 2001."

"I'm sorry about that, and I won't make light of it. So maybe part of the explanation of your actions is revenge for a lost father. That's no justification, though, for doing something morally reprehensible. You've lowered yourself to the level of the terrorists."

There was a quick flash of anger on Stephanie's face but she regained control almost immediately. "You fought a war. I'm fighting one too. We both are patriots trying to keep our country from being destroyed."

"So, the old refrain of the end justifies the means again. I bet all of you involved in this think you're patriots." Stephanie inclined her head slightly, acknowledging agreement. "OK, you're all patriots. But why the clones?"

"Don't patronize me. You have no idea of the sacrifices that we've made. There are quite a few of us of a like mind, you know. We are dedicated to carrying on the fight against the terrorists. And also against anyone trying to destroy our nation. Fools like Christy Vargas. Still, I'm not getting any younger, and most of the rest aren't either. But we can keep going a long time with a good supply of easily transplantable body parts available, don't you think?"

"You could die of other things. Like a bullet."

"Possibly. That's something in your immediate future, not mine." She stood. "Diego, hold her for fifteen minutes while I leave, then kill her." The VP turned on her heel and strode out the door.

Jay waited a moment and then turned to the marine the VP had called Diego.

"So, Sgt. Diego Chavez, are you going to carry out that order?" asked Jay.

"I'm afraid I have to, ma'am. Orders are orders. You're a terrorist."

"Come on, sergeant. Do I look like a terrorist? As one marine to another, do you think I've done anything wrong?"

Sgt. Chavez looked at the others.

"What do you mean, marine, ma'am?"

"I served six years. In the Middle East. It wasn't pleasant, though I believed in what I was doing. I still do, to some extent. The bombs in our shopping malls are real. Can you say the same thing? Do you believe in what you're doing?"

"I'm not sure I know what you're getting at, ma'am."

"Do you believe it's right to kill an unarmed citizen of this country? No soy el enemigo. You know damn well I'm not. Soldiers have a moral responsibility. Just following orders stopped being a defense at the Nuremburg trials just after World War Two, over a hundred years ago. I'll ask you again, all of you. Do you believe what you're doing is right? Let me tell you all the facts before you answer."

Jay began to elaborate on what they just heard the VP admit to. She detailed the grisly murders of John Milton, Claude Turner, and Patty Smith. She told them about the murder of Bob Martin. She told them about the DHS's persecution of Kalidas Metropolis and Chris Tanner. The killing of Richter. And she told them about the clones and how three had escaped, running for their lives, and were now dead. By the time she finished twenty minutes had passed, not fifteen.

"So, Sgt. Chavez, are you going to carry out the VP's order?"

Chavez looked at the three others. They were all shaking their heads, whether negatively or in disbelief about what they had heard, Jay didn't know.

Chavez lowered his gun.

"I guess you do have a way with words," he said. "What do we do now?"

"We leave this place and find some way to communicate with my friends as soon as possible. To warn them. Then I think we'd better find someone at either the FBI or the Secret Service that can help us. I also need to inform President Fulton about what is going on, since he doesn't seem to be involved in this."

"My commander can do that for you," offered Chavez. "I just need—"

His sentence was interrupted by shots being fired at the old warehouse.

"What the fuck?" yelled one of the others.

"I bet the VP didn't trust you," yelled Jay, as they all hit the floor hard. "You're going to be eliminated too."

They were all well trained in urban combat. As a unit, each picked a different window, broke the glass, and began firing back.

"She was going to let us kill you, then kill us, right?" called Chavez, during a momentary lull.

"You've got it, amigo mio," said Jay. "No credible witnesses that way. Toss me your pistol. I can help."

She picked another window. A quick glance showed her that there were at least ten attackers, all dressed in dark business suits. *Agents sent by Mary Beth Grogan, I'll bet. Stephanie would have used them if she could, yet all she had initially were the marines.* Jay's aim had gotten a little rusty, so she felt an immense satisfaction when she took out one of the men in black before her clip ran out.

"Another pistol," she called.

One of the other marines tossed her his pistol, and then returned to firing at his window with his rifle. Things suddenly got quiet. She hazarded a peek through the broken pane.

"Oh, shit. They've got RPGs. Is there a back way out of here? It's going to go bang mighty fast."

"In the back there's a rickety half staircase down to a loading dock next to the tracks," suggested Chavez.

"What are we waiting for?"

They had just bolted outside when the RPGs hit the little warehouse. The series of explosions tossed them into the air like rag dolls but they all rolled with practiced ease when they landed.

"Now I'm really pissed," said Chavez.

"Save that thought, marine," suggested Jay. "They've got us outnumbered. Any suggestions on where to hide?"

Chavez pointed across the tracks. There were six of them, and in the fourth one over, a long, slow freight train was leaving the area. The marines ran to it and jumped up into an open freight car, Chavez swinging Jay up, knowing that she could not make the jump herself.

"Just like old times in LA," said Chavez, panting slightly.

"I'm from there too," said Jay, as the burning warehouse got lost in the smoke and distance.

"I knew that," said Chavez. "Only a fellow chicano could speak Spanish that badly."

"Hijole, you know how to hurt a girl." But she gave him a big kiss, soot and all. "Thanks for not killing me back there."

The marine seemed embarrassed, although maybe it was just about the transfer of his dirt to a pretty woman.

"Like I said, you have a way with words."

Scherzo Thirty-Seven

Alan Grant stopped to catch his wind just a second, hoping to catch a glimpse of the clown. *Shit, it shouldn't be hard to spot him. Red mop of hair, big red nose, baggy pants. Where the hell is he?*

Then Alan spotted him, making his way through the crowd in front of the baseball toss. *If I can just cut around the merry-go-round, I can meet him head-on, as much out in the open as is possible here.*

Alan began running through the crowd again, this time at right angles to his quarry. Then he moved quickly around the merry-go-round and ended up about 30 meters directly in front of the clown, who was still looking furtively over his shoulder at where Alan had been.

It was as clear as he was going to get, so Alan drew his gun.

"DHS! Man in the clown suit, hands high!"

Most people in the carnival crowd had heard such words before, if not in real life, at least on the newsnets, where many had seen the DHS agents in action. They all dropped to the ground except one fat lady who went into hysterics. Fortunately, she was not in the direct line of fire.

The terrorist didn't raise his hands. Most of them didn't. He reached for his waist where the button to fuse the plastic explosive was located. His hand never reached it. The bullet from Alan's gun tore a path through his skull, blowing it open and scattering brain matter over the nearby crowd.

Alan walked up to the corpse, feeling like he was going to vomit. *That was a bad one. Really bad. But it could have been a lot worse. God, I hate this job.* Yet it wasn't finished by any means. When he tore open the terrorist's clown suit, he saw that the explosives were rigged to explode if anyone tried to remove them.

He took out his cell phone and dialed the office, asking for a bomb squad. It was going to be a long night.

In his office in Falls Church, the Secretary of DHS, Ben Knowland, eventually received the report. He frowned. He would have liked to interrogate the terrorist. But Alan Grant had done a good job. No other casualties, except for the fat woman who had to be treated by the EMTs for hysteria. *We don't often have that kind of success.* He permitted himself a little smile at that thought.

Chapter Forty-Five

Washington, DC, Saturday . . .

On the way to the hospital, Kalidas made two calls. One was to Sheriff Sam Fletcher. Another was to Capt. Denise Rivera. Kalidas had never met Sam but she had heard good things about him from Jay, Dolores, and Bouncer. And Chris obviously had a great deal of admiration for his boss. She was taking a chance, she knew, but when they checked into a hospital, DHS would know where they were anyway.

She gave a rapid fire account of what happened to both the cops and also described their conjecture about the clones, explaining that Jay and her group had already come to the same decision in all likelihood and were also on the run, trying to escape from the DHS. Then she went straight to Bethesda.

Jay and the marines, meanwhile, showed up at Quantico, after Jay had expertly hot-wired a van. After some fast talking between the marines at the gate and the marines in the van, they made their way into the base. In its heart could be found the FBI Academy and research center. Refurbished many times over the years, they still consisted of the original three sprawling brick buildings connected by a network of glassed walkways above ground. Below ground there was a labyrinth of labs and ops centers that tripled the space that existed at the turn of the century. The people that worked there now far outnumbered the military present on the base, testimony to the fifty year homeland security buildup to counter terrorism.

Since the sentries had phoned ahead, the disheveled group in the van were quickly led into elevators and taken to one of the ops centers. Both marines and FBI were there, in the person of Asako O'Brien, two other FBI agents, and a representative of the marine base commander. Asako and the other two agents were easier to convince than the base commander's rep, who couldn't quite swallow the whole story without checking. So it was Jake Hanlon,

FBI director back in DC, who moved first, spurred into action by a trinity of calls from Denise Rivera, Sam Fletcher, and the FBI at Quantico.

Pierce Hamilton was on the golf course when his cell phone rang. He pulled it out, took a look at the caller ID, and nodded to the two Secret Service men accompanying his party.

"Give me some space here, guys," he said. Since his golf partners were two Supreme Court judges and a senator, they understood that national security business came first. They moved on to the next hole, leaving Pierce and his bodyguards alone.

"Go ahead, Jake. What's the deal?"

Jake Hanlon was not a man of many words. He described the situation briefly and clearly. Pierce's orders were just as clear and to the point.

"First, dispatch some of your people to Bethesda. If what this Boston cop and scientist say is true, these people need protection."

"I've already got people there. Ben Knowland and his people won't get near them."

"I don't think Knowland is involved, unless he's a damn good actor. Try to check that out. He put me on to this secret DHS project, which may be connected, from what I'm hearing. We've got some homework to do. To that end, I also want that CIA analyst in my office toute suite. Have him meet me there."

"I can't order the CIA around."

"But I can. Use my name. Also, give me the marine commander's number. I'll tell him to hold the reporter and those marines. Just keep them safe for now. And can you get forensics experts to that Comfort Inn in Vienna and the warehouse in Baltimore? I want to check out these peoples' stories before I approach Fulton."

"You've got it. I've got people listening in here. They're already moving."

"I also want all the information you can get on this case from Boston and St. Mary's."

"How about the e-files that the reporter came up with? I don't know how authentic they are. We can check on that."

"Do that. And then fax them to my office. We have a crisis to head off here."

Pierce sent one of the bodyguards ahead on foot to inform the rest of the golf party that he was called away on an emergency. Then he and the other bodyguard got in his golf cart to rush to the clubhouse. They broke many grounds rules getting there, taking as nearly a straight path as possible.

Once there they got in the sleek black limo, the Secret Service man plopped a red flasher on top, and off they went back to DC.

Normally, it would have been a pleasant ride, yet Pierce was in no mood to enjoy it. He felt bad. This had all happened on his watch, so ultimately he was responsible. If it had not been for Peter Barkley, he would have been completely in the dark. He silently cursed the cloak of secrecy they had to live under, due to the constant threat of terrorist attacks. *Why did we have to become the Israel of the twenty-first century? Who said we don't pay for our past mistakes?*

When he arrived at his office in the White House, some of the information he requested was there, and other information started coming in on the secure fax as he pored over the records from the Boston Police Department and the St. Mary's County Sheriff's Department. Jay's hard copies were not conclusive, although they certainly backed up her conjecture. He then received a call from FBI forensics confirming the stories about the motel attack on Kalidas and Chris and the warehouse siege with Jay and the marines. Mary Beth Grogan's body was not found at the motel, though. *Could Knowland's people move that fast?*

At that moment Simon Multani walked in. He was unshaven and slovenly dressed, his normal state on a Saturday.

"Come in, young man. Sit down."

Simon looked around a little in awe, yet took the chair the Secret Service agent pointed to.

"You're probably wondering what's going on. Do you know Asako O'Brian?"

"What's she done?" Simon asked.

Pierce smiled and winked at the Secret Service agent.

"Don't get all defensive. She may have just saved this nation a major embarrassment. Assuming I can clean up things before the press gets hold of it."

"This is about that cloning thing, isn't it? Is Stephanie really involved?"

"You sound like you know her."

"An admirer of sorts."

"Let me guess, 'Shakedown in Rio'?"

"And other films."

"Well, if what I think happened is true, you may not be an admirer for long."

"Oh, shit."

"Precisely. It hit the fan. Apparently Stephanie ordered a bunch of marines to take out Jay Sandoval, that reporter from Crime Fighters."

"Yeah, I think I got shot at for talking to her. I've been minding my own business since then. Is Asako OK? And Jay?"

"All fine, so far. Jay escaped. Two other people were also attacked, apparently by Hank Johnson's personal aid."

"Holy crap! This is big. When I stumbled on that report from the Philippines, I didn't think it would lead to this."

"So tell me, how did you get involved in all this?"

"Well, I thought the report from the Philippines was suspicious. Asako had told me about the John Doe in Lexington Park. I saw connections."

"Did you tell your bosses about those perceived connections?"

"I did what you normally do. I passed a full report upstairs, sure that the woman in the Philippines was a clone. I thought it was some new angle the terrorists were using to replace US government officials. I don't know what action my bosses took. I'm just an analyst, sir."

"Apparently a very good one. It's just that the wheels of bureaucracy move slow at times."

"And my perception of a threat is not perceived as a threat by someone else. But who am I? I don't even qualify for full medical on the company plan because of a low GS rating."

Pierce frowned at that. *Now there's a contradiction: The government is the biggest employer in the country, yet most of our workers don't qualify for full medical. It makes this case all the more damning.*

"Can you get me copies of your report? The one you showed Asako and Jay, plus the stuff you sent upstairs? I may need all of it to build a case."

"You can't just request them?"

"It would be too slow through normal channels. I'll give you a handwritten note, and if anyone balks, tell them to call me. For the time being, you're temporarily assigned to this case and you work for me. Understood?"

"Yes, sir. I'll get right on it."

Pierce watched the young man go. *We need more like him. But now I've got to prepare a briefing for the President.*

How he would organize the briefing was determined by Pierce's long-time relationship with his boss. Privately, neither Fulton nor he were very tolerant of stupidity, although both had to publicly deal with a lot of it every day. Pierce also knew that even Fulton had his lapses. Privately, he had always thought that putting Stephanie Williams on the ticket was one of them. He never trusted the woman.

Stupid mistakes can be committed by the President of any political party. They all are human, not robots—that's why our government has its wonderful system of checks and balances. It was some real six-sigma-from-the-mean thinking that permitted our founding fathers to come up with that great compromise known as the constitution. We monkey with it at our own peril, although it is a living document that must be continuously interpreted as the years go by. You have people like Stephanie who think that life would be simpler if the executive branch had more power. Then there are those who yearn for a parliamentary form of government where the prime minister is named by the legislative body. The extremes are tempting but our checks and balances are essential. On the other hand, the electoral process offers yet another check. It means that compromises have to be made to win elections. Fulton might have been elected without Stephanie, but her presence on the ticket made it easier. He admired her as an astute politician. But had his trust in her been misplaced? A compromise to win an election may have backfired in this case.

He made a solemn oath that Stephanie Williams, if guilty, would pay for what she had done.

Scherzo Thirty-Eight

When Thompson Pharmaceuticals, the third largest drug firm in the world, proposed to buy Quality Care, the largest HMO in the US, many cried foul. Charles Ito, Senator from California, gave a famous speech in the Senate that was shown many times during the ensuing debate that surged back and forth over the newsnets.

"The pendulum of history swings between extremes," he said. "Fifty years ago we had an era of corporate greed second only to the era of the Carnegies, the J. P. Morgan's, and the factory sweat shops of the nineteenth century. Our great middle class was getting squeezed out of existence. Yet we came to our senses, recognizing that unregulated capitalism can only destroy the middle class." The senator cleared his throat and pointed a long, well manicured finger at the gallery, which was quite full for the hearings on the proposed merger. "My fellow Americans, the pendulum swung through its inexorable arc and now we are back again. In spite of all the good efforts by President Fulton and his able administration, greedy corporations are squeezing the middle class again. You all know how difficult it is to obtain full medical coverage and to get the drugs you need to keep you healthy. Now it is being proposed that we give these two major corporations carte blanche to squeeze millions of you even more. My fellow Americans, it is time we put a stop to this!"

Several lawsuits were filed against the merger. One went all the way to the Supreme Court. The Court ruled that the government could not prevent the merger on a technicality: while Quality Care was headquartered in Los Angeles, the buyer, Thompson, was an English company, so the US had no jurisdiction. The merger was completed. Senator Ito was defeated in the next election by a candidate primarily bankrolled by Quality Care—or Thompson Pharmaceuticals, depending on how you looked at it.

Chapter Forty-Six

Savannah, Georgia, Sunday . . .

Bouncer turned lazily in bed. He smiled sleepily at the woman next to him. *I could get used to this. Sandra's just about the best thing in my life right now.*

Sandra's eyes slowly opened and she smiled back at him.

"I think you need to fix me breakfast," she said.

He got up, his massive, naked frame making the bed creak. On the floor, he found his boxers and slipped them on. *Foolish. You've been naked with this woman and you now get embarrassed?*

"You make the sausage, I'll make the pancakes. How 'bout that?"

"Oh, all right. I guess I have to show I can do something in the kitchen." She got up, noticing that he didn't take his eyes off her. "You're staring, Bouncer."

"You're beautiful, babe, simply beautiful." He tossed her a bathrobe. "Put that on before I forget about breakfast."

She laughed, and it was like music to his ears.

Later, over coffee after a breakfast fit for a pair of loggers, he took her hand.

"I think we should make this permanent, Sandra," he suggested.

"Is that a proposal, you big ox?"

"'Bout all my poetic self can come up with. I'm not big on romantic words and all the fineries, yet my intentions are honest. I'll dedicate my life to you, if you'll let me."

"That's poetic enough, I guess," she said with a smile.

They both heard the board creak, the one by the front door.

"Someone's in the house," Sandra whispered, her eyes wide. "What are you doing?"

Bouncer had gone to a utensils drawer. He came up with a meat tenderizer in one hand and a meat cleaver in the other. He handed her the meat tenderizer.

"Not much against a gun," he observed.

"Daddy's got some guns in the basement," she said, testing the weight of her weapon.

"Where's that?"

"The entrance door is just to the right of the front door. You saw it."

"Yeah, right, I remember. That won't do us any good right now. I saw a back door. Off the den, right?" She nodded. "Let's go, then. Maybe we can make a run for it."

"How? It's broad daylight."

"I just want to get out of the house while the goon's in it. Whoever he is."

At that moment, Curt Forrester was stealthily moving towards the kitchen. He smelled the coffee and the sausage. Since he hadn't eaten a real meal in more than twenty-four hours, the smell of home cooking made his mouth water. But he didn't have time to reflect on his hunger. He had a job to do.

The kitchen was empty but the dirty plates told him two people had just finished breakfast. He picked up a leftover sausage and took a bite out of it. *Damn good southern cooking. So where are they?* He figured they were probably warned by the creaking floor board. *Damn old houses. You can always trust them to screw your gig up somehow.*

He moved into the corridor off the kitchen, pointing the gun one way, then the other, as if he were on a reconnaissance mission in a Teheran slum. He held the gun fairly close to his body unlike what was often seen in the stupid cop shows. He knew the ragheads could hit his extended arms with a rifle or even a shovel and send his weapon flying. They could pop up in any room, too, even kids. A buddy had been killed by a ten-year-old.

He moved quickly through the house. When he saw the back door ajar, he frowned. That would make it harder, though at least they were in the back of the house, not the front.

He peered out, seeing a gravel patio bordered by tall hedge. A weathered trellis and gate affair was an exit from the patio to a garden area with more gravel between the plants, then lawn, and finally trees, the edge of a dense woodland. The whole area was a little neglected. *This is someone's country home and they aren't rich enough to have a local gardener keep it up, so in the spring and early summer things get a little out of control.* He moved out quickly and crossed the patio.

They jumped him from behind the hedge. Two big giants, each one weighing more than he did, took him down, knocking the wind out of him. One of the giants, the white man, had a meat cleaver and was about to split Curt's head with it. Incongruously, he stopped, looked at the weapon, and tossed it. The other giant, a huge black woman, let him have it with a meat tenderizer right on the bridge of his nose. He saw stars, planets, and maybe a few asteroids.

She also threw down her weapon and both giants ran.

Curt, still stunned, went into automatic mode. He first found his gun and then brought it up to bear on the back of the woman, the closest. But her form was all blurred by his blood and sweat. She didn't make it any easier as she weaved with surprising agility and his damaged eyes tried to follow. He took out after her.

Bouncer had already crossed most of the lawn and was almost into the woods but Curt caught the slower Sandra at the edge of the lawn. It was a sloppy tackle, more like a light halfback trying to tackle a huge opposing lineman who had just by chance intercepted his quarterback's pass. Nevertheless he put a solid shoulder into her just below her butt and they both went down. The heady aroma of southern grass and sexy woman filled his nostrils. *The bitch is naked.*

Curt got to his feet quickly. He was not one to put up with fooling around. He put his foot on Sandra's back and pointed the gun at her head.

"I've got your woman, big man." He wiped the blood from his nose with his sleeve. "Your big, fuckin' black woman. If you don't come out of the woods, her brains will be spread all over this nice green grass. Now, I don't care one way or the other. I'm just here to take you out. Dirty or clean. If you come out, I just might let her go."

Bouncer peered from out behind the tree, rage and helplessness at seeing his beloved Sandra in that compromising position. He mentally shrugged. *If she buys it, it's not going to be good for me anyway.* He walked out with his hands up.

"That's better, big fella," said Curt, turning the gun to cover Bouncer, still dressed in his boxers. *God, this guy is big.*

"Let her up," said Bouncer.

"OK, honey, you can get up now," Curt told her, removing his foot. "Just don't try anything."

"Why are you doing this?" Sandra asked, tears running down her cheeks. She was holding her stomach, her hand under the fold of the bathrobe, as if she were wounded there. In that hand was a rock. "How can you people be so violent and bloodthirsty?"

"I'm just doing my job, ma'am," Curt said, wiping at the blood streaming from the gash in his nose again. His vision was still blurred. *The bitch could have blinded me.* "People give orders; I obey. You know how it is. It's just earning my pay."

Sandra moved away from him a little.

"You're a savage," she said, "a white, Nazi savage. I bet you killed John Milton."

"So what if I did? Like I said, I just take orders. I did it in the Middle East, I do it here. It's the only thing I know. So, now, what I want you two to do is get over here side by side and get down on your knees. I'll make it as painless as possible."

"You said you were going to let her go," said Bouncer.

"I lied. I do that sometimes. Doesn't everybody? Now, get over here, and you woman, get down beside him. I haven't got all day." He waved his pistol at Bouncer.

He just took his eyes off Sandra a fraction of a second, figuring that the stupid woman would be crying and sobbing right up to when he finished her off. The rock hit him full in the face so hard that he choked on his own teeth. Bouncer didn't wait when he saw what happened. Moving as fast as an NFL nose tackle, he hit Curt at the waist. The gun went flying and Curt and Bouncer hit the ground.

Curt had grown up fighting in the slums of Philly. He knew how to fight dirty—fingers-in-the-eyes, knees-to-the-groin dirty. After several seconds of skirmish, Curt was on top of Bouncer, a knee to his throat and the same rock raised high, ready to smash the bigger man's face in.

"You fuckin' bastard," he yelled. "I was going to make it easy, but now I'm just going to beat your brain to a pulp and then rape and torture your black bitch. How do you like that?"

The rock started to come down. Bouncer was seeing it in slow motion, wondering why his brain would do that, slow everything down, not let it happen fast.

Then there were five quick shots, each one ripping into Curt, jerking his body, and making his aim go wild. When he hit the ground, he was already dead. Bouncer looked at Sandra. Curt's gun was still in her hand. She sunk to her knees, sobbing.

"Shit, what a mess," was all Bouncer could say, rubbing his eyes with one hand and holding onto his crotch with the other.

Chapter Forty-Seven

Near Quantico, Sunday . . .

Asako looked at Jay and the marines, worried about how well they had come through their ordeal.

"Things are happening pretty fast. To be on the safe side, Pierce Hamilton has given orders that you should all be taken to a safe house."

"Where's that?" asked Diego Chavez. "And why do we have to go?"

"For the first question, it wouldn't be a safe house if I knew where it was. For the second, your commanding officer ordered you to do just that," said Asako, handing him some hardcopy. "But you're involved in this too. You're witnesses."

"I'll say," said another of the marines. "Just let me get on the stand and testify against the VP. They should string her up the old-fashioned way."

"Draco is from Texas," explained Diego. "He's got some weird ideas about applying home-brewed justice."

"Well, I'm inclined to agree with him, if Stephanie had anything to do with John Milton's death," Jay said. "And I bet she did."

"Anyway, come along," said Asako. "The van's out front."

It was over an hour's ride into the Virginia countryside. With all the twists and turns, Jay didn't know exactly where it was, but she had a pretty good idea. Diego kept smiling at her during the trip.

"Quit looking like the cat that ate the canary," she told him. "What are you smiling about?"

"I think the VP was wrong, that's all. You're not a ballsy bitch. You're pretty nice. Tough, but nice."

"Well, thank you, Sgt. Chavez. When we get past all this, you can invite me to dinner. You're a little young for me, though."

"Is that a problem for you?"

"No, but I don't want it to be one for you. You're a nice guy, too. And again, thanks for saving my life. I owe you all a dinner for that one."

"Maybe we should have a Texas barbecue," drawled Draco. "Unless you're a vegetarian?"

"Dios mio, how could you think that? Remember, tough, but nice. I didn't get that way eating like a rabbit."

They all laughed.

The safe house was a big, rambling farmhouse with a full length front porch and a barn. The FBI agents parked the van in the barn and opened the door of the house for them.

"How long we gonna be here?" asked Draco. He brushed some dirt off his uniform. They were still a disheveled lot.

"As long as it takes," said one of the agents. "The old man's got to figure this out."

"Old man?" asked Jay.

"Jake Hanlon. And Pierce Hamilton, of course. Things could be complicated. It's better to have all of you here, safe and sound."

"But what if the FBI's involved?" asked Diego.

"My sentiments exactly," said Jay.

"Well, you've got to trust somebody," said the other agent, a frown on his face. "Not everyone's out to get you, as far as I know."

Yeah, after what we've been through, you might think otherwise.

Two hours later they had all showered and cleaned up. Two other agents had shown up but they were from the Secret Service. They huddled with the FBI agents for a few minutes.

"Looks like some others will be joining you," said one of the FBI agents.

"Who?" asked Jay, a little worried.

"You'll see in a few moments," said one of the Secret Service agents.

About fifteen minutes later, another van pulled up. A Secret Service agent and a nurse got out. The agent and another one from the house went to the back of the van and opened the rear doors. Inside were Kalidas Metropolis and the wounded Chris Tanner.

Kalidas almost crushed Jay in a hug. Jay introduced the marines. Soon everyone was up to date about what had happened to them. Chris seemed in good spirits, in spite of his close encounter with the grim reaper. Three centimeters higher and the bullet would have smashed through his heart. The nurse was only precautionary, as much as for all of them as for Chris.

"Hell, we could have that Texas barbeque now," said Draco.

"Yeah, you could, if we weren't on government stipend here," said the nurse, whose name was Betsy Simpson. "Unfortunately, we'll be lucky to get pizza, right boys?"

The Secret Service men nodded with a smile.

"I suggest we all get back inside," suggested one. "One good reason: it's hotter than hell out here. The house really has good air conditioning. Another: the less you're outside, the fewer chances someone will see you. Believe me, that's a good idea."

So they went inside. It wasn't too bad. The refrigerator was well stocked with material for making sandwiches and there was plenty of soft drinks and beer. Everyone seemed to hit it off. The FBI and Secret Service agents lost some of their arrogance and began to trade war stories with Chris and Jay while the marines listened with great interest, sometimes interrupting with questions. Kalidas was in an overstuffed chair off to the side, conversing with Betsy.

"You know, I feel like these are the children I never had," she observed.

"Well, that must be a good feeling. They're a great bunch of people. They've all gone through a lot in service to their country."

"Yeah, so did Hank Johnson, Frank Sweeney, and Stephanie Williams. I'm trying to figure out what made the difference."

"Maybe some people just make wrong choices," said Betsy. "Most people are decent and hard-working and do the right thing. Others get a little twisted—" She touched her forehead. "You know, up here. They make mistakes then try to rationalize their actions, then just dig themselves deeper into the hole."

"I agree, up to a point. But I also believe there is evil in the world, and sometimes it consumes people."

"You mean, like the Devil?"

"Call it what you will, but how can you explain what they did to John Milton?"

"Well, I think it was the other John Milton who said that we need both good and evil in the world so we can know the difference."

Kalidas looked sharply at her. She was sure the original Milton hadn't said it exactly like that, yet the statement convinced Kalidas that she had underestimated the nurse. *This is an honest, thinking person, one that will not be snowed by bullshit.*

They talked for a little more, and just when Kalidas stood to hit the bathroom, all hell broke loose. The front wall of the farmhouse's big living room was riddled with automatic weapons fire. Everyone hit the floor.

"Here we go again," said Diego Chavez, "and I don't even have a gun this time."

"We do," said one of the FBI agents. He threw an extra gun at Diego. Among the agents, they had enough firepower to equip all the marines. Betsy whipped a sinister looking weapon from her own purse.

"Shit, that doesn't look like a stethoscope," said Kalidas.

"I'm also Secret Service," Betsy said. Crawling to the window, she smashed out the glass with the butt of the revolver, and began returning fire.

"How many are there?" cried Chris from the sofa, where he was stretched out, much more exposed than the rest.

"Jay, Kalidas, can you help Chris onto the gurney and get him into one of the back bedrooms?" asked one of the FBI agents.

"On our way," said Kalidas.

They managed to get Chris onto the gurney and wheeled him into the bigger back bedroom. The firefight in front of the house continued.

"Damn, this is getting to be a way of life," complained Kalidas.

"Especially for me. How many are out there?" Chris asked again.

"Quite a few," said Jay. "It looks like a whole DHS SWAT team. It's only a matter of time 'til they work their way around to the back."

"Or blow up the house," said Chris. "They're probably not particularly concerned about taking any of us alive. How did they find us?"

"Who knows?" asked Kalidas. "There could be a lot more people involved in this than we can imagine. Including the FBI."

"And what do we know about this Pierce Hamilton?" Jay asked. She went to the back window and peered out. "He sent us here."

"Well, I guess we have a right to be paranoid now," said the scientist. She looked at both Chris and Jay. "It's a wonder what a few bullets will do for paranoia." Then she caught her cop buddy watching carefully as Jay stretched to look over the high window sill.

"Kalidas, don't you think she's got a great figure," Chris observed. "She looks much better in person than on a cell phone."

"Hey, people, I'm in the room, you know," said Jay, turning towards them.

"I'm inclined to agree with you, Chris," said Kalidas. "But she's too young for me and you're not in any shape to do anything about it."

"Oh, but I can think about it. My love life hasn't been exactly great these last few months."

"Mine neither," said Jay. "So you can take me to dinner after Chavez."

"Chavez is too young for you, sweetie," said Kalidas. "Though he might not be a young stallion, Chris here has other qualities."

"Thanks, mother," said Chris with a smile. "Just what the woman wants to hear—she has an impotent admirer."

"Oh, I bet you're potent enough," said Kalidas, "if you ever get out of the habit of stopping bullets and dodging shrapnel."

"Yeah, I know professional soldiers who have been wounded a lot less than you," said Jay. "Myself included. But now may be my time. Duck!"

The gas grenade came smashing through the window, splattering glass all around the room. The fumes were powerful, yet Jay picked up the smoldering canister and tossed it back out the window.

"It's going to be an incendiary grenade next," said Chris. "We've got to get out of here or we'll be cremated."

"The basement!" said Kalidas.

They rolled Chris out of the room and took the gurney down the basement stairs, Kalidas in the lead to keep the gurney from running away and to keep Chris from falling off, and Jay in the rear.

As they had gone through the farmhouse halls, Jay had noticed that one agent and one marine were down. It wouldn't be long. As much as she hated to, she slammed the basement door shut and locked it with a deadbolt. If they blew up the house or fired it, they might still survive in the basement.

"Well, I'll admit I've never had so much excitement in my life before," Kalidas observed, panting with her exertion from guiding Chris' gurney down the stairs.

"I don't need this kind of excitement," said Jay. "Can you hear anything, guys?"

"Not a thing," said Kalidas. Chris also shook his head in the negative.

Jay pushed a few crates together and climbed on top of them to look out one of the small basement windows. It looked out on the front lawn of the house. She could see lots of movement, yet the SWAT team members seemed to be firing at the sky. A few died horribly, then the rest raised their hands. Three black helicopters landed on the lawn.

"I think the Mounties have arrived," said Jay.

Scherzo Thirty-Nine

Judith Wasserman knew she was going to die. That fact didn't bother her as much as the fact that her little boy and girl would be without a mummy. *What kind of childhood will they have?*

The terrorists had kidnapped her in front of the New Jersey synagogue in broad daylight with many of her friends watching. The rabbi had been pistol-whipped trying to save her.

The first irony was that she was not the Wasserman they wanted. The head of the local Jewish charity that supported the right wing movements in Israel was not even a relative. The second irony was that her husband was a Lebanese Muslim and the children were with their father, off on a camping trip.

She had told them that repeatedly. They didn't believe her.

Judith had no idea what the demands of her kidnappers were, though she was pretty sure they would not be met. Then she would die. If she were lucky, it would just be a bullet to the head. If she were unlucky, they would behead her. In any case, it would be video-recorded. She hoped her children would never see it.

She had met her husband as the peace accord was signed in Teheran. They were both UN observers. They had fallen madly in love. After several years of Middle Eastern politics, they retired, her husband to teach at Princeton, she to bear his children. It had been a very good life, until now.

In her terror she lost track of time. Occasionally, they would sit her on a chair in front of a camcorder and pull her head back by the hair so her face could be clearly seen. She had no idea who would be watching but she knew she was not the usual prim and proper university housewife. She imagined she had a look of desolation and infinite fatigue on her face. That was the way she felt, anyway.

After several days passed—she couldn't count how many—help miraculously came. She would never again complain about the quality of Papa Giorgio's Pizza.

The terrorists had even asked her what kind of pizza she liked. It seemed to Judith to be like giving the condemned their last meal. The pizza delivery man was a DHS agent. As he handed one of the terrorists two boxes of real pizza, there was a gun underneath. At the same time that terrorist was hit, an armored vehicle blasted through the back wall of the abandoned garage where they were holding her. DHS agents poured out, guns blazing.

Judith's only physical wound was a cut she picked up as some broken glass from a window scratched her forearm. The psychological wounds would last forever.

Ben Knowland knew that Judith would never be the same. But at least she was alive. He allowed himself another smile for a small success.

Chapter Forty-Eight

Washington, DC, Monday . . .

Pierce was somewhat apprehensive about the meeting with the President that Monday morning. John Fulton had flown back from Camp David late Sunday evening. Pierce had simply told him there was a domestic crisis that was being taken care of and that he would get a full briefing the next morning.

Fulton thought it was another terrorist attack. He was tired of them, yet couldn't help thinking there was irony in that. The country was getting used to them after a half century. It was just part of everyday life now, like talks of secession, militias, and riots. The country seemed to be coming apart at the seams and Fulton seemed powerless to do anything about it. Maybe Stephanie was right. Maybe a strong hand was needed. Well, she would certainly provide it when she became President. If she became President. He wished her well, for the campaign, and in her Presidency. It really was her turn.

He was already at work at his desk when Pierce came in. The younger man sat down in the chair facing the President's desk.

"I'm afraid I have some bad news and some good news, sir," he began.

"Well, let's have it. Start with the bad first. Let me guess: ten killed by a suicide bomber in some shopping mall. Or is it an amusement park this time?"

"Well, I wish it were actually that simple." Pierce cleared his throat. "First, I'd like to say, I take full responsibility. All this happened on my watch, and I should have known what was going on. I have two excuses. The recent scandal took up some of my time. Also, it all started over twenty years ago."

"Shit, Pierce, am I going to have to shake it out of you? Tell me what happened, damn it!"

Pierce began a long monologue, explaining quickly and succinctly all the facts as he knew them. Some of them he hadn't even had the time to fully digest, although he thought the story was more or less complete. Multani had been a tremendous help there, plus the information coming in from Jake Hanlon and the FBI and a joint FBI and Secret Service raid on the DHS Center.

"So, you see, sir, when we raided their Center, we found thirty-one different clone types, sir, including multiples. Fifty-one in total, just kids."

Pierce looked at his President with expectation. Fulton looked astonished.

"Counting the three that were killed, that makes fifty-four. Shit, what an operation! There weren't any of me, were there?"

"No, sir. They were all in good health, too, but terrified. They were under strict lockdown as they had actually managed to pull off a massive escape but were rounded up by the DHS guards. We believe there are a few still loose maybe. Anyway, as far as I know, there are no casualties."

"Thank heavens, on both counts." He studied Pierce's face. "That isn't all, is it?"

"No, sir. In storage tanks there were many, and I mean many, more genotypes, brainless hominoids, clones of some of the most wealthy and powerful people, from here and abroad. Apparently, when they reached maturity, they could be also harvested for body parts. The Center had perfected their techniques over time, under the direction of Richter's student, Andrew Tyler. The kids probably would have been eliminated at the time the ones in the tank reached maturity, in which case, we probably never would have found out, because no one would have escaped."

"I don't want to see a list," said Fulton. "Keep that under wraps. I probably have to deal with these people on an almost daily basis. How could I do that if I knew that they had taken part in this?"

"It's not clear that everyone that had copies there actually knew what was going on or even knew they had copies. I'd be willing to wager that some hadn't even been approached yet."

"Well, those who willingly participated, the originals, I guess you'd call them, are we going after them?"

"We're moving very carefully. I suspect that even some of the ones who knew what was going on were duped by Stephanie Williams and Hank Johnson, maybe even blackmailed. One, Vladimir Kalinin, is supposedly already dead, although I'm having Jake Hanlon check that out separately. For the others, I suggest that we just allow them quietly to resign their posts. Otherwise, this would be a scandal of major proportions, cutting across party lines. I'm not sure the country can handle it, given its present state."

"Good idea," agreed Fulton. "Otherwise it would give the militias a reason to believe that their government really is conspiring against them. And it would also give the secessionists more ammo. But aren't more of these people in the private sector, like Kalinin?"

"Yes. They're wealthy enough that they can take an early retirement, and we will make strong suggestions to that effect. By the way, we still haven't found Johnson or Williams."

"I'm sure you will. I want those two. I always knew Johnson was a scoundrel, but I had no idea Stephanie would or could do such a thing. I really feel betrayed." He stood up from his desk and walked to the window. *It's another steamy day in DC. In more ways than one.* "She was a shoo-in for the nomination, you know."

"I suppose so, sir."

Pierce felt uncomfortable. He had never seen eye-to-eye with the VP and knew that many of Fulton's progressive policies would disappear when she took office, whether she won the election or not. But what she had done was unpardonable.

"Stephanie and Hank will have to pay, sir. You know that." He saw Fulton's look, fearing the scandal that might give Stephanie's opponent a free ticket to the White House. "But we could hush it up quite easily."

"How will you manage that?"

"Simple. It's been done before. Their trials will be classified affairs. Anything they say will be declared top secret."

"They have a right to an attorney, you know."

"No, sir, they don't. We'll say they were collaborating with terrorists."

"Not many people will believe that. I'm surprised you even propose it, Pierce. No, we can't do that. We'll have to take our chances."

Pierce smiled. John Fulton had just confirmed Pierce's faith in him.

"I'm glad you said that, John. Yes, we'll have to take our chances. With Stephanie, Hank, Frank Sweeney and a few others. There are a few who can't just be allowed to quietly retire."

"My god, Sweeney? How far does this go, Pierce."

"It's quite an elite group, sir." He named a few more names.

Fulton just shook his head.

"Some of these people have contributed heavily to my campaigns," he said. He sat down heavily in his chair again. "No more names. I don't want to know. Handle it as you will but keep me out of it as much as possible. Like I said, I may have to deal with these people, especially the ones overseas. How can I do that if I think they are scoundrels?"

"Most politicians are, sir, as well as corporate CEOs, top scientists, and lobbyists. It's human nature."

"You have a low opinion of your fellow man, Pierce."

"I was a priest, sir. I saw the worst in humanity. I also saw the best."

"Well, given this prescient ability, how could you not see this?"

"I should have, but I didn't. Like I said, it started a long time ago. Maybe Richter approached Stephanie. Who knows? It obviously got out of hand, sir."

Pierce empathized with Fulton. Like Pierce, POTUS was a firm believer that the people's representatives had a sacred trust with the people they represented. His political life had been built on that premise, even though some people called him naïve.

Pierce himself believed in government's playing a positive role in the affairs of its citizens and had dedicated his second career to public service. *Every government official has been given that trust, and Stephanie has betrayed it.*

Most people wanted to trust their government and their leaders, although that trust was often betrayed by empty campaign promises, the influence of lobbyists, or simple greed and thirst for power. It was a story as old as the human race, and equally as old was the common man's need to trust and depend on someone.

As a former priest, he understood that perfectly. Often, especially with the elderly, the only person they trusted was their parish priest. Although the Church had been rocked with scandal for the last fifty years, it was still a fact of life. Pierce figured that his next career might be to return to the more basic and fulfilling work of providing support in time of need, something generally a lot less abstract than his present job. *Maybe I'll even put on the collar again.*

Independently of Fulton's desire to be spared the details, Pierce wasn't about to tell all to his boss. Knowing Fulton as well as he did, he could only concur that the man would be crippled in his dealings with foreign dignitaries, important business people, and members of his own government if he knew that they were involved. Pierce would have no such qualms as he was a man that was acquainted with both the best and the worst in human beings, and took them in stride, hoping to make the world a better place for most, while fully believing that the worst would have their just reward in the afterlife, if not this one.

Pierce had passed on requests to British intelligence and Interpol. He had given orders to the CIA, the FBI, the Secret Service, and the DHS. British intelligence, Interpol and the CIA were needed because some of the young men and women found at the Center were copies of CEOs of major corporations with headquarters outside the US. The rest of the agencies were needed to round up the guilty within the US. As he had told Fulton, many would simply be told to quietly resign, yet there were a few that Pierce wanted very much to bring to justice. First on the list were Hank Johnson and Stephanie Williams, of course.

At that same moment not far away from the White House Hank Johnson sat in his Virginia home. No one knew he was there, not even the Department of Homeland Security.

He sat in his fancy kitchen with its three natural gas ovens. He and his wife had often used them to cook two turkeys and all the fixings on Thanksgiving for sometimes as many as fifty or more guests. He had disconnected the pilots to all three and turned on the gas. The nauseous odor that was added to the gas so you would know when there was a gas leak was heavy in the air. From the living room mantel over the fireplace he had brought the box of long matches they used to light the fire there. When the odor was about to become unbearable, he lit a match.

Nearly at the same time, Stephanie Williams could be found in the old family homestead in Annapolis, on the other side of town from GeeBee's family's summer home where the marines had picked up Jay Sandoval. She sat on her sun porch, looking out on the lawn that gently sloped down to the waterway. The trees bordering one side of the property cast long shadows. Two boats, one a sleek, new motorboat, the other, her prized sailing boat, were tied to the pier. Both had enough polished brass to make them sparkle as they bobbed up and down in the afternoon sun. A cup of tea was sitting daintily on her lap.

On the table beside her was a sleek, new Smith & Wesson, a very lethal gun manufactured to the specifications of another era. Her nephew had given it to her as a birthday present the year before. She was quite the gun addict, learning to hunt at an early age with her father. *Of course, at this range I can't miss, can I?*

When she finished the tea, she put the cup down, and picked up the revolver. She tilted her head up, pointing the gun slanting into her jaw, and pulled the trigger.

That evening the news carried two items of interest to Jay Sandoval and her friends. One was the explosion in the Virginia home of Henry 'Hank' Johnson, Assistant Secretary of Homeland Security, which took his life. He was apparently the victim of a natural gas leak. The other news item was the report of Vice President Stephanie Williams' untimely death from a massive cerebral hemorrhage. Her mother had died the same way, the news report said.

Scherzo Forty

Bobby Ferreira shook her head in amazement.

"What do you make of it?" she asked.

Hiroshi Ito, her friend and thesis adviser, looked at the streaming video the underwater robot was sending back to them.

"I would guess it's some kind of squid. One big mouth at the front surrounded by all those legs. Seems to propel itself in the same way."

"At these depths? How can it?"

"Beats me. There's a lot of pressure on that thing."

"Can you get it in the cross-fire of the videocams from each robot?"

They actually had two out today, as number one had been acting up a little, and they wanted a back-up. Hiroshi sat down at the joysticks.

"What's your theory, Bobby?"

"I bet this thing is mostly water, so the inside and outside pressures are pretty much equalized. It only needs to establish a small delta P in order to keep nutrients in. It doesn't have to go against the whole P."

"And if it's mostly water, we should be able to see right through it, right?"

"Right. That's what I'm thinking."

She was only partially correct. But she was enough correct that they kept it as a working hypothesis. It suggested they would never be able to take the creature to the surface. It would be destroyed at any other depth of water. The question remained as to what it was and how it could live there.

The underwater laboratory, partially financed and run by a consortium of European and Middle Eastern universities, owed its conception and most of its endowment to Ahmed Al-Hassim, the Iraqi Nobel prize winner. Unfortunately the famous man had died before the laboratory was completed, although his ideas and ideals still shaped the laboratory's programs.

It was the leading center for deep water research in the world, out in the middle of the Atlantic Ocean. None of the scientists there thought much about the tons of water on top of them. They were just as alone down there as the scientists on the International Space Station or the ones on Mars.

Chapter Forty-Nine

Wellesley, Massachusetts, Tuesday . . .

Frank Sweeney was not in a good mood. He had put through the call from his wife's Wellesley mansion, yet his team arrived too late at the Center. *Stephanie really fucked this up royally.*

He wasn't quite sure what to do when the leader of his team reported in. Fulton probably suspected him now, since he had clones at the Center. If Fulton didn't, Pierce Hamilton certainly did. Sweeney was fairly sure that the National Security Advisor had ordered the raid on the Center. He gave crisp orders to the team leader and sat back in his overstuffed desk chair with a sigh. *I might still be able to cover my ass.* He went to the living room to find a drink.

His private study had a small bathroom attached. In it, Patricia Rivera was sitting on the toilet, trembling, still dressed in her chambermaid's uniform. When she realized that her boss had left the study, she quietly took a cell phone out of her apron pocket and dialed a Boston number.

Sweeney had just made himself a good, stiff bourbon when his wife walked in. Barbara Sweeney was loaded down with packages.

"Hello, Franky. I found a delightful new dress to wear to the Mason's party on Saturday."

Sweeney glared at her. *Everything's crumbling around me and all you can think about is a damn party dress!*

"Let me see it, then," he said.

She opened up one of the bags and displayed a cranberry colored evening gown. Sweeney had to admit that it was stunning and that she would look gorgeous in it. But his black mood quickly returned.

"Put it on," he suggested.

"Now? Don't be silly. We're in the middle of the living room."

"Put it on!" he yelled.

"OK, OK," she said, trembling. She knew his anger well.

He watched with grim satisfaction as she stripped down to bra and panties and then slipped on the evening gown. *Yes, she is gorgeous in it.*

He drew close to her. She could smell the bourbon. He toyed with the low cut of the dress, as if he were straightening the bodice. She felt some of her fear melt away. *Franky can be gentle and nice sometimes.*

Then he pulled straight down, ripping the gown off her, laughing.

"You think I'd get a hard on for a shitty dress?" he asked her, his face pushed close to hers in defiance. "And don't tell me how much it cost. I don't give a fuck. Your family has so much money that it doesn't fucking matter. It's an insignificant dress. It's all insignificant unless I can clean up after Stephanie and Hank."

"What—what do you mean, Franky? What cleanup?"

He walked back to the bar for another bourbon, leaving her standing uncomfortably in her underwear.

"Matters of state, bitch. You wouldn't understand but I'm in bad trouble."

"What kind of trouble, Franky?"

He came over to her again and she trembled in his glare.

"Like I said, you can't understand." He hit her. It was not just a slap. He sucker punched her, breaking her cheekbone. She went down, screaming. "You never understand." He kicked her twice in the ribs. "All your fine breeding bred the brains right out of you."

Actually, he knew deep down that wasn't true. His wife had more schooling than he did, although she tried to play the dutiful housewife so as not to incur his wrath. She had been a member of the Smith College debating team, as a matter of fact. He figured that was why she talked back so much to him. *She was always the one who always started it, putting on her airs, putting me down.*

She was crawling towards the fireplace. He went to her and grabbed her by the hair.

"Trying to get away, bitch? You can't get away from me! I'm your adorable Franky. The beau you showed off at all those rich people's parties. Did you know, bitch, that I fucked your cousin on our wedding night?"

Mrs. Sweeney groaned. He hit her again, then threw the bourbon in her face.

He was turning to go to the bar yet again, cursing her for making him waste good whiskey, when she hit him with the fireplace poker. It caught him by surprise and he staggered, dropping to one knee, looking at her in surprise. She had never fought back. Then she hit him again, right between the eyes. He was already dead when he hit the floor.

There was a knock on the front door. Mrs. Sweeney walked slowly to the front of the house and opened it, staggering as if intoxicated, almost falling down several times. Tears were streaming down her cheeks, mixing with the blood from her busted lip. The broken cheek bone was already turning reddish purple.

Denise Rivera was at the door. Her sister Patricia appeared in the hallway, shaking her head sadly, still trembling. From her sister's gestures together with the look on Mrs. Sweeney's face, Denise knew what had happened. She held out her hand, taking the poker.

"It's all over, Barbara. He can't hurt you anymore."

In another mansion in Virginia, Gina Preston took another dive, waving to Roger just before she did. She really loved him.

She had waited on him one night in a DC bar in Foggy Bottom. It was mostly a hangout for the press who covered the State Department, although it had distinguished visitors like Roger Preston from time to time.

He was always a real gentleman to her. He had taken her out of a life of drudgery, away from the leers of the drunks, and given her a life she couldn't have even dreamed of having when she was growing up in the West Virginia mountains.

She knew he moved in powerful circles and had powerful friends and enemies, yet to her he was just Roger. Sometimes he seemed to not be very compassionate in his political speeches but he defended his state's interests with vigor. *Sometimes to the detriment of the national ones, but everyone had their quirks.*

She came up for air, ready to wave to him again. A strange scene unfolded before her eyes. Men with guns and masks were entering their backyard, and Roger was backing away from them. *Terrorists! They must be terrorists.* She couldn't hear what he was screaming. Something about Sweeney.

She watched as three of the men shot her Roger. Many times. Then one came to the edge of the pool.

"Are you Mrs. Preston?" he asked calmly.

"Yes, I am. Who are you people? Why did you do this?" *How cool I am. I should be screaming.* "You murdered him."

"I'm just doing my job, ma'am."

The voice had a southern twang to it. Gina knew then that he wasn't your common garden variety Arab. He leaned over to offer her a hand. Without thinking much, she took it, and he lifted her out of the pool like she was a child's toy.

"You're sure one hundred per cent woman," said the killer, admiring her glistening wet body. "Sorry you had to see that."

"You're going to kill me, aren't you?"

"Wouldn't think of it, ma'am. That would really be a waste of some good pussy."

That made her furious. He was a leering bastard, just like the drunks in the bar. She clawed at his face and partially removed the mask. She was surprised to see a blond, blue-eyed American boy with a Marine haircut.

"Now I wish you hadn't done that, ma'am. It makes things so much more complicated."

From the look in his eyes, she knew then that he was going to kill her. She back dived into the pool. But just before she hit the water, something cold and sharp smacked into her just to the left of her spine. The water, well heated from the afternoon sun, suddenly felt very cold. She felt her world turning black.

They waited until she floated to the surface. The body was face down. Lt. Anderson's knife was still where he had expertly thrown it.

"A fucking waste," he said to the others. "Now why did she go and take off my mask? I was going to let her live."

"Maybe it's just as well," said a companion. "She saw everything. And you don't exactly sound like a raghead, Greg."

"Yeah, no kiddin'. Shit. Let's get out of here. We have a few more stops."

Scherzo Forty-One

The plane took off with its gruesome cargo. Rolando Guerrero, otherwise known as 'the Harvester,' looked up at it with satisfaction. It had been a profitable meeting for him, although he knew full well that the middle men in the black marketing of body parts would probably become a lot richer than he ever would. Still, he made a good living.

He and his men had just harvested an entire African village. This time his conscience was cleaner than usual. They had been only two days ahead of the rebel soldiers who would have killed everyone in the village anyway.

Chapter Fifty

Paterson, New Jersey, Tuesday . . .

Paul Church looked around the conference room. Dalton Biomedicine's CEO was a little uncomfortable with his present situation. Unlike Senator Preston, he was a member of the ad hoc committee that oversaw the Center's activities from the beginning. Together with Stephanie Williams and Hank Johnson, he had been instrumental in setting up the lucrative payoffs to Wolfgang Richter. Only one other person in the room was privy to that information. Linda Adams, his CFO, was staring at her notebook, not meeting his eyes.

Brian Wilson, Kalidas' immediate superior, was looking rather bored. Even though he was much more a bureaucrat than a scientist, he hated these meetings, as they rarely were about anything that might interest him. Rumor was, however, that this one might be different.

"I've called this meeting to make an announcement. I've been thinking about it for some time, and I finally decided to bite the bullet. As much as I enjoy your company every Tuesday within these soundproof walls, I've decided to retire." At this point, Linda looked up from her notebook, an incredulous expression on her face. "I'm not sure who the board will name to take my place. I really have no preferences. You are all candidates and very capable. It's possible, however, that they will bring in someone from outside."

"When is this happening?" asked Linda.

"My resignation letter is already at the board. They will probably meet tonight to name a successor, if it's one of you. Or they might take longer if they go outside. In any case, I'll stay on 'til they have named someone."

"This seems rather precipitous," said Brian. "I'm not sure this is a wise decision, Paul."

"Believe me, it's—" A knock on the conference room door interrupted him. Church frowned. He had left strict orders that they were not to be interrupted. "Brian, see who it is. And tell them to get lost."

Brian, the closest to the door, got up and opened it slightly. A heated exchange of words with someone ensued, and then the door was thrust open. Five men came in, guns drawn.

"What is the meaning of this?" asked Linda Adams. "Who are you people?"

The man closest to her flashed a badge which she could read clearly.

"FBI, ma'am. We are here to arrest Paul Church and Linda Adams."

"Absurd!" exclaimed Church. "I'll not be a part of this travesty."

Handcuffs were brought out.

"I assure you, sir, you have no choice. Handcuff him and Ms. Adams, please. Let's go."

"I'll call the corporate lawyers," Brian told them as they were led out, astonished by this turn of events.

The FBI agents led the CEO and CFO of Dalton Biomedicine towards the elevator. They were only twenty feet from it when the elevator doors opened and Sweeney's SWAT team poured out.

The battle that took place reminded Brian of some old western films that he had seen. Four of the SWAT team perished and all five FBI agents. Paul Church and Linda Adams along with two from the conference room were also dead. Brian and the rest lived to tell the story, although he took a bullet that shattered his jaw. Lt. Greg Anderson and the rest of his team fled down the stairs.

A little over half an hour later, Jake Hanlon and Ben Knowland, in their respective offices, were looking at the carnage via a videocam held by one of the FBI's forensic specialists. They were both shaking their heads sadly.

Hanlon was particularly pissed, seeing five of his best agents ready for body bags. *I wonder how Pierce is going to present this to the press?*

"I want a complete workup on those SWAT team members," he told his agents on the scene. "They look like special forces. I want to know who they are and who they work for."

"I hate to say it, but given the circumstances, they might be DHS," said Knowland. "I hope not."

"Ben, you can't lead if you can't delegate. Johnson violated your trust in him. Don't beat yourself up over this, even if we find they are DHS."

"Whoever they are, I want them," said Knowland. "They are marked men from this moment on."

"Yeah, well, what I'm afraid of is that, even if we find out who they are—highly unlikely—we'll never find them."

"Unless they act again. Someone has unleashed them upon those involved with the clandestine Center."

"A classic cleanup operation," said Hanlon. "I would like to know who ordered it."

"Someone who was not interested in seeing any of these people come to trial, obviously." Knowland's voice sounded bitter. "Has anyone informed Pierce?"

"Not yet. I think we need to take care to protect the others."

"The ones overseas are not our responsibility. On an emotional level, I would just as soon see all the bastards dead, but I would like to know the complete story before that happens."

"I wouldn't count on knowing the complete story. The principals who could have told it to us are all dead."

Scherzo Forty-Two

By 2020 the genetic blueprints for almost all viruses were known. As early as 2005 the genetic blueprint of the Ebola virus was archived in a database on the Internet, waiting for one of the many thousands with the skills necessary to assemble it to become sufficiently vexed with his wife or girl friend or job to do so. By 2030 several outbreaks of disease and pestilence were directly traceable to acts of terrorism. It was no wonder that people, running scared, were willing to lose some of their freedoms in order to feel a little safer. Long standing practices in democratic jurisprudence began to be questioned in the US and Europe. In Asia and much of the so-called Third World, where representative democracy had always had a tenuous hold at best, people had even less of a problem giving up newly won freedoms to corrupt corporations and governments.

Even in that most enlightened of democracies, the United States of America, citizens gave up a great deal of their privacy in order to feel safer. In 2043 a comprehensive law passed both houses of Congress. It would have given the government sweeping powers of surveillance by requiring that every man, woman, and child have a chip implant that would allow government agencies to track US citizens in much the same way police departments tracked tagged parolees and sex offenders. The technology had been available since about 2005 and had been seriously considered ever since the assassination of Sheila Remington in 2037. Fortunately President Fulton's predecessor had vetoed the bill. It had come up a number of times since then. Fulton himself had already vetoed two similar laws. Sooner or later, the Congress would have enough votes to override the veto.

Chapter Fifty-One

Grand Cayman, Two Weeks Later . . .

Dr. Andrew Tyler was enjoying himself. A pina colada in one hand and a racy novel in the other, he was allowing the Caribbean sun to sooth his soul. *My soul needs soothing. Now if I could just find some rich widow down here, I'd have it made.*

A shadow fell over him, so he looked up from his book. Against the sun's glare, he could just barely make out that it was a man dressed in Bermuda shorts and a tee shirt. He wore the kind of sunglasses that mirrored back two images of Santa Claus on vacation, something Tyler found annoying—he didn't like to admit he was overweight—and also sinister, since the man looked like a bug.

"Dr. Andrew Tyler?"

"Yes. Who are you?"

The man held out a badge. Tyler couldn't make out any details in the glare, though it looked official.

"Rafael Hurtado, Interpol. You are under arrest."

"Arrest? What have I done?"

"You're wanted for questioning in the United States in conjunction with certain illegal activities at a DHS research center. I don't have the details. Hold out your arms, please."

The handcuffs felt cold.

Twenty-four hours later Tyler was back at the Center. RP1 and SW2 saw him being brought in. They looked at each other and smiled. Some things were going OK, finally.

Later, the FBI brought them into a room. They could see Tyler behind a glass. SW2 reached for RP1's hand.

"Don't get nervous," said the FBI agent. "We just need your ID of this man, that's all. He can't see you, just as you couldn't see him when your places were switched. Is this man Andrew Tyler?"

"Yes, it most certainly is," said SW2. "He can't hurt us any more, can he?"

"No," said the agent. "He won't hurt anyone for a long, long time. We have a special place in Juno, Alaska, for people like him."

RP1 nodded. That would be good. He never wanted to see the man again.

Scherzo Forty-Three

Professor John Ballard was in good form that day. He even had the non-English students listening, if their questions were any indication. His lecture was going out to thirty-one countries spread over the globe. He was perhaps the most famous member of the elite Harvard University Center for Counter Terrorism, the most important one financed by the DHS.

Mostly, he was famous because of the Ballard Doctrine that had been adopted by President Fulton's predecessor. It stated that any government's primary job was to protect the health and well-being of its citizens.

Ballard was the first to admit that his doctrine had been twisted by many governments in such a way as to use it to justify trampling on people's freedoms. He had never quite intended it to be used in that way, yet didn't have many misgivings about that use. Some of his reasons he was giving as a guest lecturer today.

"Our century has seen a tremendous empowerment of the individual. Even at the end of the last, one could obtain gourmet recipes from a famous French chef in Lyons as well as nuclear bomb recipes from a nuclear physicist at Los Alamos, just by accessing the web. Today, individuals now have more access to knowledge, terabytes and terabytes of information, and all this information empowers the individual. My thesis today is that we have come too far." He looked straight into the camera, trying to make eye contact with more than a million students. He needed to hammer the point home. "We have seen time and time again that even the most responsible individual can make a mistake and unleash something deadly into the environment that can kill many people. Now, if we add into that mix, all those individuals who actually might want to do such a thing intentionally, we come up with a very dangerous situation. We have come to a turning point in history when just one person can literally destroy many lives or affect vast areas of our planet and its ecosystems, either by unfortunate accident or by a deliberate act of terrorism. Clearly that cannot be tolerated. The only solution is that we all give up some of our freedoms in order to save lives and guarantee a healthy environment for all. Yet, how we go about this is a very delicate balancing act indeed. Forgetting the moment about acts of perfidy such as those now occurring in our malls and elsewhere, the squelching of those freedoms can also inhibit the very innovation and creative thinking we need to insure that present human civilization does not stagnate, wither and die, just as any plant might wither and die when deprived of water, sunlight and nutrients. That is the delicate balancing act. In my series of lectures as part of this course, you will hear my thoughts on this subject. I want to get down into the weeds, as it were, and try to go into all the nuances here. And I want to hear from you. I want to hear your ideas on this subject. By the end of my three week participation in this course, I hope we can together arrive at a consensus that we can pass on. That is our challenge."

Chapter Fifty-Two

Arlington Cemetery, Three Weeks Later . . .

"Well, I guess the government can't let the public see them," observed Simon Multani. He looked admiringly at the two Stephanie Williams look-alikes playing tennis. "Does Jay know about this?"

Asako smiled at him and winked at Kalidas.

"What Jay doesn't know won't hurt her in this case," said Kalidas. "And you two are the only ones from any of the agencies to know, so treat it as Top Secret. The National Security Advisor screens all people who work here. The irony is that I'm in charge, even though I don't have a DoD or DHS clearance anymore. I report directly to Pierce Hamilton."

"A lot of us do," said Simon.

At that moment, Jay, Dolores, and Chris were visiting Arlington cemetery. Dolores had been hiding out in Tennessee at an old friend's house. She had missed all the action. Jay considered that it was just as well, since she might have had a nervous breakdown, even if she had survived.

The two women between them carried three bouquets. The sun was hot, but there were a few black thunderheads overhead. Henry, Dolores' golden retriever, was at her side, his big, wet drooling tongue working overtime to cool him off.

Jay put a bouquet of flowers on each one of the three new graves. No name was on the gravestone, only the words: "Here lies an unknown soldier who gave his life for his country."

"Sad and ironic, isn't it?" said Dolores.

Jay took Chris by the hand and squeezed. He smiled at her.

"Sad, but it could have been worse," said Chris. "They could have gotten away with it. In some sense these three are the heroes of this case."

"I'll second that," said Jay. "If I look at the big picture, I'm not sure the country can survive the upheaval it's going through. Or the rest of the world, for that matter. But at least we all did our small part to make it a better place. And these individuals, together with our dead friends, can now rest in peace."

"Amen," Dolores said. She wiped a tear away, thinking of John. It started to rain, even though the sun was shining. The full storm would not be far behind.

Close by, in a hotel in Arlington, the man who had been known as Vladimir Kalinin, stretched lazily. One of his playmates fed him an olive and another a piece of cheese. Now relaxed, he was planning again. His agile mind mapped out possible futures. The most likely one, considering the riots and the secession sentiment in the US and ethnic movements all over the world, was where the whole planet would convulse in chaos as the twentieth century governmental paradigms failed one by one. There were other possible futures. There was adventure to be had.

His first challenge was to re-establish the Center in Switzerland. Over the last few months he had already put that in motion. A team of scientists would keep another group of brainless homonoids viable and ready to provide transplants. They would also continue the lucrative business of offering the service to the wealthy and powerful around the globe. In fact, all of his pet projects were intact, and as Rupert Snyder, he was the new CEO of his pharmaceutical company. Of course, the real Rupert was dead, buried and rotting in an open-air refuse pit in Bangladesh.

Not far away, in a Pentagon office, Peter Barkley sat in front of General Roberto Vargas' desk. He tossed a paperweight in his right hand. It was a model of the Apollo spacecraft. He had given it to the general.

"You squeaked by on this one," said General Vargas.

"There was no other way. When I heard about Stephanie's secret project, there was too much risk that it would be confused with ours. Remember, I was the only one who had a plan. It worked. So cut the whining."

Vargas frowned. In spite of his brilliance, the general knew that Peter was a liability, a loose cannon. He had no use for loose cannons. He decided to ignore the insult.

"So, are we back on schedule?"

"Almost." He chuckled.

"I don't find this situation as amusing as you do, obviously. Fill me in on the joke."

"I was just thinking that Pierce would really shit a brick if he knew there really was a secret starship project."

Vargas watched the little Apollo paperweight go up and down, up and down. He remembered when he had first seen the streaming video files at NASA, scientific reports from an alien scientist that were millions of years old copied to modern media. Their secret project had started soon after. It certainly helped knowing it could be done.

He just wasn't sure they were going about it in the right way.